The Winter King

Andrion raised his own face to search the darkness outside, but it was impenetrable. I am the emperor's son, he thought. Born on the day of victory, on the cusp of winter eighteen years ago. Now spring gives birth to summer with a rumor not of life but of death. Bellasteros, the summer king . . .

"By all the gods," he said between his teeth, part curse, part prayer, "if I ever find who betrayed the legions and opened the gates, I shall cut out his heart, I shall stain the ancient altar of the temple with his blood as it was bloodied by traitors on the night of my birth!"

PRAISE FOR LILLIAN STEWART CARL'S *SABAZEL*

"Strong and thoughtful . . . gorgeously visualized . . . filled with adventure and courage and peril."

—*Science Fiction Review*

Ace Fantasy books by Lillian Stewart Carl

SABAZEL
THE WINTER KING

The Winter King

LILLIAN STEWART CARL

ACE FANTASY BOOKS
NEW YORK

For my husband Paul,
my best friend

This book is an Ace Fantasy original
edition, and has never been previously published.

THE WINTER KING

An Ace Fantasy Book / published by arrangement with
the author

PRINTING HISTORY
Ace Fantasy edition / October 1986

ISBN: 0-441-89443-7

Ace Fantasy Books are published by The Berkley Publishing Group,
200 Madison Avenue, New York, New York 10016.
PRINTED IN THE UNITED STATES OF AMERICA

Chapter One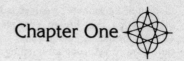

THE AGED WALLS of Iksandarun reverberated to a volley of hoofbeats. Couriers raced out of the west and plunged through the gates, scattering the marketgoers with cries of alarm. A lathered horse fell dead in the dust before the palace. The couriers swayed with exhaustion in the presence of their emperor, delivering dire news. The Khazyari had burst from the distant legendary Mohan Valley like maggots from a rotten peach. The Crimson Horde had swarmed across the borders of the Empire.

The Emperor Marcos Bellasteros listened, his features sternly attentive. He asked several pointed questions. He thanked the messengers and saw to their comfort, and then quickly sent for his generals. In the eighteen years since he had conquered the Empire, he had built it almost to its former prosperity; if it was his glory, it was also his burden.

Bellasteros, king of kings, god-king, sat that night in his private chambers. His only son, named Andrion, beloved of the gods, sat with long limbs knotted at his father's feet. "These horsemen," stated the emperor, his brow furrowed by the depth of his thought, "come around the end of the mountains, from nowhere, moving faster than seems possible. And the Empire is weak. The years since your birth have not been enough to mend it. It has absorbed us, its Sardian conquerors, and while we have strengthened it, we have not healed it."

His voice died, refusing to speak words of doom. His dark eyes, flickering with a distant flame, pierced the night that cloaked the window as if watching the Khazyari make their implacable advance from the western steppes, through the rich valley of the Mohan, to the borders of the Empire itself. The

1

diadem of the emperor gleamed in his sable hair.

Andrion's rich brown eyes were his father's; his bones were his mother's, light, strong, square. His face was his own, pure marble yet to be sculpted by time and fate. "Should we go to the winter capital in Farsahn? We could stop in Sabazel for the midsummer rites." This time, he thought, perhaps Dana will come to me. The fine, almost delicate line of his mouth twitched into a smile and then tightened, denying retreat.

"Sabazel," Bellasteros murmured. His gaze softened. He stroked his son's dark auburn hair, assuring himself the young man really existed. And he laughed, dryly, without bitterness, his teeth glinting white in the sable of his beard. "Yes, Andrion, we have lived our lives on the borders of Sabazel, not quite within, not quite without. If only we could go there and lay our worries in the lap of our mother, the goddess Ashtar. But I am emperor, I cannot hide from distasteful duty. I fear we shall have other rites to celebrate come midsummer."

A wind sighed through the window, caressing Andrion's up-turned face, teasing him with the scents of lemon and orange blossoms. Spring in Iksandarun; spring in Sabazel, and the soft odor of asphodel to sear the senses.

Bellasteros leaned back in his chair. "I shall set two legions in the path of the Khazyari, and send to Patros in Sardis for reinforcements; if worse comes to worst, we can fall back before them, shut ourselves behind the walls of Iksandarun and wait." The lines on his brow deepened with a painful irony. "These horsemen pour in from the west, but the defenses of the Empire have always looked to the north, to Sardis. Justice, perhaps, but I shall not accept such judgment." He set his jaw, raised his chin, squared his lean and powerful shoulders.

Andrion raised his own face to search the darkness outside, but it was impenetrable. And I am the emperor's son, he thought. Born on the day of victory, on the cusp of winter eighteen years ago. Now spring gives birth to summer with a rumor not of life but of death. Bellasteros, the summer king.

Suddenly the wind veered, filling his nostrils with the sharp-sweet scent of blood, and he shivered.

The mountains, rank upon shadowed rank, supported the vault of the night sky, the western vault behind the Khazyari camp. The mountains still marked the borders of the Empire, but they no longer protected it. Circumvented, they seemed to slump, fading into a dark and indistinguishable horizon.

A band of Khazyari warriors and their sturdy steppe ponies trotted over a slight rise. In the midst of the group, a cloaked figure bounced on its horse like an ungainly insect. When the escort reined up, the figure emitted an audible groan.

A white pony moved ghostlike through the night. Its rider signed peremptorily; with respectful gestures the other warriors faded back, becoming only shadows flitting among the rocks and brush of the plain.

The Khazyari rider approached the solitary cloaked figure. "Hilkar, chamberlain of the court," he said mockingly, in lightly accented common speech. "Is all in readiness?"

Hilkar swept back the hood of his cloak. His face was thin, his pale jowls dangling loosely in the starlight, like dead fish. "My lord Tembujin. I intercepted the orders of Bellasteros to General Aveyron, as you asked. I have ridden all the way from Iksandarun—"

"Which is not far." The warrior adjusted the short bow he carried. He propped one leather-booted foot on his pony's shoulder. His bright black eyes scanned the darkness, not Hilkar's face, naming Hilkar only some insignificant creature of the night. "Yes?"

"Two legions, set on either side of the old caravan route," said Hilkar. And louder, trying to draw the Khazyari's eye, "They mean to catch your forces between them."

The warrior laughed. He waved his hand, indicating the watchfires of the Khazyari camp spread as lavishly across the ground as the stars across the sky, indicating a dying moon that hung low in the east, shedding no light upon Iksandarun.

Hilkar swallowed hard. He slipped what looked like a bolt of cloth from a bag on his saddle. "Here, my lord. A gift from your loyal servant, so you may remember me after your victory."

Tembujin lazily reached out, took the cloth, shook it. A cloak, its crimson darkened into deep carnelian by the night, billowed over the flanks of his pony as it was tossed by a sudden breeze. "Yes?"

"Bellasteros's cloak. To enspell him. He is strong, my lord."

"True. He defeated you, did he not?"

Hilkar's reedy voice tightened bitterly. "He defeated the Empire and made it his own. He could not defeat my spirit.

All these years I have waited for vengeance.''

The Khazyari folded the cloak and placed it between his thigh and his saddle. "Open the gates of Iksandarun for us, and you shall have your vengeance."

"My lord!" Hilkar gasped. "That would be . . ."

"Difficult? Dangerous? No more dangerous than talking to me, traitor." The warrior smiled slowly, and his long lashes bristled about his eyes.

Hilkar groveled as best he could on horseback. "Yes, my lord. Yes, my prince. I ask only my due reward."

"That, too, you shall have." With an elaborate yawn Tembujin straightened, turned his pony, signaled to the escort. Spears and arrows stirred the night. "And I am not your prince," he said over his shoulder.

Hilkar quailed back, nodding and bowing, sputtering assurances of loyalty, flattering phrases, protestations of his own worth. The Khazyari warriors gathered around him, swept him up, carried him eastward into the night. His voice dissipated down the wind.

The moon, a pale, wasted crescent, abandoned Iksandarun. The warrior prince trotted, smiling, down into his encampment.

On the night of the midsummer moon Bellasteros's prescience was fulfilled. The shattered legions fell back to Iksandarun in little more than a rout. To the unbelieving citizens the gates of the city seemed to open by themselves. The sounds of battle echoed in the passageways of the palace.

Andrion leaned against the arched doorway of the throne room, forcing gulps of acrid air past his clenched teeth. The necklace he wore, a gold crescent moon with a gold star at its tip, leaped and sparked in the sweat pooled at his throat. His face was smudged, the linen chiton and draped cloak he wore were torn, the short Sardian sword he held was stained crimson. The Crimson Horde, he thought. Khazyari blood was as red as that of his own people.

"By all the gods," he said between his teeth, part curse, part prayer, "if I ever find who betrayed the legions and opened the gates, I shall cut out his heart, I shall stain the ancient altar of the temple with his blood as it was bloodied by traitors on the night of my birth!"

But no, his father had banned human sacrifice that very night. Andrion gulped again. His companions, sons of servants and noblemen alike, had pushed him from the battle in the streets into the momentary safety of the palace. His cloak was pinned with a brooch styled like the wings of the god Harus, and the gold necklace circled his throat; his identity was all too obvious. So he had gone, he had fled his companions, and their death screams were taunting wraiths in the air before him. Andrion, the prince, the heir, his life bought with blood. . . . "I swear," he cried, "I shall avenge you!"

Voices echoed within the throne room. Andrion turned. There, at the opposite end of the long, empty chamber, their forms winking fitfully in crimson lamplight, stood General Aveyron and his emperor.

Bellasteros sat stiffly against the glory of the peacock throne, his face scored by runnels of pain. He was not coiled like a hunting cat, blazing with anger and majesty; he was silent, his temper strangely eroded, the diadem only a band of embers on the dark hearth of his hair. He held the sword Solifrax, the gods' gift of power that was his alone to bear, unsheathed across his lap. The crystalline blade dripped red on the tile floor, blood spreading around the throne.

The general held his helmet under his arm politely, but he spoke friend to friend, his body straining forward in desperate, disbelieving urgency. "The city is burning. The Khazyari run like ravening wolves through the streets. The women's wing of the palace has fallen, and the temple citadel."

Shouts and screams and a crash of masonry echoed down the corridor. Andrion spun about; the Khazyari had brought a battering ram to the main door. If the old emperors had not built their palace as a fortress, it would already be over, his throat bared to the knife on the merciless stone of the altar. Death, and peace in the arms of the goddess—beloved of the gods, indeed! No, death was too easy.

The tapestries on the walls of the throne room seemed to smoke faintly, their images muted, as if at any moment they would burst into flame and disappear. The outstretched wings of Sardian Harus were broken; the mountain and pool of Sabazian Ashtar were muddied beyond cleansing. Gods, Andrion thought, shaking himself, even my own senses betray me.

Aveyron's voice was low and hoarse. "Your first wife, my lord. The lady Chryse. She and your daughter Sarasvati have thrown themselves from the battlements and dashed themselves to death in the courtyard rather than face the Horde."

Bellasteros closed his eyes. A muscle jumped in his jaw and his shoulders tightened in a long, sustained shiver. Solifrax glinted red, reflecting the pool of blood at his feet.

Andrion laid his cheek against the cool marble of the wall, his long, anguished breath clouding the stone. Chryse, the gentle sparrow, that one of his mothers who had guided his steps and mended his childhood wounds; Sarasvati, his spirited half-sister, less than a year younger than he.

"Declan, the high priest of Harus. . . ." Aveyron inhaled shakily. "Declan Falco lies dead in the temple courtyard, one of the falcon standards smashed in his shattered hand."

Andrion's fingers tightened convulsively on the hilt of his sword. Declan, too, wise tutor and compassionate friend; the darkness of this night consumed all hope. Tears burned the back of his throat and he choked them down into the void that had been his heart. He lived, and he would not weep.

Bellasteros opened his eyes. Their dark luster was dimmed, shadowed by defeat and death; the Sardian Conqueror was himself conquered. "So," he murmured with a quiet brutality, "the payment has come due; the sacrifice of the summer king. If only it were me alone, and not my people."

"Gods!" Andrion hissed. This despairing old man was not his father. It could not be his father. He would not let it be his father.

Another crash. The palace shuddered. A frescoed wall cracked and the images painted on it disintegrated. The hero Daimion and his companion Mari, queen of Sabazel, the hero Bellasteros and his companion Danica, queen of Sabazel, were becoming flakes of ash drifting like dead leaves to the floor.

Aveyron stepped onto the edge of the dais and seized his emperor by the arm. "My lord, no. You and the prince must escape. I let the barbarians turn my flank; I let them waste the legions. I shall stay and pay for my failure while you live for another day."

"No, Aveyron, old friend, not your failure." Bellasteros laid his hand on Aveyron's.

Aveyron shook away reassurance. "You and the prince must escape. The long leagues of the Empire lie before you, and Farsahn and Sardis beyond. You must live, so the Empire will live."

"Will your death buy the Empire? Will mine?" Bellasteros

for a moment looked into the glistening face of his general, looked into the face of Death. And he shuddered, throwing off some subtle choking drowsiness, waking the lean strength of his body. His eyes cleared and sparked into the numinous glow of the god-touched. He leaped from the throne. "Andrion," he said, his voice firm. "The prince. Where is he?"

That was his father. "I am here," Andrion called. With a tight smile more wary than relieved, he strode up the length of the audience chamber. His steps were only a faint patter on the floor.

Aveyron stepped back with a bow. Bellasteros rose, extending his hand, and Andrion placed his stained and dirty hand in his father's. Warm flesh touched warm flesh, the same sinew, the same bone. "You must live," the emperor said to his son. "I bought your life when you were born the winter king and were to have died for me. Now my life is due."

"No, no! I shall not go without you. You are the Empire. You are hope." Andrion tightened his grasp as if he could pull his father bodily from this evil despair. "I shall not go alone."

"I cannot go," said Bellasteros. The same stubborn will, no matter how oddly distorted. A slight frown marred the clean planes of his face, his words not quite his own.

"No," Andrion said aloud, his jaw set. He had never dared such defiance. He had never needed to. "The Empire is more than Iksandarun. It is your place to carry the sword and the diadem to safety. To Sabazel, my lord, my father; ever our refuge." Inwardly he cringed; no one had ever before had to tell Bellasteros his duty.

Solifrax, drained of blood, gleamed palely. A slow breeze stirred the gathered smoke, carrying in it a resonance of chimes, faint and disordered; the wind plucked at Andrion's tunic and stirred his hair. Andrion met his father's eyes, willing him to hear, and Bellasteros's eyes darkened in comprehension. For just a moment Andrion sagged, and then squared himself yet again.

An echoing crash shook the building. Shouts and cries flooded the corridors. The moment shattered. "Go," Aveyron insisted. "I will guard your back. In Ashtar's name, in the name of Harus, go now."

"So be it then," stated Bellasteros. "Perhaps the gods intend my death, but I have defied them before." He set aside Andrion's hand and glanced about him, a bright-eyed falcon seeking its prey.

Aveyron knelt at his emperor's feet. For just a moment his back bowed wearily. "My thanks, lord, for the honors you have given me."

"Well earned, my friend." Bellasteros's voice clotted. He lifted the curved blade of Solifrax and set its gleam on the general's shoulder in benediction. "May you feast this night in paradise."

Aveyron pulled himself to attention. He settled his helmet again on his head. His face was stark, gaunt, as if the skull already tightened the skin to nothingness. "My lord." He flourished his sword in salute, and he was gone.

Andrion's body rippled in a spasm of denial. "The gods shall answer for this," he muttered.

"The gods answer only to themselves, Andrion." Bellasteros's mouth curled in a black humor. His eye turned toward what remained of the painting of Daimion; it peeled off the wall before him and was whirled away. The flesh crawled on Andrion's neck; Bellasteros blanched. Lamplight glanced, ruddy brilliance, along the outstretched blade of Solifrax. "And do the gods deem it time for me to relinquish Daimion's sword?" the emperor murmured, half to himself, fading again.

"No!" Andrion exclaimed. "This despair is sorcery, whether of man or god; do not surrender to it!" And yet, he told himself, if the conqueror speaks of surrender, surely all is lost. . . . Andrion grasped the comfort of his mother's name. "Danica. We shall go to Danica. She speaks with the goddess."

"No longer," sighed Bellasteros. "Those days are gone forever." His forefinger touched Andrion's necklace, tracing the line of the crescent moon and the star at its tip. A wind stirred the air, and a beating of wings.

With a desperate, stubborn, tenacity, Andrion called, "Father!"

And again Bellasteros knitted together the raveling threads of his thoughts. His mouth set itself in a tight line of command; he thrust Solifrax into its serpent-skin sheath and jumped lightly down from the dais. "Let us see, Andrion, if any of my guard remain, so that with them we can sneak like thieves over the walls of our own city."

Andrion nodded, sheathed his sword, set his shoulder to his father's. He turned his back on the glittering peacock throne of the Empire and stretched his legs to match Bellasteros's stride.

The length of the hallway was muted with eddies of smoke, echoing with murmurs of battle. Beside the door stood the other standard of Harus. The bronze falcon seemed to strain upward, wings thrusting frantically against its bonds. "Well then, Harus," said Bellasteros. "I owe you and Sardis, though I am not even of Sardian blood." He pulled the hollow bronze figure from its pole and tucked it behind his sash.

"My lords," said a reedy voice.

Both men snapped around, their hands on their swords; Bellasteros, the famous campaigner, was a moment quicker. But it was a plump, beardless old man in the brown robe of a servant who stood behind them. "My lords," he said again. "I have lived in this palace many years. I know a secret passage."

Andrion forced his heart down from his throat and croaked, "The stories you told me as a boy, Toth? You said they were only legend."

Toth smiled vaguely and flapped a pudgy hand in the air. His clear, pale eyes sparked. "Legends become reality at need."

"True enough," growled Bellasteros. But a furtive amusement crimped the corners of his mouth. "Let the servant guide his master then, to this secret he has kept as his own."

The old man bobbed a perfunctory bow and scuttled down the passageway into misty smoke. Bellasteros and Andrion exchanged a quick glance and followed.

Five of the emperor's private guard, dirty and bloodied but as yet unscathed, waited with horses and supplies in a small dingy stableyard. "Toth!" exclaimed Bellasteros. "My thanks."

The old man smiled again. He produced a cloak, roughly woven of brown wool. "I could not find your crimson cloak, my lord," he told the emperor, "but I think this would be better."

Andrion glanced cautiously around. The sky was a black vault, etched with roiling smoke. The battlements of the palace flickered with the quickest, briefest tint of crimson. Demons dancing on the pyre of the defeated, he thought. The smoke was bitter in his mouth.

He turned abruptly and recognized one of the guards, a

young man encountered in the hallways of the palace. They had joked together, had sparred at weapons-practice. . . . Andrion could not remember the man's name.

Beyond the wall, from the heart of Iksandarun, rose a great cry. An eerie ululation offered by a thousand throats, rising and falling, that twined itself about the city and strangled it. The horses shifted restlessly, jangling their harnesses.

"A victory paean, I wager," said Bellasteros softly, detached.

Andrion spat. "Barbarians."

Bellasteros half turned, as if drawn to the sound. "But I must bring my heir to safety," he protested; he turned back again, tightened his body with an almost audible snap, and draped the clumsy cloak about himself.

Do not think about it, Andrion ordered himself. Madness stalks the night, sorcery stirs the shadows, my world turns upside down and reveals its soft underbelly.

Toth began to heave at the rough blocks of stone surrounding a well that lay against the wooden wall of the stable. Bellasteros waved and the guard ran forward. Andrion threw his young muscles against the rock. In a few moments the coping of the well lay uprooted on the dirty straw. The opening was a great blot of darkness, a cloud of darkness flowing tangibly upward. The emperor plucked up a torch and held it out. Stone-carved steps curved around the inside of the hole, their treads hollowed from much use, and dived into shadowed depths. From somewhere below echoed a faint trickle of water.

Bellasteros's eyes gleamed. "An ancient water tunnel?" he asked Toth.

"Yes, my lord." And, his hands fluttering, "Wait, wait, stack those stones here . . ."

"To conceal our exit," finished Andrion. "Very good, Toth." Odd, he had never thought the old creature capable of such cunning.

Bellasteros strode from man to man, offering a word of encouragement or a strong shoulder; he brought a length of rope from the stable and helped Andrion rip the supporting poles from the superstructure of the well. Levers took shape, the rope weaving through them like a spider's web. Andrion let himself believe that all would be well; they would escape, and Bellasteros would lead the armies of Sardis to the relief of Iksandarun.

The unearthly ululation began again, wavered and died. The stableyard filled suddenly with rosy light as flames leaped above the walls of the palace. The sky remained flat, unyielding.

"Come," ordered Bellasteros. He placed his foot on the top step, on the second step; his hand holding the torch shook suddenly, and his face in the scarlet light twisted. His other hand groped for the hilt of Solifrax.

He remembers the quest for the sword, Andrion realized. It was my mother who led him down just such a stairway, her star-shield shining before them. At the end they found the garden of the gods.

Bellasteros glanced up, searching; Andrion caught his eyes and held them. His eyes were horribly dull, terribly wrong. Perfidious gods, Andrion thought, and between his teeth he said, "If the gods mean to take the sword, better below than at the hands of the Khazyari."

Bellasteros steadied. The torch disappeared below the lip of the well. A glow fluttered within, a solitary firefly unable to illuminate the depths of the night.

The horses snuffled at the gaping black hole and started back, refusing. The guards swore; Andrion cursed. A wind whirled down from the palace walls, bearing a drift of glowing cinders, and brushed the flanks of the beasts. Whinnying indignantly, the horses plunged forward and stumbled onto the steps.

Andrion took the other torch and beckoned to Toth. "Come. We shall guard the rear."

The old man chuckled. "No, young lord; I think you will need a friend here, in the city."

"But Toth, the barbarians—"

"Will not notice an old eunuch left from the old days, before Bellasteros spread his cloak like a blessing over us. No, I shall stay and make sure this courtyard is nothing but charred wood and stone and ashes circling in the wind."

The wind—the voice of Ashtar. He was, after all, a clever old creature. "My thanks," said Andrion, and he and Toth solemnly touched hands. The old man's eyes were oddly translucent, like windows into another world. Andrion turned away.

He started down the rough, uneven stair. Slowly, he told himself. A fall could mean a broken neck. Toth would wait until the torchlight was gone before he released the levers.

There was plenty of tinder to spread over the tumbled rock; the palace, its gardens and tapestries, his own room filled with rolled maps and manuscripts and clumsy odes to Dana's beauty, the implacable beauty of the goddess. Gone, already gone. The Khazyari would find only a ruined and abandoned well. He stumbled and grasped at the wall; the slime on it burned his hand like acid. He saw only then that he had torn his palm on wood and rock.

Bellasteros and the guard were waiting at the bottom, pressing themselves against a rough-hewn wall that surrounded a dark, dank pool of water. A great rock-carved chamber arched overhead, its crevices lost in guttering shadow. Perhaps there were words carved there, perhaps not; perhaps a smoke gathered on the surface of the pool. The emperor's mouth was pinched shut in denial, but his sunken eyes were bleached into pale tinted mirrors reflecting nothing but despair. Andrion, struggling with exasperated horror, hurried once again to his side. "Father!"

With a weary sigh Bellasteros awoke. "Yes, yes, Andrion."

A tunnel exited the far side of the chamber, following the course of a stream, a water tunnel carved in the dawn of time long before Iksandarun became the seat of the Empire. The small company and their reluctant mounts splashed into the passageway.

Suddenly the earth heaved itself around them, and a wave of dust and ash boiled from behind to envelop them. Toth had done his work well. I shall reward him some day, if I ever see him again, Andrion thought. "About here," he muttered, looking narrowly upward, "would be the city walls."

"Yes," said Bellasteros. His torch threw wavering shadow on the rock. Rock shaped into leering demons? Andrion asked himself. No, it was his own imagination that saw the barbarian victory cry take form around him.

And then a breath touched his cheek, a breeze purling through the old tunnel, freshening, beckoning. Not a wind bearing the blood-and-soot scent of the city, but a cold wind singing down from the fastness of Cylandra, the white-capped mountain of tiny, remote Sabazel. Andrion smiled and turned to Bellasteros, and Bellasteros echoed his quick grin.

The exit was a tiny crevice between megaliths that might at one time have been hewn by the hand of man. Now they lay cozily together, overgrown with brambles and vines. Cursing the thorns and quelling the indignant snorts of the horses, the company forced their way through and emerged into a willow grove.

Limber branches danced and sighed, and rustling leaves played with a sky suddenly filled with stars. Andrion started with recognition. He knew this place, a grove lining the banks of a stream well beyond the city walls. He had played here as a child, dreamed here as a youth.

The wind summoned him. Beside him, his father straightened and inhaled deeply of the clean air. A full moon spun through the fingerlike leaves of the willows. Heartened, the company strode forward.

At the edge of the grove the trees parted, seeming to lift their roots and move away from the armed company like fine ladies raising their skirts to avoid a mud puddle. The plateau of Iksandarun opened before Andrion's eyes. A shroud of darkness shot with flame lay over the city. A pall of smoke engulfed the stars and reached upward, grasping at the full moon of midsummer. The moon, its great golden face tinted crimson—Ashtar's eye stained by the ordeal of Iksandarun —seemed too heavy to be borne on a breeze that failed and died.

The stench of smoke and death filled Andrion's nostrils. Faraway screams filled his ears. He quelled an impulse to run back into the trees and hide there, denying his birth, denying the gods. The grove was protected by a corner of the goddess's mantle; she loved him, yes, and whom she loved she tested. As she had tested his grandmother Viridis, who had perhaps walked here before she gave herself to Sabazel and died for her gift at the hand of Gerlac in Sardis.

Viridis's only son, his father, stood beside him. The cool shadow of the trees slipped away from him like a rent garment. His eyes dulled again, haunted by circling ghosts. "There," he said, his voice thin and taut. "The moon was there, caught in the constellation of the Tree, the night you were born. It has not been there since."

"My life come due?" Andrion heard himself say. "Or yours?" The hair prickled on the back of his neck. Blood stained the ancient altar, and blood stained the moon. Viciously he shrugged away such thoughts.

Bellasteros turned to him as if wanting to reassure him. But his words were not reassuring. "The rites of the goddess will be finished by the time we reach Sabazel, and men will have been turned away from its borders. Perhaps the queen will not let us in.''

Andrion's heart went leaden in his chest. To be turned away at the gates of Sabazel would be the final betrayal. But he raised his chin, touched his father's arm, and said stoutly, ''How can the Queen Ilanit, my half-sister, turn us away? We are the only acknowledged sons of Sabazel.''

Bellasteros shook his head, not seeming to understand. Andrion ground his teeth in frustration at the spell that must be sucking at his father's spirit. Gods, why do this to him? he demanded silently. There was no answer.

It was only when they mounted that Andrion realized his pony Pergamo had been left behind; Toth had given him a tall cavalry horse. So easily, then, did his youth pass. So terribly.

A fitful smoke hung heavy over the grassland, blurring the outlines of walls, the crumbled ashes of farmsteads. The bodies of their defenders bristled with clumps of arrows like some creeping weed. Bellasteros looked about him and moaned; a tear coursed slowly, painfully, down his hollow cheek, and disappeared into his beard. His eyes, sunken pale shadows, reflected no moonlight.

Andrion leaned forward over the neck of his horse, trying to urge them on, faster, faster, feeling almond-shaped eyes on the back of his neck. But the moon faded; they had to pick their way through the ruined land as a sullen crimson light diffused along the underside of the great cloud of smoke. The city burned; Bellasteros's challenge, to build and to grow, was forfeit. A distant wailing hung upon the heavy air; the hoofbeats of horses reverberated upon the earth.

The hoofbeats of more than the small imperial company—light steps, unshod steppe-ponies. Andrion inhaled sharply. Where? The sound could come from anywhere. . . .

Shouts tore the night, incomprehensible Khazyari passwords. As one Bellasteros and Andrion reined in their horses and spun about. The guard, uncertain, blocked their way. The horses entangled themselves, plunging and rearing.

Khazyari shouts and black-tipped arrows together split the night. One guard went down with a cry, the arrow embedded in his throat, and his horse screamed and vanished into the murk.

Bellasteros's body snapped into wakefulness. ''By all the gods!'' he shouted. Solifrax flared from its scabbard. For a moment the blade glinted crystal clear, driving the darkness before it. Andrion's breath caught in his throat, with exaltation perhaps, perhaps with terror. He drew his own sword.

The dim shapes that were the Khazyari darted through the smoke, circling like jackals. Another flight of arrows hissed downward.

And one barbed shaft struck deep into Bellasteros's right arm. He cried out, in protest, it seemed, not in pain; the sword Solifrax flew from his hand and inscribed a gleaming arc through the darkness.

"No!" Andrion shouted. "God's beak, no!" He threw his short sword away and reached up, fingers open. Solifrax fell neatly into his hand. The hilt was too large; it seared his palm and he gasped. He was not the hero who had earned its power. The glow of its path still hung in the air, the glow of its curving blade hung behind his eyelids in the shape of a crescent moon.

One quick glance, and Andrion saw his father bent over his horse's neck, grasping its mane; the diadem lay inert on his hair, his face was stark white, his teeth bared in a rictus grin of pain and of pride in his son. Then his face went blank, the last threads of his intelligence, of his courage, fraying into nothingness.

"Gods!" screamed Andrion. The outrage, the agony, the fear filled him taut as a wineskin. And burst. He shouted, realizing as he did so that he sang the Sabazian paean. The sword moved in his hand, jerking his arm out, and his thighs tightened on the horse's sides. It leaped forward. He struck, slicing right and left, and voices cried in sudden terror. Hoofs thundered behind him.

The Khazyari gave way, howling, before the wrath of the prince and the shining blade of Solifrax, and their shapes faded into the night.

But Andrion did not dare stop. Even as the sword muted itself, growing unbearably heavy; even as his hand burned, he urged the company onward. His arm could fall from his body before he would give up that sword. His father's sword, which now lay awkwardly in his own right hand.

The gods will answer for this! he told himself, seizing the far edge of sanity. I shall defy them all. The company raced on, farther, farther, as a westering moon pulled the smoking shroud of Iksandarun with it across the sky.

Chapter Two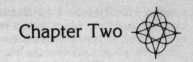

DANA PERCHED ON a boulder, settled her long bow over her shoulder, and surveyed the night with clear green eyes. Behind her rose the mountain Cylandra, its ice-crown sparkling in the moonlight; before her lay the narrow valley of Sabazel. The torches in the city flared, brazenly mortal, beneath the purity of a full midsummer moon.

Or was the moon pure? Oddly, it seemed tinted with crimson, and the stars were smudged, seen through a fine pall. Dana frowned. For the tenth time she leaped from her seat and paced up and down. Perhaps if she had participated in the rites, she could have burned away that restlessness, purged the unease in the arms of some unwitting imperial soldier.

If those men with whom she had celebrated the rites this last year had only known whose face she set upon their straining bodies. Such arrogance, to imagine the heir of the Empire in her arms. But he was, after all, her own . . . cousin? The bloodlines became tangled.

Andrion had been coming with his father to the rites of Sabazel all her life. As children they were set in the care of some older woman while their elders sang and danced and feasted together. And they were friends. Then, last midsummer, they were themselves admitted to the rites, as was custom, with partners older and wiser than they. Then the emperor and his son came again at midwinter, and again Andrion was given to another.

Soon Dana, too, would be eighteen. Soon she and Andrion would celebrate with more than stolen kisses. A Sabazian favoring a man, indeed, she thought with acerbic humor. Women counted the quiet cadence of daily life, and were therefore more important in the scheme of existence; men were sudden lightning bolts illuminating the far horizon of another world. But if her mother and her grandmother knew certain men as both friends and lovers, why not she? A slow smile shaped the fullness of her lips.

And then died. It was midsummer, the moon was full, Andrion did not come. She would not sleep alone, not yet; she guarded the city while the others slept satiated in the arms of men.

Not Danica her grandmother, though; not Ilanit her mother. They kept vigil in the temple, as restive as she. Rumors came from beyond the borders of Sabazel; the goddess Ashtar spoke grim words from her shield, from her pool, from her cavern in the mountain. But she spoke only to the queen.

Dana slipped the bow from her shoulder, braced its end against a rock, and leaned her cheek against cool willow and sinew. The city dozed, glinting black and bronze like fine armor below her. The moon hung ripe and round high above her. The wind? The wind was still.

Her spine crawled. A faint odor of smoke tickled her nostrils. Cooking fires in the city of Sabazel, of course.

Dana looked down the valley, beyond the high plains sacred to Ashtar, to the horizon. It seemed as if tiny flames flickered there, pyres consuming the flower of the Empire. It seemed as if a distant wailing of grief and pain and grotesque victory hung heavy on the heavy air.

She frowned again. Her Sight seldom failed her but the images could not be called; and when they seized her, they would not be denied, even though their meaning often remained elusive. Was this what her mortal mother felt when the Goddess spoke to her, what mortal Danica had felt when she bore the star-shield of Sabazel?

"Let the others celebrate this night," Dana said to the moon, quietly but firmly. "My grandmother rode pregnant into battle, carrying Andrion himself within her womb; by all the gods, he was conceived with a fate upon him. But I shall ride to battle empty, waiting to be filled with destiny."

Would that destiny be Andrion's, or her own? Or were their fates inextricably intertwined?

Her extra sense faded, leaving her without an answer. But then, some answers were to be dreaded. Dana straightened, tested the bow, reached into the quiver on her back and nocked an arrow to the string. She raised it up, up, until her bow repeated the gleaming arc of the moon. Her fingers snapped and the string sang with one high sustained note of music. The arrow hissed upward, bisected the face of the moon, disappeared against the muted sky.

A cold breath of wind sighed down the flank of Cylandra, stained with the scent of blood, and Dana shivered.

The Khazyari raged through the city, raping, burning, killing, until at last their blood lust was sated. Then, and only then, did the warrior prince Tembujin set small squads to putting out the remaining fires, to sorting looted silk and gold and fine porcelain, to mending the wounds of Khazyari and imperial citizens alike.

"This city will be another jewel in your cap," he said soothingly into his father's ear. "The people will work, and their work will fill our hands with riches. Go, savor the pleasures of this night, and let me oversee the dawn."

Baakhun, the great khan, nodded agreement. His burly form straddled the temple steps; his powerful arms glistened with sweat, and his thick felt boots were soaked crimson. A haggard crowd of survivors crouched at his feet. "See your gods!" he declaimed in a fractured common tongue. "They run! Khalingu strong, stronger than all!"

None of the survivors disputed his words. They lay prostrate as he and his officers, his nuryans, swept by them, and they crawled away, weeping, after he passed. The ancient temples slumped into blackened rubble; the fruit trees in the hanging gardens stretched bare and blackened limbs toward a gray sky.

In that chill hour before dawn, when the world lies stripped of illusion, each object hard-etched in silver, each sound uncannily clear, Tembujin, the khan's eldest son, rode out of the city toward the vast encampment of the conquerors. He sipped from the jeweled drinking cup in his hand, letting the strong Sardian wine, blood red, blood warm, linger on his tongue. The high planes of his face, eyes and cheekbones sculpted by the winds of faraway steppes, curved into a smile that was echoed by the curve of the bow on his shoulder.

The smile tightened as he passed the pyramid of severed heads heaped outside the gateway, defenders of the city resting uneasily. Beside the grisly tower were several poles set into the ground, each impaling the naked, twitching form of a Khazyari warrior. Tembujin's smile faded into a slight frown.

He came to the tall yurt of his father Baakhun, walls
appliquéd with scenes of battle and the hunt. A lion skin
waved in a slow breeze, and pipes wailed a hymn of victory.
Attendants, seeing the white pony of the first odlok, flocked
forward; Tembujin dismounted and flicked a drop of wine at
the cart holding the wooden idol of the god Khalingu. "Such
work you have done this night," he said quietly. "Are you
pleased, O greatest of Gods?"

"Our own kviss is good enough for Khalingu," said a voice
at his side. "Why not for you?"

He turned to see his twelve-year-old half-brother. Vlad's
swart features were not flattered by the uncompromising light;
his cheeks were stained and his nose ran. Tembujin raised an
eyebrow and sipped again from the cup. "My mother was a
Mohendra princess, given to Baakhun in alliance a decade
before yours, who is only the daughter of an insignificant
chieftain. My sensibilities are much the finer."

Vlad flushed. His lower lip pouted around a muttered
epithet.

Tembujin snorted, "Wipe your face, piglet." He ducked
into the great yurt; Vlad followed.

Butter lamps burned inside, casting a thick yellow light over
the felt rugs and hangings, over the multitude of faces turned
to the khan. Imperial officials begging for mercy, Khazyari
nuryans and their retainers waiting for rewards. Baakhun
himself sat cross-legged on a raised wooden bed, a skin of
kviss—fermented mare's milk—in his hand. His high shaved
forehead was flushed, his braid of black hair askew, his wet
lips open in a vulpine grin. The carved ivory plaque of the
khan, a rampant lion, stuck against his perspiring chest.

The hacked and mutilated body of General Aveyron lay
amid the riches heaped before him, stripped of helmet and
armor, but not, somehow, of dignity. Beside it a cadaverous
man in torn imperial robes lay prostrate, his face fastidiously
averted from the corpse. Tembujin's other brow rose, and he
slipped noiselessly into his place at his father's right hand.

On his father's left hand was Raksula, his favorite wife,
Vlad's mother. She reached out and tucked the boy under her
arm, wiping his nose on her skirts; he clung to her, whining
about his half-brother's insult. Her sharp black gaze darted
behind Baakhun's back to Tembujin, and she hissed like a
cobra who sees a mongoose.

Tembujin's teeth flashed in his bronzed face; he shook back

the fringe of black hair on his forehead and temples and
saluted Raksula with his cup. Insolent bravado, perhaps, but
his eyes went suddenly wary, and his hand closed protectively
around his own plaque, a carving of a lion's cub.

"My lord," said the prostrate man in the common tongue.
"My lord—khan, my lord prince, I beg my reward; I served
you well this night." His features were loose, pliable, ready to
be molded into whatever expression was most expedient.

Baakhun drank deeply from his skin. "Who is this worm?"
he demanded in Khazyari.

"The chamberlain, Hilkar," replied Tembujin. "The
traitor." He threw down his cup and his bow and drew the
long knife from his belt. He grasped Hilkar's sparse hair,
jerked his head upward, and set the blade against the loose
skin of his throat, drawing from it a thin trickle of blood.

Hilkar gabbled, "My young lord, please, it is I who aided
you!"

"You sent a messenger to our camp this last month," said
Tembujin in the common speech, "saying that you wished
vengeance on the Sardian conqueror. You came yourself, on
your belly like a snake. Now you have your vengeance. Is that
not enough?"

"But I can further serve the great khan!"

"What does the creature want?" asked Baakhun impatiently.

Tembujin never took his eyes from Hilkar's scrawny neck.
"Wealth," he replied in Khazyari. "Rank. Payment for his
treachery. He says he will serve you."

"Perhaps he can."

"But if he betrayed the emperor, might he not betray us?"
Tembujin's fingers tightened and Hilkar gasped. His eyes
darted from side to side, as if he could see through the
language his ears did not understand.

Raksula yawned. "Kill him. He has served his purpose."

"No," said Baakhun. "One thing remains."

Tembujin shrugged. He released Hilkar, who crumpled
back onto the rug with a gasp and quickly rearranged his face
into an empty, fawning grin.

Baakhun leaned down, his lips working to shape the common tongue. "Where the khan, the . . . king? Where the odlok
his son?"

Hilkar raised his hands placatingly. They were stained rust-brown from Aveyron's pooled blood. "They must be hiding like rats in the city. I gave you Bellasteros's cloak, to enspell him. . . ."

"Where?" bellowed Baakhun. Hilkar winced and fell prostrate again, contracting his length to an inoffensive huddle.

Baakhun straightened and spoke to Tembujin in Khazyari. "A patrol saw a party of imperial horsemen at the middle of the night, far beyond the walls. One of them bore a shining sword and carried terror with him."

"Our patrol ran from them?" demanded Tembujin incredulously. "By Khalingu's tail . . ." He stopped. "The warriors by the gate. I see."

The khan nodded. He spat, narrowly missing Hilkar's head. The throng eddied and emitted the squat form of Odo, the chief shaman. He bowed extravagantly before the khan, the battery of amulets on his chest clanking, and pulled a length of scarlet fabric from his tunic. "I cast strong spells," he purred. "Confusion, despair. But the king is strong; why else would Khazyari run from him? And the boy—I had nothing of his."

"Why did you not bring us a possession of the boy's?" Tembujin asked Hilkar.

The huddle shifted. Hilkar's face surfaced, still grinning. "He is young, unimportant."

"Evidently not," Tembujin returned. And in Khazyari, "The prince helped his father to escape. Some, then, are loyal." He stirred Hilkar's ribs with the toe of his boot.

"So," Baakhun scowled. "They are gone. Even his women are dead. A stain on my victory."

"But the city is ours," continued Odo, smiling so broadly his eyes almost disappeared in folds of flesh. "What matters a dispossessed king, a prince without an inheritance?"

"Mm," Baakhun said petulantly. His tongue was growing thick, even with his own language. "I meant to sacrifice Bellasteros and his family to Khalingu. I wanted his god-sword, that they sing of even in the Mohan."

Raksula leaned toward her husband, murmuring, "We will find him, and that power will be yours. As for today, Odo has served you well and deserves reward."

Baakhun gestured; Tembujin took a jeweled bracelet from the sleeve of his tunic and flicked it onto the rug. Odo fell upon it, tested it in his teeth, and slipped it onto his arm with a chuckle.

Guards hoisted the body of Aveyron. "A brave man," said Tembujin. "Sacrifice a horse to him." Baakhun lifted the skin and gulped.

Other guards seized Hilkar and pulled him to his feet. "My lords," he protested. "I have served you, and I shall serve you again; I shall find the Sardian and his heir. They have fled to the hole of Sabazel, I daresay."

Baakhun shook his head at the flood of common speech. "Spare him," he ordered. "His life shall be his reward."

"Your life is your payment," Tembujin translated. "Get out."

Hilkar opened his mouth, thought better of speaking, gathered his composure about him. He smiled blandly and made a deep obeisance. He strutted across the yurt, but some of the captive imperial officials spat at him, and his last steps to the doorway were a rapid scurry.

Raksula took the scarlet cloak from Odo. "I shall guard this," she said. "We shall need it." Odo smiled again. His slits of eyes glinted with a feral cunning, and Raksula's eyes glinted in return. Vlad, from the shelter of his mother's skirts, sneered openly at Tembujin.

Tembujin's mouth tightened, but he said nothing.

Raksula touched Baakhun's mighty arm in a familiar proprietary gesture. "I shall go to my own yurt now, my lord, and leave you to your celebration." Her hand pushed Vlad in the back, and he fell forward in a respectful bow.

Baakhun waved expansively; Odo led them out. He and Raksula began speaking together in low tones almost before they were outside. "Sabazel," hissed the woman; Tembujin glanced quickly at Baakhun, but the khan, grinning again, did not hear.

Baakhun conferred with his nuryans and sent the imperial officials back to the city. "And for you, my son," he mumbled at last; he drained the last drop of kviss and looked mournfully at the deflated skin. Tembujin turned an attentive expression on his father. Baakhun cleared his throat. "You are my right hand, you are my finest weapon. How may I reward you?"

"It is reward enough serving you," said Tembujin, bowing. From the corner of his eye he saw several guards escort in a brown-robed palace servant and a group of women, fair imperial women. "However," he went on smoothly, "if you insist . . ."

Baakhun saw the direction of his son's gaze and laughed. His huge hand slapped Tembujin's back, and the young man staggered. "You are indeed my son!" the khan bellowed. "Take whichever one tempts you!"

Some of the women struggled against the ropes that bound them; others stood slumped, weeping. But one stared boldly around the yurt. Her brittle lapis lazuli eyes inspected the nuryans and Baakhun's stocky form and then dismissed them. Her stare fell on Tembujin and paused. She essayed a smile, rather weak at the corners, but a smile nonetheless.

Tembujin strolled with lazy feline steps to her side. Her dress was torn and her hair, bright with the sheen of copper, was tangled, but she seemed unspoiled. He took the delicate curve of her chin between thumb and forefinger. "From the imperial harem?" he asked.

Pleased that he could speak the common tongue, her smile steadied. "This emperor has no concubines. I am a courtesan from the Street of Silk."

"Ah," sighed Tembujin. His finger traced the line of her throat, the fine bones of her shoulder, the curve of her breast. She did not flinch. "And your name?"

"Sita."

"Sita," he repeated. "Come then, Sita." Obediently she followed him. The servant, a plump, beardless old man, bobbed a perfunctory bow as they passed. For just a moment Tembujin was caught by a spark in the man's expression, by his oddly translucent eyes. But no, he was smiling vaguely, face blank. He knew his place, to serve whatever master fate gave him.

The dawn light was thin and pale compared to the luminescence of the butter lamps. Smoke tinted the still air; a bloated crimson moon rested on the western horizon. Tembujin paused, regarding it with narrow eyes as it sank slowly, inexorably, and disappeared. A warmth touched his back, a greedy sun for the new day.

Sita watched him watch the moonset. When he turned back to her she smiled and held out her hands. He unbound them. "Stop smiling," he said. "I grow weary of hypocritical smiles."

Quickly she straightened her lips, cast her eyes down, and allowed her mouth to crumple in faint, unassuming hurt.

"You learn quickly," Tembujin laughed. "Come." He guided her to his own yurt, marked by the feathered standard

of the odlok. "Tell me," he said as he ushered her inside,
"what is this place called Sabazel?"

Sita's eyes widened in what might have been bewilderment.
The fabric door fell behind them.

Chapter Three

SEVERAL GREAT SLABS of stone cast from the edge of a cliff in some ancient cataclysm shaded a rocky gully where the small company of horsemen huddled concealed.

Andrion stood at the mouth of the ravine, looking down a rough scree to the rolling grassland across which they had struggled in those dark hours between midnight and dawn. Now, at noon, sunshine glanced off the stones to assault him with waves of heat. The air moved in slow eddies, scented with the sweat of horses and men, with the dry odors of dirt and crushed thyme. The empty lands before him, abandoned long ago by the dregs of the hero-king Daimion's dynasty, shimmered and danced with mirages.

He closed his eyes. Perhaps the memories of the night were also mirages, nightmares induced by some fevered dream, terror and grief and pain circling in red-tinted darkness. If he could see beyond the heat-distorted horizon, he would see Iksandarun shining like a great peacock, unsullied, unbloodied. . . . No, he was an exile in his own land, dirty and unshaven. Following the custom of Sardis, as became the son of a conqueror who had adopted the fashion of his new Empire, he had never gone unshaven.

Sardis. It was still there, governed by his father's oldest friend, Patros; forty days' journey along the Royal Road in peacetime, more, much more, along the wilderness tracks of a conquered Empire.

Abruptly Andrion turned back into the shade. A small trickle of water pattered down the gully; three of the guards tended the horses, rubbing them with tufts of grass, offering tender shoots of the tamarisk trees that clung precariously to the rock.

25

Bellasteros was propped against a boulder, holding a cup of water untouched in his hand, his head resting on his rolled cloak. The bronze figure of Harus sat on a small altar of pebbles. The emperor's eyes, washed pale with pain and sorcery, waited for a sign. The imperial diadem rested dust-stained on his brow; the sword Solifrax lay sheathed and quiet, forgotten at his side.

I bore the sword for a few moments, Andrion told himself. It burned my hands, knowing it was not mine. But his hands were firm and clear, not singed at all.

"Harus," murmured Bellasteros. "I brought you from Sardis to the Empire, and now I exile you; Ashtar's hand once lay over all the world, but even she is trammeled by the present."

At the end the gods drove Daimion, too, mad with despair, Andrion thought. Perhaps he had deserved it. Bellasteros did not. Andrion knelt beside his father and spoke quickly, with a forced cheerfulness, "Fourteen days at least to Sabazel; we must not tire the horses. Toth provided us with dried meat and fruit and twice-baked bread, and the streams have yet to dry up in the summer's heat." You are babbling, he told himself. He swallowed the dirt, the acid in his mouth, and tried again. "We shall go across country, and they will not know where we have gone, they will not follow."

"The traitor," said Bellasteros, "will know Sabazel." His glazed eyes never left the tiny face of the falcon. The falcon was silent, its bright bronze muted with dust.

Andrion's lips tightened. Horrible, to see the mighty Bellasteros stunned by defeat, eaten by an evil spell; a demi-god desecrated. Andrion wanted to shake him, scream at him to wake. But only Danica, who once bore the power of the goddess, might be able to ward such sorcery. "No," Andrion said, a trifle too loudly, "Sabazel is our refuge."

He focused on his father's arm, bound with a bloody scrap of his own chiton. The shaft of the arrow had snapped in his hands sometime during the cold paralyzing dawn, snapped like living bone. "We must withdraw that arrowhead, Father. It will not wait for Shandir and Danica."

A frown flickered over Bellasteros's face. He glanced down at his arm and seemed to notice the wound for the first time.

"I will do it," Andrion stated firmly, but his stomach was anything but firm.

"Danica," stated Bellasteros. He stirred, sat up straighter.

His eyes cleared, darkening, and turned to Andrion. His hand touched the necklace at Andrion's throat and his seamed and weary features softened in a smile.

Ah, my father . . . A movement; Andrion started. But it was only the fourth guard, the one little older than he, offering a helmet full of water. Andrion dredged his name from the well of memory and tried to smile. "Miklos, thank you." The young man was hollow-eyed, pale beneath his sun-darkened skin, trying to comprehend the incomprehensible.

"My lord," said Miklos, "I campaigned against the bandits along the Royal Road when I came out from Sardis two years ago. I have seen something of surgery."

"Good, you may help me." Andrion's hands trembled; he choked back a scornful oath and clenched his teeth. Delicately he touched the bandage. Bellasteros winced and looked away, beyond the shadow and the stones, to the distant insubstantial horizon. The bloody scrap unwound, revealing the barbed head of the black Khazyari arrow imbedded in raw, scored flesh halfway between elbow and shoulder.

"We must push the arrowhead through," Miklos said. "A barbed head will only tear the wound further if we draw it out the way it entered."

"Mm," said Andrion. His jaw ached, but he ground his teeth even tighter. Spoiled princeling, grow up. "Here, hold the arm steady." Miklos inhaled deeply and grasped his emperor's arm in two strong hands. Andrion took the arrow-shaft between thumb and forefinger.

Bellasteros began to speak, quickly, his voice thin and strained. His eyes never left the horizon, but it was not the horizon that flickered in their depths. "Chryse, my first wife, I tore you from your home in Sardis and brought you to Ik-sandarun on the day of my victory. My victory, and therefore yours. But you were torn from our daughter Chrysais, never to see her again, for she married the king of Minras in the Great Sea."

Andrion pushed, slowly. The barbs sliced even more deeply into the wound. Blood gushed, burning, over his hand. A sparkling mist swam before his eyes; impatiently he shrugged it away.

Miklos averted his face and gazed intently at the image of the falcon. His lips moved. But his hands were steady.

Bellasteros's breath caught in his throat. "Chryse, you raised my children as your own: Andrion, son of Danica the queen of Sabazel; Sarasvati, daughter of the imperial princess Roushangka. Dead in childbirth, Roushangka, and now Sarasvati's blue eyes are closed forever. . . ."

"The lady Sarasvati," Miklos blurted. "Is it true, did she leap from the battlement?"

Do not remind me, Andrion pleaded silently. Do not speak of it, and maybe it will not be true. But the other man's dark gaze was fixed unwaveringly on his face, pleading in its turn. "Can you imagine," replied Andrion, forcing the words between his teeth, "what the Khazyari would have done to her?"

"Yes," Miklos hissed. And added lamely, a moment later, "My lord." His gaze fell. His hands remained strong on Bellasteros's arm.

Andrion worked the arrowhead as gently as he could, pushing it deeper; the blood welled up around it, spilled over, ran down onto the dirt.

Bellasteros's left hand clutched awkwardly at Solifrax. "Aveyron, my old friend, what a fool I was to let the enemy take me from behind." He gasped, closing his eyes. His words tumbled from his lips, spinning into delirium. "Gods, gods, take me as your sacrifice, the blood of the summer king healing his land—"

"No!" Andrion exclaimed. "Your strategy was sound; we were betrayed." His gentleness was only giving Bellasteros more pain. He thrust, and the barb burst from the back of the arm, blossoming from torn scarlet muscle. Scarlet droplets pocked the dust where Andrion knelt. His stomach heaved and he forced it back down. His father's voice abruptly ceased, leaving a sudden silent void in his mind.

Imperial blood, he thought, as warm and red as the least peasant's. "Forgive me," he murmured, not sure just why he asked forgiveness.

Andrion grasped the barbed point of the arrowhead and pulled it from the poor shattered flesh. It pricked his fingers, and his own blood mingled with his father's. He considered the evil weapon. Was it tainted? But the emperor's madness came from a more subtle poison. And there was no remedy, not here, not now. With a curse he threw the arrowhead away.

Bellasteros's face was so pale as to be faintly green. A cold sweat glistened on his forehead. Andrion cleaned the arm with water from Miklos's helmet. His own sweat ran stinging into his eyes but he ignored it.

"Patros," sighed the king, his voice drawn into a feeble

thread. But it was his voice. Andrion inhaled, trying to absorb that voice into his own body. "I grew up with you, your brother in your father's house. You helped me gain the Empire I have now lost. Declan, I brought you to your fate in Iksandarun. Chryse . . ." And he roused, opening his eyes, seeing nothing. "If I had given Sarasvati to Sabazel, she would be safe now. I owed her to Sabazel, in return for Andrion. But I owed Roushangka, dead in childbirth; I owed Chryse for my neglect. I owe the gods themselves. . . ." His words dissipated and died; his hand went slack and fell away from the sheath of Solifrax. His eyes faded again, taken by pain and madness.

Andrion bound the wound with the ragged edge of Bellasteros's cloak. A brown peasant's cloak, not his crimson one. He realized his teeth were sunk deep into his lower lip. Salt-sour sweat stung his eyes, salt-sour blood clotted his mouth, his stomach fluttered and his head swam, thoughts spinning like dried willow leaves in a fall wind, like the ashes of Iksandarun scattered to the sky. Something in Miklos's voice caught him then, some carefully hidden agony. Yes, he had been assigned to the women's wing of the palace. . . .

Andrion's thought steadied. He glanced up. The young soldier held one end of the bandage, his eyes opaque, his face set. I can hardly ask, Andrion thought, just how closely the guard guarded his princess, or if she encouraged such devotion; but then, such a grave and delicate game would have been worthy of her temper.

His lips crimped in a bittersweet smile as he tied the rude bandage around his father's arm. Miklos slipped away, disdaining thanks.

Andrion hovered as Bellasteros dozed uneasily, muttering strange phrases under his breath, waking only to take food at Andrion's insistence. The sun passed its zenith and began to glide toward the west. The wind stirred slow whorls of dust down the cliff face, and the shimmering mirages were sucked up into a flat blue sky burnished like a blade.

We have to go, Andrion thought; we shall surely be pursued. He rose, stretching. His body ached as if it had been beaten.

His father leaned on his arm, silent, and struggled silently onto his horse. Andrion settled Solifrax at Bellasteros's side, but the emperor stared into the distance as if listening for some music in the wind that he could no longer hear.

Indeed, there was no message in this searing breeze. Andrion picked up the bronze falcon; with a quick prayer, Mercy, Harus, for this your servant, he stowed it in a saddlebag. He sent a prayer upward into the sky, to the flaring disk of the sun, and the moon that hid its face from the sun's harshness: Ashtar, we are your sons, have mercy. And he thought, Everything will be well when we reach Sabazel; my mother Danica, my sister Ilanit, my cousin Dana with her challenging smile will heal us. We shall find direction in Sabazel. His necklace burned his throat and blood clotted on his hands as he led the company into the hot breath of the afternoon.

The shadow of the great rocks moved away from the black arrowhead and the blood-spattered dust. The edge of the sunlight spilled over them. A serpent glided from beneath the boulder, considering the world through eyes like cut sapphires; its shining scales clicked by the barb and smoothed a crescent across the stained ground.

Chapter Four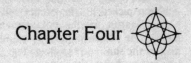

TEMBUJIN DOZED IN the heat of midday, luxuriating among the quilts of his raised bed, wearing only his plaque of rank. A breeze plucked fitfully at the hangings of the yurt, and sunlight flickered around the door; motes of golden dust swirled in the warm air.

There was a movement beside him. Tembujin's muscles tightened, his black eyes glittered briefly between slitted lids. Sita thrust the quilts away and sat up, groaning, looking about her with a moment's confusion. Then her mouth tensed with memory. She sat unmoving for a time, only her breasts rising and falling with her breath. The fall of red hair down her back lifted in the breeze as if stroked by invisible hands. Tembujin smiled, let his smile fade, did not stir.

Then Sita sighed and raised her chin. She glanced down at the sleek body of the Khazyari prince, her nostrils flaring with distaste. His long knife lay among his clothes on the carpeted floor; stealthily she crept from the bed, picked it up, drew it from its sheath. She turned it in her hand and a brief ray of sun glanced down the blade.

Slowly she stepped to the side of the bed and sat beside Tembujin's still form. Slowly she raised the knife so that the shining blade just touched the arch of his throat.

Her teeth indented her lower lip. The blue of her eyes, the blue of evening before the first star, glistened with shifting depths of fear, anger, conscience. Tembujin's face remained as impassive as a statue cast in bronze, but his hand snaked silently through the covers behind Sita's back, tense, ready.

"Harus! If I kill I am no better than he!" She turned and hurled the knife across the yurt. It struck deep into the carpeted ground and stood there shivering. Tembujin's hand leaped upward, closed on Sita's hair, and yanked her down.

She yelped in terror, and yelped again as Tembujin fell on her, pinning her to the bed. Her hands set themselves flat against his chest as if to shove him away. But she moved only her eyes, averting them when his face pressed close to hers.

"Why did you throw the knife away?" he asked.

She looked right and left, seeking an escape. But the Khazyari's hand was tight in her hair, his weight crushing her. His black eyes searched hers. She swallowed. "Whoever strikes you down would die. And I have compromised so much already to live."

Tembujin laughed shortly. "If it were a slave who struck me down, retribution would indeed be swift and unpleasant. There are those, though, who could perhaps strike with impunity." He released her hair and raised himself on his elbows, continuing to contemplate her face. But her eyes revealed nothing. The long tail of black hair tied at the back of his head fell forward and rested on her shoulder like a coil of binding rope. "You are no courtesan," Tembujin said. "A virgin, certainly. Did you think I would not know?"

Sita's lips thinned as she closed them even more tightly.

"You have fair skin, smooth hands. You have never worked."

Her cheeks slowly drained of color.

"A rich merchant's daughter, perhaps, a precious jewel among his wares?"

She exhaled suddenly, as if relieved; her eyes flicked across his, searching in turn. "Yes, quite."

"So," Tembujin said. "Live, then. You are mine now, and if you behave yourself, no one will hurt you. Do you understand?"

"I understand," she replied, her words tinted with bitter gall. "I shall live, and suffer the indignities of living, such as contempt so great you would not even bind me after using me."

"Shh," he said soothingly. "Be glad you were not taken by my father Baakhun, who would squash you like a flea, or by Odo the shaman, who would work evil magic on you, or my pig-brother Vlad, who would torture you, knowing no other way to pleasure himself with a woman." Tembujin abandoned her eyes and bent his cheek to hers, inhaling the lavender and anemone of her scent. "But I, Sita, know how to pleasure you."

Her lip curled in denial. She stared up at the center pole of the tent, removing herself from her body, and sighed, lightly, shakily, "Ashtar . . ."

The wind stirred the cloth doorway of the yurt and played with the prince's feathered standard that stood outside. The guard next to it leaned on his spear dozing. Toth, carrying a clay pot of water, approached quietly.

Warriors did not deign to notice slaves. Toth bent, set the pot on the ground, and glanced through the opening. The dim interior danced with dust motes that formed shifting shapes and figures in the corner of the eye, not quite seen, not quite unseen. A knife stood upright in the floor.

The sturdy bronze body of the Khazyari prince arched above Sita's rounded whiteness; black hair and copper mingled on the quilt like the design on some exotic vase. The son of the lion played, not ungently, with his prey. As Toth watched, her hands reached upward above Tembujin's shoulders, clenched into fists and then loosened, opening, perhaps, in supplication. Perhaps in offering to a goddess who could sanctify her sacrifice.

Toth's plump face withered like a sun-dried apricot. He straightened, turned, shuffled away. His dark-circled eyes glanced toward the bleakly silent walls of the city. The pile of severed heads before the gate was almost obscured by a great swarm of buzzing flies, and the sickly sweet odor of death lay heavy on the wind. Under the eye of Khazyari warriors, a squad of slaves, boys who had yesterday been freeborn citizens of the Empire, stacked brush around the grisly pyramid. Another squad dragged cartloads of mutilated corpses to the mound that had risen eighteen years ago, the tomb of the Sardians who had died for Bellasteros and the Empire.

The traitor Hilkar straddled a horse atop the mound, smirking like a grotesque puppet, head held high and thin chest outthrust in a counterfeit majesty that both imitated and mocked Bellasteros's regal manner. "The emperor," muttered Toth, "tempers his pride with grace. We welcomed his conquest, for he freed us from a pitiless rule. And Danica of Sabazel placed the diadem upon his brow."

Vlad wandered through the carnage, poking here, probing there, as flies crawled across his greasy face. Women and children quarreled over looted riches.

The old servant turned away from the scene, shuddering. Outside a nearby yurt he found another water pot. Only dead eyes watched him; he hoisted it to his shoulder. He skirted the guards by the khan's great yurt. A low sound of heart-rent sobbing echoed within, punctuated by thunderous snores.

No guard stood outside the residence of the shaman; the rumor of Odo's protective spells were enough to frighten away even the boldest Khazyari. Toth, grimacing, made the sign against the evil eye. Again he bent and set a pot before the door, again he glanced inside.

Another dim interior. But these dust motes were black, not golden, and swirled in wraiths of acrid smoke. Here were grasping claws, there sharp, leather-covered wings. Bright spots of eyes, amber and chalcedony, glinted in the mist. Toth strangled a cough. The yurt reeked of nightshade and hemp, those herbs that excite the mind and create visions.

The mist rose from the burned upturned palms of a woman whose body lay in the center of the tent surrounded by butter lamps. A carved stone axe lay across her face, the focus for her blank, staring eyes; the focus for her contorted features, frozen dead in an extremity of terror. No wound marred her pale skin.

Carefully spread beneath her was Bellasteros's crimson cloak. As the lamps guttered in the breeze, the cloak rippled like a lapping pool of blood.

From the shadows at the rear of the yurt came an odd noise, a grunting like a wild boar in rut, a rhythmic striking of flesh against flesh. As Toth's eyes adjusted to the dimness he saw Raksula leaning over the squat body of Odo. Her scrawny legs wrapped the folds of fat that were his waist, pressing them into intricate hills and furrows; her hips thrust at him, slapping wetly. He grunted, his glazed eyes staring into some other dimension, his mouth hanging open. But Raksula's eyes, points of brightness amidst the damp tangle of her hair, were those of a feral animal. Under the glare of those eyes the amulets on Odo's chest leaped and danced; Raksula seized them in clawlike fingers and made of them reins to guide the heaving body of the shaman. She laughed, and the black mist swirled through the yurt.

Toth gagged. He spun about. The cart of Khalingu blocked his path. The form of the god seemed to shift and move behind its hangings, multiple arms reaching greedily outward, shaking weapons above a face split into the rictus grin of a skull.

Again Toth made the sign against the evil eye. He trotted away quickly, into the depths of the encampment. The humps of the yurts stretched to the heat-shimmering horizon like a crop tilled from the soil of Iksandarun, watered with blood. Ravens whirled overhead, rending the sky with their cries, and the howling of jackals echoed down the wind.

Chapter Five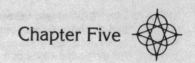

THE SETTING SUN was a crimson flare on the western horizon. The new moon was a ghostly crescent floating in the pink luminescence that swept eastward across the arch of the sky. The walls of Sabazel blushed, and the ice-crown of tall Cylandra glistened rose and amber.

A hush fell over the city. Small shepherdesses stilled the bleating of their flocks and lowered the gates of the pens behind them; chickens clucked drowsily to their roosts; bees buzzed to their hives replete with nectar. The guards above the Horn Gate leaned on their spears and gazed warily at the bedraggled company waiting outside.

It had been a harrowing journey. Fearing to stop and rest, Andrion had driven them onward over rough country, sparing neither horses nor men. He had sustained himself by anticipating this sanctuary. Now, at last, he was here, and he breathed deeply of the scented air of Sabazel. No asphodel to sear his senses, not now; no exotic perfumes to remind him of Iksandarun or Sardis. The subtly familiar odors of charcoal fires and fresh herbs filled his mouth and nose, and he felt his sweat- and dirt-caked face split into a smile.

Then he stole a sideways glance at Bellasteros, and his smile died. The emperor clung with a desperate tenacity to his horse, his back bent, his face seamed and flushed. His hair and beard were flecked with gray; his eyes were no longer a rich brown but bleached taupe, seeing nothing. The madness followed him even here, and he was sick unto death.

Gods, Andrion prayed, wrenching the thought yet again from some deep core of faith; gods, whatever your names, let him live. I am not strong enough to see him die.

The gates opened. A Sabazian sentry appeared, her javelin

at the ready. "The queen directs that only you, Prince Andrion, and the emperor may enter. The others must camp outside. Food will be sent to them, and they shall be under the protection of the goddess Ashtar."

Ashtar, give me strength. "My thanks," replied Andrion. He signed to the soldiers; obediently, their lined faces blank, they began to dismount. Only Miklos's eyes still gleamed with thought, asking if the exotic folk of Sabazel could be trusted. Andrion nodded reassurance to the sceptical Sardian.

Thank the gods—or perhaps it was Toth to whom thanks were due—that Miklos had come with them. His stoic perseverance had carried Andrion through more than one despairing midnight. Truly, he thought, if Sarasvati had lived, Miklos would be worthy of her.

"Follow me, if you please," said the sentry, and once again Andrion kneed his poor wheezing horse into shambling movement. Exhaustion sucked at him, and his grainy eyelids started to close. With a start he forced them open. Not much longer; Danica and Ilanit and Dana were close. Dana, he called silently, let me touch you.

The small stone houses, the temple square, streamed by him in a vague golden haze. The clopping of the horses' hooves blended with the cooing of doves; it was a soothing rhythm, a mother's heartbeat. . . . He started awake again. Sabazians lined the narrow streets, watching him and his father and the sentry, incredulous, perhaps resentful. Perhaps merely curious at the sudden admittance of men into man-forbidden Sabazel.

Bellasteros swayed in his saddle. Andrion leaned over to seize the reins of his father's horse, overbalanced, grabbed at his own mount. "Not much farther," he whispered.

Bellasteros's features were wiped clean of any thought, any feeling.

"Danica," whispered Andrion, louder, urgently. "She is here, she awaits you with healing in her hands."

Something like comprehension flickered in Bellasteros's vacant eyes. He sat a little straighter, trying to square his shoulders; the bloody bandage on his arm tightened and he gasped in pain. The flush drained from his face, leaving it pale and cold.

"Not much farther," said Andrion. "Just up the street and around the corner to the queen's garden." He realized with a sinking heart he was talking in the bright high-pitched murmur one would use with a child. But this was Sabazel, and all worries were to end in Sabazel.

A face was before him. Strong angles, clear planes, fine brows arching upward beneath smooth blond hair. Steady green eyes holding him transfixed between one breath and the next. He leaned forward, drawn into that face.

"Well, little brother," said Ilanit, "once again I break the laws of Sabazel for a man. For two men, this time; lawbreaking becomes easier, as one grows accustomed to it."

Andrion stared stupidly at her. Yes, she had lain with Patros during the campaign before Iksandarun, outside Sabazel, outside the turning of the year. They had suffered for their crime, but not overmuch, for their passion had flowered into Dana, and could not have been wrong. No, he had the story backward, the whole world shifted and ran backward and he and his father found their strength slipping away, their manhood disappearing; the emperor and his heir became supplicants, returning to infancy and seeking the warm womb of the mother.

"My sister," he groaned, "I have brought you such a dilemma."

"Do not apologize, Andrion." She smiled, and her eyes softened. "Of all the women of Sabazel, I alone am blessed with a brother." She stepped forward, reached up, caught him as he slipped from the horse.

The ground heaved beneath him, his knees wobbled, and he clutched at her. She propped him against her shoulder and gave some command; other hands took Bellasteros gently from the saddle, placed him on a litter and bore him away.

Andrion winced. That feeble shell was not his father; his father had been stolen from him. "Ilanit, his wound has become inflamed and I fear his mind is muddied with sorcery." He explained the defeat, the journey. Gods, he thought for the hundredth time, and for the hundredth time the thought struck him harder than a black-barbed arrow, my sister Sarasvati is gone. Tears ran suddenly from his eyes to hang shining in the beard on his cheeks.

"Come," murmured Ilanit, grim and sorrowful, cajoling in her turn. "Rest now. And tomorrow we shall wash you clean of fear and shame, and of dirt, as well."

He had to smile at that; he sniffed and swallowed his tears. Surely Ilanit was another mother to him. She was that much older than he, the child of Danica's girlhood as he had been the child of her maturity. He leaned against her gratefully as she guided him up the steps to her garden.

The leaves of the trees, laden with apricots and figs and almonds, stirred toward him and spread the last of the sunlight in his path. A breeze purled past his face and he could almost hear the words in it: Come, beloved, come to me. The flank of Cylandra rose before him, reflecting the sunset like a faceted stone; the high plains of Sabazel faded into dusky illusion. A solitary raptor, a falcon, surely, coasted down the wind, its bright eye solemnly regarding its sons' entry into the stronghold of Ashtar.

Andrion's thoughts stumbled as awkwardly as his feet. Something about the falcon god . . . The bronze image was still in the saddlebag. Forgive me, he told it silently, I shall rescue you tomorrow. His head fell forward, and once again Ilanit buoyed him up. She led him to the little house built close against the side of the mountain, and opened the door.

Ah, thought Andrion, the queen's chambers. The great bed surrounded by gauzy hangings where he had, no doubt, been conceived; the walls frescoed with the exploits of ancient Sabazians. The face of Mari, the companion repudiated by Daimion, gazed out at him. But Bellasteros never repudiated Danica. Why, then, had the gods let him be cursed?

The hangings of the bed had been tied back. The emperor lay among the pillows like a carved effigy, unmoving, eyes closed, his sword sheathed at his side. A figure leaned over him, wiping his face with a cloth; Shandir, who had lifted Andrion from his mother's body long ago, on a legendary midwinter's night.

"Father?" he croaked.

A light flared. A hand lifted an oil lamp from a small table and held it high. Emerald eyes fixed him, held him, sustained him. "Mother," he said. He withdrew from Ilanit's grasp and with one last effort of will stood tall, his hands upraised in worship, in supplication. "Mother, please help us." He could not tell if he spoke to his mortal parent or to the goddess herself.

Danica handed the lamp to Ilanit. "Such a sorrow, such a burden," she murmured, and her voice was as clear as the breeze in the garden.

He fell into her embrace. Yes, the fragile scent of asphodel clung to her, comforting and soothing. He tried to speak, but his lips could only stammer. The lamp flickered into pennons of flame. Ilanit's face shifted before him and became Danica's, bone sculpted by years and wisdom, bottomless eyes seeing all, condemning nothing.

The women were easing him down onto a pallet beside the stand holding the queen's armor, crested helmet, breastplate, shield. The shield was emblazoned by a many pointed star, a star humming with latent power. Andrion raised a trembling hand, touching the star, and he thought it thrilled for him. His hand fell heavily to the bed. Ilanit spread a coverlet over him, and Danica arranged the golden necklace, moon and star, at his throat, arranged the winged brooch on his shoulder. "Rest, my son. Here, for now, is your sanctuary."

Her hair was two wings of smooth-spun electrum contained by a silver net; her eyes were green. Green eyes bent over him, the small imperial princeling—grave women called Sabazians rode into Iksandarun—the scent of asphodel and a star offered to his tiny hand. One day the shield passed from his mother's arm to his sister's, but the star always shone for him.

My sanctuary, he realized she had said, only for now.

A door opened, shut again. The eyes swam, circled, became three pairs, parted. One pair remained, emerald eyes bright with youth, with spirit, with an uncanny vision of more than this world. His breath sighed from his body, "Dana."

"Sleep," she said. She smiled, but her smile wavered at the corners. Her mouth brushed his forehead, leaving a trail of flame, leaving the fleeting images of her Sight: Iksandarun burning, smoke billowing upward and blotting a crimson moon, a crimson cloak spread carefully on a smoke-stained carpet. . . .

The lips disappeared. Andrion slept, deeply, dreamlessly, in the glow of the star-shield of Sabazel.

Dana tucked the covers around Andrion's body. He was thinner than when she had last seen him, his jaw and cheekbones more sharply defined, almost a stranger. A copper-colored beard did not soften his face; it was tight with worry. She stroked his brow, his cheek, until his features relaxed.

Such a burden, she thought; the weight of it hangs on him like a cloak. Darkness gathers around him. She touched him again, but some dim barrier separated them.

A cloak. She frowned, trying to seize the image, but it was gone.

Ilanit held the lamp high over the bed as Shandir mixed

herbs into a cup of steaming water. "Wormwood for infection," the healer said. "Valerian, willow, and almond milk to ease the fever of mind and body."

Danica bent over Bellasteros. Her hand brushed the matted hair from his brow, tested the heat in his cheeks. He muttered something and twitched. His eyes opened, the pupils rolling wildly. "Danica . . ." Her name was an incantation.

"Marcos," she returned. Something caught her voice and drew it taut. "So you come yet again to this bed. Even though it is no longer mine you come, drawn by the years of memories."

Shandir touched Danica's shoulder and they shared a glance. Only a glance, but the need for words between them had ended long before Bellasteros first came to Sabazel.

Dana stepped closer to the bed. The king was gray-haired and gray-faced, and the diadem of the Empire was gray on his brow. Gods, she thought with a pang of sorrow, he has aged twenty years. At the midwinter rites he and Andrion had played side by side in Ashtar's games, and if Bellasteros had not been quite as lean and limber as his son, he had still been a vital presence, his teeth flashing with laughter in his handsome face. Now he was no longer a man in the prime of his middle years, but aged beyond measure.

With firm, delicate fingers Danica unwound the bandage. Bellasteros groaned, a cry of soul-deep agony; Danica blanched in response. The arm was swollen, the gaping wound festering yellowly, and streaks of red ran in evil tendrils up to the shoulder. His hand, his right hand, lay like the dried claw of a dead bird beside Solifrax. The serpent-skin scabbard reflected no light.

The fine hair rose on the back of Dana's neck. Sorcery. A black mist hovered about the figure of the emperor, sucking at him; death, but no peace in death. A stench filled her throat, rancid butter and blood, and she gagged.

Ilanit thrust the lamp on Shandir and hurried to her daughter. "What do you see? What do you feel?"

"Evil magic," Dana choked. She swallowed, and the taste, the vision faded. "It is more than the wound that pains him."

"Yes," Danica stated. "Bellasteros would never acquiesce so meekly to defeat; he once fought the gods themselves for his son, and won." Her eye strayed to Andrion's still form, lingered on it, moved back to the bed. "But I cannot fight such evil, for sorcery corrupts anyone it touches; I can only fight this wound, and that in but one way. . . ." Her voice broke. Suddenly she, too, seemed old, ravaged by time, no longer the proud queen of man-hating Sabazel but a weary woman despairing of her man's weakness.

The room was silent. A breeze plucked at the shutters, stirring the flame in the lamp. The fruit trees sighed. Shandir touched Danica on the hand and she straightened, setting her chin sternly. "I choose to be a healer, a warrior no longer. Therefore I must heal him. The juice of the poppy, Shandir."

Shandir nodded, her plump face tight. She reached into her bag of herbs and shaved a few morsels of brown paste into the cup. Then she took a case that lay nearby and set out a row of obsidian-edged knives that glowed with a dark luster in the lamplight. Once, Dana thought, Bellasteros's eyes had glowed like that.

Danica lifted the diadem from his head as she had once placed it upon him. She unbelted the sword from his side. She handed the symbols of his kingship to Ilanit, and Ilanit laid them carefully beside the sleeping heir.

Shandir placed a cloth-wrapped board beneath Bellasteros's wounded arm. Danica tipped a drop of the infusion between his lips. He groaned again and swallowed. "Always trust you, my lady," he whispered. The effort it cost him to speak sent a tremor through his body.

"Once you did not," Danica said. "And once I did not trust you." She lightly kissed his mouth. "Here, my lord, drink this." And he took the drug from her hands.

Dana turned away. The door closed behind her, shutting away the scent of herbs, the glitter of knives. Shutting away oblivious Andrion. "Forgive me," she murmured, but she knew not to whom she spoke.

Night had fallen over Sabazel. The garden was a shadowed tapestry sewn in shades of black and gray; even the scarlet anemones were the color of dried blood. Stars pricked the sky; cold, distant lamps. Dana hurried along familiar paths, up a flight of steps cut into the living rock of Cylandra, and burst out of breath into a hollow in the mountainside. She fell to her knees beside a large bronze basin of water.

Her breath stirred its dark surface. The starlight gathered itself and eddied through the water in slow sparkling spirals. "Ashtar," she said softly. "Ashtar, spare me."

But the goddess spoke only to the queen, through the pool and through the star-shield. The water was silent. Dana slumped against the cool bronze, her hands pressed to her ears as if blanking out some unwelcome sound, but the sights and sounds continued unabated in her mind: the heavy, gasping breath of the unconscious king, exhaling a low moan; the careful snick of knives and needles and a sudden, sickening crack of bone; Shandir removing one blood-soaked pad and placing another one; Danica's still, white face, and eyes that glistened with tears she stubbornly refused to shed.

At last Dana raised her head. She heard a door open and shut; Ilanit, bearing a cloth-wrapped bundle to the temple fire, a pyre for the strength of the emperor. Andrion slept dreamlessly, so Dana would weep for him, for Danica, for them all, until he woke to the harsh light of day and wept himself.

The wind blew cold from Cylandra's icy peak, murmuring a dirge over the city of Sabazel.

Ilanit sat slumped on a bench in the temple atrium, her elbows on her thighs and her head hanging. The brazier set beside the shallow pool emanated a thick coil of smoke that shaped itself into tangled limbs, into faceless wasted bodies, before dissipating through the opening in the roof and into the night. Doves shifted uneasily in the rafters, cooing soft complaints.

Ilanit's nostrils flared at the smell, and yet she did not move. "This much I owe," she said to herself. "Little enough for the man who secured Sabazel."

A figure approached from the doorway, glanced into the brazier, recoiled. "By Ashtar's blue eyes, Ilanit, this is an evil night."

"In the dark of the moon," the queen responded. "Come, sit by me, Lyris. Cheer me."

"My words will not cheer you," Lyris said. She stepped to the bench and with a clanking of her armor sat. She laid her javelin down and removed her helmet, shaking her hair free. Her face was thin and keen, etched with the memory of suffering and with the quest for certainty; her eyes, uncompromisingly steady, reflected the flames in twin points of fire.

"Well?" asked Ilanit after a moment.

Lyris blinked, freeing herself from the reflection. "You should not have allowed men into Sabazel. Men may only be allowed into Sabazel for the rites of the goddess at the solstices and the equinoxes."

"Do not lecture me, Lyris. I know the law."

"If the law is not obeyed, we shall pay for it."

"If we do not show mercy, we shall pay for that."

Lyris picked up the javelin and tapped its butt end against the floor. "The law was made to shield us when our very existence was threatened. Now that we have won peace and the respect of our neighbors, we grow soft and shall be undone. One breach, and then another, and Sabazel shall be lost."

"Spoken with the zeal of the convert," said Ilanit with a wry smile. "To think you were catechized with the litany of Harus when you were a girl in Sardis."

"I forswore the falcon god after what his high priest Adrastes did to me. Raped and possessed by Gerlac's demon spirit. . . ." Lyris shivered, glancing quickly from side to side, as if even the name chilled her. The shadows stirred. "I was only sixteen, as you were, and Danica showed me mercy even when the demon forced me to attempt her life."

"Mercy," stated Ilanit, "to those who come here wounded."

"But I am a woman!"

Ilanit's brows shot up. "I am queen and you my weapons master!"

The javelin cracked against the floor, and Lyris looked away, teeth tight between her curled lips.

Ilanit slumped again. "Forgive me, my friend, my pair. This night drags my thoughts into some dark pit. I would not make light of your travail. To this day you will accept the touch of only one man. But your taste is impeccable, I must admit." She cast a tentative look sideways at Lyris, offering peace.

Lyris let the javelin fall, flinging her anger after it. "I am pleased to receive Patros's offering, when he comes to me scented with your body." She chuckled. "You turn me cleverly from my purpose, Ilanit, reminding me of happier times."

"I am not at all clever. If I were, I could remedy this trouble that has come upon us. Do you not think I fear our law-breaking? This time I shall not gain a daughter. This time we shall draw the wrath of a new enemy upon our heads, and whether Ashtar will protect us, I know not. Her voice is silent, leaving me to choose."

"But you will not choose to cast out Bellasteros and his son?"

"How can it be right to hate all men because some have hated us?" Ilanit glanced back at the brazier and the pitiful embers within. "No. Bellasteros might soon be leaving us for another realm; Andrion will find his own destiny. The Khazyari will not wait while we split hairs over our loyalties. We are bound to the Empire now."

"Indeed," Lyris growled. "Safe, but no longer free." She set her hand upon Ilanit's shoulder, drawing her gaze. They eyed each other, Lyris's tensile strength testing the strength of Ilanit's conviction. At last the weapons master bowed slightly. "Of course I shall do your bidding, my queen; I shall even understand why you bid it. But I cannot like it."

"Neither can I, Lyris, neither can I."

The flames in the brazier subsided to ash. A cold, clean wind blew the smoke away. The doves fell silent. Ilanit and Lyris leaned together, talking quietly in the half phrases of long acquaintance, and the night spun itself out.

"Andrion!"

He sensed the damp coolness of a summer's morning. Birds sang riotously. No doubt Toth would have warm bread and cheese; his stomach felt as empty as an abandoned well.

"Andrion!"

No, it was a woman's voice. This was Sabazel. What was her name, that warrior he had bedded last year? Or who had bedded him, rather, to his mingled chagrin and delight.

"Andrion!" Fingertips stroked his cheek. "My son, awake to me."

His eyes opened. Danica's face hovered over him. His mother's face, drained of light and peace, cut by anguished sleeplessness into the furrows of age. But her eyes were calm and steady, doggedly guarding the depths of her soul. "Mother, what—"

Searing memory flooded him. Gods, he chided himself, can I think of nothing more than food or sex? "Mother, forgive me, I slept." He scrambled up and staggered, his muscles knotting themselves. His father's diadem lay on his pillow, beside the hollow where his head had rested; the sword Solifrax lay mute at his right hand. No, I cannot, he thought. I am not strong enough!

"You needed to sleep. Now your strength has returned."

Had it? Andrion felt as wobbly as a newborn colt. He shook himself, organizing his limbs, and tried to smile at his mother. He was, strangely, taller than she. Had he grown, or had she stooped?

"Your father lives," Danica said. "He is weak and tired, but he begins to break free of the oblivion of the poppy. We . . ." Abruptly she turned and braced herself on the edge of the table.

No, Andrion thought, you are strength itself, Danica the warrior queen, the shield borne beside the sword. He gazed past her to the bed. The hangings swayed gently in the breeze. Through them Bellasteros's face was as pale as some ancient fresco faded by storm and time.

Andrion inhaled deeply, calming himself. He gave Danica his arm and together they walked to the bed as if the few steps were a long ceremonial passage. Something was wrong, he thought, something terribly awry. He reached out and jerked the hangings away.

Where Bellasteros's right arm had been there was now only a stump. Carefully bandaged, well cleaned, but a stump. The hand that had lifted Solifrax from the grasp of the gods and with it won an empire, that hand was gone.

A rushing filled Andrion's ears and brought the blood surging to his face. No, the emperor could not be a frail mortal. He must be strong and whole and sturdy to hold the hand of his son, guiding him, teaching him, laughing with him. . . .

Andrion steadied himself. And what then should Danica have done? Let the wound rot and the fever drain Bellasteros inexorably of life? A shameful death for the conqueror. Better to live, and grow strong again, and win back his realm.

"Father," Andrion said. His teeth were clenched so tightly his jaw ached.

Bellasteros's eyes opened. Taupe eyes, drained of madness, containing only a resigned sorrow. "Andrion?" a voice whispered. "Andrion, you are my heir, take the diadem." His eyes rolled upward, clouded, closed again. His face was spent almost to the skull.

No! Andrion realized he was trembling. "But this is Sabazel," he protested.

"Yes," said Danica. "What did you expect, my son?"

"Healing . . . healing and direction." She did not answer. He turned, gazed full into her face. Her great green eyes, malachite mirrors, reflected the image of his own face. "Healing," he persisted.

"Andrion," Danica sighed, "I once carried you and the power of the goddess as well, but now I carry neither. You are my strength, and his, and the gods'. . . ." Her voice shattered, and she struggled not to weep. Whether at Bellasteros's agony or at the passing of her own strength, Andrion could not tell. He did not want to know; he had never seen her cry.

He carefully set her upon the edge of the bed and kissed her brow. He tenderly drew the coverlet to Bellasteros's gray-bearded chin and tucked it in. And he ran, bursting out of the small house, through the gleaming green and gold of the garden, up the steps to the hollow in the mountainside. "Gods! Gods!" he cried, but none answered.

Dana sat by the bronze basin. "I waited for you," she said. "I knew you would come."

He fell to his knees before her and bent his face onto her breast. Before his eyes the surface of the water stirred, sunlight glinting from its depths. Understanding rent his mind like the beak of a raven feeding upon the dead.

What did you expect? he asked himself brutally. What did you expect? An ending like a story told to a princeling tucked away safe in his palace, his patrimony secure? Or a beginning? He was empty, his youth cut away, cauterized and bound; he was full to bursting with the unutterable agony of its amputation. Sobs of grief wracked his body, inescapable.

Dana held him, her cheek against his hair. Her last tears, the dregs of her own grief, fell upon his head. The water in the basin swirled and splashed over the rim. He could not tell which drops were her tears and which the anointing touch of the goddess.

Chapter Six

THE FEATHERED STANDARD of the odlok fluttered lazily in a slow evening breeze. Tembujin looked up at it, as if hearing something strange in the wind. But the constant and varied voices of men and beasts, punctuated by the cries of ravens, were louder than the murmur of the breeze here on the great central plain of the Empire.

He shrugged and turned back to the bow laid on his crossed legs. It was made of horn and sinew on a wooden frame; now, unstrung, it was almost circular in shape. He dipped his brush into the pot of lacquer at his side and applied yet another shining layer.

Sita, kneeling behind him, was dressed in the thick felt bodice and short skirts of a Khazyari woman. Her face glistened with sweat.

"Well?" asked Tembujin peremptorily. She passed an ivory comb through his long tail of hair, grimacing as if the sable strands would dirty her fingers. But they did not. The shimmering cloth of the shirt he wore was spotless.

"All Khazyari wear silk shirts," he informed her. "An arrow will not cut through one; it will still enter the body, true, but if the shirt is pulled carefully, the arrow can be brought out without tearing the flesh any further."

"You think of war," Sita said between her teeth, "nothing but war."

"We are strong. We are destined to take tribute from soft city dwellers, and to rule the Empire."

"It is not your Empire," Sita retorted. The comb jerked. "Bellasteros might have welcomed you, for the Empire has long needed people."

Tembujin glanced back, one black eyebrow arching upward

in challenge, before dipping his brush once again. Quietly, almost to himself, he said, "These lands are indeed empty, unlike the country around Iksandarun. Unlike the valley of the Mohan, where I was born. Our progress north is slowed for lack of supplies. . . ." The pall of haunted Iksandarun rustled over the plain, and his voice died.

The sun sank toward the horizon. A band of warriors trotted by, their extra horses following like dogs behind them, and the air turned gold with suspended dust. The nuryan made obeisance to Tembujin; he nodded graciously in return.

The shadow of the feathered standard stretched out, longer and longer, toward the east. There a faint glimmer paled the deep blue of evening, presaging the rising of the almost-full moon. Sita eyed it with something like hunger in her expression, hunger tempered with caution. Several Khazyari women, Tembujin's cast-off concubines, passed by and made pointed remarks in her direction; the massive form of Baakhun left his yurt, Raksula jangling with Sardian jewelry in his wake. Sita quickly dropped her gaze back to her task.

"You are accustomed to being served, not serving—" Tembujin began, but Baakhun appeared beside him. "Ah, my father, my khan," he said in Khazyari. "Greeting."

Baakhun vented an enormous smile, every stained tooth glinting. "My son, my finest handiwork indeed."

Raksula growled, deep in her throat. Her hair was braided in a multitude of tiny plaits, each one supposedly a prayer to Khalingu; it had no doubt been the work of many hours for some hapless slave. The woman's head seemed like a seething nest of serpents, her eyes hard chips of jet.

Tembujin's features set themselves in a caution not dissimilar to Sita's. "Greeting, my father's wife." With a swift, smooth motion he strung the bow and snapped the string. It emitted a taut note of music.

Raksula's leather-covered toe stirred the carpet upon which Tembujin sat, a bright and intricate pattern of trees and birds. "A Mohendra rag. You are too good to sit upon the ground?"

"My mother gave this to me. I keep it as a remembrance of my youth. I see many Khazyari now sitting upon imperial tapestries."

"Your mother," said Raksula, not to be swayed, "was worthless, a princess with blood so weak she could not even withstand a winter journey to the steppes. She should have been sacrificed to Khalingu."

"And the worth of a prince?" asked Tembujin. He sealed the pot of lacquer and casually inspected his bow. Under the silk of his shirt his shoulders knotted. Sita released her hair and sat back, shrinking into herself, pretending no interest in this conversation in a strange language. The sun touched the rim of the world, washing the sky with a brilliant crimson glow.

"A prince," Raksula scowled, "is worth what his father the khan decrees he is worth."

Baakhun threw back his head with a howl of laughter, enjoying the game played by his wife and his son. "And this prince is worth everything to me. Such strength from such weak stock, is it not so?" His great hand closed on Raksula's arm, pinching it.

"Indeed," she snarled. The word might have been acid, dripping upon Tembujin's bowed head.

His black eyes darted upward and thrust Raksula back a step. "A prince's worth is measured in loyalty to his khan," he stated. He rose to his feet and bowed to his father, insolently turning his back on Raksula.

Baakhun howled again. "No one would be disloyal to me, least of all you, Tembujin."

Raksula's lips tightened to a slit, the mouth of an irritable reptile drunk on its own venom. Her eyes sparked like tinder catching fire.

An ovoid moon rose, tinting the rosy twilight with clear silver. Sita bowed slightly, as if to the moon itself; the wind lifted her hair and the light stroked the red gleam from it, leaving it a colorless fall of satin.

Tembujin raised his face to the glowing near-ripe face of the moon, seemingly struck by some omen written upon it; even Baakhun and Raksula turned, and the camp for a moment fell silent. Then two squat figures waddled out of the shaman's yurt; a cadaverous form strolled diffidently up to the gathered group, a servant in a brown cloak shambled by, carrying a pot of water.

Everyone stirred as if released from a spell. Tembujin glared at Raksula, and she turned his glare with a gentle and affectionate smile. He recoiled, and his bronzed skin blanched.

"Mighty khan," Odo called. "The nuryan Obedei sends you this, found by his scouting party."

"And why," muttered Tembujin, "should you be the one to take Obedei's report?"

Vlad thrust forward a silk-wrapped bundle; Baakhun took it, opened it, held up a black Khazyari arrowhead. "So?" he demanded.

"This," Odo answered, savoring every word, "was found in a rocky cleft a day's ride from Iksandarun, lying amidst blood-stained dirt. In the direction of Sabazel."

"Sabazel," repeated Raksula. "The scouts went on to its borders, then."

"Yes, indeed. The information that Hilkar gave us was actually helpful." Odo made a mocking bow toward the thin figure of the traitor.

Hilkar elbowed his way into the group, puffed like a pig's bladder with self-importance. "As I told you of the pass at Azervinah and the road to Farsahn, and as I told you of Sardis itself. I have been there, you see, as an ambassador, and I have a kinswoman in the governor's household—"

Vlad's shrill voice cut through Hilkar's rambling. "Is it true that the Sabazians have women warriors? What sport, to kill one!"

Raksula shot him an evil look, and he subsided.

"The scouts made only a brief sally across the borders, and did not contact the inhabitants," Odo murmured placatingly.

Tembujin's chin went up, alert, interested. "What of the arrowhead, Odo? Do you believe one of the emperor's party was wounded?"

"Yes. The emperor himself, Khalingu willing."

"Can you use the emperor's cloak to discover that?" asked Baakhun.

"The cloak that I brought to you," Hilkar purred. He thrust himself eagerly forward.

"Yes, yes, my khan," said Odo.

Baakhun waved Hilkar away as if the man were no more than an annoying flea. He laid one great arm across Tembujin's shoulders. "Shall we organize a hunt, my son? Not for boar and lion and antelope in the midst of winter, but for an exiled king and his heir in the midst of summer." He paused and wiped his brow. "By Khalingu's teeth, is the summer always so hot here?"

"The nuryans with their best warriors on the flanks," nodded Tembujin, "and you commanding the center. We shall sweep the entire country of game, both animal and human, feeding ourselves and closing on Sabazel as we shall close on that legion now marching south on the Royal Road."

He cast a quick look at Sita's bowed head. "Perhaps I should scout the area myself, Father."

"You know that I trust your judgment." Baakhun's eye followed Tembujin's to Sita. "And your taste. If you ever tire of this one and her red hair . . ."

Tembujin smiled thinly. "Not yet, Father. Not yet."

Sita's clasped hands tightened convulsively, her knuckles glinting white. Raksula glanced at her in cool appraisal, and her eyes fogged.

Baakhun chuckled and slapped the young prince on the back. Odo smiled, his eyes squashed into slits by his cheeks; Vlad pricked his fingers with the arrowhead and inspected the welling blood. Hilkar, oddly, was no longer grinning and bobbing obsequiously, but was peering at Sita's shadowed features, as if something in her profile had struck his interest.

"So," said Baakhun. "Our prey Bellasteros turns at bay. We shall have him soon. And if I cannot sacrifice him to Khalingu, then I shall offer the prince Andrion instead. And the sword Solifrax shall be mine."

"Yes, great khan," said Odo. "A pleasure to anticipate."

And Vlad chirped, "A pity that Bellasteros's women chose their own deaths."

The words lay uneasy on the wind, stirred by an odor of roasting flesh. Baakhun lifted his head and sniffed the air like a hound. "Ah, the evening meal. Gazelle, perhaps. Raksula? Tembujin?" He started off. "Vlad?" he called over his shoulder.

"Stop it, Vlad," said Raksula, suddenly waking. She seized the arrowhead from the boy. "Odo needs that."

The boy shrugged, began to suck on his finger.

Tembujin picked up his bow, flexed it, called, "I shall join you in a moment, Father." And quietly, for Raksula's ear, "What is Prince Vlad worth? As much as a pot of night soil?"

Raksula growled under her breath, turning her back on Tembujin. She wiped Vlad's hands with the silk rag. As she gave the arrowhead to Odo, she gazed long and hard at him, delivering some urgent if silent command; then she strutted after Baakhun. Odo trotted off toward his tent, humming under his breath, and then stopped as another scout approached the camp.

Hilkar, forgotten like some useless piece of baggage, still craned to see Sita's face. But she crouched, her face averted, her shoulders rounded, beneath the gravid moon. He shook his head as if the light dazzled his eyes, and he realized that Tembujin was glaring at him. "Ah—g-good evening, my lord," he stammered; hastily he scuttled away.

Tembujin spat into the dust at Hilkar's heels. Then he extended his hand to Sita. "You may get up now," he said in the common tongue. "No one remains to bite you."

Perhaps it was the delicate moonlight that made her face seem so pale. "What were you saying?" she asked quickly, her words tumbling from her lips. "Something about a legion on the Road, something about Bellasteros and Andrion and sacrifice . . ."

"What is it to you?" Tembujin returned. He pulled her to her feet, caught her chin in his hand and tilted her face up to his. His thumb pressed into the softness of her cheek. "Why should it concern you that my father seeks to sacrifice Bellasteros, or failing that, his remaining child?"

Sita gulped and closed her eyes, denying him their expression. "I try to learn your language." Her voice squeaked. "You and your . . . Raksula speak the common tongue so well."

"Slave tutors," Tembujin said dryly. "I would know my enemy." And, inspecting her closely, "I wonder whether that worm Hilkar recognized you tonight?"

Her chin trembled in his fingers. His grasp gentled into a caress, but did not weaken. "Look at me, Sita."

Slowly, reluctantly, her eyes opened. Lapis lazuli eyes, the color of the sky at evening, dusted by the moonlight with silver. Tembujin leaned so close that his face brushed hers. "I would advise you," he whispered, "to call me 'my lord,' as Hilkar does. He is accustomed to such courtesy, although I daresay you are not."

"Please, my lord," she gasped, "Please . . ."

He kissed her, stilling her panicked breath, and close against her lips he murmured, "I told you. If you behave yourself, no harm will come to you. You are mine now." He released her, saluted her, slung his bow over his shoulder.

Odo was interviewing the newly arrived scout. Tembujin elbowed the shaman aside and beckoned the man, questioning him closely. Odo followed. Words echoed fitfully down the wind, "Legion . . . Road passes through a valley . . . surprise attack . . ."

Sita stood unmoving, the print of Tembujin's finger on her cheek, shaking like a willow leaf until they had all disappeared into the khan's yurt. Toth slipped around a nearby wagon. "Are you well, my lady?"

"Do not call me that," she hissed. "As for my health, it depends on Tembujin. On whether that relief column can turn the barbarian advance."

Toth turned his shrunken face to the sky. His pale eyes filled with the lingering light of the sun, with the glow of the waxing moon, but the sky revealed nothing.

From the sanctuary atop the great ziggurat of Harus, Sardis's two rivers seemed strands of light dividing sunset from moonrise.

Patros's dark eyes, creased at the corners with years of sunshine and command, turned from the neat velvet-green squares of farmland to the east, past the jumbled tombs of the city of the dead, to the north where the port of Pirestia lay in a lavender haze against the rim of the sea. And on, to the west and the Royal Road to Farsahn, to Sabazel, to Iksandarun.

Shurzad rustled her finely pleated gown. Getting no response, she rattled her jewelry—a wide enameled collar, a headdress of golden leaves, earrings of cascading beads. Still her husband gazed silently into the gathering night. She lifted the veil that in deference to Sardian custom she wore in public, and her red lips whispered, "My lord, the ceremony is over."

"Ah," said Patros. He shook himself and nodded to the black-clad priest. "A fine ceremony of jubilee, Bonifacio."

"Thank you, my lord." Bonifacio bowed deeply in return. "I had hoped that my master Declan Falco would return from the emperor in Iksandarun in time to lead the ceremony."

Patros cleared his throat. "Indeed." As he offered Shurzad his arm, his eye fell upon the slight form of their daughter Valeria. Above the clinging veil her cornflower-blue eyes were great with the wonder of the ceremony and the height of the temple; her fragile hands were clasped in worship. "You are my finest jewel," he whispered to her; she flushed with pleasure.

"And the proper setting for such a jewel," murmured Shurzad, "is in the arms of Prince Andrion. . . ."

"Let him choose his own wife," Patros said.

"Because you could not?"

Patros's mouth tightened. He escorted his women with punctilious courtesy to the long stairway, leaving the garland-draped altar, leaving the incense to coil in a thin gray smoke to the darkening sky and be spread into gauze by the wind.

Gold faded in the west and silver lit the east. The gilded helmet Patros wore sparked, its crimson plume nodding; the helmet Bellasteros had worn on the trek to Iksandarun was now a relic in the chief house of Harus. Patros chuckled humorlessly. "We honor King Gerlac's birthday on the night of the full moon, implacable enemy of the moon that he was."

"Is it true," asked Shurzad, reaching protectively for Valeria's hand, "that Gerlac's hatred was so strong he became a demon after death?"

"Quite true. But his evil was vanquished by the spirit of the wife he murdered, Bellasteros's mother Viridis."

"The royal family in Iksandarun never stooped to such . . . unpleasantness. Even my kinsman Hilkar, ambitious as he was, would not resort to outright murder."

"Hilkar has gnawed the dry bone of resentment these many years, profiting nothing from it."

Shurzad's kohl-thick lashes fluttered. "Poor soul. He was to have wed the princess Roushangka, but he saw her given to Bellasteros. As a lesser wife. It was Chryse, after all, who bore Andrion."

Patros glanced at her, a brief secret gleam. He peered over the walls and down the western road. No couriers approached.

The shrines of lesser gods crouched on a wide pavement at the feet of Harus's ziggurat. To one side rose a new one, open to the sky, planted about with scarlet anemones that stirred in the wind. Patros nodded obeisance; to Shurzad's suddenly stony face he said, "We must honor all gods, my lady. Even the emperor bows to Ashtar of Sabazel."

"Sabazel," she hissed. Her eyes narrowed. "Yes," even the emperor can be beguiled by the moon." She bobbed perfunctorily.

The girl Valeria nodded, too, and looked curiously at the small temple. But the priestesses of Ashtar disdained to show their faces on Gerlac's anniversary; the old king had ordered the original shrine destroyed and its women killed. Only under the rule of the conqueror, who could name any deity he wished, had the worship of Ashtar been restored to Sardis.

At the doorway of another shrine, before the sculpture of a reclining cat, Shurzad bowed deeply. Her manicured hand closed about the amulet, a stylized eye, she wore at her throat.

"Qem is but a minor god," Patros remonstrated. "Probably an aspect of Ashtar. Why should you be his high priestess?"

"It was I," returned Shurzad, "who bought Qem from the Empire. The wife of the governor of Sardis must honor all gods."

Patros, rolling his eyes in silent supplication upward, agreed. He paused, removed the helmet, delivered it to a waiting acolyte. He bowed before it with a grimace of unease that could have been a grimace of pain. The wind caressed his crisp black and silver hair.

The moon, untainted by Sardian torchlight, hung round and bright and clear on the horizon.

Sita peered through the doorway and pressed her hand to her mouth. Khazyari warriors dragged imperial soldiers triumphantly past the yurt; some were already dead, others lived only moments longer to be sacrificed by knife and by fire before Khalingu's cart. Their pale faces were stunned, incredulous, stricken. Sita shuddered, choking back the bile in her throat, strangling her screams of outraged horror.

The full moon hung cool and serene at the horizon, remote from the last scarlet flare of the sunset, from the scarlet-tinted ground and the scarlet fires where Odo danced grotesque thanksgiving. Pipes wailed eerily, celebrating another victory. Khazyari women and children fought over mounds of imperial armor and food and clothing from the shattered army's baggage train.

Tembujin, slumped with weariness, stood talking to the nuryan Obedei just at the rim of flame-gutted twilight. "Yes," he seemed to be saying, as much as Sita's fluttering senses could comprehend, "the southern provinces of the Empire have collapsed. But the great generals of the north, Patros and Nikander, were not with this legion. They underestimated us. Let us not underestimate them." His eyes scanned the death and disorder about him and darted suddenly to the doorway of his own yurt, striking Sita like a blow. His eyes were black, flickering with fire and moonlight, and she could not read them.

Several drunken warriors quarreled over a Sardian sword. Obedei's face darkened. "Our own men are beguiled by the riches of the Empire."

"Indeed," Tembujin growled, and released Sita from his

gaze. Her knees buckled and she sat suddenly onto the carpet.

Twilight gave way to darkness. Sita waited numbly until Tembujin came in and threw down his weapons and his stained garments. He washed himself, but the faint reek of death still hung about him. She averted her face and lay inert when he touched her, while he sought with grim concentration for something within her, something perhaps to respond to that black flicker in his eyes. But he could not find it.

After a time he rose and went wordlessly to the victory feast. Jackals held their own feast on the battlefield, under the merciless gaze of the moon.

The thick felt sides of the yurt repelled not only the moonlight but also the fires and shouts of celebration. Inside was a darkness relieved only by the feeble flames of three butter lamps placed around a smoldering pot of hemp. An iridescent swirl of smoke licked at the roof and the center pole, seeking an escape.

Odo squatted over the black arrowhead, his hands and arms still splashed with gore. He inhaled, shivered as the smoke seared his throat and lungs, coughed. He began to speak, his voice hoarsely intent, and saliva sprayed in droplets from his lips to fall upon the mounded shape of Bellasteros's crimson cloak.

The tent flap stirred. Raksula bowed to the statue of Khalingu and slipped inside; kneeling beside Odo, she thrust her face into the smoke and breathed open-mouthed of it. She, too, shuddered. Then she threw back her head and laughed a deep throaty laugh, a response to the growls of the feasting jackals.

Odo's voice never wavered. Raksula's joined it, two different timbres blended into one; not harmony, but an oddly compelling discordance.

Something moved just at the boundary of light and dark. Eyes glinted, blinked, glinted again. Shadows coiled from the edges of the yurt, drawn on the words of the incantation, snaking lithely along the stained carpet. The lamps, engulfed by the darkness, guttered. The cloak rippled uneasily.

The shadow flowed over the arrowhead and sucked at it. Jerkily, it lurched toward the cloak. The cloak rippled again, starting back. Darkness blotted the center of the tent; the incantation stopped between syllables and its echo hung heavy in the silent air.

Then, suddenly, the lamps shone again. Lingering tendrils of shadow retreated into darkness. The arrowhead stood quivering in the center of the cloak, rent threads fluttering like welling blood around it. A faint and distant cry like that of a soul in agony plucked at the outside of the yurt and then faded.

Raksula and Odo sat silent for a moment, molding their spirits back into their bodies. Then Raksula turned to Odo with a smile of satisfaction. "So it was the emperor who was wounded. Khalingu is indeed with us."

"But he still lives."

"Not much longer. Leave the arrowhead there, let it continue its work on him." She turned, took Odo's hand, and pressed it to her breast. "We shall be honored indeed when Baakhun learns of this. And soon we shall rule."

Odo's face crumpled in doubt even as his fingers moved greedily into Raksula's bodice. "Tembujin is strong, and has the allegiance of the nuryans. Shall I poison him?"

"No. We must not make him a martyr. He must be discredited and disgraced. We shall pit him against his father's pride, and in the end both will perish." Raksula leaned close to the sparse fringe of hair on Odo's skull and began whispering into his ear, lips moist.

His face cleared, his tongue lapped out and back. "Henbane for persuasion; I understand. And I shall talk to Hilkar again."

They lay down on the carpet, whispering and chuckling together. Their bodies twined like the stems of some choking weed. The statue of Khalingu shifted in its cart, settling back to rest after performing this last of its many tasks of the day. Its face leered up at the moon. The black arrowhead pinioned the cloak.

Chapter Seven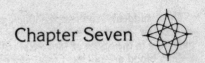

ANDRION THRUST THE rattan shield forward. The sword whacked against it, and his arm shivered from the blow. He lunged to the side, parried another blow, struck. Lyris spun away. "Not bad for a boy," she taunted.

"My father—" Andrion began indignantly.

Lyris spun back again. The blunted edge of her practice sword turned the rim of his shield and jabbed him in the stomach. His breath started from his body, sparks pinwheeled behind his eyes, the ground leaped upward and jarred against his knees.

He crouched, doubled over in pain, gasping, "By the tail feathers of the god, Lyris!"

"If Harus teaches you nothing else," she said, "he should teach you never to lower your guard." Her left hand grasped his hair and the dull point of her sword pressed his throat. "See?"

Andrion found himself eyeing the taut muscle of her thigh, exposed by the short practice tunic. Hastily he cleared his throat, cleared his mind, tilted his head back so that he could see her face. She smiled at him in affection and challenge mingled, and tickled his chin with the tip of the sword. "I see," he said stonily.

Lyris laughed. "Sulk then, Andrion. But remember that those Khazyari scouts would have been less gentle with you."

"True," he admitted. "Though they would have come here in any event."

She lowered her sword and released his hair. Groaning, he found his feet; evidently his ribs were not broken after all. Lyris started to help him, thought better of it, turned to put her sword and shield away.

The row of faces on the wall of the practice field watched raptly. Andrion was growing accustomed to the audience of little girls who followed him about. This evening the gallery included some older girls, almost Dana's age; warrior acolytes, evaluating the competition.

Suddenly he grinned. How absurd it was, the heir of the Empire on show like a monkey in a menagerie. He bowed extravagantly to the row of faces. They dissolved in giggles.

"Go on," Lyris called to them all. "There is ample work to be done." Reluctantly the girls drifted away. The weapons master turned back to Andrion. "When your father was your age, he commanded an army."

Still she taunted him. "For Gerlac, his demon stepfather," he returned, "who goaded him to conquest."

Lyris paled. "Not a fair blow, my prince."

"Neither was yours." They eyed each other; Andrion offered his hand and she clasped it.

"Ashtar smiles upon you," she told him, "but your will is your own."

"Is it? Is it indeed?"

Her brows shrugged away the question. "Danica waits for you. We shall meet again on the morrow."

"Thank you," he called after her. "I think." Gingerly he placed his sword and shield in the nearby rack; gingerly he started for the bathhouse. I once held Solifrax in my hands, he thought; it should be mine, but I have yet to earn it. I have yet to earn the Empire.

Cleaned and shaven, but no less sore, Andrion sat in the queen's garden and watched the sun hide itself behind the western horizon. Another sundown, he thought, and still I dally in Sabazel, waiting. Waiting for what?

The evening was clear, the sky a crystalline lapis lazuli like Sarasvati's eyes, so deep and vivid that it seemed as if it should reflect the entire world: Iksandarun, clotted with the tents of the invaders, where Aveyron and Declan, Chryse and Sarasvati slept uneasily; the small figures of Miklos and the other guards creeping along the Royal Road, over aqueducts, through tunnels, to Farsahn and thence to Sardis with messages for Patros. I should go to Sardis, too, Andrion thought. But how can I go without Bellasteros?

Ashtar's star hung like a solitary jewel in the depths of the sky. The full moon rose up the flank of Cylandra, and Sabazel was washed clean in its light. Somewhere in the town a lyre began to play a song of welcome, a skein of music spun through the gathering darkness to bind day to night. The quiet hum of insects filled the twilight like the insistent patter of tiny cymbals.

Andrion shrank from the moonlight, as if the moon were the accusing eye of the goddess. Why bother to shave? he asked himself. Why keep my hair cut short? To imitate the young Bellasteros? I love him, and would avenge him. I hate him for laying such a burden on me. . . . The Sabazian shirt and trousers he wore chafed him, too tight across the shoulders, too loose in the hips.

With a glimmer of moonlight Danica walked among the asphodel, the anemone, the fruit trees. She set a plate and a cup before Andrion and settled herself on a low wall above him. "Eat," she said softly. "You cannot nourish yourself with worry."

He ate. The bread and cheese, fruit and honey, were ashes in his mouth. The thin pink wine was gall.

The door of the house opened. Bellasteros, supported by Ilanit and Dana, tottered out into the evening and was seated in a comfortable chair. The moonlight fell upon his face, smoothing it, tinting his hair and beard with silver; his eyes gleamed darkly again. His ruined arm was only a bulge in his carefully draped cloak.

"To think of the years I hid from women, fearing them," he said. But his smile was bittersweet; a warrior brought low, cared for like an infant, with only dignity to call his own.

Ilanit brought out the star-shield. She seated herself and with a cloth began to burnish it, brushing slow sparks from its emblazoned star. Dana sat beside the conqueror. "Sing to me," he asked. "Sing the lay of Daimion. Not the Sardian version, which forgets Mari, but the true one."

She took his remaining hand, cradling it in her own. Her voice floated like distant chimes down the wind.

"When the world was young and the sunlight red,
Daimion walked among the children of the gods."

Andrion sipped once more at the wine, and it was a little sweeter upon his tongue. His mother's hand touched his hair, gently, as if reassuring herself he really existed. "Auburn hair," she murmured. "Dark, like his, but tinted with the fires of a midsummer's passion, of a midwinter's battle.

"It used to be that a king went willingly to his death so his land might live; failing that he sent to death his chosen surrogate, the summer king twinned with the winter king. But the goddess no longer demands such sacrifice. Compromise, ever compromise, and love as strong as death."

"Then why are we now betrayed?" Andrion asked.

"Are we? Or are we trusted to begin again?"

He shook his head. His uncertainty was like a wound improperly healed. With a sigh he folded his long limbs to lean against her knee.

> "Daimion, beloved of the gods,
>   sought the tree at the end of the world.
>   Sought the sword forged in the world's dawning."

The diadem and the sword still rested beside the shield of Sabazel. Bellasteros refused to take them up again, a wounded king incapable of healing a wounded land. Andrion could not bring himself to touch them, feeling himself a naughty boy playing with things not meant for a child. He had taken the image of Harus to Ashtar's temple and set it where it could see the pool and the sky. The aged priestesses left offerings of grain, but still the bronze figure seemed worn and wasted, grain alone not enough to feed it. "Forgive me," Andrion muttered. "Please, mighty Harus."

A breeze purled past him, kissing his cheeks. "Forgive me, Ashtar," he said.

> "Mari of Sabazel was her name;
>   she met Daimion on the field of battle, sword to sword.
>   But their eyes met, their swords dropped,
>   and another kind of fire passed between them."

Danica laughed softly. "Another kind of fire indeed." She touched the necklace at Andrion's throat. "A sword in the shape of the crescent moon, and the star-shield at its tip. Sardis and Sabazel meeting on the field of battle, mating, making an empire."

Andrion drifted on the familiar song, on the purity of Dana's voice and the breeze that carried it. Daimion and Mari found the tree and the sword just as Bellasteros and Danica had. But Daimion betrayed Mari and her shield called him to his death, in a cavern deep underground, shorn of the light of sun or moon.

Dana came to the end of the song. Her voice rippled away down into the wind. Bellasteros gazed up into the sky, thoughtful and silent. Then it was Danica's voice that filled the evening, reciting the familiar story of Sabazel like a soothing catechism. "Once the goddess Ashtar, the great mother, ruled the world. Once everyone bowed to women, for from a woman's body comes new life.

"Then the role of men in the making of children was realized, and the goddess took a consort, as was right and proper. At times she killed her consort, more often she gave him life; the world prospered.

"But the pride of men demanded a father god. Women reminded them of their broken vows to the goddess, and they scorned women. Those who would remain free came to Sabazel. For a time Sabazians rode openly through the world, and their queen did not have to be a warrior. I hoped such a time had come again."

"Yes," said Andrion. And then, "But not all men are evil, Mother."

Danica laughed quietly. "I thought, once, that they were. I was wrong. Compromise, Andrion, and change."

"Yes." He leaned against her, inhaling her scent, the scent of Sabazel itself. He watched the stars, Ashtar's lamps, blossoming in the sky above him. But the radiance of the moon, the radiance of the shield, drained the light from the stars and filled his eyes with a silver glow like a translucent liquid. If only he could slip into it, he mused, drown in it, forget who he was.

"Sardis almost forgot Ashtar," continued Danica. "The Empire, more indulgent, allowed her discreet worship even among their noblewomen. So it was that Viridis, given to Gerlac of Sardis to end the endless war between them, came through Sabazel to consecrate herself to Ashtar in the rites. But proud Gerlac took offense when Viridis bore a nine-month babe in seven moons, suspecting her visit to Sabazel. He killed her for it and challenged the child, challenged him to be strong."

"He was," said Andrion. "He is." But the name of Gerlac

tightened the back of his neck, pulling each fine hair erect. Surely the old demon had been laid to rest. Why shiver, except at the horror of an old tale?

Bellasteros said something quietly to Dana. She rose and went into the house.

The emperor's dark, pellucid gaze turned upon his lady and his son; his eyes were haunted, clinging desperately to the tattered edge of sanity. I shall heal you, Andrion shouted silently. But his thought mocked him. How?

Danica's voice softened. Her eyes rested on Bellasteros's face, its familiar lines a pleasing scroll for her to read. "When Bellasteros became king, there were those who suspected his birth, who would have used it against him. Only when the goddess, through me, brought him here to Sabazel; only when he had the courage to acknowledge her, and I the courage to acknowledge my love for a man, did the war end at last. And you were set as a seal upon the victory, not as an ending, but as a beginning."

"A victory not without cost," said Andrion.

Danica chuckled under her breath. "The ways of the goddess are subtle indeed."

"Yes," he said acidly. He shifted again, restless. "The queens of Sabazel carry the star-shield; the king carries Solifrax; Dana, for good or ill, bears the Sight; for a time you even bore the power of Ashtar herself. But what do I have, Mother? The goddess will not even speak to me."

"The shield, the sword, the magic of the gods is meant only to supplement our own wills. More would be sorcery and corruption. You can hear the goddess, if you listen."

He shook his head, not understanding. The wind sang down from the vault of the sky, flowed over the height of Cylandra, danced among the trees; the moonlight was so bright that the shadows were dense and black. Andrion's neck was tense, his shoulders tight with a strange urgency.

Dana came from the house bearing the sword Solifrax solemnly across her hands. The moonlight flickered in quick crescents of light along its snakeskin sheath. Bellasteros straightened, moved with his right shoulder, grimaced and reached for the sword with his left hand. Ilanit laid down her cloth and stood, lifting the shield onto her arm.

Slowly, tentatively, as if he expected the sword to turn upon him, Bellasteros pulled Solifrax from its scabbard and held it to the sky. The curved blade, so highly polished as to seem like crystal, flashed in the moonlight. Andrion rose, drawn to it. But even as he stood, its light failed and the blade dulled. The wind was suddenly chill.

Dana's eyes widened with a glimmering green light. Andrion reached toward her, but did not dare touch her.

"Andrion," said the emperor. He lowered the tip of the sword; it wavered a moment, and he steadied it, wincing with effort. "Andrion, come to me."

The young man stepped across the dark-dappled grass, his blood stirring with some strange lust; he felt again the hilt of Solifrax searing his hand. The hilt made not for his hand, but for his father's.

"Take this sword," said Bellasteros. "Take Solifrax."

"What?" The unease of the evening gathered itself, crashed over him.

"Listen to me. Take Solifrax and place it in the water of Ashtar's basin, there, on Cylandra's flank."

Andrion heard Danica gasp in dismay. Or perhaps it was the wind that hissed suddenly in his ear. He could not move. No, I am not hearing this final rite, he thought. It cannot be. But the sword was given to Bellasteros because he was strong enough to bear it, and now neither he nor his son was strong.

The emperor's smile was thin and taut. The darkness in his eyes ebbed. "You heard me. Do it, Andrion."

Swallowing his grief, he replied, "Yes, my lord." He knelt, extended his hands, received the soft sheen of the blade across his palms. And it was not hot; the metal was cold, drawing the warmth from his hands, from his arms, so that his body ached with it. "Father . . ."

Bellasteros's eyes were stern, for his son and for himself. Andrion could only grasp the sword, set his jaw against the pain, stand and turn. Danica stood draped with shadow, watching, her hands clasped before her. Dana knelt suddenly by the chair, bowed over the now mute and dull scabbard. "Sorcery," she whispered. "Black smoke, reaching even over the borders of Sabazel."

Ilanit saluted the sword, and the shield gleamed in some faint memory of their combined power. No! cried Andrion silently. They cannot be separated, from them I draw my life! But he turned, spurred by his father's will, forcing his legs to flex and loosen.

The garden lurched past him. Dim tree shapes withered, and gray flowers folded their petals. Shadow lapped his mind, swallowing thought, swallowing hope. "No," he cried aloud, but his voice was a thin wail snatched away by the wind.

The steps up the mountainside were narrow and well worn, and Andrion stumbled. Ten steps, twenty—surely the stair would stretch on forever, surely he could bear the sword into some eternity and there preserve it. Thirty steps, and the stairway twisted beneath his feet, throwing him into the murky hollow in the mountainside. The water in the great basin waited, dark and still. He stood staring into it, the ragged thuds of his own heart counting irrevocable time. I must!

I cannot. The sword was too beautiful to abandon to a tub of water. The wind muttered in his ear, murmuring reproof, but if other words were in it, he could not understand them. Carefully Andrion laid the sword on a great boulder, released it, turned way.

The blade sparked in the corner of his eye. Tendrils of noxious black smoke swirled around it, muting it. He turned back. No, the sword was as smooth and clear as the face of the moon. Slowly he walked back down the steps, rubbing his hands together to warm them. To warm his shame.

Danica knelt beside Bellasteros, holding his hand in her own. Dana huddled on the ground at his other side. Ilanit crouched, wary, holding the faintly glowing shield. "What did you see?" asked the emperor of his son.

"Ah." Andrion took a deep breath. "I saw the wind ruffling the water and drinking the stars."

Danica and Bellasteros exchanged a glance, rue eroded by grief and fear. "Did you?" asked the emperor.

Andrion's hands were still cold, and the cold flowed through every vein in his body, turning his blood to strands of ice. He shivered. "I could not put the blade in the water; I laid it down. Forgive me."

His father's weary smile was worse than any reprimand. "Go, Andrion. Give the sword into the goddess's protection. Quickly." Bellasteros's voice cracked. He turned his face to the sky, surrendering to it. The moon sheen faded from his eyes, his face went pale, he gasped in sudden pain. Ilanit strode across the garden and called to a passerby, "Bring Shandir."

Andrion turned, turned back again, rent by uncertainty. Dana's eyes were upon him, not seeing him, churning with horror. "If the sword is not returned to the gods," she said, "it will be taken by the sorcery that seeks it, that seeks—" She choked.

Some evil did indeed darken the sky and dim the stars. The moon faded, covered with a dim mist. Andrion's heart wrenched in his chest and every nerve quivered. You can still mend your disobedience, hurry! he told himself. But his feet were leaden weights. A barrier pushed against him, thick shadows stirring in the folds of the moon's cloak. Mother, please! He forced his body to struggle up the stairway.

Solifrax lay on the boulder where he had left it. Darkness gathered around it, gnawing at it. Andrion threw himself forward, plucked it up, brandished it. The sword shimmered quickly, briefly, and then lay cold again in his hand. The shadows, cut by the sharp gleam of the blade, shredded into trailing wraiths and then thronged again.

Darkness sucked at him. Tiny teeth and claws seemed to rake his back. He fought to the edge of the basin and leaned into the blinding swirl of light and shadow that was the water. With a cry of agony, tearing loose part of his own existence, he cast the sword away.

Glittering droplets rained upward as the water surged to meet it. Andrion felt no dampness, only the biting kisses of a cold so deep it burned his shivering flesh. The sword and the water flashed so brightly that his own shadow leaped across the hollow, a great black figure climbing the mountainside. Come, beloved . . . "Yes," he gasped. "Yes, I shall come."

The sword was gone. The pain was gone. The shadows were gone. Starlight and moonlight together illuminated the depths of the basin, and nothing was there save a slow sparkling whorl, leading down, down, to some other realm.

Andrion shook himself and straightened. Now he felt the wetness of his soaked shirt. Now he felt the chill of the night breeze. An owl hooted amidst the rocks, locusts buzzed. He went trembling down the steps to see lamps flickering in the house and the chair empty. His heart jerked crazily—of course, the spell was not only for the sword, but for the bearer. He plunged through the door.

Bellasteros lay again in the bed, eyes closed, cheeks hollow, a desiccated waxen figure. Shandir bent over him. "Black sorcery," she sighed. "By the gods, Danica, I can do nothing. He is dying."

Danica grimaced in a terrible bitter desperation. The lamps

leaped, fire licking the gathering darkness. The star-shield glittered on Ilanit's arm.

Dana threw the scabbard of Solifrax down by the diadem, discarded toys. She rounded upon Andrion, her eyes wild. "The arrow," Dana demanded hoarsely. "Andrion, what of the arrow that struck him?"

Andrion reeled back, his thoughts scrabbling for purchase.

"The arrow!" insisted Dana.

The words exploded from his lips. "I threw it away. In the ravine where we stopped at dawn. They found it, did they not?" He smashed his fist into the door frame, unable to deny his folly. Heal him? his mind howled. I have killed him!

"And the crimson cloak was missing?" Dana asked. "Great mother, they have that, too!" She swayed and reached blindly for support. "No, no, his task is not yet done!" Ilanit pulled her tight against her side and covered her with the glowing shield.

Shandir's eyes swam with despair. "The arrowhead. It works its way to his heart."

"No!" Danica cried, her voice echoing, strong and fierce. She laid her own body over the emperor's supine form. "Love is as strong as death, and I chose long ago to love him. Ilanit! Bring the shield. Bring Dana. We must ward this evil spell. Ashtar, grant your son, your consort, continuing life!"

Shandir clung to the bedpost, hand pressed to her mouth. Ilanit and Dana stepped forward. Danica seized the edge of the shield and lowered it over the silent form of the emperor.

Three sets of eyes, matched emeralds, gleamed as one. The emblazoned star in the center of the shield hummed with power. It flared, filling the room to bursting with a clear white light, the moon and the sun, unsullied. The darkness fled.

Andrion stood numbly in the doorway, not inside the room, not outside, grasping the necklace at his throat like a powerful amulet.

The light of the shield ebbed. Bellasteros's face still gleamed, freed of despair and grief. The three women parted, queen-that-was, queen-that-is, queen-yet-to-be. Andrion shook himself. His mind crumbled to ash and floated away down the cold, clean night wind.

Shandir touched the emperor's cheek. "He lives," she whispered. "A waking death, a deathly sleep. How long his soul can exist like this, I know not."

Danica collapsed on the bed. Her features were furrowed by

anguish, chalk-white, as if part of her own vital force had
passed into Bellasteros. Her voice now was stretched taut,
close to breaking. "I have done this—compromise to him. I
shall stay by him to the end, until his task is done."

Ilanit bent over the now dim shield, grimacing as if straining
after some voice in the wind, in her mind, and not hearing it.
Dana turned to the doorway. Her empty eyes, slightly unfocused, sought Andrion's. He could not read them. Accusa-
tion? Scorn? Or sympathy, the worst of all? In one lunge he
was out of the door. The garden rushed by him in streamers of
black and silver and dark carnelian like dried blood. The steps
heaved under his feet.

Again he came to the hollow in the mountainside, the place
of the basin. "Mother," he gasped, "take my life for my
father's, which I have thrown away. I am the winter king."
But the basin held nothing but moon-dappled water. The wind
stroked his hair.

His shadow had leaped up the mountain. There was the
stairway up Cylandra's flank, the path to the cavern of
Ashtar, the heart of Sabazel forbidden to men. Andrion raised
his chin and gazed up the mountainside. It was a dangerous
path, they said, even in daylight.

The chill of fear, of grief and despair, drained from his
limbs. His face flushed hot as anger sang through his body.
Anger, and the ultimate defiance. The sword was gone, the
man who had wielded it was gone, nothing remained but to
test himself against the perfidious gods, will to will. "Yes, I
shall come to you. If you call me to my death, payment for my
weakness, so be it. If I deserve to live, then you will speak to
me."

He paced across the pavement and started up the stair. "I
am yours," he called to the mountain, to the moon, to the
night, "sacrifice or consort, as you will. Now let it end, or let
it now begin!"

The wind murmured wordlessly in his ear. The water in the
basin rippled with shimmering moonlight and then grew dark.

Chapter Eight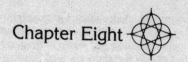

THE WRITHING TANGLE of clothing and limbs that was Raksula and Odo suddenly froze. Their two faces, swart and flat in the feeble light of the butter lamps, rose from the tangle like cobras from their baskets.

A cold breeze knifed through the yurt. The lamps flickered; the two faces melted into gape-mouthed, open-eyed astonishment.

A silver shimmer gathered about the cloak and the arrowhead, shaped by the breeze into the form, perhaps, of long delicate hands. Shaped perhaps into the elegantly feathered wings of a falcon.

The shape beckoned. The arrowhead rose from its bed in the cloak, hovered in midair, plummeted into one of the lamps. Fiery butter splashed. A tendril of flame lapped at the crimson cloak, tasted it, consumed it in a quick flare of light like a many pointed star. The stench in the tent cleared.

Odo and Raksula reeled back, covering their eyes against the light; when they looked again, the cloak was only a pile of glowing ashes, the arrowhead a lump of gleaming slag. "Magic," gasped Raksula. "A warding spell, turning ours back upon itself." She pushed Odo away and scrambled across the carpet, grasping at the remains of her sorcery. But the breeze laughed, swirling the ashes around and around the dim tent, dusting its furnishings with silver.

Odo waved his arms, trying to repel the ashes. Raksula grabbed at the arrowhead and choked back a scream as the heat of it seared her hand. She dropped it, and it, too, was plucked up by the wind. A cold wind, like that from the top of an ice-crowned mountain.

The ashes, the arrow, the wind were gone. Only the faraway

70

sounds of revelry disturbed the night. One of the butter lamps lay spilled and extinguished on the sooty rug.

Raksula slumped down. "Magic," she stated between her teeth. "By the short hairs of Khalingu, Bellasteros's gods are powerful. We almost had him, we almost had the damned sword!"

Odo's voice squeaked. He swallowed, steadied it, said, "Did you see that star? The shield of Sabazel, I hear, is emblazoned with a many pointed star."

Raksula spat upon her burned hand. "Sabazel," she hissed. Her thin lips curled with hatred. She brushed Odo aside and burst through the cloth covering the door of the yurt.

Khalingu's image huddled in its cart, shifting uncomfortably under the onslaught of the moonlight. The hangings hung still and lank around it. Behind them one clawed hand opened and shut, opened and shut, dimly. Raksula spat again. "Yes, Khalingu, we shall avenge this insult."

The celebratory bonfires subsided into dull embers. The moon rode high, serene, implacable across a star-studded sky.

Chapter Nine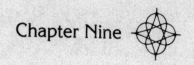

SARDIS WAS OVERARCHED by the great crystalline bell of the sky, every small night noise reverberating again and again in its moon- and star-embedded vault: rattling carts delivering goods to the city's shops; rivers lapping at their piers; the creaking of many masts; the guards' footsteps measuring cadence through the courtyard of the palace; hoofbeats, not measured at all, but broken, as if the horses had been ridden far and hard.

Patros leaped from the bed and seized a loose robe as the guards' shouts echoed through the night. Shurzad twitched, opened one eye in puzzled annoyance, burrowed farther into the bedclothes.

Patros flung open the door just as the guard outside was raising his hand to knock. Behind him was the panting, disheveled form of a secretary. "My lord, messages from the emperor at last." The young man's eyes rolled white in the light of the lamp he carried, more fearful than relieved.

Patros ran, his bare feet hammering down the long marble corridors to the travertine staircase and the entry hall. The statues of long-dead kings shifted, startled, and peered after him. A statue of Bellasteros stood at the head of the steps, hands outstretched in generosity, stone lips smiling, stone eyes blank. "Marcos," Patros pleaded softly, under his breath.

Most of the men below wore the livery of Farsahn, an escort, evidently; at the core of the group were four ragged guards from Iksandarun. They were hollow-eyed, gray with exhaustion, their clothing stained and torn with the urgency of their journey. Patros began a headlong rush down the stairway, caught himself, managed to descend with some semblance of dignity. A soldier with four parchment scrolls in his

72

hand bowed and began, "My lord, I am Miklos of the emperor's guard—"

"What of Iksandarun?" demanded Patros. "What of the emperor?"

"Iksandarun fell to the Khazyari under the last full moon."

Patros's cheeks went stark white under their stubble shadow. "Fell?"

"A traitor opened the gates," Miklos said bitterly. "Only through the loyalty of an old servant, and that of Prince Andrion, did the emperor escape. He lies wounded but safe in Sabazel."

"Sabazel," Patros repeated, like the response of a prayer. "No, Ilanit would not turn him away. But what of the others?"

"The lady Chryse is dead," stated Miklos, as emotionlessly as if through repetition he had wrung all emotion from the words. "And the lady Sarasvati. And Declan Falco, the high priest—"

"No," commanded Patros, cutting off the terrible litany. He turned away, averting his face, allowing it to twist suddenly in grief. His voice faded to a whisper. "Andrion lives, you say?"

"Yes, my lord. He lives. Here, I have letters for you." Miklos grimaced. "And from Proconsul Nikander in Farsahn. The relief army was turned back in a bloody battle, and has retreated north of the pass at Azervinah."

"Gods," Patros hissed. "I expected evil news, but this . . ." With a deep inhalation he steadied himself, smoothed his features, and turned back to the pitiful remnants of Iksandarun's legions. He took the stained and crumpled scrolls from Miklos's hand. "You came from Iksandarun through Sabazel in only one month?"

"Ten days from Sabazel," said Miklos, as if such a trip were well within the bounds of his duty. "I fear, however, that we killed three horses."

"Gods," Patros said again. "Your efforts shall be rewarded, I assure you. Now rest." He turned to the secretary. "Send the captains-general of the army to me. Send scribes. Summon Bonifacio from the temple." And, under his breath, "Harus, he is not strong enough to be high priest."

Attendants scattered. The soldiers vanished down the hallway. Patros, turning to the stairs, glanced at the scrolls. Brisk, controlled letters—Ilanit. A deliberate if uneven hand

—Andrion. Short straggling sentences, smeared and drooping dispiritedly off the parchment. . . . A shudder rippled through Patros's body. "My lord, Marcos, this is the writing of an old man!"

He did not open the message sealed with the insignia of Nikander at Farsahn. He looked up. There, at the top of the sweeping expanse of white stone, stood Shurzad. The hand that grasped her gown about her was clenched into a fist; the other held her amulet. "Iksandarun has fallen?" she asked faintly. "The southern provinces are lost?"

"Yes, my lady. But Bellasteros and his son live."

"In Sabazel?"

"Yes." Patros bounded up the stairway and paused at her side. "Return to your sleep, my lady. I must plan—"

"Sabazel?" she repeated, her features contorted in bewildered outrage.

"Allies, my lady," Patros said tightly. "Our allies." And he was gone, striding down the corridor with his back as straight and taut and stubborn as a banner blown outward in the wind.

Shurzad slammed the bedroom door behind her. Her cat Qemnetesh waited, yawning, tongue curling between sharp teeth. "Come, my pet," she said. "We must have the courage to venture a little farther, a little farther." She pulled aside a tapestry at the head of the bed and pressed a lever; a panel of the wall slid away.

Inside was a small dark chamber, illuminated by solitary oil lamp. The light flickered as the door opened, and the carved jade statue of a cat seemed to stretch, flexing its claws. A cloud of incense swirled about its tail, and its tail twitched.

Shurzad knelt before it. "Qem, please, guide me. The Empire must be preserved. Andrion must be delivered from Sabazel, or he will be devoured as my husband was long years ago. . . . What can I do, what?"

The tiny lamp fluttered. The living cat leaped onto the statue and settled on its shoulders. Topaz eyes and jade eyes fixed dark slits of pupils on Shurzad's flushed face.

"Who is the Khazyari god?" she demanded, shriller, faster. "How can I placate him, turn him aside? How can I bring Andrion here, to safety and to your guiding Eye?"

A distant yowling echoed through the night, as if some great feline hunted its prey deep below the palace. Shurzad bowed her head, wringing her fingers, contemplating a small offering bowl set before the image. In the bowl was a curl of dark auburn hair.

Andrion struggled upward. It seemed to him that the path was marked, rocks smoothed by generations of feet and clinging hands. The moonlight gathered in shining pools on each shaped stone; the slowly moving moon watched him, pouring its light over Cylandra to guide him. "You call me," Andrion said between his teeth. He grasped another spire of rock, pulled himself over a narrow crevasse. "You goad me."

The jagged, untouched stones were obscured by dark runnels of shadow, black like Khazyari arrowheads. The shadows circled him like accusing faces, moving just at the corners of his eyes, but his eyes were dazzled by the light.

He skirted a waterfall, a veil of stars softened in their passage to the boundaries of the earth. He slipped on a wet stone and fell. The shadows licked out at him. For a moment the mountain heaved, trying to throw him off; Andrion clung to the ground until the moment passed, then stood again. "Not yet," he said. "This is not the testing place."

He had wrenched his leg and scratched his hands, leaving the mountain an offering of his flesh. He moved on, limping slightly, denying the physical pain. The night wind cooled his face. He had been here before, he realized; in his mother's womb, no doubt, and in his dreams. He wanted to plunge forward, throwing himself from rock to rock, but some clinging shred of common sense counseled caution. Slowly, he thought. The cave has been here forever, and now it waits for you.

Dana had told him about this place, where those girls seeking to become warriors fasted and slept. Their dreams accepted some of them into the Companions of the queen. But nightmares came to those unsuited, terrifying visions that could mark a woman for life, and many girls would not even attempt this initiation; Sabazel was not served only by warriors, and initiation came to all in time.

Dana, Andrion told himself, the descendant of queens, had been honor bound to try the cavern, had been honor bound to succeed. And I am a dishonored descendant of those same queens.

He realized the ground was no longer rising. He stood on a narrow terrace in the mountainside, bordered on the right with a sheer cliff, on the left by the yawning gulf of night. The moonlit world was laid before him, shades of black and gray and silver, silent and serene, as if mocking his agitation.

There was the tunnel. He inhaled deeply and ducked into it.
I should not be denied this rite, he thought, simply because I
was born male. A cool breeze, murmuring with voices, with
distant music, touched him. His shoulders tightened, waiting
for the blow, but none came.

The tunnel was dark, not black but a deep, clear indigo. His
questing fingertips touched walls that had been smoothed by
human hands. A faint luminescence drew him on.

He came out onto a promontory and stood, blinking, bracing himself against a sudden vertigo. He could see no border
to the cavern, no ending, just eternal crenelations of gently
sparkling stone, shaped by the song of wind and water; it was
as if the earth opened under his feet, sucking him into some
blue depth, not land nor sea nor air but an ethereal combina-
tion of all three.

There was the solitary flame in its basin, a beacon beyond
the shadows. Andrion found a stairway and stepped carefully
down its hollowed steps. A trail led through the cavern,
following close beside a water channel. The path was
treacherous with bits of rock and slithering creatures; a
serpent passed by his sandals, and each scale gleamed on its
undulating back. Each scale gleamed like the sheath of
Solifrax. Heartened, he went on.

The fire had burned in its carved stone basin since time
began, fed by some seepage in the rock. Andrion paused
beside it; the flame fluttered, bowing, and he bowed in return.
Behind the basin was a small grotto, filled with soft golden
light and the echo of rushing water. Here, he told himself,
here . . . He stepped in.

There were the clay statuettes of goddess and consort,
shaped by fingers long dead. Andrion did not dare touch
them. He knelt by the slender waterfall that filled the stone
channel and splashed his face and head, but the cold bath did
not still his trembling or soothe his aches, body and mind.
"Mother," he sighed, and looked up.

Painted figures danced across the wall before him, human
simulacra engaged in some ancient and terrifying rite. The
summer king was sacrificed by his queen, the priestess of the
goddess, as the land died in the autumn. His son or his twin,
the winter king, met his fate by the same hands as the land
awoke. But it had been millennia since men and women had

believed such sacrifice necessary to ensure the great cycle of the year.

"Do you betray my father and me to a superstition, Mother?" Andrion asked. "Or do you place some greater trust in us?"

Sistrums rattled in the outer cavern and he started. Sistrums, like those held by the aged priestesses at the quarterly rites, a rattle like racing pulse and heart and fevered blood.

The noise ceased as suddenly as it began. Andrion cried, his tongue rasping in his mouth, "I am not strong enough to save my father or even his sword; how can I be strong enough to be your consort?"

A brief rattle. A scent of anemone and asphodel. Distant voices chanted harsh, uncompromising words that he could not quite hear. Yes, his heart raced. The drops of water clinging to his forehead seemed as hot as drops of molten gold. Gasping for breath, he tore off his shirt and trousers and stood as naked as the clay dolls before him; his necklace, moon and star, glinted and sparked rhythmically on the pulse in his throat.

A breeze probed his body, and the fine hairs on his neck rose. Andrion extended his scraped hands in supplication and surrender mingled. "Speak to me!"

And the goddess spoke. *So then, find strength in forgiveness, or peace in death.*

Andrion's senses reeled. The cavern swayed around him, and he fell onto a bench strewn with fresh rushes, clawing among them as they flew from his hands. His vision spun in wheels of light. Was this, he asked himself with one last tendril of rationality, what Dana felt when the Sight came upon her —merely a vessel for some greater thought, some greater feeling?

Rationality dashed itself against the stone, shattering, spinning away, disappearing. The light winked out. The rushes were hot, tendrils reaching up to coil about him and tie him with rich bands of searing metal.

The rich scent of flowers filled his nostrils—anemone, the wind flower, and asphodel, the lily of love and death. He was dead, and this was the otherworld. No. He still lived; this ceremony was a wedding.

Torches blazed suddenly and he winced, trying to cover his

eyes. But he was still bound, tied at ankles and wrists and throat. Faces circled around him, the faces of women, many different women and yet the same one. Green eyes, blue eyes, the sky-blue eyes of Ashtar herself.

She was insubstantial, an image molded by a fitful wind. A young face, yet to be tried, or a face strong in maturity, or an aged face engraved by wisdom; Andrion could not tell. Her hair spilled over him like a shining mist and he tried again to reach up, to embrace her, to pull her down beside him.

Her lips were solid. They touched his, burned his, seared away his mortal flesh; her hands caressed his body, plucking it like the taut string of a lyre. He moaned with desire, straining toward her, aching in every fiber for the consummation. But she was gone. The torches danced and leaped, the flames doubled and redoubled by shining bronze knives, held aloft, falling. The blades struck and struck again; the pain was sharp and sweet, and he heard his own voice scream in agony, in ecstasy—they were the same. His blood flowed from him, draining away dishonor.

The torches went out. He was cold, heavy and cold, wrapped in a shroud, and darkness encompassed him.

No, not complete darkness. There was a long tunnel, and a pinprick of light at the end. Andrion tried his limbs. He was no longer tied, and was, it seemed, unwounded. He struggled up, brushing away the brittle shafts of dead rushes and flowers. He fought free of the linen shroud.

Voices chattered in the gloom, hooting derisively at him, "Bastard, Sardian bastard." He quailed a moment; then, gathering himself, he shouted back, "My father and I, the only sons of Sabazel, wear the label *bastard* like a badge of honor!"

The light was pure, crystalline, unsullied by any evil spell. He took a step. He was as weak as a newborn babe, and fell. He rose and took another step. And another. Each step was steadier.

The voices eddied about him, softening. Wings beat against him like rough caresses. The light at the end of the tunnel summoned him. Slimy things crawled over his feet, tried to swarm up his legs, but he kicked them away. The light grew closer.

It was not a doorway, but a hole in time, a passage from this world to the next. The voices called him affectionately, "Andrion, beloved of the gods, come." Music and sunlight and the scent of spring filled him to bursting, and the pain ebbed.

No more pain, and eternal peace, here, in this green-gold shimmer . . .

With a hideous effort he wrenched his mind back into thought. Bellasteros lay suspended between life and death, waiting for redemption. Ilanit crouched over the rim of the star-shield, caught between two worlds. The rumor of war echoed in the courts of Sardis, and the Empire was sorely wounded, circled by hooting demons.

"No!" Andrion cried, and he turned away from paradise. Tore himself away, flaying alive some part of his soul, and stood numb with regret while the music ebbed and died. The silence was absolute; he could hear the surge of his own living blood. He looked up. He stood in a doorway, beneath a painted stone lintel, gazing into a tomb. But still the light beckoned him.

He stepped forward. The tomb might have been furnished with rich enameled grave goods, but shadows hung over them, obscuring them; he could see clearly only the great sarcophagus in the center of the chamber. There, the light was there. Dust stirred around his ankles. The statue of a cat blinked solemn topaz eyes at him. Suddenly he heard a dry clicking sound, like fingerbones tapping at the coffin lid, trying to get out. But the light was also coming from inside, welling through the crack between lid and base.

Andrion's head spun. It was Solifrax, not safe in the hands of the gods but caught between light and dark, trapped. . . .

He saw then the shining gold effigy, saw its twisted, vulpine face. The hollow eyes turned and glared at him, scornful; he read the words carved like a weapon on a figure's massive chest, *Gerlac, King of Sardis.*

Andrion staggered back with a cry of dismay. He had himself cast the sword into this snare, into his worst nightmare. The tapping paused, began again, stronger. The lid began to shift. The light wavered and grew thinner; Solifrax faded, eaten by evil, destroyed forever.

"So then, I shall be strong!" Andrion stepped forward, thrust the lid from his demon grandfather's grave, reached for the shining blade.

And awoke, deep in the heart of Cylandra, trembling, wheezing as if he had indeed moved a great gold lid and looked evil in its decaying face. His body was drenched with sweat. He sat up, shaking himself, seizing waking life and pulling it securely about him. His terror had melted into stoicism, but the desire roused in him by the goddess still seared his veins.

Silence. No sistrums, only the rush of water and a faint odor of asphodel. "Mother," he said quietly, "I understand. If you did not love me, you would not test me by showing me my path, by letting me find my own forgiveness." He rose quite steadily and knelt by the basin. His leg no longer hurt, his hands were healed. In fresh, cold water he washed himself clean of sweat and blood and indecision. The water steamed from his body in a fine, golden mist, and he waited.

Dana clambered carefully up the mountain. If Andrion came here, she told herself, he is indeed possessed. Possessed by the goddess, to her own purpose. She half expected to see his smashed body lying below a rocky scree or, bloodied and wet, in the basin of a waterfall, but he was not there. Fleeting wisps of shadow curled across her path like the tattered rags of sorcery, but she burst through them.

Dana was supposed to be on guard, but she had pleaded with her friend Kerith to replace her. She knew, she sensed, she felt where Andrion was. He needs me, she thought. She had not confided in Ilanit, who struggled with the contradictions of the night, nor in Lyris, who stalked through the garden, up and down, up and down, as if her pacing would return the emperor's life to him, discharge him and his son through the gates, and seal the borders of Sabazel behind them.

Dana paused on the terrace before the cavern's entrance and adjusted her bow on her back. The moon hung low in the west, too ripe to sustain itself across the sky. A faint pink blush rose up the east. The east, and my father in Sardis, she thought; I shall see you soon, I think. The wind murmured reassurance in her ear. Suddenly she heard the faint echo of a cry.

She sprinted into the cavern, hardly botherng to mind her steps, searching. No sign of Andrion. But wait. She heard a faint splashing noise, more irregular than the usual song of the water. Dana hurried down the steps and across the floor to the flame. She peered warily into Ashtar's sacred grotto.

Andrion knelt on one knee beside the water channel, contemplating a wall drawing of a slender woman with a bow. His upturned face was shorn of immaturity, cheek and jaw etched by clear, square lines; his mouth was firm, almost tight, guarding against any importunate remnant of youth and uncertainty.

He realized he was being watched, but he did not start. Slowly he stood and looked around. The fire in the basin was reflected twofold in his eyes, distant but uncompromising flames. And yet he spoke lightly, wryly, with a lopsided smile, "You have caught me trespassing."

Dana inhaled, trying to calm herself. His boldness was intriguing, his smile compelling, possessed by some primal simplicity beyond the complexities of logic. "Already you break the laws of Sabazel," she admonished him lamely, "and this, this is—"

"Sacrilege? I think not. Not now." His smile wavered for a moment, as if touched by a memory of weakness and pain; then he assumed confidence like heavy armor. "There is madness here, Dana. Can you not feel it? Does it not tempt you, too?" He stepped forward, pulled the bow from her shoulder, and set it against the wall.

Not quite in protest, not quite in question, she said, "Andrion . . . ?" Her blood stirred, responding to the spell he had called upon himself. His body glistened in the firelight, draped with a numinous cloak, god-touched; his hair lay damp across his forehead like fine red-brown feathers, and his brows were straight wings over the bright depths of his eyes. Incongruous and yet right, this vision of manhood here in the ancient place of Ashtar. "Harus," she said. The words spilled from her mouth, unbidden, "Harus, Ashtar's consort, called to the secret crevices of her body."

"Out of time," said Andrion, continuing some ancient litany, "neither daylight nor dark, neither winter nor summer, beyond the world we know and yet undoubtedly within the borders of Sabazel." Even his voice was firmer, more even. He lifted the quiver of arrows from her back and laid them down. He untied her shirt.

Dana's head spun. The sacred marriage of the ruler and the priestess, she thought; love as strong as death. Her heart lilted, repeating the rhythm of the whispering water, the sistrums that rattled in the outer cavern, and the pulse that made Andrion's necklace flutter like a tiny flame against his throat.

And she laughed. "A divine madness, surely."

"A gift." Andrion's eyes were wide in amazement at his own presumption, even as his fingertips sought her body beneath her clothing.

Her clothing suffocated her. She slipped out of it and tossed it aside. Their hands touched, entwined. Their bodies entwined. They were the same height, the same length of supple muscle, the same suddenly urgent strength.

With some distant, lucid part of her mind Dana saw the rough stone roof of the grotto undulate like the surface of a wind-brushed pool. She lay inside the pool, deep in some moon-dappled depth; no, it was the fire and its shadow that danced over the rock. It was Andrion's body hot against hers, and his lips and tongue sketching a delicate, fiery filigree across her flanks; it was Andrion's face, intense, serious, close to hers.

"Accept my offering." His hoarse voice pronounced the words of the rite; even here, even now, he would remember the courtesy due to her and to the goddess.

"Yes," she responded, equally hoarse. "In your name, Ashtar!" She circled him, guiding him, and gently he filled her. They were one, held in the goddess's hand, possessed of a timeless, worldless joy.

Dana heard her own voice waver upward into a soft cry, saw crystalline beads of sweat spring out on Andrion's forehead as his voice caught and repeated hers. The darkness of his eyes reflected green, mirroring her own awed gaze. The moment was sharp, sweet, ungraspable. And was gone.

Dana set her hand against Andrion's suddenly sober face and groped for words to preserve the spell a moment longer. "We have always been destined for each other. Our fathers like brothers, my mother the daughter of yours, both of us conceived with Bellasteros's empire."

"And yet we are no longer children," he replied.

She glanced at their damp, tangled limbs and had to smile. "Innocent no more." Andrion's necklace was imprinted on her breast, the sword and the shield branded on her flesh. He kissed the image, stroking it with his fingertips until it faded.

The cave steadied, the rush of the water slowed, the sistrums fell silent. The two mortal bodies clung together as the beguiling madness ebbed, leaving exposed the hard stones of reality—Sabazel and the Empire and their own separate lives.

"I must go to Sardis," Andrion said at last. He propped his head upon his elbow and gazed bemusedly at Dana's body spread beneath him. "My father's sword is there and I must reclaim it. Will you come with me?"

"To play Danica to your Bellasteros?"

"Bellasteros had an army at his back."

"You will."

"And at the beginning Bellasteros and Danica hated each other." Andrion's mouth tightened and he looked suddenly away.

But his thought was tangible; if we love at the beginning, then how will it end? Dana pulled Andrion's head back down to her and kissed him fiercely, trying to recapture an already fading passion. "So you will have your father's sword. For yourself? For the army of Sardis? Or for him?"

"Yes," he answered, and he answered her kiss with one much more delicate, accepting the end of their rite.

She sighed. "Then I shall stand by you."

Quietly, deliberately, he asked, "And by Sabazel?"

"Always by Sabazel." She shifted; his body, which she had borne so lightly a moment ago, was now heavy.

He slipped away and sat up on the edge of the bench. "Sabazel is all your life, Dana; it is only part of mine."

"I know, Andrion. I know." And they shared an affectionate if rueful smile, understanding each other only too well.

They washed in the water channel silently, as befitting the end of a solemn rite, and they allowed the icy droplets to damp the last embers of their madness. Chilled, they dressed, and Dana armed herself again. She could have wept; no longer could she anticipate the moment of their union, now that it had been consumed. But she would not cry before god-touched Andrion, the heir of the Empire.

She considered the rushes tangled and matted on the bench. "We shall pay for this. Enspelled, sanctified, and still condemned."

"We choose to be tested." Andrion grimaced.

They gave the rushes to the flame. As the light flickered on Andrion's still face, Dana thought, I have lost the boy I loved; I have found a man. And yet I must not love a man lest I be devoured by his world, by his name, which matters there far more than mine. But the flame warmed them, and the joy of their embrace lingered even as they left the grotto and the cavern behind.

A shining dawn mist obscured the horizon and transformed the city of Sabazel, nestling at the base of the mountain, into gauzy lace. As if they had stayed years in the cave, Dana told herself, and emerged only to find Sabazel a half-forgotten legend. But no, Sabazel waited.

• • •

Andrion heard Lyris's voice, rising and falling through the
mist, even before they had reached the place of the basin.
"Duty . . . honor of Sabazel . . . Companion disgraced . . ."

"Why is she so angry?" he asked Dana. But he knew the
answer.

She groaned. "I asked Kerith to take my place on guard
duty. She was discovered, it seems."

We are discovered. Andrion writhed in a moment's embarrassment. Then that, too, peeled away like an outgrown skin,
leaving only sorrow. That magic moment, so long anticipated,
had been forever consumed and would now lie gutted at the
impenetrable boundary of two worlds. But he would no longer
weep before this warrior of Sabazel. I have lost the girl I loved,
he thought, and found a woman I must not love; it can be no
other way.

He turned and kissed Dana's cool and reluctant lips, and
she summoned a smile for him. With his own grim smile he
said, "Let us divert Lyris's wrath from the innocent."

They hurried past the bronze basin. Andrion glanced back;
mist gathered above the still water, wavering into a shape, into
clear blue eyes and glimpses of the sky beyond the clouds. The
queen's garden held muted images of trees and flowers. Even a
seated Ilanit was the ghostly shape of a dream. Only Lyris,
fully armed and armored, and the slender shivering form of
Kerith bent before her, were distinctly defined. "Please,"
Dana called, "the blame is mine. I was called to Andrion in
the cavern."

The weapons master turned. Her keen eye quickly appraised
the pink cheeks of the pair. Her nostrils quivered in outrage.
She dismissed Kerith, small game, with a wave of her hand;
the girl, with a wild glance from her friend to her queen and
back again, fled.

Lyris's steady, blazing gaze scoured Dana's form, as taut as
an upraised saber, clean of pretense. Then it leaped onto
Andrion. Their eyes locked, struggling for dominance. You
shall not catch me off guard again, he told her silently, and she
snapped away, disdaining the struggle.

"So," Lyris hissed at Dana, "you would abandon your
duty to serve a man."

"I serve no man," returned Dana. "And none serve me. We
were called together."

Ilanit awoke. Her features crumpled and she choked, as if strangling either a laugh or a cry. Her eyes began to focus on the garden around her. The mist thinned and shimmered, diffused with the light of the morning sun.

"I would expect nothing else from a man," Lyris stated, "than to dirty the sacred places of Sabazel, thinking himself above the law. But you!"

"Not above the law," insisted Dana, "but caught within its meshes, as are we all."

Lyris snorted, and her glance again stabbed like a javelin at Andrion. He stood firm, determined and yet respectful. "I am sorry, Lyris, that we offended you. It could not be helped."

"Self-righteous prig," she spat. She turned, indignant, to Ilanit. "You and I have borne sons, my queen, and we traded them for girls as the law requires. Why should this boy be not only acknowledged but favored?"

Ilanit looked toward the house that sheltered Danica and Bellasteros. "This boy is beloved of the gods," she said. She almost sang, as if chanting a liturgy. "His birth secured Sabazel from slavery to Sardis, to the Empire."

"And tied Sabazel too close to the outside world."

Ilanit fixed Lyris with the glow of her eyes, asking with dignity and love for mercy. "The goddess's winds blow strange and subtle, Lyris, and who are we to question them?"

"I do not question the law," Lyris muttered.

Ilanit turned to Andrion. "Why did you enter the cavern?"

"I wanted the goddess to speak to me."

Ilanit smiled at that. "And did she?"

"Yes. I must go to Sardis."

"Soon?" asked Lyris hopefully.

"Soon. With Dana at my side."

"Ah?" exhaled Ilanit, as if pierced to the heart.

Lyris drew her sword and regarded it as if it were the only certainty left to her. "But they must pay for their crime," she persisted. And she, too, was pleading. A sudden breeze swirled through Sabazel, shredding the mist, and a thin, watery sunlight brightened the colors of the garden.

Ilanit set her jaw and raised her hand in judgment. "Their rite was a valid one," she pronounced. "If penance is due, then their journey will be it, I think. But the letter of the law must be obeyed. For taking a man outside the quarterly rites I was shorn of my hair, and the Companions mocked me for my frailty. But Patros paid only with blood, not with his manhood." Her hand fell to her side and closed into a protective ball. "Token payment, Lyris."

Lyris bowed to the queen's verdict. She turned narrow-eyed to Andrion, her sword twitching. He rolled back his left sleeve and extended his arm. "I entered the cavern and Dana both, illegally," he said. "Strike."

The sword darted out and bit. He stifled a gasp. A runnel of crimson appeared on his forearm, welled, and dripped onto the ground. The wind quickened. "Nothing personal," Lyris told him.

"No offense taken," Andrion returned between clenched teeth.

Lyris grasped Dana's hair, pulling it so hard she winced. Again the sword darted, and a long flaxen lock spun away into the wind. The mist burned away and the warmth of the sun poured down upon mountain and city. For a long moment the world was silent except for a faint chiming in the wind, and Andrion tried to pray. But he had spent prayer as he had spent his passion between Dana's thighs, as his blood spent itself upon the ground, offerings to Ashtar, to Harus, to Bellasteros. Perhaps to himself.

Lyris sheathed her sword and strode away. The morning filled with the song of birds, the hum of bees, the voices of women and children.

Ilanit touched Andrion's shoulder hesitantly, as if afraid his flesh would burn her hand. "You tread a narrow path. A dangerous one."

"Yes," he said, with a sideways look at Dana. She was staring off into the distance, listening to some other sound. "Have I a choice?"

"No. None of us do." Ilanit laughed shortly. "Ask Danica to bind your wound." And, to Dana, "Come. We have work to do, small things like winnowing grain and weaving cloth, pleasant things that tie us to this world." She turned and walked away, her head tilted to the leaf-latticed sky, blue sky winking between olive and laurel leaves like Ashtar's amused glance. Dana smiled at Andrion sadly, and was gone.

With a weary sigh he opened the door of the house, stepped into the dim interior, went to the bed and leaned over the still form of the emperor. Bellasteros could well have been asleep, deeply, serenely, his face illuminated as if by the glow of the basin, as if he looked into the otherworld where Solifrax now waited. With a tremor of sorrow Andrion kissed the cool, waxen skin of his father's brow. "Forgive me," he murmured to the unconscious face. "I shall try to redeem us both."

"He has not stirred," Danica said.

Andrion turned to her. She sat by the bed, separating fragrant herbs into small parcels. The sharp odor of thyme cleared his head, and he frowned. "But you turned the evil spell away."

"This one, yes. But the first spell had ample time to eat at his will, his strength; now I hold him in a life he might no longer choose."

"No, no, death would be too easy; he never shirked duty, no matter how distasteful. . . ." Andrion's thought spun away and disappeared. Mutely he held out his wounded arm.

"So," said Danica. "You escaped lightly." She reached for a bandage. "To think I should condone your boldness, to think I should condone your life itself. To think I should allow this man to bring the troubles of the world here." She chuckled in dry resignation, turning to laughter, apparently, because grief would be useless. "The goddess sets us into a game, as she did before you were born."

"Do we choose our fates, Mother? Or does the goddess order fate, allowing us to believe we choose?"

Danica cleaned his arm and snugged the bandage around it. She looked up at him, eyes uncannily clear jade. "Once I carried the power of Ashtar, and yet even then I did not know who directed it. When the power left me, when you were born, I was not left empty but changed. I wanted to heal, to kill no longer. Perhaps it is all the same game."

"I would like to believe it is." Andrion flexed his arm. "Thank you. I shall sleep now. Dreamlessly, I hope."

"And alone," smiled Danica, brows raised in gentle admonition.

"Gods, yes," Andrion swore. He settled himself on the pallet by the shield, looked up at it, touched it lightly. But the shield was quiet, only a great disk gathering golden motes of dust, supporting the abandoned diadem of the Empire and the dull empty sheath of Solifrax.

He watched Danica bend to her task, her veined hands moving purposefully. He saw her hands, young and firm, lifting the shield, lifting a tiny infant. He saw Bellasteros, clean-shaven, dark-eyed, touching her with a heart-hunger that he could only now comprehend. Ah, Dana. I had so many romantic fancies about you, and me, he thought. But the truth of it hurts: No man can ever truly touch a Sabazian.

Andrion's sleep stirred with the slow phantoms of nightmare. The great stone sarcophagus of Gerlac waited, dust-rimed but not quite silent, in Sardis.

Chapter Ten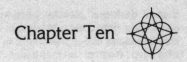

WAVES OF HEAT shimmered above the plain as if it burned. The sky was clear, infinitely high, washed of color by the glare.

The throng of Khazyari warriors shouted in delight. Ponies raced in a great golden dust cloud down the field, stopped with many protesting rearings and whinnyings, turned and raced back again. A small bloody bundle bounced ahead of the scrum, was overtaken, disappeared under thrashing hooves.

The watching warriors shouted again, some urging one team in the game of pulkashi, others another. The women sang wild songs of mockery and encouragement.

Tembujin leaned low from his speeding pony, reached precariously far, seized the bundle. He sat back into his saddle, rising high in his stirrups and flourishing the bundle with a laugh. His eyes and his teeth glinted, black and white, beneath the patina of dust on his face; his tail of hair floated behind him like the tail of his pony as he swung the beast about in a tight circle. Leading the pack, he galloped wildly to the goal line and flung the bundle to the feet of Baakhun.

Baakhun, seated cross-legged on a raised dais under a canopy, saluted his son with his drinking skin. He gulped and threw the skin to Tembujin. The prince caught it and drank while his pony curvetted under him. The bundle, burst open in the dust, emitted a mangled, severed head.

The slave's only crime had been his reluctance to serve. With a sigh Toth turned away from the spectacle and shuffled behind Baakhun's dais to the one occupied by Raksula. Hilkar squatted before her, his scrawny neck outthrust like that of a gabbling vulture. "Yes, my lady, my kinswoman Shurzad is the wife of the governor of Sardis, Patros, the closest friend of Bellasteros."

"And what god does she worship?" Raksula asked rather too casually. She held a horsehair whisk, brushing the flies from her face; she did not look at Hilkar but at the game before her, and her eyes glittered, hard, like two shards of obsidian. A slave restored the grisly trophy to its bag and flung it onto the field again. The watchers cheered. The ponies neighed. A few tethered camels screamed their approval.

"Qem," said Hilkar. "A local deity here, whose idol she took with her to Sardis. There she had herself proclaimed high priestess. She is full of herself, you understand, my lady."

Raksula laughed shortly. "A fitting trait for your kinswoman, yes." And with a slow, thoughtful sweep of the whisk, "So she worships Qem. I know that name, the cat god . . . ." She snapped her lips shut as securely as if she sealed a secret missive, muttered something in Khazyari, and darted a sharp, suspicious look at Hilkar. But his face was eagerly obsequious. Toth stared into the distance, as if hearing and caring nothing.

Tembujin tossed back the skin of kviss and bowed to his father. He spun his pony about, organized his milling warriors, and led them in a swift descent onto the bundle. The other team rushed forward. Vlad, kicking his fat pony in a vain attempt to gain the lead, leaned out to seize the bundle. He overbalanced and hung screeching to the girth as the pounding hooves sprayed dirt into his face.

Tembujin spun his horse expertly about, plucked Vlad from his precarious perch, and flung the boy like a slaughtered sheep over his saddle. He galloped to the edge of the field and with a sneer dumped Vlad at his mother's feet. Baakhun howled with laughter.

Raksula snorted in disgust, and the look she sent Baakhun would have stabbed him deep, if he had seen it. She threw Hilkar her whisk, rose, brushed by him. She picked up Vlad, shook him like a cat would shake a rat, and wiped his dust-smudged face with her skirts.

Toth, frowning, left the edge of the field and retreated toward the white-feathered standard. Sita sat on the Mohendra rug, supposedly mending one of Tembujin's tunics, but the stitches straggled sloppily across the cloth. Her face was so pale as to be a sickly green, her eyes half-closed, hidden by her lashes, and sweat trickled down the sides of her face. She plucked fitfully at her thick clothing. Toth quickened his step. "Are you well, my—" He caught himself.

The mass of horses and men seethed like maggots in a rotting carcass. The voices of the Khazyari crashed through the encircling yurts and rolled like thunder across the land. The plain as an oven, the sky a lid of blue-glazed tile; the mingled odors of sweat, dust, and lathered ponies hung heavy in the air.

Sita grimaced weakly. "Indigestion, I hope. Spoiled food; they do not know how to cope with the heat, do they?"

"Indigestion?" repeated Toth warily.

She threw down her work. "I think I am with child," she said between her teeth.

"It is the will of the goddess," Toth said quickly, blanching almost as pale as she.

"Is it?" Sita glanced toward Tembujin's distant figure. He again leaned low from his pony, swept up the bundle, sped away. Her eyes glistened, and she dashed away any suggestion of tears. "He could die playing that foolish game. What would happen to me then? He uses me, and yet he cares for me; he protects me from those who are much more the barbarian than he. How can I hate him? But he seeks to kill my father and my brother, and he brought about my stepmother's death; how can I like him, even if he is the father of my child?"

Toth listened, his pale, translucent eyes resting on her face, seeing more, somehow, than just her sickly features.

"Is it the will of the gods?" continued Sita. "Do we choose our fate, or do they order fate, allowing us to believe we choose? Do they use me, do they care for me?"

"Whom the gods love they test," said Toth. "Ashtar moves in subtle ways."

Sita looked at him, sceptical, and yet wanting to believe. "That night the city fell. Who held me back, took my hand from Chryse's in that moment when she and her handmaiden leaped? The doors were broken and the palace burned, and we ran, the three of us, with the servant carrying my jewels, as if my jewels were important. We had thought at first to escape, but there was no escape, so we ran to the roof, and the screams of abused women followed us. We must choose between our lives and our honor, Chryse said; she leaped and the girl leaped, but at that last moment my courage failed me and I fell back. The pavement was . . . unforgiving. I could not look to see their bodies so far below, mortal flesh and blood and bones; Chryse's love for me, for Andrion, gone."

She gulped, but again suppressed her tears. She whispered, "It must have been my choice to live, and suffer the indignities of living. Even now, Toth, even now."

"If only I had known you yet lived," said Toth, "when I showed the emperor and the prince and Miklos the old tunnel. But I had seen Chryse, and beside her a young woman carrying your jewels; I found you too late."

"I understand, Toth."

His plump face attempted a smile. "Console yourself then, my lady, by thinking of Bellasteros and Andrion, safe in Sabazel."

"Sabazel," Sita repeated, her tongue lingering over the name. The color returned to her cheeks. She clasped her hands in her lap and sighed deeply. "I have seen it only in the eyes of Dana, in the faces and voices of Ilanit and Danica herself. They never condemned me for a life trammeled by men's customs, as some would condemn them for their freedom."

A slight breeze stirred the air, bringing a brief, elusive freshness and coolness to the afternoon's stench. The racing warriors clashed again. Someone fell off and was trampled. Horses squealed, women screamed. Sita gasped, her hands to her mouth; Tembujin emerged from the scrum, laughing again, and trotted his pony to the sidelines. There he dismounted, allowing the nuryan Obedei to take the reins. The two warriors stood close together, sharing some confidence.

Sita exhaled shakily and spoke, so softly Toth had to lean forward to hear her. Or perhaps she was not really speaking to him. "Dana would scorn me for what I do now, submitting to a man because that man preserves my life."

"The goddess saves you for some purpose," insisted Toth.

Her voice was still quiet, abstracted. "And Andrion would be ashamed of me, child of the moon that he is." She stopped, looked sharply at Toth.

He met her look with a self-conscious nod. "Yes, I know who his blood mother is. You need conceal nothing from me, my lady."

"So it seems." She summoned a smile. "It is a comfort to have you with me, Toth. Someone before whom I need have no pretense."

He bowed to her. "With all respect, my lady, only the gods see all."

Sita tightened her lips resignedly and picked up the needle again. Tembujin clapped Obedei on the back and started through the throng. The people parted before him, bowing, and he nodded graciously to all.

"You are most accomplished," Sita said to him under her breath. "You would like to excite me, but I will not let you. The bow and smile of Miklos, the guard at my door, meant more to me. . . ." Her voice trailed away, and she flushed.

With a tactful nod Toth vanished. A whorl of dust stirred the sides of the yurt. Tembujin swept by, calling for water, and ducked inside. Sita followed. "Are you well . . . my lord?"

"Of course. Why not?" He peeled off his tunic and his shirt, shook the dust from his hair, turned to Sita with a grin. "Our games are too rough for you?"

"I am not accustomed to such games. Athletic contests, certainly. Sword duels. But not outright battle."

Sita proffered a full water jar, awkwardly and with more than a tinge of resentment. Tembujin picked up a dipper of water and splashed it over his face and shoulders. The water gilded his supple body, and Sita looked away. Tembujin turned her face back to his. "You were concerned about my safety? May I assume I am no longer quite so distasteful to you?"

She could not move her face, held firmly in his damp hand, but she averted her eyes. "Is it your concern that makes you so pale?" he murmured.

She closed her eyes, refusing to reply.

"Stubborn," he chided. "Hiding, always hiding. One would think you had something to hide." With a short laugh he released her, leaving a muddy fingerprint on her chin, and dried himself. As he reached for his clothing, he said, "I shall be leaving tonight to scout the pass at Azervinah. You disavow all knowledge of Sabazel; I do not suppose you have been to Farsahn?"

"No," she replied. She opened her eyes, but they were still averted, staring into some distance far beyond the walls of the yurt.

"So be it then. I shall question our tame traitor yet again and hope that he does not have the courage to betray me."

"Who would?"

"Ambitious and arrogant folk," Tembujin said, a sudden sharp edge cutting the smoothness of his voice.

Sita glanced around at him warily. "And what of me?" she asked.

"Hm?"

"While you are gone. To whom will I belong?"

"Ah, so that was your concern then, your own lovely body." Tembujin tossed his tail of hair behind him, like a spirited beast before a race, and settled his shirt over his chest. "You are still mine, Sita. You will stay here with my household, and if the other women tease you, you will bear that as nobly as you bear my embraces."

Sita flushed and looked down at the ground. "You would mock me?"

"I would like to see you smile," he said acidly. "But then, you must have something to deny me."

Her look darted upward, and she met his eyes with the wide lapis lazuli of her own. He stepped forward, interested, watching her keenly. Something moved in the depths of those eyes, some determination; she blinked, breaking the moment, and turned away again.

Tembujin shrugged. "I have asked Obedei to watch you. I hope you enjoy your respite from my company." He turned on his heel, picked up his bow and quiver, and was gone.

Sita stood unmoving. "I cannot hurt you," she whispered under her breath, trying to memorize a difficult lesson. "I am only a toy to you, and I could not hurt you if I tried."

Tembujin strode glowering back through the crowd, his mouth crimped tight and unyielding with irritation. He threw himself down on the edge of his father's dais and watched an archery contest begin. The sun slanted into the west, its light burning gold on the planes of his face, and a soft breeze played with his hair.

Baakhun handed over the skin and Tembujin drank deeply of the kviss. Hilkar's thin figure scurried like a furtive insect down the sidelines; the prince hailed him.

Bobbing and bowing, Hilkar asked, "My lord, may I serve you?"

"I suppose you can tell me nothing more of Sabazel. Odd, how no one has been there!" The skin was as flaccid as Hilkar's face; Tembujin threw it down. "So tell me again of the Royal Road to the north, beyond the place of battle. Tell me of the pass at Azervinah and the cities of Farsahn and Sardis."

"Farsahn is not as great as it once was. It was burned by the Sardians. Accidentally, the usurper Bellasteros always claimed, but I know better. It has now been rebuilt, and is, as I was telling your lady mother, governed by one Nikander—''

Tembujin's alert eye darted to Hilkar's face and stopped his words in his throat. "Raksula, who is not my mother, asked you these same questions?"

Hilkar's face wavered among several possible expressions, trying in vain to gauge Tembujin's mood. "Er, yes. Questions about Sardis and my kinswoman Shurzad, the wife of the governor. She even asked for something of hers. I found an amulet of Qem, a small bauble."

Tembujin's eyes narrowed. "Ah. I see."

A shadow fell on him, and he concealed a start. Raksula, trailing Odo and Vlad, brushed Hilkar aside and jogged Baakhun's elbow. She trod upon Tembujin's foot and he kicked surreptitiously at her, succeeding only in rustling her skirts. She stepped on him again. With a snarl he rose. Raksula stood shoulder to shoulder with Odo and Vlad, leaving no opening; Tembujin thrust his chin outward and stepped to the side in scorn of their association. Hilkar made little sallies left and right behind them all, jockeying for position.

Odo handed Vlad a full skin. Vlad, with a bow, passed it on to Baakhun. One of the archers made a remarkable shot and the crowd cheered. Baakhun opened the skin and drank. He smacked his lips. His mighty bulk shifted, wove an uncertain circle, settled back again clasping the new skin. "A different flavor," he pronounced. "Tasty, though."

"Herbs to increase your stamina, my lord," Odo grinned.

"Ah. My thanks. The heat is indeed tiresome for us all."

Raksula smirked, but her eyes were flat, like tightly shuttered windows, watching enspelled as Baakhun drank again. Vlad stood self-absorbed, his finger thrust up his nose in an apparently successful quest for something of interest.

Tembujin's eyes narrowed farther, but Hilkar gabbled on, going so far as to grasp at the prince's sleeve. "Shurzad and Patros have a young daughter, my lord. See, her name is also engraved on the amulet I bring."

Raksula whirled. Her fingers, curved like the talons of some predatory bird, seized the amulet dangling from Hilkar's hand. The chain caught around his fingers as she yanked it away, causing him to gasp in pain. Tembujin caught a glimpse of the stylized slanted eye of a cat, carved of glistening green nephrite, about the size of his palm. And yes, tiny letters coiled like a kohl rim around the eye: *Shurzad and Valeria humbly beseech the favor of mighty Qem.*

Raksula waved the amulet before her face and exchanged a triumphant look with Odo. "Surely Khalingu orders the world for our victory," she said.

"Surely," repeated Tembujin loudly. His eyes were now gleaming slits. "Father, shall I shoot for you?"

"Yes, yes, show us your prowess, my son," bellowed Baakhun. He drank again and wiped his mouth on the bulging muscles of his arm.

Tembujin shoved Vlad aside and marched out onto the field. The watchers shouted; the other archers gave way. He gestured, and attendants moved the wicker target farther back. With a twist of his body he strung his bow, tightening its horn and sinew into a crescent. Smoothly he plucked an arrow, nocked it, aimed. His thumb snapped and the string hummed. The arrow flew swift and true to the center of the target. The crowd roared its approval. Tembujin smiled faintly, chose another arrow, fired again.

Raksula sidled closer to Baakhun and curled up at his feet, swinging the amulet. "You will need stamina," she purred, "when the odlok Tembujin departs and leaves his red-haired girl with you."

"He has not offered her to me," responded Baakhun. "She will stay with his own household, I suppose, served by that eunuch." And he chuckled, a rumble emanating from deep in his chest, amused by his own cleverness. "But a eunuch could never serve her the way I could."

Raksula laughed heartily. "True indeed, my lord. Tembujin keeps her so close, there are those who name him selfish." She reached behind her, dragged Vlad onto the dais, and seated him at his father's right hand.

Baakhun peered inquisitively into the skin of kviss, as if Sita were kept within. "A waste of a pretty girl."

"Unlike the odlok, to so insult his father." Raksula barely murmured the words, but the wind lifted them to Baakhun's ears. His lower lip protruded, injured, and he gulped the kviss.

Hilkar abandoned the effort to understand this exchange in Khazyari. He turned and feigned great interest in the archery contest. Tembujin shot a third time, again perfectly, and the other contestants bowed to him. Another cheer rose from the crowd. He glanced around at Baakhun, but Baakhun, petulant, would not meet his eye. The prince's face clouded.

Raksula smiled, but her eyes were still flat. The wind stirred the afternoon light like water in a bronze basin.

• • •

Darkness lay heavy over the world, a mist dimming the face of a gibbous moon. Mist lay over the plain south of Azervinah, where the humps of the Khazyari yurts stretched horizon to horizon.

The image of Khalingu stretched and yawned, lipless mouth with brittle, sharp teeth opening, long tongue licking out. The hangings stirred as if by a fetid breath.

Raksula and Odo bent together over a solitary flame. Between their clasped hands dangled the amulet of the Eye. At their side lay the trussed shape of a prisoner, a Sardian captured in the disastrous battle along the Road. His eyes rolled up in their sockets, his breathing was shallow; he had been drugged into docility.

The Eye twitched like a cat's tail, back and forth, back and forth, over the fire. Shapes oozed through the shadows and streamed out through the smoke hole of the yurt, flowing upward into a shrouded sky.

In Sardis, at night under a waning moon, Shurzad knelt naked before her secret shrine of Qem. All was ready: knife, lamp, incense, an empty chased gold offering bowl beside another containing a curl of dark auburn hair. "So," she said to the cat, Qemnetesh, "we begin. Such little magicks I have done before, such insignificant ones, love philters and elixirs of strength."

The gray cat lay along the altar, delicately cleaning its paws. It did not look up at her.

Shurzad's voice quickened and rose, leaving the rhythm of her own breath and taking up Raksula's. Darkness oozed around her, sucking at her; her body swayed, its soft shining curves seemed to waver, slip into another shape, waver back again.

Raksula lifted a long curved dagger, touched the amulet with it, traced an arcane pattern on the face of the prisoner. His eyes disappeared, leaving only vacant white crescents beneath his lids. Raksula cut his throat.

Shurzad looked up into the eyes of Qem. They were deep topaz mirrors, spinning, pulling her down into some depth. Her voice stopped with a gasp in her throat. She picked up the knife, and it twisted, alive, in her grasp. Blood welled from her wrist, flowed into the empty offering bowl, became a shifting vermilion pool that lapped out, farther and farther.

Raksula's teeth glinted. Great beads of sweat stood out on

her brow. Each tiny braid on her head stood on end and waved, as if trying to swarm from her head and follow her words across the darkened expanse of the world.

She spoke a word of command. Shurzad screamed in pain. Her eyes started from their kohl-rimmed sockets. And yet, except for the cut on her wrist, her body was unscathed.

Valeria slept, secure in her bed in the palace of Sardis, guarded, doted upon. She tossed, moaning in nightmare, and the shadows of her bedchamber coiled like strangling ropes around her.

The blood in Shurzad's bowl leapt upward in a garish red fountain and sprayed the other bowl. The coil of dark auburn hair was inundated. It sparked, writhing, and burned. The incense emitted an evil stench, as of a charnel house, a battlefield where only jackals and vultures moved.

Shurzad crumpled before her altar, motionless, hardly breathing, her eyes staring unseeing before her. The flame of her lamp stood straight and unwavering, touched by no breeze here in the secret, ensorcelled room. Shadows hemmed her in, harrowing her soft flesh with darkness and then fading. Laughter echoed around her, faint and distorted, like a feverish hallucination.

A guard passed the outer door, his footsteps steady, ordinary. Shurzad slowly lifted her face. It was sunken like a grape that has been crushed and sucked dry. Her eyes contained only a tiny image of the solitary flame. "My husband readies an army," she whispered, as if she had no voice, no will, left. "Andrion comes to claim the army. To claim Valeria, as you promise."

The offering bowl held a curl of charcoal, and ancient rust stains. The statue of Qem was silent, only carved stone. Qemnetesh emitted one sharp gleam between slitted eyelids and then lowered its head, asleep.

Raksula held the amulet of the Eye before her and gloated. "Shurzad. Valeria her daughter. What pleasure, Odo, to turn Bellasteros's flank. To strike at Andrion in a place he feels secure. Shurzad, you simpering fool, I own you."

The body lay silently, head twisted back, blood running sluggishly from the gaping wound in its throat. Blood soaked into the dark carpet and lapped at the hem of Raksula's skirt. Odo squatted over the butter lamp, nursing its tiny flame; it flared, sending his shadow shooting up the walls of his tent, a hulking and twisted gargoyle bending over Raksula.

She laughed, Odo sat down, the flame steadied, and the gargoyle disappeared. "Qem," she said, "an aspect of Khalingu as snow leopard, brought here to Iksandarun by the caravans, and carried by Shurzad herself to Sardis. How pleasant, indeed." She stirred the body of the prisoner with her foot, sneering, "Sardian weakling."

Odo's face was furrowed with a different thought. "My lady, to put henbane into Baakhun's kviss so that he may heed those suspicions we plant in him is inspired, certainly inspired. But Tembujin is strong. You saw how the warriors cheered him at the games four days ago, before we left. We must enspell him to what appears to be treachery."

"Fool," said Raksula. "Of course we must enspell him, even as we enspell the other prince, Andrion. Khalingu has planned it all."

"Yes, my lady," Odo replied.

Raksula swung the amulet in slow circles, round and round, and Odo's eyes, black currants in rolls of dough, followed it. Outside the yurt the statue of Khalingu sat, still and content, under a shadowed moon.

Chapter Eleven

THEY LEFT THE city in darkness. Ilanit's shield, raised in farewell, glowed like a beacon behind them. At dawn they guided their horses across the borders of Sabazel, and the sun rose before them like another shield, flourished in greeting. The wraith of a waning quarter moon hovered uncertainly above the still-shadowed horizon at their backs.

Andrion and Dana had hardly seen each other in the eight days since they returned from the cavern, kept apart not by some conspiracy of their elders but by some elusive reluctance to test the depths of their new bond.

Lyris had insisted on scouting the entire country of Sabazel and beyond while Andrion chafed to move on and Dana went gravely and patiently about her business. Not, he thought, that he was in any hurry to test his fate in Gerlac's tomb. He shivered and put that thought out of his mind.

He realized Dana was looking at him, and smiled at her. She smiled back and began to laugh, somehow bewildered that there was still a constraint between them. It was as if the old wall had burned away, revealing another just behind.

Andrion repeated her laugh and her bewilderment. "I shall be clumsy at this," he said. "I always thought of my father as the hero."

"But you were born a hero," Dana returned. "Ashtar's will, set long before our births or even our mothers' births."

Andrion grimaced, both pleased and resentful to be a pawn of the gods. Cylandra shrunk behind them, faded, became only one peak among those that anchored the southwestern horizon. The grasses of the high plains bent and sighed like the waves of a golden-green sea stroked by a morning breeze. The sky deepened to blue. Billowing clouds, still tinted pink with

100

dawn, thronged low in the eastern sky.

Dana shifted irritably in her long skirt and high-laced boots. "I would have preferred to ride bravely out in armor," she grumbled.

"Of course," Andrion replied. "But if we are to be a merchant couple, we must look the part. Subtlety now, and then when I find Solifrax . . ."

"And my father's army," shot back Dana, but she was teasing him.

He bowed graciously over his saddle and arranged his cloak around him, much more comfortable in an embroidered chiton than in Sabazian trousers. He carried no weapons save for a short dagger behind his wide leather belt; Dana wore a dagger concealed under her skirt. Her bow was wrapped in a bolt of cloth, her arrows hidden among pots of honey and grain laid on a packhorse, ostensibly goods for trade. Also hidden was the sheath of Solifrax, now only a dry cast-off serpent's skin, the bronze image of Harus, and the winged brooch. But the crescent and star necklace still gleamed against Andrion's throat; it seemed an innocent enough affectation for a young merchant, and he could not bear to put it away.

A young merchant, he thought, and his sister? His wife? Sacrilege indeed. "How fares Kerith?" he asked. "Will she speak to you again?"

"She was not angry with me. She understands the demands of friendship."

"And of love?" he asked quietly.

Dana looked at him with a slight frown, trying to fathom his question. "We are lovers, if that is what you ask."

"Ah," he replied. He sternly reminded himself that Patros shared Ilanit with Lyris, Bellasteros shared Danica with Shandir—no, it was each woman's pair who was the constant in her life, the steady daily cycle of sun and moon compared with the brief if insistent thunderstorm of a man's presence. He cleared his throat. "Do you think you will pair with her someday?" he asked, knowing even as he spoke that he picked at a scabbed but still tender wound.

Dana's mouth twitched, too considerate to show amusement. "Perhaps. But not yet. We do not pair ourselves until our first pregnancy, so that the babe may have two parents. You know that."

"Ah," Andrion said again. "But I never thought of you

pregnant." There, he had said it.

Dana chuckled, leaned over and lightly slapped his thigh. "I will let you know when I know. And that, Andrion, is more favor than other men receive."

"Thank you," he said, rather stiffly. But she was right, he deserved no preference. And if Dana did bear his child, be it boy or girl . . . He abandoned that thought as well. The complications of the heart were an indulgence he could not allow himself, not now.

"Soon," said Dana quietly, probing her own wound, "they will find a wife for you."

Andrion cringed. "Some general's daughter, who will lie whimpering while I steal her nurtured innocence?" He guided his horses carefully across a gully, through a warm cloud of crushed thyme and the song of locusts, and waited for Dana to follow. "My father did not meet Danica until he was twenty-seven, and he had no heir before then. But I have known Sabazel since birth—"

"And are beguiled by the daughters of Ashtar?" Dana asked, not without sympathy. "Some men would use us and then reject us, true, but not Bellasteros, not Patros, not you." She, too, cleared her throat. "Shurzad will not be pleased to see me with you. She intends a general's daughter for you, her lovely, cosseted Valeria."

"A fragile blossom; I would bruise her with a kiss. When I gave her a lock of my hair last year, she blushed and stammered."

"Shurzad would not even let us play together," said Dana, "fearing, I suppose, that I would contaminate her."

Andrion was only too ready to abandon such difficult topics as his potential marriage and his possible children. "When were you in Sardis?" he asked.

"I was a child, without breasts."

"Many years ago, then."

Dana laughed, refusing to rise to the bait. "Indeed."

"Poor Shurzad," said Andrion, swallowing a grin. "She never forgave Patros for leaving her on their wedding night and going simply to sit with Ilanit and the unborn child that was you. As Bellasteros, I hear, left Roushangka to sit with Danica and me." Roushangka, the ill-fated imperial princess, Sarasvati's mother. . . . The sunlight faded. "Gods," he muttered. "Even if in the end we drive the Khazyari away, we have lost so much, Dana, so much."

"I always sensed in Sarasvati the free spirit of a Sabazian, well hidden though it was. Even to herself, I think. Such a waste."

They moved on across the plain. It seemed to Andrion that they stayed in the same place while the ground slipped away beneath them and the clouds rose across the sky like a creeping curtain. I am clumsy, Andrion said to himself. I must learn to be strong.

"We shall make better time when we reach the Royal Road at Bellastria," said Dana after a time.

Bellastria, thought Andrion. Where my father and my mother first met. "Sardis was once a world away from Farsahn, and Sabazel was only legend. Now, with the roads and bridges Bellasteros built, with the maps he had drawn, the world shrinks."

"But grows no less deep," Dana returned dryly.

A falcon coasted high above the plain, its bright eye fixed on the riders beneath. Andrion saluted it. "I come to your city, Harus, I come."

Egrets flew upward, blinding white against clouds like blue-black iron. Thunderheads blotted out the sun. The world softened into an artificial twilight, but the two riders rode on and on, until the storm broke at last. They sought shelter in a village, and played their roles to perfection for their hosts.

Andrion tried to imagine himself as a villager, complacently ignorant, untouched by the gods. But he could not. And neither, he decided, could Dana.

A cool, brisk wind rolled up the clouds and thrust them away; the morning sun glinted off each stalk of grass, each branch of the willows lining a swollen stream. Andrion and Dana bade the villagers farewell and set their faces to the east.

By afternoon they came to an escarpment. The land fell away into a thick forest that edged a glistening rim of the sea, azure water blending in hazy sunlight with azure sky. There was the settlement of Bellastria, founded behind the palisade of an old Sardian encampment. Not too old, Andrion corrected himself. Less than twenty years ago his father had summoned his mother here, and here he tried to kill her. How often Bellasteros had told that story, shame-faced and yet amused at his distant impetuous self.

The ditch that had protected the camp was almost filled in, and houses lay beyond the remaining logs of the palisade; the

forest was pocked with farm plots, and boats were drawn up
on the beach. Beyond the town, a wide river wound like pieces
of glinting mirror through the lowlands.

Dana and Andrion guided their horses down into the damp,
verdant stillness. Unusual stillness, Andrion noted; the drooping oak leaves murmured among themselves, stirred by a
whisper of a breeze, but above the town plumes of smoke
reached unwavering upward. No birds sang, no small animals
moved, even the hum of insects was muted; no human figures
were about.

"Something is wrong here," said Dana, her nostrils flaring.

They followed a muddy track through the wood, the plop-
plop of their horses' hooves sounding like reverberating
drumbeats. The outskirts of the town, whitewashed walls
and red tile roofs, appeared through the thick oak boles,
beyond a stubbled field.

And then a puff of wind brought a distant murmur of
voices, not shouting voices, but taut, cautious ones, gabbling
faster and faster and then cut, suddenly, by a word of command.

As one, Andrion and Dana dismounted. They tied their
horses to a nearby tree trunk, concealed behind a tangle of
blackthorn and oleander. They crept forward across the field
and into a narrow alley between high limestone walls. A few
pigeons hopped through the dirt, searching for scraps to eat,
cooing softly.

"We shall take tribute," stated a smooth, lightly accented
male voice, "and leave you to ponder the lesson of our coming. Lessons, perhaps, for Nikander in Farsahn, for Patros in
Sardis." He spoke easily, accustomed, it seemed, to being
obeyed.

Dana and Andrion pressed against the side wall of a house
and peered around its corner into the marketplace of the town,
cobblestones surrounded by low columned buildings, a well,
piles of melons, grapes, flyspecked fish.

The center of the square was thronged with people, probably the entire population of the town. All were hunched over,
as if waiting to be beaten, their hands upraised in supplication
toward—

Andrion choked down a gasp. The gasp exploded into rage.
He closed his eyes, opened them again, but the scene before
him did not alter. A Khazyari warrior stood on the public
speaker's stand, his hands on his hips, his long black tail of

hair tossing behind him. His gleaming black gaze raked the
faces before him, and his lips parted in a lazy smile. "Boo!"
he cried suddenly, and the entire crowd jumped back.

The warrior turned to his twenty or so heavily armed companions, laughing, teeth flashing, saying something in his own
language. Andrion did not need a translation. Such was the
evil reputation of the Khazyari, he told himself acidly, that
several hundred people allowed themselves to be bullied by a
mere handful of warriors.

"How did they get here?" hissed Dana in his ear. "Surely
Patros's army stands athwart the Road from Iksandarun."

"I wager that army stands there no longer," Andrion
growled. "And a small force like that could well follow the
river bottom right past Azervinah."

The chieftain turned and accepted the reins of the only
white pony in the band. "Tribute," he said again. "We shall
collect it then." He indicated a sun position just over a roof,
late afternoon.

The crowd still stood petrified. "Go," he shouted, and the
people scattered like a startled flock of pigeons. The Khazyari
retired to a nearby inn. The owner, to judge by his leather
apron, stood in the doorway bobbing like a feeding duck; a
togaed individual who must have been the chief magistrate of
the town shuffled downcast behind. A couple of warriors remained in the square, grooming and watering the horses, ignoring the quick scurryings of the townsfolk.

"That chieftain struts," spat Andrion, "as if he owns this
place." Red streaks glanced across his vision and he blinked
them away.

"At this moment he does," Dana returned. And she
frowned, puzzled. "Handsome demon, is he not? Do you suppose that if a Khazyari came to Sabazel for the rites, we should
let him in?"

"Dana!" exclaimed Andrion, aghast.

She met his eye frankly. "There was a time when the Sardians seemed as evil to us. And as yet the Khazyari are only
our enemies because they are yours."

"Dana," Andrion protested; but it was foolish to let her
words hurt, especially now. He inhaled, calming himself. "We
must report this to Nikander. They are too close, too bold."

She nodded taut agreement. They turned. A hulking
Khazyari warrior stood behind them, his felt-clad body like
some great bear filling the alley. He jumped up and down with

glee at having surprised them, burbling something in his own tongue.

"Damn," said Dana, more annoyed than frightened. The breath went out of Andrion as surely as if the warrior had struck him in the pit of his stomach. He reached for his dagger; Dana fumbled exasperatedly at her skirt. Two bowmen looked over the edge of the roof above, arrows at the ready. "Damn," Andrion said. And he thought, I am a fool.

With massive hands the warrior took Andrion and Dana each by the scruff of the neck and dragged them into the sun. The light was like a slap, bright and hot. The warrior stank of stale sweat.

The interior of the inn seemed dark, sweet and cool by contrast; a window admitted only one gold-dusted ray of sunlight. The Khazyari deposited his booty like squirming puppies before his chieftain.

Andrion thrust his chin out belligerently and then lowered it, biting his tongue to keep from speaking. His cloak was askew and Dana's dress was smudged with whitewash from the wall they had leaned against; perhaps they would appear harmless enough. Meek, pretend to be meek, he told himself. But meekness was not a word Dana knew, and her body was as straight as ever.

The band of Khazyari, their spears and swords and arrows prominently displayed, dismembered some roasted chickens, tore off gobbets of bread, and slurped from tankards of ale. The innkeeper fluttered on the periphery of the group, holding a dripping pitcher; the magistrate, old, balding, eyes hollow with shock, knelt at the chieftain's feet pleading for mercy.

He lounged in the midst of his warriors, his felt boots propped comfortably on another chair, his tunic open, revealing a silk shirt and a carved ivory plaque. His oddly small bow lay over the back of his chair, his long dagger lay along his hip. He held a cup of wine, and his tip-tilted eyes watched the crimson liquid swirl around the sides of the cup. His high cheekbones were the prows of ships, cleaving not the sea but the world itself.

"Stop your whining," he said to the magistrate. "I give you my word that I shall harm no one, so long as you deliver the tribute I asked. I shall not even take any women from you; my men must remain alert, guarding against a counterattack." He snickered into his cup.

The old man shut his mouth with a pop. His eyes rolled to

the side, saw Andrion and Dana, stared. "So," said the warrior. "You do not know these people." He looked up. Andrion almost started back, so keen was the glance, sharp as a flaying knife. He forced his own gaze down, to where his heart had sunk into his boots. No, the enemy must not be this intelligent.

The magistrate glanced apologetically away. Not knowing what to say, he said the truth. "No, my lord. These are strangers. Merchants, I would say."

"Merchants? Trade goods? Where are your supplies?"

Bolting for the door would do more harm than good. Andrion waved vaguely in the air, remembering at the last minute to make his hand limp instead of a balled fist. "Edge of town, out there."

"Good. Then you, too, may pay tribute. And while you collect your goods . . ." The Khazyari's black eyes turned to Dana.

She returned his look, never thinking to drop her gaze demurely; the green eyes locked with the black, curious, angry, hinting at challenge. The warrior smiled. "And what is your name, lovely?"

Gods, Andrion said to himself, writhing inside. Dana, he will think you are playing with him!

"Dana," she replied evenly. "And yours?"

Pleased by her impudence, the chieftain smiled even more broadly. "Tembujin," he said. "First odlok of the Khazyari."

Gods, Andrion said to himself again. He must be a prince. Let me kill him, Harus, let me kill him. His breath quickened and he struggled to still it. He turned slightly, and the ray of sunlight found his necklace. He felt the heat against his throat as surely as he heard the Khazyari's pleased intake of breath.

A strong if slender hand closed on the moon and star and yanked it from his throat. He staggered, spun back around. Tembujin held the necklace before him. "I know a woman," he confided, "who might be pleased with such a pretty bauble." And he tucked it inside his tunic.

You dirty it! Andrion wanted to scream. Take your filthy hands from my patrimony! His blood shrieked in his veins, and he clenched his teeth, clenched his eyes to keep from lunging for Tembujin's throat. Cool, he told himself. Be calm, survive this humiliation, and you can have a gross of necklaces.

Dana's lips thinned; she, of all people, knew what that

necklace meant. But neither could she speak.

Tembujin lowered his feet and stood. He considered Dana's hair, flaxen waves streaming down her back. She did not take her eyes from his face as he stroked the shimmering fall. "Blond," he said bemusedly. "The women in this village are dark." And he asked Andrion, from the corner of his mouth, "Your sister? You have something of the same look."

"My wife," said Andrion, not daring to unclench his teeth.

"Ah, good. It is so tiresome to break in new stock."

Andrion glanced at Dana, her face suffused with mirth and resentment mingled. By the three ages of Ashtar, she thought Tembujin's remark amusing! Something burst in his mind, and the sparks of it flew through his senses, burning away common sense. With an incoherent oath he leaped.

Tembujin, with a supercilious half smile, stepped aside. Andrion found himself confronting three greasy warriors. One seized him and pinned his arms behind him. One lay a dagger against his throat. Its cold sharpness cleared his head: Fool, fool, she is Sabazian and can care for herself. Fool, get yourself killed now and it ends, it all ends. The blade pressed against his pulse and a veil of shining star-stuff clouded his vision.

Somehow he saw Dana's face freeze into carved alabaster, terror and rage mingled, and behind them a flicker of cunning. Somehow he heard the magistrate, still kneeling, dare to protest. "But these are not of your town," Tembujin said blandly. "If I kill him, if I take her, I do not break my word."

The magistrate's eye rolled to Andrion and he grimaced. Good man, thought Andrion with one part of his mind, to risk himself for a stranger. I must commend him.

The blade was sharp. A drop of blood ran down his throat, past the ghost of the necklace on his tanned skin. Commend him when? Andrion thought. Humiliation, gods, burning humiliation; but I must live, for Bellasteros, for the Empire. "My lord," he choked, "spare me, please." For a moment he thought he would be ill, right here before them all, and viciously he swallowed the bile in his mouth.

"So," Tembujin laughed to Dana. "He does not wish to die for you. Sensible man." He turned and stroked her hair again, letting it run like spun gold through his fingers. Dana's vitriolic glare ran like water from him, unnoticed. At last, too late, she dropped her eyes humbly.

"Let him go, my lord," she purred, with only the slightest quaver in her voice. "He will bring you tribute while we . . . amuse ourselves."

Tembujin's brows rose. "You interest me, Dana." And he leaned forward to kiss her, lightly, in blatant promise not so much to her as to Andrion. "Go to the room above and wait for me. I shall come presently, after I collect my tribute." He turned. "And for this brash young cock . . ." He spoke an order in his own language.

The Khazyari's scorn was a whiplash. Andrion bit his lip so hard he drew blood. Dana's tight nod as she turned to the stairway was no comfort. Did she mean, never mind, I am accustomed to strange men using me? Did she mean, never mind, I will kill him with my own hands?

Andrion's mind shattered into a thousand spinning shards. The room fluttered as he saw Dana's determined mouth, Tembujin's sneer, the magistrate's sickly face. The floor vanished from beneath his feet, and the glare of sunlight seared his eyes. A mud puddle, surrounded by a flock of squawking chickens, came up underneath his head and struck him a glancing blow. Other blows landed on his ribs and stomach as the warrior kicked him. Stunned, he could not move, could not think.

Felt boots swaggered away. The shadows lengthened as the sun sank. The people of the town walked by with their burdens, paused, hurried fearfully on. The heir of the Empire lay in a dirty alley. Waterbirds screeched raucously overhead, taunting him. Bellastria, named for the greatest warrior of the age. Andrion, son of that warrior, clumsy beyond contempt, lowering his guard out of—damn, perhaps it was jealousy. They had not even taken away his dagger. The ultimate insult.

Andrion curled into a ball, shivering with rage and shame. Images of Solifrax's gleaming blade danced through his mind, Solifrax lopping off Tembujin's demonic head and parading it before his own warriors.

The bile rose again in his throat, and this time he spat. But I am neither a peasant nor a merchant, Andrion thought, but more a prince than he. I am the son of the falcon. I must live, and suffer the indignities of living. I must rescue Dana. He staggered to his feet.

There she was, as if called from his thought, peering out of an upper window. He waved, confidently, he hoped, and slipped around the corner.

• • •

Dana leaned against the shutter covering the window, her fists clenched at her sides. Between the slats she could see Andrion lying in the mud. Gods, he was so still; had they killed him? Then she would kill as many of them as she could, before they killed her.

He moved, curling into a ball like a wounded animal, suffering under the burden of his birth, Sabazel and Sardis and the Empire combined. She could not bear to watch him. She turned from the window and inspected the room. It was small and dusty, with whitewashed walls and plank floor. Planks taken from old ships, judging from the pungent smell of salt and weed. There was a basin, a bench, a sagging bed, a mouse chittering nervously in the corner.

The sun dipped into the west and long beams of light glanced through the shutters, rendering the shadowed room only an illusion. She glanced outside again. Andrion was staggering to his feet. Dana wrenched open the shutter and signed to him: I shall free myself, meet me later! He waved in stubborn bravado and disappeared around the corner. Dana sagged in relief against the shutter, trying for a few moments not to think, not to feel.

After a time she heard voices rising and falling, like the distant murmur of the sea. Ah, yes, the Khazyari collecting their booty from the townsfolk. Every now and then a yelp indicated that some hapless soul had not produced the proper quantity or quality of "tribute."

Tembujin would be here soon. Dana gathered her wits and squared her shoulders. Easy as it would be to climb out the window, drop down to the ground, and sneak away, she could not leave without wiping that infuriatingly complacent smile from the Khazyari's face. It would be simple enough to kill him; her dagger nestled, cold and hard, against her thigh. But something stirred, deep in her mind, like a breath of wind stirring the asphodel in Danica's garden. No, he must not die.

She shook her head, but the insistent something—not a thought, an impression rather—would not fade. And she had learned to trust such impressions. Well, she told herself, so I must not kill him. She must not, after all, give his warriors an excuse to wreak havoc on Bellastria. She must not fight him; that would be a waste of strength, and might attract the others, and would end in her death, at the least.

That impulse of low cunning returned. Ah, she thought, he really is an attractive man, for a barbarian. Or would be, with a touch of humility. That sleek hair, like the lion's cub on the plaque he wore. But no, this was the wrong time, and the wrong place, and his intent was most certainly not sacred but profane. I must not enjoy him, but get the best of him, she concluded.

A door crashed downstairs. Male voices bellowed. Footsteps sauntered up the stairs. Dana braced herself and greeted the opening door. "How went your collection?"

"A few silver coins. A glass vase or two. Some woman tried to give me a piglet." Tembujin snorted. "I do not need a piglet." He slammed the door behind him.

Pinfeathers! she thought. He has left his tunic downstairs, with the others, and Andrion's necklace is in it. I should retrieve that for him; I owe him that, I think.

But Tembujin's hands closed warm on her arms, pulling her toward the bed. She was as tall as he, she realized; his face, a cast bronze statue, touched hers and his breath fanned her cheek. At least this one did not stink. He might not even be of pure Khazyari blood; he was less broad, more supple and more subtle than the others.

She laughed, low and throaty. She set her hands against his shirt. "If I have no choice," she murmured, "then I shall enjoy myself."

A spark ignited, deep in his eyes. "You will smile for me?"

She did not try to deduce what he meant by that. "Of course, if you make me feel like smiling."

"I shall." His lips were against hers, demanding, devouring; his mouth tasted of honey and spices. For a moment Dana's head spun. I cannot let this creature of darkness beguile me, she thought; your will, Mother, your strength! She returned his kiss, drawing him backward until she sat on the edge of the sagging mattress.

He braced his arms on either side of her and tossed his tail of hair, grinning. The sublime confidence of the man, Dana thought. If he is their prince, no wonder the Khazyari are victorious. And she wondered suddenly, just who is their god?

Tembujin's stance was perfect. She smiled, letting him believe her smile was for him. She lifted his hand, twitched her skirt aside, set his fingertips against her thigh. Again his eyes sparked, tiny flames reflected again and again, prisms of light and shadow. She moved her leg up the inside of his. Ah, yes, he was nicely rampant. His hand plunged home.

Her hand jerked the dagger from its sheath. Her knee darted upward in a sudden thrust of her entire body. And struck, with a terrible crunch of bone against flesh. She winced even as she pushed him away.

Tembujin had no breath even to gasp, let alone to cry out. His eyes widened and glazed over, his mouth formed a circle of exquisite agony. He crumpled, and Dana was on him as he fell. She pulled the coverlet from the bed, slashing it into strips. By the time he recovered his breath and emitted a ragged exhalation, part gasp, part moan, she was already binding and gagging him.

His cheek lay against the floor, his body curled on its side. He swiveled his head upward, trying to look at her. For a moment his eyes were strangely hurt; then the hurt faded into incredulous affront.

She tickled him with the tip of the dagger, just at the angle of his jaw. "And you so intelligent. Have you never thought that women might not be playthings?"

He grunted indignantly.

The shutters crashed open. Thick sunlight flooded the room. Dana leaped to her feet, dagger at the ready, crouching. Tembujin glanced up.

Andrion clambered over the windowsill and landed, remarkably, on his feet. His hair was a burnished red in the light, his face dirty and pale beneath the dirt, but composed. He took in the situation at a glance. "Very good, Dana," he said.

Tembujin rolled his eyes upward, amazed Andrion would risk himself for a woman.

Dana shuddered in relief and allowed herself a laugh. "I did not hurt him overmuch. Just where it was appropriate. If his warriors were to find him trussed like a sacrificial animal, now that would hurt him. The predator felled by its prey."

Andrion paused, considering that delightful prospect. He bent down, lifted Tembujin's tail of black hair, let it slide across the blade of his dagger. "Shall I take a trophy?"

Tembujin mumbled some Khazyari oath and turned his face away, disdain written in every line of his body.

Andrion let the hair fall. He sighed extravagantly. "But no. We do not want this . . . odlok to be demeaned before his troops. He must keep their charge, so as to lead them"—he leaned over, enunciating into Tembujin's ear—"away from this town and back to their own sty."

Tembujin's shoulders twitched.

Dana realized what Andrion meant. She sheathed her dagger and bent again over the makeshift ropes, tightening this one, looping that one.

"You will be able to free yourself before long," Andrion said. "Anticipate going back downstairs and listening to the lewd jokes of your comrades, who, like you, are sick enough to believe that rape is pleasurable. Anticipate remembering that you gave your word to preserve this town. Or is your word worth anything, barbarian?"

Tembujin twitched again, as if Andrion were only an annoying fly and could be flicked away.

"Your necklace is still in the room below," said Dana. "I am sorry, I meant to recover it for you. But someday you may have a gross of them."

The corners of Andrion's mouth pinched themselves white. She realized too late that those words were not the ones he wanted.

The sun faded and the room was filled with soft-silvered twilight. Carousing Khazyari voices boomed through the floor. Andrion and Dana rose and glanced at each other. But the brown eyes and the green shared nothing. Silently Dana cursed her clumsiness in a man-ruled world.

She turned and peered out the window into the gloomy alley. The horses were tethered beneath. So that was how he had gotten in, standing on one of the horses. Without a backward glance Andrion sheathed his dagger, swung himself out of the window and down. Dana turned for only one moment. Tembujin lay, an indistinct, unmoving lump on the floor, wrapped in sullen silence. Mercy, she thought, is to him worse than death.

She clambered over the sill, lowered herself to the back of the horse, settled upon it. She and Andrion did not speak while they passed the edge of the town, slipped throught the stubbled field, gained the shadow of the woods. A wind chimed through the oak branches and an owl hooted. The west was filled with a crimson light, Bellasteros's cloak spread over his namesake town. But the town was now only a jumble of pale blotches behind them.

They turned their horses toward the bridge over the river Jorniyeh. Just beyond lay the Royal Road, forking east to Farsahn and south past Azervineh to Iksandarun. Dana looked at Andrion, a tight, unbending shape mantled in darkness. Did I ever think, she asked herself, that it would be easy to love a man? Her hand reached toward him and fell back, empty.

His hand touched his throat. Nothing was there. The rhythm of the horses' hooves played a counterpoint to the wind that lit the stars.

Chapter Twelve

ANDRION RODE IN a spiky carapace, brooding on his impotence. The darkness was an encompassing mantle, he thought, smothering him with the amused tolerance of the gods. The night should be lashed by a storm, claps of contemptuous thunder, lightning bolts like arrows of anger. But the gods ignored his weakness—Dana ignored his weakness —with a mocking indulgence.

Slightly strangled, Dana called, "Andrion, was it my fault?"

"No." It was my own jealousy, he thought. Not only the banal canker of lovesickness, but jealousy of that chieftain, of his confidence, of his strength, of his power—that he could walk openly through the land his father had bought with blood and pride. Not a canker, but a deep abscess.

"Andrion," said Dana, as tautly as if trying to channel her words into another language to explain herself to this man. "I laughed then, at the inn, because what Tembujin said about breaking in new stock; do you not see, it was what you said about stealing the innocence of a general's daughter. You were compassionate, and he arrogant, but still I was struck by the similarity between you."

"I am not like that barbarian," Andrion snapped. He glanced back, but her face in the darkness was closely guarded, unreadable. "You did nothing. I lowered my guard."

She muttered testily, "A woman outside the borders of Sabazel is expected to do nothing."

Andrion hated her. As a Sabazian she was aloof from the struggles that consumed him, free of his search for confidence and power; to her he was the pair of that animal Tembujin. How could she say that name so calmly? Andrion guided his horse around a great oak tree whose branches coiled almost to the ground, whose shadow writhed across the Road, resenting the twilight that would consume it. My blood, Dana, he thought, spilled on the earth of Sabazel; my pride trampled into the dust at Bellastria, where my parents first met.

The last of the sunlight faded, the stars spread across the vault of the sky, distant, implacable lights. Andrion turned his face upward, appealing to the night.

And he thought brutally, Yes, I am the same as the barbarian. He has, and I seek, a power Dana does not need. Always she has seen the strengths of men eddy about Sabazel, but Sabazel disdains any power save that of Ashtar.

He seized the self-control that befitted his father's son. "I meant no insult, Dana."

"I know," she replied. Her features softened, and once more she struggled with that strange, unaccustomed tongue. "I, like my mother and my grandmother before me, must pay the price of loving men."

"These men help to preserve Sabazel. Is it so hard, then, to love?"

Her reply was a humorless laugh. "Forgive me, Andrion." Dana leaned from her horse to touch his extended hand. Another barrier was burned. What new one would arise, Andrion wondered, and when?

The bridge lay before them, arches of stone leaping from bank to bank of the Jorniyeh. The river was black liquid shadow. A mist lay on the water, wavering uncertainly in the wind, and the water whispered through the arches as if weeping softly. At this end of the bridge was the still-smoking shell of a guard post. The bodies of the guards were blotches in the night, clumps of darkness tufted with black-barbed Khazyari arrows; shocked eyes were only points of phosphorescence.

Andrion turned away from those arrows. Dana reined in her horse but he motioned her on. "We cannot stop to bury them; the Khazyari might well ride after us." And to the soldiers, "Forgive us what we owe you all." As they hurried across the bridge, they heard no sound except the murmur of the wind in the reeds and willows lining the river and the quiet sobbing of the river itself. The mist reached upward, flowing over the parapet. They broke free of its grasping fingers.

Farsahn lay ahead, and Sardis. Andrion's vision leaded the panes of his mind, vivid and bright; the great ziggurat of Harus, and the tomb of Gerlac, and the sword—his father's sword—the sword of Daimion. I shall return the sword to you, Father, he thought. The Empire is in dire straits, and needs your firm hand . . . But he knew that firm hand was gone. It must now be his own that raised Solifrax.

The smooth, hard-packed dirt and flagstones of the Road were a ribbon unfurling before them, beckoning them on.

The Khazyari moved implacably north, long wings of mounted troops leisurely raking the land. The barbarian army passed some deserted villages and caravanserais; other settlements disgorged clots of frightened people flocking forward with cries of obeisance. Baakhun, basking in victory, extracted tribute from them and allowed them to live. But the pickings were slender in these still ailing lands, and the Khazyari quarreled like jackals over their kill.

A dim, clouded twilight promised a dark night when Sita emerged from Tembujin's yurt and stood, a solitary figure under the standard with the white feathers. The other women of the prince's household had set up the shelter and then dispersed throughout the camp, looking for better sport than one lonely girl; not even a guard stood outside the doorway, since the odlok himself was gone.

Sita clasped her hands protectively and watched the sun plunge into a retreating mass of storm clouds. The west was red, like the red of her father's cloak, fading and dying. The stars were muted by shadow, unattended by any moon. The sounds of the camp—voices, piping music, the grunts of animals—seemed muffled by a curtain of uncertainty.

Toth hovered nearby, the dusk concealing his withered face and uncannily bright eyes. As Sita crumpled onto the spread Mohendra carpet, he reached out consolingly, but figures moved around the fires that burned before the evil image of Khalingu, and he stopped, wary.

Odo danced before the image, amulets jangling on his hairless chest, flames reflected in his swart face, singing in cracked falsetto a prayer of lust and greed. Vlad squatted, holding the offering trays, mouth hanging open in anticipation. A goat squawked and died; in the rushing torrent of light and shadow, the many armed shape of Khalingu seemed to shift and reach forward, pointed tongue curling to lap at the blood. The gathered crowd sighed in satisfaction. Vlad giggled.

Baakhun lumbered unsteadily from the mass of people.

They bowed and murmured fealty. He saluted them all with his drinking skin and drank again. Raksula was a ferret-thin shadow at his side, Hilkar a wisp of darkness an arm's length behind her.

Sita shrank into an inconspicuous huddle. Words drifted to her ears, and she studied them, understanding them. ". . . how Tembujin is faring in the north, so close to our enemies?" Raksula was saying.

Baakhun grunted. "He should be returning soon."

"Yes, he should; but he is so independent, so proud. What does he do all this time, far away to the north, close to the armies of the Empire?"

"Proud," repeated Baakhun. "He is too independent and proud."

Raksula's eye fell upon Sita's bowed head. "And he would not leave you his prize, as a loyal son would."

"Ah," Baakhun said. Attracted by the faint gleam of copper hair, a reflection of the sunset's embers, he staggered into a sudden turn and bent over Sita. "Ah," he boomed in common speech, "red hair alone. Come, we play." He sloshed the drinking skin before her, fanning her with his fetid breath. She gagged, contained herself, shrank even farther.

"Look up, pretty girl," Baakhun ordered. He fumbled at her chin.

Reluctantly she raised her face. It was glistening pale, not reflecting the ruddy light of the fires or the sunset, but some distant silver gleam. Raksula's brows shot up. "Are you ill?" she demanded.

The shadow that was Toth shifted uneasily. The shadow that was Hilkar emitted a gasp of recognition, quickly quelled.

Sita's eyes darted to the side, saw Hilkar, saw his expression. She became even paler. Raksula turned and snarled at the man, sending him scurrying away. He almost collided with Toth. For a long moment the two stared at each other, Hilkar's jowls flapping, Toth's translucent eyes steady and unblinking. Then Hilkar quailed and darted into the night.

Someone called Baakhun. He sighed, tweaked Sita's breast, tugged her hair; he stalked heavily away, like an elemental molded of the earth itself. Raksula coiled down beside Sita and peered closely at her. Sita averted her face, but it was too late. "So," Raksula hissed, in a long release of breath and inspiration, "you are pregnant."

Sita swallowed and knotted her hands in her lap.

"You are not pleased to bear the child of such as Tembujin." The name, on her lips, was a curse.

Sita's eyes flicked suddenly to Raksula's face, wary and yet fascinated, a bird enspelled by a snake.

Raksula's talonlike fingers jabbed at Sita's belly. "You would like to rid yourself of this small parasite."

Something small, frightened, and yet malevolent moved in the depths of Sita's lapis lazuli eyes.

"When you hate the fine arrogant odlok enough," Raksula crooned, "come to me. Bring me some part of his body, a nail clipping perhaps, and I shall cast his spawn from you."

Sita's eyes crossed, unfocused. With a rustle of her skirts Raksula was gone, leaving only her words to shift in the breeze like some provocative charm. Then the words were gone, and the breeze as well, and the stars melted across a damp sky. But Sita did not move, did not blink.

Toth rushed forward and fell to his knees before her, hands extended to shake her awake. "What did she say to you, child?"

Sita started and looked around her, unsure for a moment just where she was. "Hilkar recognized me," she whispered.

"Do not fear that worm. Fear Raksula."

Sita's hands held her belly as if Raksula's touch had seared through her flesh to her womb. If she heard him, she did not reply.

The new city of Farsahn rose upon the rubble of the ancient one. Raw bricks and stone, thatched roofs and tiled ones; tall, fast-growing poplar trees stood high upon their mound, as if eyeing the horizon for invaders. But Sardian invaders had freed it from the old imperial dynasty, and the northern provinces flourished, safe between mountain and sea.

An encampment lay outside the gates, ordered rows of tents and wagons and neat wooden buildings dozing under a late afternoon sun. Andrion squinted at it as he and Dana left a guard post and followed a sentinel up the Road. Those were the legions wounded in battle? Those were the huddled refugees from Khazyari greed? Nikander had done well.

But then, he had always done well. One of Bellasteros's legionnaries before Iksandarun twenty years before, he was now third behind Patros and Aveyron. Second, Andrion corrected himself, for Aveyron was dead. Death scoured every familiar landscape.

They met crossed spears and a challenge. Their escort passed them on. And there was Nikander himself, attended by scribes and staff, inspecting a freshly raised palisade when many officers would have retired for the evening meal.

"My lord," called the guard. "Andrion, the emperor's heir, is here."

Nikander and his staff, a cluster of faces glinting with sweat, turned like sunflowers to Andrion. The grimy soldiers levering a log into place quickly laid the log back down and squatted in the dirt, grateful for whatever respite this youth, prince or no, could bring. A wind hummed down the taut blue dome of the sky.

"My lord Nikander," Andrion called. He saluted, then extended his hand. Dana hung back, looking surreptitiously about her, ignoring the curious glances bent upon her by officer and legionaire alike.

Nikander raised his hand, wiped it on his tunic, firmly clasped Andrion's. The proconsul's long neck protruded from his light cuirass, seeming barely strong enough to support his helmeted head; his lips were thin and tight, his eyes hooded by bushy brows. His glance moved deliberately across Andrion's face and form, inspecting his lashes, his beard, his brooch shaped like the spread wings of a falcon. He seemed to sense in the features of this youth some veneer of Bellasteros's face and manner, some echo of Bellasteros's strength.

His thought resolved, he spoke. "Welcome, my lord."

Nikander reminded Andrion of a great sea turtle, slow to move, but once roused, crushing any opposition. "Thank you." He smiled. "May I present Dana, a Companion of the queen of Sabazel."

The turtle nodded. Dana nodded, her eyes dancing, amused perhaps at the contrast of this stolid general and Andrion's mercurial self.

As they turned into the encampment, Nikander signaled almost imperceptibly to a centurion, and the man hurried off. The proconsul then began to report the messages that had recently passed through Farsahn. Andrion only half heard the imperturbable drawl; his mind leaped ahead, finishing each sentence and gauging its significance. Patros had sent word by faithful Miklos to leave only hidden sentries in the valley of the Jorniyeh and beyond, lulling the Khazyari into underestimating imperial strength. Nikander had sent Miklos on to Ilanit, suggesting that she do the same in the small land of Sabazel. I am the least competent of them all, Andrion thought glumly. Patros, Ilanit, Nikander, even Miklos, they do not need me; it is my father who deserves to lead them. . . .

He should tell Nikander the extent of Bellasteros's wound, he thought, but he could not bring himself to speak the words.

Shouts and the frenzied neighing of a horse echoed through the evening. Andrion turned and was transfixed.

Soldiers scattered like leaves driven before a wind, the exasperated centurion waving his arms futilely. A magnificent black stallion plunged after, teeth bared, hooves lashing out. The reins of his halter dragged in the dust.

The horse stopped, dancing, shaking his head. The soldiers, with sheepish glances at Nikander's dour face, cautiously circled the animal. The horse's sides glistened, ebony polished with a patina of red, in the slanting rays of the sun. His rolling eyes were somehow amused; he feinted at the soldiers, his tail and mane floating, and the men scattered again. In spite of himself, Andrion could not help but be reminded of the Khazyari chieftain, Tembujin, teasing the people of Bellastria with his power. He realized he was holding his breath in awe. He exhaled, and the wind stirred.

Nikander said, "I was given the beast in tribute. I saved it for you, a gift from Farsahn to the heir of the Empire."

The horse reared, hooves slicing the air. So, Andrion said mutely to the old turtle, you give me a chance to prove myself before my father's veterans. Or do you test me on your own behalf?

Nikander's seamed face did not change expression. He leaned on his saddle bow. Dana opened her mouth, thought better of speaking, closed it.

The proconsul's motives did not matter. "My thanks," Andrion said, and he grinned. This horse was the mount for a warrior. This was a familiar worthy of the man he should be. He dismounted and walked toward him, drawn by his beauty and strength. The gathered soldiers and civilians parted before him, their murmuring voices only notes in the humming of the wind.

The great horse shied, snorting. His eyes were as dark as Andrion's own, flickering with intelligence. "So," Andrion said softly to him. "You are surrounded by strangers, and choose to strike rather than run away. Good. We understand one another."

The horse's ears flicked. He snuffled at Andrion's shoulder.

The animal's scent was strong in his nostrils, its presence fanning a desire in him he had only realized a moment ago he could feel.

A wind pealed down the sky. A falcon coasted high above Farsahn and the gathering people. The sun was a brilliant circle of fire, a shining shield set against the horizon. The shadows of tree and building and man lay like offerings to the coming night. "Ventalidar," Andrion whispered to the horse, naming him. "Ventalidar, come to me." Andrion laid his hand on the animal's neck. He shied, though not violently, and allowed Andrion to grasp the reins. A murmur, quickly quelled, ran through the crowd.

Ventalidar reared and neighed. Yes, Andrion thought as he clung to the reins. Fight, yes. The horse's luminous eyes blinked, stilled, peered inquisitively at Andrion. Nikander's eyes widened perceptibly. Dana started to smile.

Andrion petted the horse and he did not shy. Andrion murmured sweet nothings in his ear and it pricked forward, intrigued. Andrion leaned heavily against his side. And now, some part of Andrion's mind told him, you will probably be thrown onto your face before them all. But that thought burned to ash in the heat of his desire and dissipated down the wind.

He pulled himself as slowly and carefully onto Ventalidar's back as he would enter a woman. And yet he had never had to woo a woman with this delicacy. He chuckled at his importunate thought. The horses's broad back was warm and pleasant against his skin. Assurance flowed like sweet liqueur through his veins.

The watchers gasped. The stallion started, rearing. Andrion clutched at his mane and tightened his knees. "Ventalidar," he whispered, "who goes upon the wings of the wind." For a moment the horse stood, braced and shivering. And then he shrugged, his coat reflecting that quick red gleam. Divine intervention, perhaps; Andrion did not care. "So then," he said to the horse, "we each have our roles to play, have we not? Pawn or hero, in the end it is the same."

He flicked the reins and Ventalidar moved off, tossing his head and stepping as proudly as if he had tamed Andrion. Only then did Andrion realize they were surrounded by an immense crowd, so silent that the distant cry of the falcon echoed eerily, seabirds chuckled overhead, and the wind itself laughed.

Dana, grinning, stood in her stirrups and saluted. Andrion, bareback, waved jauntily to her. Nikander's features broke into a smile. "A beast worthy of your mettle, my lord. Lead us to victory."

My mettle, not my father's, Andrion thought. "Victory indeed," he called over his shoulder.

A ripple ran through the proconsul's staff and spread in ever-widening circles outward. A thrumming in Andrion's ears, wind and Ventalidar's hooves, became the chant of a thousand voices, "Andrion, Bellasteros, Andrion!" Hands reached out to god-touched horse and god-touched rider. Andrion found himself surrounded by a cordon of centurions, called by one of Nikander's invisible gestures. He commanded his troops with the subtle motions of a rider practicing dressage. Of a rider riding Ventalidar.

Gods, Andrion said silently, thank you for this favor; the joy is all the sweeter for being unexpected. He laughed out loud. Ventalidar carved a stately swath through the people and led them, singing and cheering, up the ramp toward the city gate. Nikander and Dana fell in just behind, each bowing and gesturing for the other to go first.

Andrion cared for the horse before realizing how dirty and hungry he was himself. Bathed and shaved, he hurried to dine, glowing with an achievement so intense it almost shamed him to feel it. Dana, reclining beside him, allowed his glow to illuminate her wit and began exchanging comradely jests with Nikander's officers.

Andrion regarded the candied rose petals, saffron rice, and larks in honey set before him; he would have preferred a hearty meal of beans and fish, legion fare. But Nikander obviously felt that a prince, beloved of the gods, ate such delicacies. The proconsul reclined stiffly opposite, his hooded eyes gazing avuncular approval. Andrion glowed even brighter; he ate his rose petals and was grateful for them.

Later he and Dana, left diplomatically alone, sat sipping cool sherbet in the twilit atrium of the proconsul's residence. Nikander's wives and children peered from the surrounding colonnade like so many exotic birds, chirping about the Sabazian woman's familiarity with the prince, cooing about the prince's dark, even features, so like his father's. "Andrion, master of man and beast," someone said.

"Nikander has so many wives," whispered Dana.

"He was ennobled many years ago," Andrion replied.

She giggled. "He must have many hidden qualities." And then, sobering, "Why, by Ashtar's tresses, did you take such a chance with that horse?"

"You should not have to ask that."

"I am surprised that you did not name him Tembujin."

She does not goad me, Andrion chided himself as irritation fluttered in him. She challenges my complacency, as well she should. "You noticed the resemblance, then. Did you also notice that the horse submitted to me?"

"He was frightened; you soothed him." She paused, as she would when the elusive Sight stirred within her; but no, she lost it, and she shrugged it away. "Your stallion will make a fine mate for my mare."

"Does your mare go into heat only at the solstices and the equinoxes?"

But Dana would not accept his challenge. She tried to smile, but her lips faltered and tightened instead. "Andrion, I am not pregnant."

"Ah," he said, the syllable a stone falling suddenly into deep water. That interlude in the cavern had been some other time, some other world. No wonder she burnished her own glow this night, rejoicing at her release from such a burden. Or did she rejoice? Did he? His eye went reluctantly to her face, not really wanting to see her expression; she stared up into the sky with a faint, closed smile. Let it go, he ordered himself. Soon you will have your own atrium and caged wives chattering like peahens over their big bellies.

The twilight was muted as if, with no moon to guide them, the stars hid their brilliance. The horse was, after all, only a horse. "The moon will be new tomorrow," Andrion sighed. "We shall not see it again until we are well on the way to Sardis." Sardis, and a faint resonance in the back of his mind, the dark tomb of the demon king.

Dana smiled at him, and he at her. Conscious of the watching eyes they dared no more.

The days were woven like a tapestry, the warp the unfurling Road consumed by Ventalidar's tireless stride, the weft Andrion's desperate eagerness to touch the future, to make the future, with its fearsome uncertainties, into a secure past. The escort hurried behind, led rather than leading.

Causeways, forests, fields, and marshes fell behind. They outdistanced the rocky hills that were the last thrust of the great southern mountains; they passed the ancient border between the Empire and Sardis.

At last the Road wound in lazy curves, past stands of cypress and oak, down into the floodplain of the Sar. The setting sun glinted off the twin rivers, and the city that lay in their confluence seemed like an intricate child's toy. Smaller towns and villages lay about the walls of Sardis, dividing the land into tidy blocks of wheat and barley and olive trees. An indigo smudge on the horizon was Pirestia and the sea.

An irrigation canal, a mirror reflecting a gilded sky, was suddenly creased by an ibis. A boy guided a herd of harp-horned cattle across the Road; harvesters sang in the fields. Row upon row of tents lay ahead, the last rays of the sun pricking light from the spears of the guards.

The great ziggurat continued gleaming faintly even when the sunlight drained from camp and wall, as if illuminated from within, the heavy stones parchment thin. Can I see into your heart, Harus, as you see into mine? Andrion asked silently. Sardis lay at last at his fingertips, and the scents of dust and cattle and freshly scythed grain were like a heady ale. Ventalidar pranced as if the journey had just begun, nostrils flaring.

The necropolis was beyond the city, beyond the two rivers. I come to the reckoning, Gerlac, Andrion called; I have none of your Sardian blood, but for Sardis and the bastard Bellasteros I offer my life.

Dana's face was gray with dust and weariness. She would not have chosen to come here. Gods, he thought, I offer many lives. He saluted her, and she summoned a smile as taut as the bow which arched above her head.

The sentries of the long bridge crossing the clear Sar Azurac saw the livery of Farsahn and the falcon brooch and snapped to attention. The traffic on the bridge pulled aside. The stones rang like bells under Ventalidar's hooves. The moon rose, an elliptical lamp glowing orange just above the ziggurat, a flame lit at its peak. Tomorrow it would be full. And you, too, Ashtar, Andrion thought. You can see into my heart and set strength against weakness.

Doves spun upward from the temple precinct, their wings dark brush strokes against the face of the moon. The moon shed its orange gleam, shook off the embrace of Harus, mounted higher into an indigo sky. The evening star hung beside it, a clear, pure white. Andrion reached for the hundredth time to his throat, but even the mark of the necklace had faded.

Soldiers flocked from the encampment, shattering the evening's lull with their shouts. The gates of the city stood open; but then, they had not been closed for years. Andrion and Dana passed under the carved archway into flickering torchlit streets, into a flood of ruddy faces and reaching hands. "Andrion!" the cry went up. "Bellasteros, Andrion!" He had come, the axis upon which their mingled hopes and fears now must turn.

Dana quailed back, set her teeth, plunged after the escort into the throng. Ventalidar started and Andrion soothed him. The world stuttered, the faces and fires up close and definite one moment, wavering distant and misted the next. The streets were haunted, filled with people looking like Chryse his stepmother, Declan the priest of Harus, Aveyron. . . . The faces lingered only in his mind. There is something of me that is Sardian, he thought, that they gave me. He raised his hand to wave to his people.

They swept Andrion along like a piece of jetsam. Soldiers fended off the surging crowd, their helmets tilted rakishly as they, too, tried to see the prince. Ventalidar danced down the cobblestones. Were his hooves striking fire, or did the torches gutter in a sudden breeze? The colonnades of the agora and the staircases of the forum flowed by. Monuments to those men thought to be his ancestors shifted on their pedestals, but they did not mock him.

They passed another gateway, guards in black and gold standing to attention, a glitter of short Sardian swords. Great flaring lamps reflected crimson in marble walls. The escorting horsemen fell back, so that Andrion and Dana beside him emerged alone in the center of the palace courtyard. Still the cry went up, ringing against the clear night sky, "Bellasteros, Andrion." The wind took the names and bore them away.

Andrion floated from his horse's back to the ground. Dana's blond hair gleamed briefly copper in the lamplight. His elation chilled as he thought, Sarasvati, I shall avenge you.

Ventalidar suffered himself to be led away by a solicitous groom. Great brass-bound doors swung wide. Light, pouring down a long stairway, drove back the night.

"My father," said Dana, in a suddenly small voice. Patros rushed down the stairs, choosing in his delight to forfeit dignity. Gods, Andrion thought, how the waiting has told upon this old friend, crevasses cut at the corners of his mouth and eyes, the silver at this temples consuming his sable hair. He, too, grows old. . . . But then the crevasses were erased by a great boyish grin. Not knowing which to embrace first, Patros took them both into a massive hug.

"Patros," Andrion said, sternly quelling a quaver like a weary child's, "Bellasteros has lost his right arm."

Patros looked Andrion in the face, seeing, apparently, that same veneer of Bellasteros's courage that Nikander had seen. And perhaps he saw something of Danica's integrity, as well. His features furrowed again, but his shoulders squared themselves. "Andrion, you are his right arm."

Andrion straightened. Yes, he thought, solace is only a moment's embrace; the game will be played to the end, and I am the king upon the board. I am strong. Steadily, he said to Patros and to Dana both, "We are all his right arm."

Patros nodded and grinned again. He clasped Andrion on one side and Dana on the other and carried them to the top of the stairway. Servants flicked by like hummingbirds. In their midst appeared a statue of Gerlac. Andrion returned the glare of the empty marble sockets. My father's strength was forged in hatred, he told it, but mine is forged in love.

Clothing swirled before him and twin veiled faces confronted him. Dana stiffened, settling her bow on her shoulder.

Valeria's eyes were warm and wide and shy, if oddly troubled; Andrion bowed punctiliously over her damp, trembling hand, and wondered why she trembled. He bowed over Shurzad's cold hand and suppressed a start. Some power hummed in her, some acid coursed through her veins and shocked him. A half-healed cut marred her wrist.

He looked up into her eyes. They were hard, like beads of jet. Odd, her eyes had not been that dark before. He seemed to teeter on the edge of a precipice, his mind plucked by the darkness of an abyss. But within the abyss something squirmed pitifully to be free.

He closed his eyes, shook himself, opened them again. Shurzad stared into the distance over his shoulder. Her face had something in it of Ilanit's when the goddess moved in her mind, of Dana's when the Sight came upon her. And yet Shurzad was as drawn and pale as if rent by her vision, not filled by it.

I see too damn much, Andrion told himself. She is only jealous.

Patros's eyes rested upon Andrion, too noble to suck another's strength, and yet strengthened by his presence; relieved, as if Andrion were the star-shield gleaming against encircling darkness. "Come," he said, and his eyes turned fondly to Dana. "Tell me of your journey."

But Shurzad looked stonily beyond her husband's daughter. Dana's wary green eyes followed, widened, and fixed upon a shadow in an angle of the hallway. Andrion turned. No, not a shadow but a gray cat, crouching, tail twitching, topaz eyes scanning Andrion's body with a glare so intent he could feel it. He shuddered. Surely there had been a cat in his vision.

Dana spun abruptly and paced off. Andrion followed at Patros's side, ordering the scattered mosaic of his thoughts. Valeria attempted to match her half-sister's stride and failed. Shurzad stood alone in the hallway, a pillar of silence repelling the shouting from the street, the echo of footsteps from the palace. "Your will be done, Qem," she murmured. The cat slipped away, shadow blending into shadow.

Chapter Thirteen

THE KHAZYARI CAMP lay strewn beside the Road. Behind it stretched the vast plain of the southern provinces, shimmering in wind-stirred waves of grass and tree and rock gilded by the late summer heat.

Toth stood at the edge of the camp, shading his eyes against the rising sun, squinting to the north. An uneven blotch, the faintest suggestion of a cloud bank on the horizon, faded and was absorbed into the clear blue sky even as he looked at it. It was only a mirage of the dawn light, a transparent reflection in the colored glass of the sky above the mountain range that divided the northern Empire from the south.

Figures moved on the Road, coming from the pass at Azervinah and the cleft of the Jorniyeh. The sentinels set up a cry. Toth slipped away. The iridescent smoke wavering over the camp swirled in a sudden gust of wind, stirred by an unseen hand.

Baakhun lumbered from his yurt like some great beast from its lair, blinking around him in a vague, disturbed somnolence. Raksula and Odo popped out of the shaman's shelter. Vlad, torturing a small bird in the shadow of Khalingu's cart, looked up, shrugged, returned to his play. Sita glanced from the doorway of Tembujin's yurt, her eyes indigo dark, guarded.

Tembujin rode stiffly, his red-rimmed eyes haunted by some dread knowledge. His hand went again and again to a necklace at his throat, a gold crescent moon and a star at its tip, reassuring himself of his strength, perhaps. Or perhaps the necklace drained his strength and he sought in bewilderment a way to seize it again.

Obedei ran through the gathering crowd, took the reins of Tembujin's pony, helped him down. For a moment the prince swayed, scourged by weariness. Then he straightened and in

129

sudden afterthought grinned, but his grin was no longer sublimely confident; his face was as tightly drawn as his bowstring.

"Welcome," said Baakhun, distracted, reciting lines by rote. He patted at Tembujin's shoulder and missed. Raksula and Odo bobbed up and down in unison, smiling in bland malevolence. Hilkar materialized at Tembujin's elbow and stood mesmerized by the necklace.

"My lord," Tembujin said to his father, the words pouring from him as if his troubles poured, too. "We traveled to the end of the Jorniyeh, where it meets the great water of the sea. We skirmished with a few guards, and collected tribute; we touched the borders of Sabazel and found them guarded only by girl children. The north is ripe for the plucking, the people abandoned by their leaders. . . ." His voice ran down, stopped.

Baakhun peered at his son, his heir, as though he were a stranger. Suspicion furrowed his high shaved forehead. "Empire unguarded, eh? Well, well, we shall see."

Tembujin licked his lips and said even faster, trying to repulse those troubles as they came tumbling back toward him, "The pass at Azervinah is difficult, a flanking movement, perhaps, to the west."

Baakhun turned his back on his son and thrust through the crowd as if no one were there.

Tembujin looked after him, his lips parted in dismay and hurt. Raksula and Odo still watched him, still smiling expressionlessly. Hilkar leaned forward and blurted, "Where did you get that necklace?"

Tembujin focused on Hilkar's bulging eyes, and his face froze in anger. Anger, a more tolerable emotion than dread. Coldly he strode away. Toth drifted in a slow spiral behind him. Hilkar scurried like a rat.

Odo and Raksula chuckled, congratulating each other on their subversion of Baakhun, and returned to the shaman's yurt and some evil-smelling potion they brewed inside.

Sita composed herself, bowed her head, folded her hands before her in feigned docility. But her shoulders coiled with a tenseness equal to Tembujin's.

He burst into the yurt, ripping away the doorway with a vicious sweep of his arm; he threw off his tunic, seized a dipper of water and drank thirstily, washing away a bad taste in his mouth. Over the rim of the dipper his eyes fell upon Sita,

and for just a moment, softened. "So," he said, "you are still
here."

"Where would I go?"

"You do not prefer my father's embraces?" He threw the
dipper down.

Her head was still bent. Her voice was not docile but as
uncompromising as flint. "No."

Tembujin pulled her to him and inspected her closely.
Perhaps he thought to find some surcease from his worry, a
minute's solace. But her gaze went through him. "Here," he
said with a studied lightness. "Here, I brought you a present.
My regard for you, after all." He pulled the necklace from his
throat and held it out to her, clasped in his hand so tightly that
at first it appeared to be only a gold chain.

"Something you stole?" she asked, still looking beyond him.

"Believe me," he said, one corner of his mouth tucking
itself into a bitter smile, "I paid for it." He opened his hand,
let the chain unfurl, and the crescent moon and the star
gleamed before her.

Her eyes snapped and dilated so widely that the soft shine of
gold was reflected like a kindling fire in their depths. "Where
did you get that?" she demanded hoarsely.

His look went hard and cautious. He muttered, "This must
be a remarkable bauble to interest so many people."

"Where did you get it!" The intensity of her look stabbed
him, thrust him back a step.

His breath caught in his throat. His black eyes stirred with a
sick comprehension. He snarled through his teeth, a cornered
leopard striking out, "I took it from the body of a man I
killed. A young man, dark auburn hair, brown eyes like those
of a fine, well-bred horse."

Sita's face went gray and hollow.

Deliberately, unrelentingly, Tembujin's voice went on. "He
rode with a blond woman, young, supple and yet strong, with
gleaming green eyes. Good sport she was, before she, too,
died."

Sita's hands rose to her face, pressing a cry back into her
mouth. Her eyes raked him, not wanting to believe, but believ-
ing all.

Tembujin seized her shoulders, dragged her to the bed, and
threw her down on it. Her body heaved beneath his but he
pinned her. She spat at him. He did not deign to notice, and
the moisture glistened on his cheek like a tear. He dangled the

necklace before her eyes. Sparing neither himself nor her, he
asked, "Who was he? Who was the woman? Tell me, Sita,
who you really are."

She was not weeping. Her eyes were dry, burning with
hatred and despair. "My brother Andrion, son of the falcon,"
she said, clearly enunciating each word. "His cousin Dana of
Sabazel. And you know my name."

"Sarasvati," he hissed. His face was so close to hers that the
sibilants of her name sprayed over her. She did not flinch.
"Not just a noblewoman, but Sarasvati, the daughter of
Bellasteros."

"Make the most of it," she snarled. "Barbarian carrion-
eater." He drew back his hand as if to strike her, but she did
not take her eyes from his face. "Go ahead and beat me. Force
me, for I shall no longer yield to you. Or is your lust at last
satisfied, blood-drinker?"

His hand fell. His features collapsed. He rolled away from
her with a sound almost like a sob, his anger caught and consumed by a weary terror. The necklace fell from his suddenly
slack hand.

In one swift movement Sita swept it up and cradled it
against her breast. She glanced at Tembujin, tensed to fight or
flee. But he lay face down among the quilts, his body racked
by the shocked quivering of a wounded animal finding its
strength useless to free itself, trying to understand why its
strength no longer sustains it.

Sita jerked herself away. She sat on the edge of the bed,
rocking herself back and forth, the necklace clasped in her
hands. A shaft of morning sunlight withdrew across the floor
and was absorbed into the daylight outside. Still Tembujin did
not rouse. After a time his quivering ceased and he lay as if
dead, finding some measure of freedom in an exhausted sleep.

Sita allowed a tear to spill down her cheek. "Ashtar," she
muttered, "Harus, help me. Help me to hurt him. . . ." She
stopped, gulping. Her head went up, as if listening to distant
words. And slowly her mouth hardened with decision.

She reached for Tembujin's knife and held its shining blade
before her, letting quick refractions of the sunlight play across
her face. But the light did not illuminate her expression.
"No," she murmured, "death would be too merciful for
you." She leaned over his prone body and in a few delicate
strokes severed his long tail of hair. It coiled around her hand
as heavy and smooth as a serpent. He groaned in his sleep,

caught in a nightmare, but did not wake. "Dream," said Sita. "Dream the despair you have cost me."

She threw away the dagger and rose. She stared at the necklace, lifted it to her lips and kissed it. Then she dropped it down the bodice of her dress. "Andrion," she said, "I shall avenge you."

Sita slipped out of the yurt into the brilliance of the noonday sun. She ran furtively from shadow to shadow until she reached Odo's shelter. A huge warrior ambled away, his face set in innocent puzzlement. Hilkar stood in the doorway, bowing and nodding and squealing fealty to Raksula's dim shape. Sita dodged behind Khalingu's cart. The image seemed to shift and mutter, disturbed from sleep, but Sita's upward glance was more impatient than fearful.

Hilkar scuttled away. Sita whisked across the open space and paused in the doorway. Darkness stirred before her, dim, malevolent shapes swooping toward her and then swirling away. The faint light of a butter lamp tended by the squat figure of the shaman. Odo looked up, smiled in pleased surprise, and gestured. From the deepest shadow Raksula stepped forward and bowed, gloating, to Sita.

Sita stepped back, confused by this sudden mocking courtesy, but her face was still hard with anger and pain. "Here," she said, thrusting out the coil of hair. "Here. Drive Tembujin's spawn from me. Hurt him."

Raksula, realizing what it was she was offered, lit with pleasure. She took the hair into her hands with a slow, sensuous motion, her sharp fingers not tearing it but caressing it. She glanced covertly at Odo, and he grinned and jiggled up and down, his flesh rippling with delight.

Raksula looked again at Sita, her teeth gleaming, her eyes bottomless pits sparkling in an ecstasy of evil. "Thank you, child, thank you."

Sita paled at that look. She spun about.

"And would Tembujin have shown you a gold necklace, my child?" Raksula asked, her voice exulting with secret knowledge.

Sita jerked as if stabbed between the shoulder blades. "No," she said hoarsely. "I know nothing of any necklace." She leaped forward and confronted Khalingu's cart. The image leered at her. She gasped, veered, ran. Her hair streamed behind her, flaming in the sunlight. Howls of laughter followed her.

She rounded a yurt and ran headlong into a body. She squeaked in terror. It was Toth. "What have you done?" he demanded, discarding courtesy.

With a mighty effort Sita caught her breath. But she could not still her trembling. Wordlessly she reached into her dress and displayed the necklace. "Yes," sighed Toth. "I saw it at his throat."

"He killed Andrion," Sita said. The long-delayed tears swelled in her, clogging her throat, swimming in her eyes. "He killed Andrion and Dana and he mocked me with their deaths."

Toth frowned. "No. I cannot believe that. They are in Ashtar's hand as surely as we are. There is a plan, my lady, a reason."

Sita crumpled to the ground, drained of anger and of resolve, drained of thought and left only with grief. She held the necklace to her face and sobbed. Toth took her into his arms and held her against his chest. His translucent eyes mirrored the sun and the sky, a preternatural patience at last reaching fulfillment.

Hilkar stood just at the side of Odo's yurt, his face contorted, his body shaking in a rapture of malice. "So," he muttered, "princes fall, and princesses, as well. I am powerful indeed."

Raksula's grasping hands moved quickly. They fashioned a manikin from Tembujin's hair, a little creature with arms and legs and head and a tail of hair of its own. She impaled the doll on a sharp stake and set the stake in a circle of butter lamps. As she worked she sang spells, and Odo danced around her, transported by evil glee.

Raksula sat back and considered her handiwork. Odo hunkered down beside her. "Surely," he said, "Khalingu decrees that Tembujin's hour has come. He shall not even be able to speak, let alone defend himself."

"How fine it is," crowed Raksula. "His necklace belonged to Bellasteros's son, his woman is Bellasteros's daughter. And the imperial bitch herself delivers him into our hands!"

Odo giggled happily.

"And I thought Hilkar would be no more use after our victory at Iksandarun," Raksula chuckled. "Well, Odo, forgive me for that mistake."

"A minor misperception, my lady," returned Odo.

"Hardly a mistake. It is Tembujin who makes mistakes."

"And Baakhun who will act on them, and we who will profit by them." She turned to Odo, her eyes glinting with joy and lust. "Come, pleasure me for a time. Until the feast for Tembujin's return. For his downfall."

Odo's tongue darted between his lips. His pudgy hands reached out to Raksula's skirts and lifted them. She was moaning in delight before he even mounted her.

The sun passed across the sky and plunged behind the western horizon. A full moon rose, shedding an uncanny silver light over the camp. Sita looked up, pleading for a blessing, but the moon was silent. The fires of the Khazyari muddied the clear light.

With a sigh Sita ducked into Baakhun's great yurt. She folded her hands meekly and took her place behind the other women. The air was close and warm, redolent of singed meat, stale milk, spices, and sweat; slowly the color drained from her cheeks and she gulped, nauseated. But her eyes were flickering lamps of hatred and dread.

Toth hovered nearby, his features expressionless, serving huge trays of imperial delicacies to the assembled warriors. More than one of the faces that had been lean and feral before Iksandarun was now swollen with dissipation.

Tembujin sat cross-legged by Baakhun. They glanced at each other once, as stiffly suspicious as strangers set on the chieftain's platform by chance, and they did not look at each other again.

Tembujin lifted the drinking skin again and again to his lips, until his face flushed and his eyes dulled. But then, his eyes had been strangely dull even before he began drinking, his body as flaccid as that of a corpse impaled upon a stake. Warriors shouted jests and compliments alike to him, but he did not hear. He seemed not even to be aware that the short ends of his hair stirred uneasily about his shoulders.

Baakhun did not drink at all, as though he grew tired of the herbs in his kviss, as though he no longer wanted strength, fearing what he might do with it.

Raksula and Odo sat chuckling. Vlad's greasy face shone with joy at the food laid before him, unaware of any other reason for pleasure. He threw the leg bone of a pheasant into the crowd of feasting Khazyari and reached for the stuffed haunch of a boar. Grains of cracked wheat cascaded down his tunic and Raksula indulgently wiped them away. Hilkar fawned behind them, shooting glance after glance between his sparse lashes at the solitary copper-colored head in the group of women. One corner of his lip shivered into a sneer.

Obedei sat close to the chieftain's platform, picking at his food, not sharing in the shouts and cries that gusted about the yurt. He looked from Tembujin to Baakhun and back again, cautiously. But even he did not dare look at Raksula.

A minstrel played his harp in a minor scale and began wailing about some past victory of the odlok's. Tembujin did not respond. Baakhun shifted in massive irritation, his lower lip beginning slowly to jut out.

The song ended and was applauded with louder shouts. Emptied skins of kviss sailed through the air to land with moist splats at the minstrel's feet. Raksula stood and signaled for silence. Obedei tensed.

Feeling some change in the thick, odorous air, Tembujin at last stirred. His dark eyes flickered with a grim awareness, trying his bonds; then they blurred into vague futility. They crossed Sita's unblinking stare and passed on without reaction. Sita lowered her hands to her stomach as though it had suddenly knotted.

The shouts and cries subsided to a dull murmur. Raksula began a speech punctuated by expansive gestures. Sita caught a phrase here and there, words darting about the huge domed tent like demons. It seemed as if the gathered warriors were only shapes of light and shadow, not living people but simulacra, summoned and controlled by the shrill voice of the Khazyari witch. Only Raksula was real.

Beads of sweat started on Sita's brow, joined, ran down her temples and throat. Her face was icy cold, dead flesh. Toth stood alone on the opposite side of the yurt, eyes closed, hands clasped, waiting for the blow to fall.

Raksula's words had sharp teeth, striking again and again, leaving jagged wounds. "Tembujin dares to challenge the rule of the khan, his father. He had the odlok Andrion in his hands, but he returns with only a golden necklace, a token of friendship, perhaps. Perhaps a bribe. What conspiracy now waits to catch the Khazyari in the northern provinces?"

Sita swayed. The words were not quite what she had anticipated. Maybe she simply did not understand them.

Tembujin also swayed. He seemed not to hear the charges against him; he raised the skin and drank thirstily, fueling his slide toward oblivion, a man so sorely wounded he no longer felt pain and could not resist the final blow of the executioner.

Raksula produced the men who had been with Tembujin in Bellastria. The hulking, somewhat simple warrior testified that he had captured a young man and woman there. Another warrior described the man's golden necklace, how Tembujin had taken it and then left the man abandoned in the street.

Abandoned. Not slaughtered, abandoned. Sita slumped against the fabric of the yurt. Her lips began to tremble. Dark red hair matted her brow.

Raksula was grinning now, her teeth glinting like a death's head. With a flourish she summoned Hilkar and translated his words: Yes, Prince Andrion had a necklace like that. Yes, he was tall and auburn-haired and dark-eyed. And the tall blond woman with gleaming green eyes was no doubt Sabazian, one of the spawn of Danica.

Raksula turned with a triumphant gesture to Baakhun. Baakhun stood, shaking off his torpor, eyes burning. Tembujin laid down the drinking skin, crumpled, hid his face in his hands.

The silence in the yurt, the silence of the mob gathered outside, was absolute, no voice, no breath, no protest. "And," crowed Raksula, "Tembujin's pride, his audacity, is so great . . ."

Again the flourish. Hilkar turned and dove through the throng, his robes flapping, his outthrust bald head and wattled neck like a vulture swooping onto its prey. He dragged Sita from her shelter behind the others. She gathered all her strength and struggled, but his scrawny hands bit like claws into her flesh. "No!" she cried, not so much to him as to the night.

Toth turned away, hiding his face.

Hilkar thrust Sita sprawling onto the carpet before Baakhun, seized a handful of her hair and dragged her face up. "The daughter of Bellasteros," he said in well-coached Khazyari. "Tembujin kept her, knowing who she was. See, he gave her a gift, binding himself to your enemy, mighty khan. . . ."

Hilkar's hand ripped Sita's bodice, dragged the necklace from it, waved it high into the air. He said nothing; he did not have to. The necklace shone hard and bright in the torchlight. A shout went up, drunken epithets, hurt protests.

Baakhun paled, stabbed deep. Tembujin looked slowly up-

ward, and for a moment his eyes touched Sita's, as openly as if
they together played some intricate game and he begged some
knowledge, any knowledge, of the rules. Then his eyelids
shivered, his eyes thinned to black slits between his lashes, and
he looked down again. Sita cowered, her face reflecting the
same horror and confusion as Baakhun's.

The warriors leaped up and surged in drunken chaos forward. Vlad, grinning open-mouthed, beat cadence with a bone
upon his tray. Raksula glowed, exalted by joy and malevolence. Hilkar released Sita and preened himself. "For your
father," he muttered to her below the clamor. "The conqueror who took my bride Roushangka and killed her." He
tucked the necklace inside his sash.

Sita wrenched herself away from Baakhun's sickened features, from Tembujin's bowed head. Her eyes lit with a bright
blue flame. She set her teeth into her lower lip, rose to her feet
and confronted Hilkar. "Roushangka was my mother," she
snarled. "Your filthy tongue desecrates her name. Better that
she enjoyed one night with Bellasteros than suffered a lifetime
with you!" She struck him across the face. He staggered,
yowling; she seized the necklace from his sash and thrust it
into her dress. Hilkar fell back into the swirling mob and was
swept away.

Sita turned, colliding with Obedei. The warrior was frowning, incredulous, hurt; he took her shoulders in a firm but not
ungentle grasp and leaned toward the huddle that was Tembujin. "My lord, defend yourself!"

Tembujin raised his head. But his face was blank, his eyes
veiled with the film that floats on a stagnant pool. He looked
at Obedei and through him as if he had never seen him before.

Obedei's hands kneaded Sita's shoulders in a paroxysm of
frustration and defeat. She pulled herself away but was
hemmed in by the storm raging about the great yurt. The
necklace seared her breast, fell through the torn fabric and
hung at her waist.

Vlad pounded on the tray. Someone trod upon the minstrel's harp and it twanged as it shattered. Voices screamed
from outside. Raksula slithered to Baakhun and whispered in
his ear. The khan's great chest heaved. He turned to Tembujin
and bellowed, "You are no son of mine. You are no Khazyari.
I renounce you."

Tembujin jerked, closed his eyes, opened them again as if
hoping to see himself in a new place. But nothing was changed.

Baakhun plucked him to his feet; his body flopped like a child's puppet as his father ripped the plaque from his chest, tore the tunic and shirt from his back, took the bow that lay beside him and broke it over his knee. "You will not even deny it!" sobbed Baakhun through his teeth. "Half-breed!"

Raksula spewed orders. "Take him north, to where his crimes were committed, and let him die slowly, slowly." Two warriors grasped Tembujin's arms; an aisle opened suddenly in the throng and they dragged him through. He stumbled, deathly pale, unresisting, his vague gaze touching no one. The screaming voices poured upward, broke, dissipated. Silence fell. Raksula's glittering eyes touched every face in the gathering; Odo made arcane gestures with his amulets. Every warrior looked at his fellow, wondering who shared in the guilt, denying any knowledge of it.

Baakhun raised his gray and ghastly face. "Do not shed his blood," he choked. "He was once an odlok, he must die bloodlessly, by starvation." And the khan turned away. Raksula licked her lips and chuckled.

The footsteps of the warriors, Tembujin's shambling tread, reverberated through the yurt and then were gone. A sudden breeze tautened the felt fabric, and it flapped explosively. Obedei, his hands balled at his sides, kept his gaze fixed on his boots. Sita's fiery eyes fastened upon Raksula.

Raksula started at that stare. With an evil smile she leaned against the broad, damp expanse of Baakhun's chest. "Kill her," she said. "She is Bellasteros's daughter, conspiring with the traitor Tembujin, kill her."

Baakhun's huge hand reached out, seized Sita, pawed perfunctorily at her breast. He inhaled to give the order. She seized the knotted muscle in his arms and looked up into his eyes, forcing his gaze to her face. "Great khan," she said, in heavily accented but clear Khazyari, "I carry Tembujin's child. All you have left of Tembujin is his child, of your blood and his mingled."

Baakhun's empty eyes stirred, woke, focused on her. Raksula hissed, her hands darting out to rend Sita's body. But Baakhun's massive arms closed around her, protected her for a moment, then shoved her toward an astonished Obedei. "You, you will be governor of Iksandarun. Take her with you. And take that maggot Hilkar as well. Imperial maggots, take them away!" The khan crumpled to the platform like a huge cypress tree falling, slow and ponderous, shaking the ground. He reached for a skin of kviss and drank deeply. He turned his face, twisted like a hurt child's, away from his people. Tears spilled down his cheeks. Raksula snorted in disgust.

Sita collapsed against Obedei, trembling violently as her desperate strength drained from her. It was as if she had not even spoken, as if the words had come from outside herself and now hung in crystalline drops above the sudden vortex of sound that buffeted her. The yurt billowed, torches spinning out into pennons of flame, faces swirling into a demon's dance.

Toth was there, looking at her, nodding some kind of encouragement, perhaps; Andrion and Dana are still alive, there is a plan, a reason. . . . He, too, was gone. And the golden necklace no longer seared her waist.

The necklace had fallen through her dress. Sita gasped, pulled herself up, scrabbled about her clothing. But Obedei was dragging her through the crowd, away from the platform, silent and tight-lipped.

Odo wiped Vlad's face and thrust him forward. Raksula seized him and called, "The new odlok will have gifts for his loyal followers!" The yurt erupted with cries and shouts. She picked up Tembujin's plaque and set it upon Vlad's flabby body. With Odo she stepped behind him, smiling threats and promises at the entire assemblage. The screams of the people were deafening, edged with resentment and puzzlement, but were screams of acclamation nonetheless. Baakhun, huddled over his drinking skin, nodded weary acknowledgment. Vlad emitted a high-pitched giggle, strutted across the platform and smeared his boot through a tray of food.

Raksula's arm shot out, seized a fawning Hilkar, dragged him to her side. "Give me the necklace," she commanded.

He snickered and searched his sash, at first with self-congratulatory confidence then with hurried fear. His face froze in the snicker, loose-lipped and grotesque. "I . . . it is not there!"

"Fool," hissed Raksula. "Idiot, worm! See if you can redeem yourself by killing that bitch and her whelp before they reach Iksandarun!"

Hilkar, bowing and scraping, stepped backward and fell off the edge of the platform. Odo, bloated with pride and venom, plucked at Raksula's sleeve. "All is well, my lady. Tembujin is gone. And you have the amulet of the Eye."

Raksula sighed and reached into her bodice, pulling out the amulet Shurzad had given Hilkar. "Yes, yes, we are stronger than ever; and in time Khalingu will deliver that necklace into our hands." Her thin lips split into a complacent smile.

Baakhun drank, dazed, oblivious, forgotten.

Obedei propelled Sita from the yurt and fought through the throng swirling outside. For a moment she was blinded by the darkness. Obedei thrust her toward the yurt that had been Tembujin's. "Save what you can," he told her.

Her eyes cleared, the cool night wind fanned her face, the moonlight poured its innocent radiance upon her. "What have I done?" she whispered. "I have killed him, so I am less than he is; and yet he lied to me. . . ."

From the far edge of the camp horsemen moved toward the north; a figure staggered behind them, wrists tied to a leash-like rope. A plump form on a spavined nag was only a blot of darkness following. "Toth!" Sita gasped. "No, do not leave me!"

She turned in breathless circles toward the great yurt of the khan, where Andrion's necklace had disappeared; toward Obedei's still, taut figure, which gazed toward the silvered mounds of the northern plain; toward Tembujin's yurt, which was being gutted by a shoving, grasping group of women who cast guilty looks over their shoulders even as they seized what they could.

"God's beak!" Sita cried. She ran toward the women, kicking, shoving, striking out. They jeered her, pulling her hair. She seized the Mohendra carpet, staggered with it to a shadowed place several yurts away, and sank down upon it. She clasped her arms about herself, shivering, retching in desperate spasms of denial. "Gods, help me!" The wind lifted her hair, stirring it in slow circles about her face. Her anguish poured itself out and was gone.

She laid her hands upon her belly. "So, little one, you saved me even as you bought your father's death. I live, still I live, for what purpose I know not." She raised her tear-streaked face toward the moon. "I shall try to be strong, I shall try." The wind was as cool as if fresh from an ice field, cleansing her nostrils of the miasma of the great yurt.

Sita folded the rug, hid it in the shadow, staggered up. The camp heaved like a disturbed termite hill, horses stamping, camels bellowing, human voices caught in revelry as feverish as if the revelers tried to forget to what they had acquiesced; shouts and cries shattered against the expressionless face of the moon.

Sita crept unnoticed through the camp. She skirted the shadowed image in the cart and approached the shaman's tent. It was dark, untouched by moonlight. A foul odor hung about it. Her skin prickled, as if touched by tiny claws, but nothing was there. She plunged into the tent.

A solitary butter lamp burned before a stake holding what at first appeared to be some thick effluvia of darkness. But no, it was a manikin formed of Tembujin's hair, still as dark and glossy as it had been on his head. Sita's lip curled in disgust. She forced her hand to touch the manikin. It was cold, so cold it burned; gasping, she started back. Something moved in the corner of her eye. But it was only her own distorted shadow, cast by the tiny flame in the lamp. She smiled tightly and tilted the melted butter so that it ran onto the dark, fetid rug. The flame followed its path. Hissing yellow fire leaped from the carpet and Sita's shadow leaped taller and taller against the fabric. She turned and fled.

There were eyes upon her, glittering eyes shining in the depths of Khalingu's cart. But the moonlight poured down upon it, making of the hangings an upraised gleaming shield. Sita skirted the image, hurried away. The yurt behind her looked like a black beehive oven filled with incandescent flame.

She returned to the pile of rags that had been Tembujin's yurt and sat down in their midst upon the Mohendra rug. The moonlight sparked on the woven pattern, as if there were some meaning in it; Tembujin's life, Sita's life, the Crimson Horde and Iksandarun. She slumped over it, her hair a shining hood around her. "Forgive me, Andrion, I lost your necklace," she murmured. "For whatever I have done, forgive me." She did not stir when the thick felt of Odo's yurt at last caught fire, sending a shower of sparks upward to mingle with the stars. Dim shapes rushed by her, their drunken shouts the unintelligible gibbering of ghosts.

The night lasted into eternity, and still the moon hung silent in the silent sky. When Obedei appeared at her side, Sita did not start. She rose meekly, rolled the rug, followed him to his own yurt. She lay on his bed, waiting numbly for him to touch her, but he did not. When at last she slept, she whimpered through fire-streaked nightmares, and the night at last ended.

Chapter Fourteen

ANDRION WONDERED IF the doves spiraling from the temple precinct would pierce the hazy sky and plunge through it into black, star-pricked night, or if they, too, were trapped by the uncompromising light of day.

The birds spun across the flat white disk of the rising sun and disappeared. Andrion, blinded by the glare, looked away. The mist would soon burn away and the day would be hot. Not that it should matter to him, where he was going. He felt slightly drunk, observing himself and his surroundings from a great height.

The ferry creaked beneath his feet and a tentative puff of wind fluttered the great lateen sail. The muddy waters of the Sar Cinnabran murmured just beyond comprehension. Ventalidar's ears pricked. Absently, Andrion stroked him. "No," he said, "you cannot come with me into the tomb. You will wait, guarding my back."

Dana stood at the gunwale beside a silent Patros, staring at the low, jumbled buildings of Sardis cleft by the lightning stroke of Harus's ziggurat. The city was muted by dusty haze, as if by legend; her eyes seemed to envision it as nothing more than a pile of rubble, an occasional broken column or the mutilated head of a statue. My own head, Andrion thought, my own eyes staring vacantly at the passing years, and Sabazel enduring still. . . . He shook himself.

Something sparked at the peak of the ziggurat. The bronze falcon, perhaps, that Bellasteros had saved from the sacking of Iksandarun. It had been before dawn, under a spectral moon, when Patros had conducted Andrion up the long flight of steps, past the great statue of Harus in the wing-stirred darkness of the sanctuary, to the altar at the peak of the

143

artificial mountain. There Andrion, trying not to condescend, had given the falcon to Bonifacio. But poor fawning Bonifacio made it so tempting to condescend.

Andrion had bowed before the images of Harus, large and small, but they looked through him and would not speak. He had bowed before his father's crimson-plumed helmet, but it, too, was as silent as a cast-off carapace, the creature who had worn it gone. Bonifacio muttered prayers and blessings, made small protests at the coming violation of the tomb of Gerlac, Harus's servant, urged Andrion to visit the ancient oracle instead. Andrion had longed to tell him that Harus, Ashtar's consort, needed no servants like Gerlac, that he had already heard from an oracle in Sabazel. But he had said something polite and reassuring and walked numbly beside Patros toward the east, away from the setting moon.

Andrion looked away from the living city and toward the city of the dead. Not much farther now, and the penalty for a moment's disloyalty to Bellasteros would be paid. The sunlight, diffused by the hazy sky, poured like a pale, vinegary wine over the dun-colored hummocks of tombs and monuments, blending all into an indistinguishable shimmer. The brightness of the sun, and the brightness of Solifrax waiting in shadow; Andrion touched his throat, seeking the emblems of sun and moon united, but they were gone.

The ferry ground against the riverbank. The soldiers of the guard scrambled out. Patros reached to aid Dana and thought better of it, leaving her to leap from the boat alone. Andrion grasped Ventalidar's reins and jumped. Ventalidar landed beside him with a reassuringly solid thunk of hooves against ground.

Dana's hair streamed down her back, a gleaming veil; her eyes were as flat as jade beads, whether concealing fear or resentment, whether racked by the Sight or bereft of it, Andrion could not tell. Her forehead shone with gelid sweat. She smiled tightly at Patros but the muscle in her jaw writhed, her teeth clamped shut. And is this, Andrion thought, her penalty for a moment's disloyalty to Sabazel?

The party mounted and rode toward the great pylon gate of the city of the dead. Patros looked eagerly ahead, the line of his cheek and jaw set less in dread than anticipation, a desire exalted by its depth. He wants that sword as much as I do, Andrion told himself. He wants to worship me as he worshipped my father. He will not, he cannot fear Gerlac as I do, for he knew the living man and I know only the demon.

Dana shrugged her bow from her shoulder and offered it to her father. He laid it across his arm like a ceremonial sword, a companion to the flaccid snakeskin sheath of Solifrax which he wore at his waist. The pylon rose before them, a tall pile of brick and stone carved with the names of ancient kings now almost weathered away. Ventalidar danced sideways, restively, as if a cold breeze blew through the gate. But the day was hot and still. Patros returned the salute of several guards and led the company under the cracked lintel, into the necropolis.

Lemon and orange trees clung to crevices in the paving stones, above windrows of rotting fruit clouded by wasps. A lizard sunned itself atop a stele, and colonnaded tomb was half-displaced by a gnarled weeping cypress. The monuments were broken and dusty, long ago despoiled and forgotten. The buzzing of insects was the distant murmur of lost souls.

The avenue turned and curved down into a great basin. "Here," Patros said, "is the quarry from which came the stone for the great ziggurat. And for many of those old tombs by the gate. The later kings and nobles wanted their tombs carved in the rock, to better protect them from grave robbers."

The rock was honeycombed with elaborately carved niches, memorial inscriptions, closed tombs. Asphodel, paler than any that grew on Cylandra's slopes, clung beside straggling lemon trees. The pale gold stone gathered the sunlight, filling the basin with a pool of liquid heat rimmed high above by a bleached blue sky.

There was the doorway. The huge slab had subsided, leaving a dark fissure at its top, but the seals were intact, faded but still readable: *Adrastes Falco, Talon of Harus, protects this tomb of the godling Gerlac.* The evil Adrastes, Andrion told himself, contaminated with sorcery, who met well-deserved death in Iksandarun only a few hours before my birth. The muscles in his neck and shoulders knotted, as if burning eyes glared at his back. He knew he was frightened, but he saw his fear from far above, dispassionately, someone else haunted by this old terror. The taste of rotten fruit coated his throat.

Dana knew well the names of Gerlac and Adrastes. Her face was pale and set, and beads of sweat left tracks down her cheeks.

"It was another lifetime when the procession came here

with Gerlac's coffin," Patros mused, leaning on his saddle-bow. "Chanting and incense and the weeping of the servants who were to die . . . we no longer commit such sacrifice, of course, thanks to Bellasteros's compassion."

Are you sure? Andrion thought as he crawled slowly, heavily, from Ventalidar's back. He handed the reins to a soldier. The horse snorted and pawed at the ground.

Andrion was standing on a grave stone, a slab placed flat in the floor of the basin. He bent, narrowing his eyes. *Viridis, wife of Gerlac,* read the almost obliterated inscription. So, he thought, my grandmother deserves only this hole in the ground, beneath the feet of the man who murdered her. The gods burden me with this old evil. He turned to the escort and gestured.

Reluctantly they clambered from their horses and approached the tomb of Gerlac. Dana shivered, gathered herself together, followed. With his dagger, his only weapon, Andrion's numb fingers cut the seals on the tomb. The dagger tingled, sending ripples of pain up his arm.

Grunting, heaving, the soldiers rolled the stone away. Bats exploded from the opening, pulling with them a cloud of almost palpable darkness. Dana started; if not for the watching men, she might well have screamed. Andrion seemed to fall down a long, smooth curve, faster and faster, shattering his numbness upon sharp pinnacles of mortality and fear. Sweat slipped in cold beads like stroking fingers down his back. He set his teeth into his lip, and the pain of it was sharp and immediate, steadying his resolve.

Patros ordered a torch lit. The flame was swallowed by the glancing sunlight. Andrion saw his own hand take the torch, raise it high. He heard Dana make some faint sound in her throat, not quite a sigh, not quite a protest. She stepped to his side; their trembling shoulders touched, jarred, touched again, warm living flesh to flesh.

"I shall wait here for your return," Patros called; he tightened his mouth, refusing anxiety. The bow and sheath lay reverently across his arm. The accompanying soldiers shifted uneasily, pretending interest in other things. Ventalidar's dark eyes reflected a pinpoint of light, a torch tiny in the circle of darkness that was Gerlac's tomb.

Dana and Andrion saluted Patros and turned to the shadow. "You have no power over me," Andrion said. "Gerlac, I have none of your blood, and you have no power over me.''

Dana's teeth glinted between her lips. She took her dagger from its sheath and clutched it before her. They stepped through the doorway into a narrow passage.

The sunlight failed, and the torch leaped high in gouts of yellow flame. The faint breath of a breeze moaned through the corridor, as cold but not as clean as the breeze from Cylandra's icy crown. The dank chill of twenty-five winters was gathered in the tomb; Andrion felt his sweaty skin break into gooseflesh, each tiny hair questing nervously upward.

The walls of the passage were carved and painted gaudily with bas-reliefs, warriors and gods dancing in the flicker of torchlight. Andrion tried to focus on one particular scene of his father Bellasteros, young but never untried; the light leaped, the images shifted and whirled away and made taunting gestures in the corners of his eyes.

He turned, trying to look everywhere at once, following the faint afterimages clotting the boundary between light and shadow. His foot crushed something; he lowered the torch. Human bones, desiccated into crumbling husks, lay along the corridor.

''Sacrificed servants,'' hissed Dana. ''Think of them lying here, forced to drink a poison draught, feeling dark death creeping horribly through their bodies as the stone rolled across the mouth of the tomb. Barbarians! Give me a battle in the open air, and death shining like Ashtar's tresses!'' Her voice echoed down the passage, doubled and redoubled into a rushing murmur of disapproval. Her hand trembled and the gleaming blade of her dagger sent reflections wavering across the bodies; headdresses of enamel and gold blinked like awakening eyes. Andrion and Dana, as one, started back. The broken strings of a lyre stirred in protest beneath their feet.

''I used to play a lyre,'' said Andrion, grasping at some kernel of calm sanity. ''I sang love songs for you, Dana.''

Her face in the torchlight was all harsh planes and pinched angles. ''And I for you,'' she replied.

''Oh?'' And his voice, too, was caught and stolen by the echoing currents. They walked on leaden feet, stepping between the bundles of dried rags that had been human forms. The dust was heavy, swirling in slow eddies, cold and slick. The quick glints of cup and jewel and statuette could well have been the gleaming scales of wary snakes, glancing out at the warm and solid flesh passing by and then retreating into blackness.

The corridor turned. They hurried by a spot slimed with bat dung and the crawling creatures who lived on it. A vault, its edges lost in shadow, opened before them. Here were more bodies, and the glints of sword and armor; soldiers, dying for Gerlac as surely as those killed in Sardis's many battles. Was this death as honorable? Andrion wondered. What was honor? A few steps would carry him into the free air, into shame and scorn. I cannot leave, he told himself, until I have Solifrax, or until my bones, too, are a sacrifice to Gerlac.

Dana's cold arm shuddered against his. The musty air of the sepulcher stirred; a shadow cloaked in shadow, no more substantial than smoke, came toward them. Pretending no chill crept through his body, Andrion lifted the torch higher. Sparks snapped against a low ceiling painted with outspread wings, Harus in the aspect of hovering Death.

The shadow was a man, or rather the image of a man, a suggestion of face and form wavering uncertainly in uncertain light. It was Bellasteros. A beardless youth trammeled by his father's pride, features guarded by his own protecting arrogance. He turned blind eyes toward Andrion and Dana, unaware of their existence; and indeed, they did not exist for this memory of the prince who had become king at Gerlac's timely death.

"Father," Andrion breathed. But the ghost was not his father, was not even properly a ghost, because Bellasteros yet lived. . . . With the searing pain of a sudden sword thrust, Andrion thought, Did he yet live?

Dana's fingers clawed his arm. "Look, he searches," she whispered, and her words stirred slow spirals in the dust. The figure turned dark, blind eyes toward them; yes, he was searching, Andrion realized, the young man for victory and love, the old for victory and death.

The misty image moved noiselessly on. The eyes looked through them and beyond. Andrion thrust his dagger into its sheath and raised his hand. "Father, your search has ended; you are with Danica in Sabazel."

Those names, anathema in this place, plummeted into blackness. The shape stopped. The dark eyes fixed upon Andrion, sensing their mirror image, and besides it the echo of Danica that was Dana. The torch guttered.

The vaporous shadow that was Bellasteros swirled. The eyes paled, the skin tightened, cracked, sloughed away. It was a fleshless skull, teeth bared, sockets filled with blackness, that stared at Andrion. And the entire body of the image was a skeleton, for one moment complete, then with a dry cascade of chimes scattered over the dusty stones of the floor.

Andrion knelt among the bones, hands outstretched and yet unable to touch them. "No," he cried, "you cannot die. I still need you!" His voice boomed across the room and returned, subtly altered, mockingly.

"It is only a spell," squeaked Dana past some obstruction in her throat. "The evil in this place, racking us with illusion."

"Illusion?" Andrion asked. "Gods, if only it is!"

A gust of icy wind, reeking of natron, spices, and decay, scoured the room. The torch fluttered wildly, and grotesque shadows leaped across the walls and ceiling. The wings of Death beat slowly, fanning the wind, and the torch flared and died.

Impenetrable darkness. Utter silence. No wind, no movement, nothing but the chill malodorous air. Andrion's intestines convulsed within him; he heard his own pulse racing in his ears, and he heard Dana beside him gasp. But nothing happened. After an eternity Andrion pulled himself together, forcing each knotted tendon to loosen, and tried his voice. "Dana!"

"I am here." A wisp of sound, but her voice nonetheless.

"What if this darkness is also illusion?"

"It is still darkness."

Outside the sun shone on Patros's gilded helmet and on Ventalidar's sleek coat; on the city of Sardis crouching like a hunting raptor abreast the two rivers. His heart sent warm blood through his veins. "If I cannot have hope," Andrion said between clenched teeth, "then I shall take honor." He laid down the burnt-out torch and groped across the floor. The bones lay about him, hard and dry to the touch, quite real.

"What?" asked Dana.

"We shall have illusion dispel illusion," he said. His fingertips touched the skull, started back, then gingerly, lovingly, traced the line of jaw and brow. He lifted it. He held the simulacrum of his father's head, and prayed that the real head still held the living spirit of Bellasteros. "Harus," he called, "I am your son as well as Ashtar's. Aid me."

A faint gleam. Two gleams. The eye sockets of the skull lit with a clear crystalline light. The light of burnished Solifrax, shining where Bellasteros's dark, pellucid eyes had once reflected it. Carefully Andrion stood.

The light emanating from the skull was colorless, consuming the darkness without being tainted by it. Andrion turned to Dana; her face was starkly pale, her eyes so wide that glistening white rimmed silver-green irises. "Ashtar," she quavered, short of breath, "see us from this sorcery-ridden place."

"See us to the sword," Andrion returned, "and after, thence."

Dana muttered, "You and that sword." He pretended not to hear. How could she understand? It was enough that she came.

Close together they walked across the vault, skirting the desiccated bodies of the guard, and passed through an empty doorway into yet another chamber. Here were the grave goods Andrion remembered from his dream, gold-plated furniture, alabaster vases, an entire chariot inlaid with sardonyx and ebony. And in the midst of the jumbled riches lay the carved sarcophagus of Gerlac.

Andrion faltered. The light of the skull dimmed. Shadow shapes coiled like smoke in the corners, and the bas-reliefs on wall and ceiling mumbled curses. The air was close, reeking with spices and decay, and despite the chill Andrion began again to sweat.

Dana's dagger flashed as she turned from side to side. "Get it, quickly," she said, "for the evil gathers itself."

Andrion forced his body forward. Stiffly, with awkward steps, he approached the sarcophagus. Dana moved warily at his back. If she had not been breathing so loudly, he might perhaps have heard fingers tapping within the coffin. And yet her ragged, racing breath was comforting.

A brazier filled with ashes stood next to the sarcophagus. He laid the skull upon it, balancing it upright, and the light shone out clear and bright. His shadow moved against the wall, sweeping away lesser darknesses, as he bent over the great slab of stone.

The image of Gerlac, granite carved in an eternal vulpine sneer, gazed up at him. Granite, not the gold of his vision. Andrion set his jaw and gazed steadily back. "You have no power over me, Gerlac." He pushed against the lid. It was too heavy, or he too weak; it did not matter. The great slab would not move.

"Gods," hissed Dana, trembling.

He had never seen her so frightened, at the limit of her self-control. But if she saw something he did not, he certainly did not want to know it. He muttered something reassuring, to which she did not respond, and drew his dagger again. He worked the point into the slit between sarcophagus and lid and turned it. The metal was well forged, holding the weight, and with a low creak the lid lifted.

Dana saw what he was doing and hurriedly set her shoulder to the stone. She groaned, wrenched to the heart; Andrion, lifting beside her, turned his dagger and set it upright between rim and lid. Dana slipped exhausted down the side of the coffin to crouch on the floor. "Are you well?" Andrion asked, even as his eyes were drawn to the interior of the sarcophagus.

"Get it, get it!" she exclaimed.

Darkness welled from the narrow crevice between coffin and lid. The dim light emanating from the skull faded. But then a similar light glimmered, died, glimmered again from within the sarcophagus. Andrion felt his face pulling into a grimace of resolve, felt his hands tightening into fists; he looked in.

A band of light curved across tattered grave-wrappings, Solifrax gracing the face of Gerlac himself. Andrion recoiled in disgust and glanced wide-eyed at Dana. She staggered to her feet, averting her face from the coffin. He slowly edged head and shoulders into the crevice, holding his breath against the choking stench of natron and rot.

The face of the old king was not regal, not serene in death. It was twisted with hatred, dried lips drawn back on brown teeth, hollow cheeks, empty sockets lidded with parchmentlike skin that seemed, in the uncertain light, to be straining to open. The shroud, stained with unguents, was torn, revealing wizened, shrunken limbs. The body was petrified in a writhing motion, as if it had been put into the tomb alive.

Again Andrion recoiled. He exhaled, and his breath was a cloud of mist in the cold. Dana was motionless, half crouched, watching with slitted eyes something behind his back. His skin crawled.

He reentered the sarcophagus. Solifrax lay, pure and unsullied, across the crumbling body. The hands, fingers like sharp talons, grasped at the sword but fell short. The mouth moved, muttering soundless curses; Andrion seized the sword and pulled it from the bone and granite trap.

It flared, light dancing along the length of its curved blade, just as it had flared outside Iksandarun. But the filigree hilt had shrunk, it seemed, or else his hand had grown to fit it. Dana glanced at the sword, her eyes glinting in its light, and said, "Come now, come."

The skull of Bellasteros was gone, leaving only a print in the cold ashes of the brazier. But the sword glowed, clear and white, casting shafts of luminescence about it and driving back the shades that gibbered in the corners of the chamber. At last, Andrion exulted, *I* have won this sword. Surely I shall win the Empire, and win back my father's life.

He looked again at the remains of Gerlac, King of Sardis, no longer a king or even a demon, vanquished long before. He tried to feel sympathy for this man devoured by hatred, but he remembered Viridis and Lyris and his own mother, and could feel only satisfaction and the smooth, cool hilt of Solifrax in his hand.

"Come!" insisted Dana, plucking at his arm.

He was oddly reluctant to leave, mesmerized by the wasted face of Gerlac. As he stared at it, it twitched. One hand rose, reaching for him. Dana lunged forward and interposed herself between Andrion and the body. He started, waking. The desiccated hand twitched the dagger away. The lid of the sarcophagus fell with a resounding crash.

Dana screamed. Crash and scream reverberated together through the tomb, through the earth itself, pounding like Andrion's heart within his body. He was no longer cold, his limbs leaden; his head swam with sparkling coils of light, and every fiber in his body fired, ordering flight.

He fumbled for Dana's hand, grasped it and ran out of the chamber into the room where the warriors lay, the radiance of Solifrax like a torch before him. Her breath was a great bellows, opening and closing, sending gooseflesh down his back. The dead warriors stirred, bony fingers reaching for their weapons, skulls turning, blind eyes searching for their prey.

"Hurry," he said to the dim shape at his elbow, and the shape turned its face and grinned at him. A face with only a thin aperture for a nose, lips like dried papyrus, lidless eyes opening onto dark, bottomless pupils.

His cry of horror echoed in receding circles of sound into

the blackness and was swallowed. He dropped the hand he held, leaving stinking particles of dried flesh on his own skin. The demon threw back its head, neck bones rippling like falling axe blades, and laughed. It was not Gerlac; it was something else that had once been human, Adrastes, perhaps, who had given himself to evil and whose shade now crouched eternally at the feet of his master, Gerlac.

Andrion's body surged with hatred: My father and mother withstood you, you have no power over me! "Ashtar!" he cried. Solifrax sang. Blade and name alike cleft the thin neck of the demon, sending dried flakes of flesh and bone spinning away into darkness.

Andrion gasped for breath. The warriors struggled to their feet around him. God's beak! his mind exclaimed, what if the demon were only illusion and he had just beheaded Dana! But no, he would not believe that. He spun, knowing that if he ran now, he could escape the tomb, but knowing that he could never escape without finding Dana. Dana, child of the clear moonlight, must not be left to molder in this airless place.

He sprinted back into the pitch-black chamber, illuminating it with his sword. Dana slumped against the sarcophagus, dagger at the ready, eyes staring in a paroxysm of terror and courage. Her long hair had been caught by the falling lid of the coffin. Andrion swept her up in his free arm; she was cold and yielding—was she dead? No, she breathed, her eyes blinked, and for a moment she actually clung to him.

"Forgive me," he gasped. "I did not mean to leave you here, I thought you were with me." He was babbling. She did not hear.

Andrion raised Solifrax and with a trembling hand sheared her hair, freeing her. So, he told himself, his mind reeling with relief into wry and irrelevant thought, now she pays indeed for lying with me. Her shining hair will remain here, an offering to my lust for power and for her both.

Dana shuddered, released Andrion as if his body were a burning brand, straightened. She croaked, "Can we go now?"

His body flushed with anger, at himself, at those who had made this tomb a place of evil, not of peace, at the gods who tested him with illusion and with darkness. "Come," he snapped, taking a fold of Dana's shirt securely in his hand. And together they confronted the dead guards.

The warrior bodies stood in uneven rows, not quite remembering how to soldier, bony hands grasping rusted spear and sword, eye sockets staring vacantly. Andrion did not pause. Shouting, raising Solifrax, carrying Dana with him, he dove straight for the center of the warriors' line.

And Dana, desperately denying her fear, shouted also. Solifrax flamed, its brilliance exploding the shadows that shielded the skeletons. Sword and dagger struck, and bones fell rattling to the floor. The bite of the rusted weapons were only brief stings of ice against warm flesh; the wrath of the living prevailed, and the dead fell back into uneasy sleep.

Andrion and Dana gained the passage. They skidded through the bat slime, crushing small slithering creatures beneath their feet. They careened past the dead servants and scattered enamel and gold behind them. They catapulted from the tomb entrance into the light of day.

"By the tail feathers of the god," Andrion gasped, "I never thought the scent of rotten lemons could be so sweet."

Dana turned away from him, head bowed, shoulders shaking, alone.

It was, surprisingly, evening. Storm clouds massed, layer upon layer of blue-black billows, in the east. Shafts of yellow sunlight streamed through apertures in the cloud, but the basin was in shadow. The waiting soldiers started up; Patros rushed forward.

He looked with unconcealed joy at the sword Andrion held. Then he looked at Dana's stark, pinched face, and her shortened hair fluttering about her neck. His face clouded, caught between extremes. The soldiers set up a feeble cheer, dispersed by a gusting wind. The gaping tombs and monuments in the basin seemed like staring eyes.

Andrion leaned to Dana, asking quietly, reluctantly, "What did you see there, in the darkness?"

She replied in a small, stiff voice, "The same that has gnawed me since the dawning of the day. My death."

"And still you came with me?"

"I told you I would stand by you." Her lips thinned. "And I did not understand my vision, did I? I was wrong. I did not die."

Her courage was greater than his; her loyalty greater than his lust. Honor above hope indeed. Andrion stared for a moment uncomprehendingly at the sword in his hands, his triumph somehow stained. And yet he had gone back for her. He did have Solifrax, his own now. If only you could be pleased

for my triumph, he said mutely to Dana. But still she stood
aloof.

Andrion turned, bowed, handed the sword hilt first to
Patros. It flared in a brief moment's promise. Patros bowed
deeply, took Solifrax, and with a slow, reverent gesture
slipped it into its sheath. It entered with a hiss, its light winking out. He returned the sword to Andrion, and Andrion hung
it on his belt. The sword was heavy, murmuring of power. He
let his hand rest lightly on the hilt. Ventalidar tossed his head,
and seemed to gaze at Andrion with amused scepticism. No,
he thought, do not doubt me; I can no longer doubt myself.

No dead flesh clung to his hand. He could tell himself it had
all been hallucination. He had lost the sword to evil, and he
had paid to reclaim it, whether or not it was his legacy from
the god-king Bellasteros his father.

Patros handed Dana her bow. She glanced at it, and up at
her father's concern, and she summoned a smile. But her eyes
were haunted by terror, her cheeks pale, and when Patros
dared to pat her shoulder consolingly, she stepped away from
him, unable to take comfort from a man.

Ashtar, Andrion thought, do not show me her vulnerability.
She must be certain, so that I can be certain, too. Dana, as if
hearing his thought, straightened, firmed her shoulders,
turned toward the horses.

The soldiers, without waiting for orders, were rolling the
stone back across the entrance of the tomb. Did tendrils of
shadow still flow from it? But they were powerless now. The
sun's rays were blotted by cloud, and the evening air took on
an oddly hazy, muted quality, as if tombs and soldiers, Patros
and Dana, were all hidden behind a gauzy veil.

Suddenly Andrion was tired, and he wanted nothing more
than a bath.

Silently the company mounted and rode, jostling against
one another in their haste, out of the city of the dead. And the
dead stayed behind, the wind moaning about their abandoned
monuments.

Chapter Fifteen

RECLINING WAS A preposterous way to eat, Dana thought. She shifted again on her couch, achieving an even more awkward angle of arm and leg. She nibbled at an herbed mushroom and eyed with irritation the food arrayed before her: honeyed larks piled in intricate towers, suckling pig lying as if asleep on its platter, molded sugar palaces guarded by ranks of rose petals.

This is Sardis, she told herself, more style than substance. Twenty years ago it had been the implacable enemy of Sabazel. But the wind brought many changes; not only did she know her father, she knew him to be a Sardian. Faintly nauseous, she threw down the delicacy.

The lamps in the banquet hall glared yellow-white. To Dana, still shadowed with the darkness of the tomb, the light struck with an almost audible clangor on the bronze-plated armor of the sentries, on their bronze weapons, on the gold vessels lining the tables. Jewels gleamed, and exotic perfumes rose like a warm mist from a hundred bodies.

A harp player sang the lay of Daimion, daring to say the name of Mari; he sang the lay of Bellasteros, mentioning in passing that the queen of Sabazel had come to him a supplicant. Dana scowled. The young noble beside her refilled her wine cup; it was unwatered Sardian wine, bloodred, blood warm, and already her head spun.

Patros watched her from the head table, dark eyes resting fondly on the image of her mother. Her mind envisioned him as a skeleton with gleaming, empty eye sockets. Her mind veered around the crash of a granite slab falling and the sudden tug on her hair like dead hands seizing her. She could have cut herself free, but she had submitted to fear, waiting for Andrion to save her.

The Sabazians, she thought, burned their dead, purifying the mortal flesh; they did not preserve it, worship it, dread it. She set her cup down with a crash and wine splattered the tiles of the tabletop.

There was Andrion, beside Patros. Did they hear the lying words of the bard? Yes, they exchanged an amused glance. Only amusement, to hear Danica so slighted. Dana writhed. The man beside her touched her hand, beginning some flirtatious query; she snarled at him, and he retreated in confusion.

Valeria, on Andrion's other side, looked up at him with luminous eyes, hanging on his every breath, her unveiled cheeks becomingly pink. Well coached by Shurzad, Dana thought, to sell herself. She allowed herself only slight sympathy for her sister.

Shurzad sat beside Patros, her eyes bruised with the exhaustion of a long battle fought and lost. Her eyes saw everything and passed secret judgment upon it, touching Dana, darkening, moving on. Her gaze fixed with unblinking calculation upon Andrion. Her hand rose again and again to her throat, where the Eye of Qem glowed a pale phosphorescent green.

Dana realized her hands were knotted fists against the rich fabric of her couch. Valeria would indeed be a worthy match for him, she scolded herself. But Ashtar! He would dash himself to death on her innocent sweetness. And Shurzad—something unhealthy held Shurzad.

Andrion, maddeningly unaware of Dana's surly thought, of Shurzad's steady look, of Valeria's adoring gaze, tipped his cup and drained it. His face was flushed, and he laughed gracefully, but too often. The sword Solifrax rested on the couch beside him, the snakeskin sheath shining in brief ringlets of light, taut and full. His hand rested on the sword, stroking it proprietarily.

Patros turned to him, saying something, smiling. Andrion laughed again. Shurzad passed him another cup and again he drank. Of course he would drink, Dana thought scornfully. He has triumphed. The legions await his word, and despite the storm that gathers above them, the populace stands outside the palace calling his name and the name of his father and the name of his new toy, Solifrax. What has he to fear, now?

The priest Bonifacio came forward, and over the burble of voices began an unctuous prayer. The name of Harus, legendary Gerlac, glorious Bellasteros. Dead Chryse, Andrion's mother. At that Andrion looked up, met Dana's icy gaze, shrugged sheepishly.

I hate you, she thought. You hypocrite, I hate you.

The banquet was over. Patros rose, thanking all the guests. To raucous cheers he bowed Andrion from the hall. The two figures were both lean and straight, Patros's hand resting on Andrion's shoulder; it never occurred to him to resent this princeling who came in Bellasteros's place.

Dana spurned the smiles of Patros's officers and hurried into one of the upper passages of the palace. There she paused by a window; the moon would be just past the full, perhaps she could catch a glimpse of it. But the storm had begun. Lightning, sudden stark blasts of searing light, defined every rooftop and then whisked them into impenetrable blackness. She turned away, suddenly frightened, as thunder rolled along the streets of Sardis and sent mysterious vibrations through the stone of the palace.

Rain burst from the sky, thousands of tiny drumbeats combined into one great roar. Perhaps the stone at the mouth of the sepulcher had been left ajar, Dana thought. The water could run in, swirl away bone and jewel, lap at the sarcophagus where her own hair hung lankly, fill the tomb with a cool sapphire light like that of Ashtar's cave, clean and pure.

She huddled for a moment in a dim corner behind a statue, shaking herself free of fear and resentment and longing for Sabazel. Footsteps clicked along the marble corridor; voices drifted on the heavy air, Shurzad's as hollow as though emanating from a deep well. A well filled with acid, no doubt. "But she is your own daughter!"

"So you admit that, at least." Patros, in the presence of Andrion, never seemed tired. With Shurzad he spoke like an old man ridden by time and worry. "But she is Sabazian, living by different rules than yours. If she has lain with Andrion, it was under the blue eyes of Ashtar." Dana realized with a start that they spoke of her, not Valeria; peering around the pedestal of the statue she saw that the girl walked with them, eyes downcast in fascinated embarrassment.

Lightning flared. Thunder shivered the city. Valeria squeaked, but Shurzad did not notice. "Sabazians," she sneered, "are not proper women. Do not hasten to defend your bastard; it is she who would use Andrion, I daresay."

"Harus," Patros moaned. "How can I make her understand?" And wearily, by rote, "Andrion is a man of honor, like his father."

"Indeed," mused Shurzad. "Indeed, that he is."

Dana crept from her hiding place, more indignant at Shurzad's meddlesome words than shamefaced at having overheard a private conversation. She stamped down the hallway and gained the door of her room.

Lightning rent the night, followed by an immediate peal of thunder. Dana blinked, and realized that Shurzad was standing alone at the end of the darkened corridor. The gray cat sat beside her, its tail twitching from side to side. The beast's eyes glinted. Shurzad bowed in some odd acknowledgment, her hand on her amulet.

Dana shivered; indeed, the taint of sorcery ran like a black thread through the bright tapestry of the palace. Perhaps the opening of the tomb had released some loathsome shade. But last night Shurzad had already been possessed by . . . what? Petty jealousy, yes, but even Dana had never thought her evil. For a moment she spiraled downward through her thoughts, sifting them, following that dark thread, but her Sight eluded her.

Shurzad disappeared. Dana turned across the hall to Andrion's door with some vague notion of warning him about Shurzad's scheming, with some notion of apologizing for her resentment at the banquet. This man's world was difficult, but Ashtar knew that it was his own world and he had his role to play in it.

She knocked and stepped inside without waiting for a reply. Andrion stood as she had, before a window, his head cocked back, his face turned toward the sky. For a moment lightning illuminated his body; he still glowed brightly against the darkness outside, even after the flash of light winked out.

He turned at Dana's entrance, not at all startled. A cool, damp breeze puffed the curtains beside him, and his carefully draped cloak fluttered. Solifrax hung at his side, gleaming in the faint light of two small lamps, just as the winged brooch gleamed, and the ever-shifting depth of his gaze. She fell dizzyingly into those dark pellucid eyes.

Andrion stepped toward her. "I was thinking of you." His hand never left the hilt of his sword.

She said nothing, not trusting her voice. The pit of her stomach churned, and sternly she quelled it.

"I was hoping you would come." His voice was silkened by
the wine he had drunk. His full lips were moist, his hair clung
in auburn ringlets to his brow. The scent of his body was salt
and sandalwood, filling her nostrils with searing memory as he
kissed her.

She cursed herself for remembering and wrenched herself
away. The room reeled about her, but she steadied it. "I am
not some reward, to be taken at your pleasure," she said,
more harshly than she had intended.

Andrion's face crumpled like a hurt child's. "Are you not
pleased for me?"

Gods take the man! "The Khazyari still contaminate the
southern provinces and approach the borders of Sabazel; do
not let your new toy beguile you into thinking the battle is
already won."

"Toy?" he asked, and his face cleared. He offered her a
formal bow. "I would never have left the tomb but for you.
My thanks."

"I would never have left but for you," she replied, with an
equally formal nod. "But then, I would never have gone there
but for you. And I would not have needed to be rescued if you
had stayed by my side, instead of running off with your toy."

"Perhaps," he snapped, "you should have let Lyris cut
your hair, then you would never have been trapped."

"Perhaps," she spat, "I should have let Lyris kill you, and
spared myself your arrogance!"

His eyes flared. Another breeze rippled the draperies. The
lamps fluttered. Thunder rumbled in the distance and the rain
slowed to a swishing murmur, as if the palace were at the base
of the waterfall in Ashtar's cave . . . No, Dana ordered
herself. No, forget that, it is over. This is a man, and he grows
more dangerous every day.

"What is wrong with you?" Andrion snarled. "Where is
your good humor?"

"It was cut off in Gerlac's tomb!" She sprinted for the
door, hurling one last taunt. "Do you really think Tembujin
will be impressed by your new play-pretty? He will not worship you, and neither will I."

Andrion stood as hard and still as a statue of Bellasteros,
white-knuckled hand clasping the hilt of Solifrax, shoulders
taut, face averted. Dana grimaced in pain, and almost turned
back to him. Something fills the air this night, she told herself,

something beyond the wasted shade of Gerlac and the warlike aura of Sardis.

"Leave me." Andrion growled, as if it were an order. "I do not need you."

So be it! Dana silently replied, plunged through the door and slammed it behind her. She ran across the hall and burst into her own room, seized a pillow from the bed and threw it, raging, across the room. It burst and a cloud of feathers spewed into the air, eddied, drifted down.

Her flaming anger drifted like the feathers and subsided. "Mother," she pleaded, "I know it is my fear that angers me, and the burden you have given me; forgive me." And, more quietly, "I know I cannot have him, I know I cannot even want him, but why, why, must I hurt him? He has every right to savor this moment, as it will pass too quickly. And he did come back for me."

A breeze swirled through the room. Thunder rumbled distantly. A tremor passed through her thoughts, the slow stirring of the Sight. Her blood prickled. She inhaled deeply and let the vision fill her.

Shurzad padded like a cat down a darkened hallway and entered Valeria's room. She lifted a lamp, poured fiery oil on her daughter's sleeping form, stood calmly while the girl burned.

Dana shook herself, and the images spun in whirling scintillants of flame. Surely this was not to be taken literally; she had taken literally the intimation of her death in the tomb, and had been wrong. She pressed her hands to her temples as if her mind were a winepress from which she could squeeze more images.

Andrion held the erect blade of Solifrax before him. The crystalline metal melted, burning his hands, his body. His eyes, pale taupe like the ensorcelled Bellasteros's, mirrored only the fire, no will, no pain.

She lowered her hands, trembling. The night was still, the storm over. A guard paced across the courtyard. Soft steps padded down the hallway. Ashtar! It begins! Dana blew out her own lamp, crept to the door, opened it. Something, someone was there. At first the shape was unclear, obscured by darkness; then she saw. It was Valeria.

Dana's heart started into her throat at seeing the object of her vision. But the girl was as luminous and pale as a waning moon, not flushed with fire. Her diaphanous nightdress revealed the lines of her slender child's body. Her eyes were wide and unfocused, tinted with dream; was she sleepwalking?

Then Dana saw Shurzad. The woman slipped like a shadow behind her daughter, turned her toward Andrion's room, guided her inside. And stood leaning against the door, her eyes hidden but her teeth glinting eagerly between parted lips.

Dana's mouth curled in contempt. So the shepherdess sent her lamb to the sacrifice, baiting a snare for a prince. And she had dared to accuse Dana of using him!

It took all Dana's willpower to quietly close the door, creep to the bed, perch upon its edge. Still her mind reeled, slow eddies circling rather than seizing thoughts, skirting some barrier, some power outside herself. Andrion, in his present mood, might well fall for this trick. Shurzad had probably even spiked his wine with an aphrodisiac. Fire, indeed; drunken passion, more likely.

But Valeria is intended for him, Dana insisted. I cannot interfere.

And yet, and yet . . . A chill settled like a heavy drapery over her. Dana again pressed her hands to her temples, trying to thrust herself through that mantle that her Sight could not penetrate, trying desperately to discern the significance of her vision. And slowly, painfully, the threads of the curtain began to tear, shreds of dark stuff floating away to be consumed in a growing flame of certainty.

Andrion stood so stiff and still that his muscles cramped. He cursed himself for his rash words. Dana, he moaned silently, did I ever think it would be easy to love you?

His tension snapped and he sat, hard, on the edge of the great canopied bed. The gauzy hangings moved, slowly inhaling and exhaling the cool dampness of the breeze. Andrion took a deep breath, steadying his thoughts.

He had drunk too much, he admitted that. He had sought to erase the memory of the tomb, of his folly in leaving Dana behind; he had sought to erase the knowledge that the evil of past generations followed him as closely as the good. He had held his father's skull in his hands, as he had held the hand of a demon, and whether his own hands were stained or sanctified, he could not tell.

Dana spoke the name of Tembujin. Harus, how could she

speak that name, corrupting her lips! But she should remind him of the task ahead. He drew the sword, considering its line, its light, its perfection. He ran his thumbnail up the burnished blade and spilled a faint spray of sparks over the coverlet. So I have Solifrax, Andrion told himself; I have succumbed to its spell. And yet it is not itself an end.

His glow, and the angry pride that was its edge, drained from his body. He fell back on the bed, fully clothed, and laid Solifrax beside him. A toy indeed, he thought with wry amusement. Never that. But Dana, how can I make you understand?

His mind fluttered into that twilit country between sleeping and waking. Tomorrow he would seek out Dana and apologize, and they would be friends again. When the legions went west, they could pass the fall equinox in Sabazel. There he could touch her, stroking her firm body as he now stroked his sword. He could bury himself in her, for a time forgetting who he was. He shifted uneasily on the bed, his body stirring with desire, with the image of her face and form this night, a beauty etched of both spirit and flesh.

The door opened. Drowsily he turned, but failed to wake himself. Dana, he thought, coming back to take him; an offering to Ashtar here in the heart of Sardis, how appropriate.

The woman was clad in a diaphanous gown that shifted around her like an illusory mist, teasing him with glimpses of her form. Dana seemed, Andrion thought fuzzily, to have suddenly lost weight. Her arms were taut at her sides, a soldier standing to attention, not lithe, not supple. Intrigued, he sat up. The room spun around him. He shook his head, but the motion only dizzied him further. The woman stepped stiffly toward him.

The sword shimmered, hissing. The body of the woman shimmered, beckoning. He pulled her down beside him. Jerkily, she yielded.

Dark hair, cornflower-blue eyes, face as fragile and open as a snowdrop. Dana, Andrion puzzled, you disguise yourself. Will it be easier for you this way? She lay stock-still, staring beyond his back as if seeing something move in the lamp-chased shadows.

Wings beat uncontrollably inside his mind, hiding something, revealing something. He closed his eyes, opened them again, and found the same face, the same delicate body before him. The same odor of lotus bathed him, a scent too heavy for this girlish figure but enticing nonetheless, hinting of dark delights beyond his meager experience. Tentatively but firmly Andrion ran his fingertips from her throat to her thigh. His body responded even if hers did not, lifting and hardening like the naked steel blade of Solifrax beside him, aching to be ignited.

He pulled her into his arms and pressed his lips to hers. Her lips were cool and tinted with venom, her tongue as cold as a serpent's. Venom coursed into his mouth and sent shivers of pain, sharp and sweet, through his body. Intoxicating pain, drawing him on and on. But some rational part of his mind hammered at him, an insistent rhythm beating countermeasure to the pounding of his blood. The sword sparked, just at the rim of his vision.

Surely it was his skin that sparked, blazing bright and hot. He devoured her mouth, letting her fiery venom take him, glorying in it; his senses filled to bursting like fruit ripe for the plucking. A sudden wind was cool against his heated face, but did not clear his mind.

Andrion clasped the woman tightly against himself, rolling her over him, rolling on top of her and fumbling at both their garments. His whole awareness was intent on only one goal, to plunge himself into the inferno of ecstasy this woman promised him, and there to lose all identity.

She looked up, roused by the intimacy of his touch. Her mouth opened in a long, silent scream. Not quite silent; the sound rent his mind and he started back. He fell against the sword. Its sharp edge pricked through his cloak and chiton, ice condensing the steaming cloud of lust that veiled his senses. Drops of horror showered him and his mind convulsed with reality and illusion, wrenching itself awake. He looked with clear eyes at the face close to his. It was Valeria.

No, it was not Valeria. That one scream was the last protest of the enspelled girl. Now a demoness glared at him, cold fire leaping in her narrowed eyes and licking at her parted lips, her flesh glowing and smoking without heat. She slipped toward him as sinuously as creeping flame. Her hand searched his thigh, demanding his manhood, his name, his life.

"No!" exclaimed Andrion, and the sound of his own voice steadied him. "No, by Ashtar, no!" He seized the sword, batted away the grasping hand, held the bright, clear blade between them. She reeled back, her arms raised against the crystalline glow. "In the name of Harus, Valeria," Andrion cried, "wake up!"

The flame in her body died, and the fire in her eyes became gray, cold ashes. Her own consciousness filled her face. With a scream of uncomprehending horror she threw herself into the pillow and began to sob.

Andrion sat numbly, Solifrax heavy in his hand, mouth hanging open in appalled amazement. His thoughts scalded him more deeply than Valeria's kisses had as he berated himself for his stupid, drunken lust.

But sorcery was at work here. His eyes had been clouded by more than lust and heady Sardian wine. He closed his mouth and raised his hand to comfort and reassure Valeria, but she started back, trembling violently, eyes rolling at him from behind laced fingers. He snatched his hand away.

A movement stirred at the edge of his sight. He spun about, still clutching the sword. Dana stood in the open doorway, holding Shurzad by a fold of her gown, her hand on her dagger. Dana's mouth was pinched tight, her face contorted with fear and fury and loathing mingled. Shurzad seemed only half conscious, swaying, eyes glistening slits of white.

Her eyes were like those of the dead sentries at the Jorniyeh bridge. Andrion shook his head, jarring his mind into coherence. His throat was scorched. "God's talons!" he croaked. "How long have you been standing there?"

Dana looked steadily at him. "Only a moment. I realized too late what was happening. I almost abandoned you." She swallowed as if her throat, too, was parched.

"I did not," Andrion began, stammering, "I did not . . ."

"I know. If you had, you would have died."

Valeria curled into a tight ball, shivering, still crying. Shurzad fell against Dana's side, and Dana thrust her away. But she did not release her. Shapes stirred in the darkness of the corridor, gaping servants, guards, Patros himself. Patros's gaze darted to each figure in the room and widened in shock. He ordered a guard to disperse the crowd and firmly shut the door behind them.

Which was worse, Andrion demanded of himself, to be found assaulting Patros's daughter with his body or with his sword? Solifrax fell from his limp hand and landed with a muffled thud on the coverlet. Its light failed, its blade grew dull and chill. Groaning, Andrion crawled off the edge of the bed. His cloak flopped lopsidedly over one shoulder.

But Patros passed no judgment. He went quickly to Valeria, embraced her, cradled her tearstained face against his strong shoulder. Her sobs ceased and she clung to him, her hands knotted in his robe.

Gods help me, thought Andrion. I have violated her as surely as if I did enter her. But she came to me. Or was it her? His eye moved reluctantly to Shurzad.

Every eye in the room went to Shurzad. The woman seemed to wake, gather herself, straighten. She realized that Dana was holding her, and she wrenched herself away. Her hand clutched the amulet at her throat; her lips pouted, like a small child caught in mischief.

"What is this?" Patros asked wearily, not wanting to know but unable to turn away from the truth. His cheek rested on Valeria's tumbled head.

"I slept," said Andrion. "I dreamed. I thought Dana came to me. . . ." He trailed off lamely. To have thought it was Dana was not much better.

Tersely, Dana told her father of how she had seen Shurzad lead a sleepwalking Valeria to Andrion's room and thrust her inside. Of how she had sensed sorcery at work, and Andrion in peril of more than just marriage.

Patros frowned, turned to Andrion.

"She was not Valeria," Andrion shrugged, feeling utterly foolish. "She was a . . . a succubus, consuming me with fire. Forgive me."

Patros sighed, "You are young, you are ruled by your body." His eye touched Dana. "As I once was."

"I saw Shurzad pass him a cup of wine," muttered Dana, looking at her feet. "An aphrodisiac, perhaps."

Lighting a fire already lit, Andrion sneered at himself.

Patros, pale as if a dagger stabbed him to the heart, looked squarely at Shurzad. His voice was quiet and even. "So you spell our child into seducing Andrion, knowing that he would burden himself with the deed and marry her? Unworthy, Shurzad, of us all."

Shurzad's face collapsed. Her eyes were dark, writhing with some furtive struggle; no, they were flat and dull. "What difference?" she pouted. "You do not care about Valeria or me. Only those whores from Sabazel." She saw Dana's baleful glare upon her and stopped.

The dagger in his heart turned, and Patros flinched.

"Hear me." Dana leaned forward urgently. "It was not that simple a spell. Valeria was possessed of a demon, and if Andrion had taken her, he would have died. Even I cannot believe that that was Shurzad's purpose."

The lines in Patros's face deepened. His body shivered and then stilled itself. He patted Valeria's shoulder and helped her up, and he offered his other arm to his wife, regarding her with sadness, not anger. "Come. Show us your secret shrine, where you practice these sorceries. Where you have sold yourself, it seems, in your spitefulness."

Shurzad looked at him, through him, uncomprehendingly. Her own personality seemed to be only a glaze on her shadowed eyes. She set her hand, a dried claw, on her husband's arm and let him lead her from the room. Dana glanced warily at Andrion. Andrion grimaced, hoisted the weight of Solifrax, and followed them down the dark corridors of the palace to a sumptous bedroom and through a hidden door into a small, dark shrine.

Dana's nostrils flared, and Andrion, too, noted that the air was dank and still, not unlike the tomb's. An odd acrid scent permeated the shadows, that of a distant fire, perhaps. The jade statue of Qem lay cold, silent, hard, disdaining the tiny flame that flickered before it. Shurzad knelt, her hands upraised in worship, but there was no sign.

"I thought her small magicks would keep her amused," said Patros, his voice tight almost to breaking. "I did not realize her hate was so deep that it would turn on her like this."

Something stirred, some dark shadow fleeing through the open door. Andrion spun, the sword lancing out. His arm tangled in his cloak. A hiss, and a supple shape flowed over the suddenly glinting blade. Shurzad's gray cat vanished into the night. Andrion's knees went weak. Demons! I can no longer trust my perceptions; this day has sucked them dry.

Dana sniffed again. "The scent of grass," she stated, "like the great southern plain. . . ." Her voice failed. She shook her head. "I sense nothing but the faded, broken threads of power. Patros?"

"Yes?" he said distantly, frowning at Shurzad's bowed head. And then, catching himself, he turned to Dana with courteous attention. "Yes?"

"Shurzad and Valeria are in great danger, eaten by sorcery.

You must bring them on the campaign, to Sabazel and beyond, to Iksandarun. . . ." She sighed. "I am sorry I can offer so little."

Patros allowed himself a light touch on her hair, gold muted by shadow. "Thank you."

Valeria stirred and turned, still safe in the circle of her father's arm, to Andrion. "I woke from nightmare to see you with me, and was startled; it was not you that frightened me."

She was as generous as her father. But her eyes were still vague, distracted, not quite in this room. Andrion bowed deeply over her damp hand. "Harus knows, Valeria, I should be begging your forgiveness."

"No, someone else should ask forgiveness," said Patros, and his voice broke. He turned again to Shurzad, raising his hand toward her, letting it fall. "Why, my wife, why?"

As if his gaze, his words, were an unbearable weight, she crumpled, prostrated herself before the statue and began to weep with small inconsolable whimperings. "I do not know, truly I do not."

May I never again, Andrion prayed, see Patros's face bearing such pain. Bearing it uncomplainingly, with dignity, as Bellasteros had borne the knowledge of his own weakness. He caught Dana's eye; as one they left the room and hurried down the haunted corridors of the palace.

"It is not some evil from the tomb?" he asked, quelling an impulse to glance over his shoulder.

"No more than it is domestic drama. It is something other, something else. Our enemies are the Khazyari, but how could they touch us here?" She snorted. "Devils take them all, Khazyari and Sardian and . . ."

"Me?" asked Andrion.

One corner of Dana's mouth indented itself with weary amusement. "Surely the gods protect you, Andrion."

"Indeed," Andrion responded dryly. "Forgive me, Dana, for excluding you from that favor."

"Forgive me for trying to rip it from you." They permitted their fingertips to touch awkwardly, and parted.

Andrion found his lamps guttering, the oil burned out. Like his body. He sheathed Solifrax, set it carefully aside, stripped off his clothing and fell across the wrinkled bed.

The moon rode high above Sardis, a cool shining pearl searching the fleece of clouds surrounding it. A wind puffed the curtains and caressed his body like the purifying touch of the goddess.

Raksula sat unmoving, staring through slitted eyes at the dancing flames of her small fire, her hand grasping the amulet of the Eye. After a time she swore and threw the charm down. "Weakling!" she snarled. "Shurzad, you are useless." She stamped at the fire and sparks licked at her skirts. Deep lines grooved her brow and lips, as if she had worked hard and long to no purpose.

"The sword," she said musingly. "Is the power in it, or is it in the bearer? Ah, I must have both sword and prince. I must have that necklace."

She bolted from the yurt and stalked through the camp, spitting venom at everyone she met. Spitting venom at the moon, a day past the full, that rode serenely high above the plain.

A squat shape outside the great yurt scrabbled to its feet. "Obedei took Hilkar and Sita away at midday," Odo reported.

"Hm," snarled Raksula. "And you, fool, have you saved anything from the ruins of your yurt?"

Odo indicated a pitiful pile of singed bags and boxes. "Enough, my lady." He reached familiarly out to her. She snapped at his hand, shoved him aside, and burst through the door hangings. He followed, his soft, round chin trembling with hurt.

The torches guttered. Several nuryans scrambled aside. A minstrel stilled his pipes, and the wailing music died away. Baakhun, a sunken pile of flesh on his dais, did not look up. Neither did Vlad, pinching and poking at a slave girl, the plaque of the lion's son hanging greasily awry on his chest.

Raksula made a jerky if gracious gesture at the musician. Tentatively, the keening began again. The nobles turned back to their food and drink. Their voices were oddly muted, as if damped by the ghost of Tembujin.

Raksula pulled Vlad away from his toy and wiped at the kviss staining his chin and tunic. He flailed at her. "I am the first odlok," he squealed, heavy-lidded and insolent. "I no longer need you."

Raksula bared her teeth in a grin. She saluted mocking acquiescence, but under her breath she hissed, "Do not test me, my son!"

Vlad's plump cheeks paled. His lower lip thrust itself out.
She grasped the scruff of his neck and deposited him at
Baakhun's side.

Still the great khan did not look up. Trays of meat and
sweets lay untouched before him, his skin of kviss was drained
dry, a blond slave lolled beside him as safe as though she were
a hundred leagues away.

"My lord," Raksula called. "My lord!"

Baakhun looked up, but he saw nothing. His eyes were red,
his shaved forehead wrinkled in futile inquiry. "Tembujin?"
he mumbled.

Raksula turned away in disgust. She almost fell over Odo,
who hovered just behind her. "Find that gold necklace,"
Raksula ordered him. "Find it!" And she stood quivering
with frustration in the center of the yurt, the torchlight casting
her face in tarnished brass.

Chapter Sixteen

THE GREAT STATUE of Harus loomed like an avenging god, silent and yet alert. It seemed to shrug off Bonifacio's droning voice and look beyond the dim, wing-stirred sanctuary to the lightening eastern horizon.

But I am going west, Andrion thought. Toward the sunset, toward the ending. The last ten days had been tedious, forged into a heavy coat of mail by details of food, arms, men. The nights had been anxious. Andrion had kept looking over his shoulder, waiting for some new illusion to strike him. But Sardis remained rooted in reality. Do you weary of testing me? Andrion mutely asked the image of the god. Or are you saving the greatest tests for the end?

He shifted. The greaves on his shins creaked. His cuirass chafed his neck, and the skin beneath the vambraces on his forearms prickled with sweat. His new armor was only the outer layer of the shell he now wore. But Solifrax hung at his waist, as alert as the god, humming. Am I a vessel for your strength? Andrion asked it. Or are you for mine?

Patros stood beside him, holding the small bronze falcon again affixed to a tall pole. The governor wore a similar shell, decision and courtesy tempered by an undercurrent of difficult thought. Shurzad and Valeria stood cloaked and veiled just beyond him, cold wax candles waiting only for a spark to melt into nothingness.

And Dana? Andrion glanced at her. She shrugged her bow higher on her shoulder, uneasy. It was no longer shameful for a Sabazian to bow to Harus, just as a Sardian bowing to Ashtar might suffer ridicule but no longer death. But she had refused Patros's offer of armor, taking only a few arrows to replenish her stock. If Andrion were anxious to be gone, then

171

she was no doubt doubly so; Sabazel beckoned with its own tangled skein of illusion and reality.

He caught her eye. She let a corner of her mouth shiver at him. At least the barrier between them was no higher. Bonifacio waited politely for recognition. Andrion cleared his throat.

"My lord," said the priest with a flourish, "I offer you this, to bring success in the coming campaign." He held up the helmet with the red plume that Bellasteros had worn to win the Empire. The bronze was carefully polished but the horsehair plume hung lank and dispirited.

Shall I wear his skull for all to see, using his image to usurp his army? Andrion stifled a shudder. But I must be polite. "Thank you," he said with a bow. "I . . . cannot take this relic from you."

Bonifacio's face fell. Gods, did he think such cannibalism would please me? Andrion wondered. Hurriedly, he said, "But you may bring it to Bellasteros himself. He will be pleased to see it." I hope. I plead. I pray.

Bonifacio, mollified, smiled. Patros's lips thinned, perhaps with amusement, perhaps with pain. A sudden shaft of sunlight struck deep into the sanctuary. The statue of Harus seemed to stretch, wings flexing and feathers rippling in the warmth, beak and talons lifting and eyes glinting. The small bronze falcon gleamed, cleansed of its misadventures.

Andrion led the group onto the long flight of steps that scaled the side of the temple mound. The sun lay like a crouching lion on the horizon, red and hungry; a cool wind purred down the flanks of the ziggurat and into the city, searching for prey. In the temple square, in the streets, beyond the city gates, gathered an army twenty thousand strong. The soldiers saw their prince emerge into the sunlight, and as one they cheered.

Ah, thought Andrion under the onslaught of so many eyes, we who are to die for you salute you. He drew Solifrax—a remarkably natural gesture already—and thrust it upward to catch the light of the sun. It cracked like lightning, flashing gold and crimson. You will follow my father's sword, will you not, even if you might not yet follow me? Again the soldiers cheered.

"Here are the cloak and helmet you requested," Patros said. "You are certain you do not want crimson like your father?"

A retainer stepped forward, holding a black cloak over his arm, holding a shining helmet with a floating black plume. "No," said Andrion, sheathing the sword, "I do not want crimson like my father." He draped the cloak about his shoulders and pinned it with his brooch; he set the helmet on his auburn hair and looked out across the world from its shadow, dark brown eyes reflecting the glow of bronze. The black plume lifted in the wind and fluttered like a banner.

Patros watched him. Dana watched him. Their eyes were mirrors, impenetrable, showing only his own face. He set his jaw, squared his shoulders. "Come," he said, and they stepped down the stairway, bowed to the shrine of Ashtar, and led the legions of Sardis to the relief of Iksandarun.

The moon waned, vanished, reappeared beside the sun. Soon it will be the equinox, Dana thought, and we shall pause in Sabazel. Andrion, can I touch you then? Or does it matter, in the goddess's scheme of things, whether I ever touch you again?

She rode beside him. His face was soberly introspective between the cheek pieces of his helmet, his black cloak flowed over him like a shadow of death. They talked quietly, even laughed together, but they remained an arm's length apart.

Shurzad and Valeria rode in an ox cart, with the supply train behind the marching infantry. The cat was a taut lamp of fur and muscle in a gilded cage, preening itself, scanning the passing world with glazed amber eyes. The women sat aloof, their eyes, too, glazed with the vastness of the world unfolding before them.

On Dana's eighteenth birthday Patros tore himself away from attending his women and his army; he presented her with a fine wool cloak and his best wishes. His face even in this light moment was grave and dark, and Dana ached for him. But she could not touch him, either. She accepted the cloak, thanked him, and turned away, choking on the best wishes and on remorse.

Her discomfort grew. The army came to Farsahn, where Proconsul Nikander joined them with ten thousand men, including several newly formed squads of cavalry. Miklos brought messages of welcome and promises of assistance from Sabazel; Andrion, glowing in a rare grin, made him a centurion and let him bear the falcon standard beside him.

Dana's skin prickled with the Sight. She found herself drift-

ing to the south time and time again; she began to ride on
Andrion's right hand as the column snaked along the Road in
the cool, clear days of early fall. Peasants left their grain and
their grapes to gawk, holding their children high to see the
chariots, the bright falcon borne by Miklos's steady hand, the
scarlet pennons, the prancing black horse and the black prince
who bore Bellasteros's sword. Then the legions entered the
wilderness.

As the leagues rolled away behind them, Dana grew frantic.
She strained her senses, listening to the blackbirds, smelling
the fine wine-bright air, but she could not grasp the image that
tantalized her. Until they came to the bridge over the Jorniyeh, where the Road turned south.

She saw then, in a waking vision, the pass at Azervinah. She
saw the curved blade of Solifrax gathering the sunlight, re-
fracting it into myriad colors. She saw a face that seared her
memory. But the vision could not be denied. Wearily she told
Andrion, "When the scouting party rides to Azervinah, we
must ride with them."

He knew better than to ask why.

A cool breeze stirred the leaves into cascades of gold and
green. Like Dana's eyes, Andrion thought, shifting depths of
color and shadow. She rode beside him, pale but steady, staring into the deep blue of the sky as if seeking some sign of the
goddess. Andrion, wanting nothing more than to finish this
uncertainty, had to hold himself as tightly in check as he held a
frisky Ventalidar. "No Khazyari?" he called to the leading
centurion.

The man shook his head. "No, my lord. None, even past
the fort itself and into the opening of the plains."

Strange, Andrion thought. Had they abandoned an attempt
on the pass? Farsahn and Sardis itself were protected from the
south by the mountain range, towering ever higher toward the
east; they could not break through there except with small
bands. Only one other place might allow the passage of an
army from south to north: the high plains of Sabazel.

Dana, sensing his thought, winced. He tightened his legs on
Ventalidar's flanks and the horse leaped across a thistle-
choked gully. Something crashed through the underbrush, and
his heart jerked.

"My lord," cried another scout. "Something odd ahead."

Dana's head went up, and the glimmer of sunlight in her eyes was extinguished like a candle snuffed. "Yes," she whispered. "On a great flat rock above a bend in the river."

The man glanced at her, brows raised, and nodded. Andrion sent scouts right and left and told the other soldiers to hang back. In a few moments he could see the stone, glinting with tiny points of crystal between leaves that danced in a fitful breeze. The water of the Jorniyeh swept by, rushing toward the sea with the murmur of a thousand voices.

Andrion dismounted, patted Ventalidar's nose, pushed through the brambles without noticing their tiny barbs in his flesh. Dana moved just behind him, so close he could feel her breath on his neck. He glanced around; it was really Dana, not a demon. He wondered if he would ever again trust his own senses.

She looked past him. He stepped through the last whipping branches. There, before him, a man clad only in ragged breeches lay spread-eagled, tied to stakes driven into fissures in the rock. A hooded figure huddled nearby. The sun glinted so brightly off the stone that the two shapes shimmered in fluid waves of heat. Were they dead? Then the bound man stirred, a faint shivering twitch, and the hooded figure roused itself and reach for an empty waterskin.

Toth. Andrion stepped forward, caught himself. Was this a Khazyari trick, or some new divine test? He set his hand on the hilt of Solifrax and stepped again, nerves quivering like the bowstring to which Dana nocked an arrow. The rushing of the river was suddenly loud. The wind gusted.

Andrion's cloak unfurled, casting a shadow across the two figures. Toth looked up and his eyes bulged with the image of the black warrior. His features had melted into flaccid, hanging folds of skin, the plumpness eaten away; his cheeks were bruised, his lips scabbed. Andrion inhaled to say something reassuring and stopped, the breath held burning in his chest. The man on the rock was painfully thin, his ribs standing out in sharp-etched lines, his cheekbones axe edges cleaving the sunlight. Tangled strands of black hair blew over his face, over caked, dry lips, over swollen tip-tilted eyes that opened onto ebony pools of despair.

This beaten animal was the elegant Khazyari prince, Tembujin. Andrion spun toward Dana; she remained at the edge of the rock, unmoving, unblinking, eyes still and cold.

Andrion whipped back around, grimacing in a fierce joy. At last, at last! He drew Solifrax with a hiss and a flare of light. Tembujin stirred. His eyes focused on the shining blade, on the face beyond it. His mouth twitched in what was almost a laugh. He lifted his chin, closed his eyes, and bared his throat to the sword.

"Andrion," Toth croaked, realizing who this warrior was. He raised a palsied hand. "My lord, mercy for this man, please."

Mercy? The sword keened in Andrion's uplifted hand. Mercy, for this vile creature?

Dana lowered her bow, looked away, looked back again, compelled to interfere. She took a step onto the edge of the rock and called something that clotted in her throat. And you, too, would beg mercy for this creature? Andrion asked silently. But yes, she had realized who it was who awaited them, and why; her Sight had brought her here.

Andrion swallowed his anger, and his stomach curdled. But he could no longer afford the luxury of anger.

"Tembujin was condemned to death by his own people," Toth said urgently, clutching at Andrion's greaves. "The warriors who brought him here to starve beat me when they found me following, but thinking me worthless, they left me alive. They never discovered that I carried food. Tembujin must live, lord, he must live."

I know that. Gods, I know it. Andrion lowered Solifrax; killing this sick, helpless animal would stain it forever. His head spun, and he stilled it. So, Tembujin had done something to earn the hatred of his own people. Interesting, most interesting. Perhaps, then, he would not be reluctant to serve the Empire.

Solifrax flicked four times, and the ropes that tied Tembujin fell into ash. His wrists and ankles were chafed raw. "Why did you not untie him?" Andrion asked Toth, sheathing his sword, sheathing his animosity.

"You needed the proof of his predicament," the old servant replied. His eyes reflected the pale gleam of the sword.

"You knew I would come?" But Toth did not need to answer. The hair on the back of Andrion's neck prickled. He glanced again at Dana. She was gone. With a sigh of resignation, he knelt and levered Tembujin to a sitting position.

The odlok looked through bleared and resentful eyes at his

rescuer, swallowed, croaked, "Damn you."

"And you, I am sure," Andrion replied equably through his teeth. His cloak billowed in another gust of wind, encompassing them both.

Soldiers ran from the woods, lifted the two wasted forms, bore them away. Dana crept across the surface of the rock, waiting for reproval. He could only wonder if his face were quite as grim and tight as hers, the face of an older, wiser person who grasps at fate and finds it to be a carnivorous animal, stalking him, mangling him, spitting him out and abandoning him to stagger on.

The river rushed heedlessly by. The wind murmured of comfort, healing, and rest. Sabazel lay before them. Andrion and Dana walked silently away from this place of suffering.

Andrion squinted into the sunset, trying to see Cylandra's peak silhouetted against the scarlet glow. But no, Sabazel was still too far away. The army was encamped just south of where Bellasteros's great army had camped a generation before. That army had fought for two years to get to this spot, Andrion thought. This one came from Sardis in seventeen days, and still had time to thank a stunned magistrate in Bellastria for his charity to a young merchant.

Bellasteros fought for six months to take the southern provinces and Iksandarun, with fifty thousand at his back, without a major defeat at the hands of his enemy. As for us—well, we still have Bellasteros, Andrion mused, and turned his eyes upward. A waxing moon hung like a silver egg among clouds like pink and lavender feathers. He felt the stiff muscles of his face draw into a smile. He had, it seemed, forgotten how to smile.

The wind whipped the scarlet and purple pennons above the pavilion where he stood, playing with the hair on his helmetless head. A work detail stepped briskly down the avenue, led by the scent of roasting meat. Dana sat outside her tent, also contemplating the moon. He started toward her.

Patros beckoned from a nearby tent. Gods, Andrion moaned silently, can I never rid myself of that Khazyari? Squaring his shoulders, stilling his smile, he responded to the summons. Dana, frowning slightly, did not follow.

Andrion nodded companionably to Miklos, who stood guard outside the tent. Inside it was already night. A flaming brazier drove away the chill; red light flickered unevenly on the two thin faces laid on camp beds.

Nikander and Patros watched a surgeon fold away his packets of herbs. He turned to Andrion with a bow. "My lord." His hand indicated Toth. "This one is old and frail. I have given him what strengthening brews I can, but still . . ." His voice died away. Toth seemed to sleep, unhearing, eyes closed and ravaged face still.

"But this one," the surgeon continued, turning with a firm nod toward Tembujin, "with some heartening food, should be up and around tomorrow."

Tembujin, awake but distinctly subdued, inquired, "Up and around? That is for the son of the falcon to say."

Andrion thanked the surgeon and bowed him out, using the opportunity to collect his thoughts. Patros and Nikander waited. Odd, he thought, how accustomed he'd become to even the generals of Sardis deferring to him.

The dark, numbed hollows of Tembujin's eyes were fixed upon him. Well, he said to himself, we seem to be set in this game together; I shall play it to the end, if you will. "Would the son of the lion like vengeance on those who betrayed him?" he asked.

"Indeed," replied Tembujin. "But you yourself are at fault."

"My prayers were answered?" Andrion replied caustically.

"Your necklace," said Tembujin, raising himself with effort onto one elbow, seizing some of his old spirit. "Your god-cursed necklace."

"The one you stole from me at Bellastria?" Unwittingly Andrion's hand touched his throat.

"The same. I wore it back to my camp, and was haunted by it. . . ." He shivered. "There were those who recognized it."

"Who?" interjected Patros. Nikander's expression did not change. Toth stirred, and his eyes glinted pale between his lids.

Tembujin licked his lips and said, with a weary if bitter relish, "Hilkar the chamberlain. He who opened the gates of Iksandarun."

Whorls of light spun before Andrion's eyes. "By the blood of the falcon," he spat, "so that is who it was. That sneaking worm, what did we ever do to him?"

Nikander's long throat bobbed in slow swallow. Patros paled and cursed under his breath. Of course, Andrion real-

ized, the whorls chilling into cinders, Hilkar was a kinsman of
Shurzad.

"A worm," continued Tembujin. "I quite agree. It seems
that he did not care for your father's taking his intended bride,
Roushangka, and has nursed his anger all these years."

"Roushangka," repeated Andrion. "She was—"

"Sarasvati's mother." Oddly Tembujin smiled, his lips
lingering over the name. "You do not know, do you, that your
sister is still alive?"

Nikander's eyes widened by a fraction. Patros paled even
further, to a sickly green. He turned to Toth. "Surely he lies,
seeking to taunt us."

Andrion turned, too, part of him praying that Tembujin
was lying, part of him praying that he was not. He would
almost prefer Sarasvati dead to being enslaved, to being *used*,
by the Khazyari demon. A void opened beneath his heart. The
tent flap stirred and Miklos stood in the opening, for once
forgetting his position, his eyes aflame with Sarasvati's name.

"No, he is not lying," said Toth feebly. "My apologies, my
lord; when I left you I did think she was dead. But I found her
later, and we agreed it was best she give herself to a chieftain."

Andrion's heart plummeted. Miklos's mouth fell open in
horror.

"I was foolish enough," Tembujin sighed, "to give her
your necklace, telling her I had killed you. In her hatred she
cut my hair and gave it to my enemy, Raksula, my stepmother.
With it the witch enspelled me to silence, and told my father
the khan that I had your necklace because I was your friend.
He believed her." He fell back against the pillow and closed
his eyes. His body seemed to wither, drained.

"Sarasvati," Andrion said. He swallowed something large
and jagged into the place his heart had been.

"Ah," said Tembujin, "I did not know she was your sister.
I knew her as Sita. But she is so lovely I would have taken her
in any event."

Miklos lunged for Tembujin. Andrion seized him. Damn it,
Miklos, he shouted silently, I need him! He wanted to laugh,
he wanted to cry. Patros grimaced in anguish and turned
away.

Tembujin looked up at Miklos, one brow rising in a thin
shadow of arrogance. "So," he said, "I had something you
wanted."

Miklos lunged again, spitting obscenities, suggesting mutilations. Andrion tightened his grasp on the young soldier's arms. "This barbarian stud," he snarled, "has already been gelded. Only in spirit, unfortunately, but that should serve."

And Nikander, taking Miklos's shoulders firmly in his huge hands, thrust him out of the tent. "It is much too late to mend the situation," the general told him. "Get outside until you calm yourself."

Calm yourself, Andrion repeated silently. He wondered why he, too, was not writhing with fury. Gods, Tembujin's hands violating Dana, his body violating Sarasvati. . . . But was death indeed better than what Sardis would call dishonor? The Khazyari, cast out and left with nothing but the memory of his betrayal, had felt his own pain. Justice, perhaps. Or perhaps some divine jest at the expense of Sarasvati, of Tembujin, of himself.

I become too calm, Andrion told himself. I lose myself, accepting too much. He met Nikander's wise, hooded eyes, and the old sea turtle shrugged slightly. Such was a hazard of maturity, it seemed.

"My lord," said Toth. "The lady Sarasvati carries Tembujin's child."

Tembujin gasped.

Andrion noted somehow that the tent flap trembled; Miklos, still listening. He noted his own blood pulsing in his mind. He noted Tembujin's face, struggling to choose between resentment and affection, failing. He noted Patros, stricken, cloaking himself with desperate dignity.

"So," Andrion heard himself say to Tembujin in an oddly firm voice, "she had good reason to betray you. But where is she now?"

"Perhaps Obedei, who was once my friend, will care for her."

"It seems she can care for herself." Andrion found that thought reassuring; racked with sympathy as he was, he knew he could spare none, not now. "Are you worth this pain you bring us?" he demanded.

Tembujin's face, too, was grim and tight, scoured by fate. "Probaby not," he replied. "But we have no choice."

"We have a choice," Andrion told him, told everyone within earshot. "We choose to win back the Empire. Will you aid us?"

"Not one of my people would defend me against the witch, Raksula," Tembujin said bitterly. "I would see her dead. I would see them all dead."

"Even your father?" asked Andrion, and he marveled at the words his own voice said.

For just a moment Tembujin looked Andrion in the face, allowing him to see the bleak void of his soul. "Even him."

"So be it." Andrion spun about and plunged out of the tent, away from the firelight, into moonlight. He stood in the darkness as the cold wind, Ashtar's breath, cleansed his mind. He pounded his closed fist into his palm. I cannot afford to hate him, he thought. I will *not* hate him.

Dana still sat before her tent, head bowed over clasped hands. Something in her attitude told Andrion that she had heard it all, in her mind; good, he could not bear to repeat it. Behind him the voices of his generals spoke. Nikander calmly drew word after word from Tembujin and Toth and set each into a pattern; Patros, suppressing his agony, darted like a dragonfly from point to point. Numbers, tactics, disposition. The Khazyari people lay gutted.

Andrion realized that Miklos stood beside him. "My lord, you must not let him live. You must avenge Sarasvati's honor."

"She has avenged herself and helped us," he said placatingly. "We have no time now for personal vendettas."

"Gods!" Miklos exclaimed, stung, "she is your sister!"

"Miklos, it galls me as much as you that we left her behind. We can only repay her by winning our battle. For that we need Tembujin." Andrion set his jaw and laid his hand on Miklos's shoulder, willing him to understand, to obey. "He is our ally now. That is an order."

The soldier's face fell, wounded, struggling not to resent. "Yes, my lord," he muttered. He jerked away, leaving Andrion's hand empty. Yes, Andrion thought ruefully after him, I have feet of clay. And a heart of clay, it seems. He recalled how just this evening they had sparred with practice swords, laughing as each of them in turn won a match.

"The gods work in subtle ways," Dana called softly.

"Indeed they do." He spread his cloak like the shadow of his thoughts around him, and joined her. They sat, each in their silent shells, watching the moon cross the sky.

• • •

In the depth of the night Andrion awoke with a jolt, realizing that his necklace was still in the Khazyari camp. He tested his thoughts and feelings; no, he did not seem to be enspelled. But then, apparently, one never did. When dawn came he had prayed a hundred times that Sarasvati still had the necklace with her. He could do nothing about it if she did not. For the son of a god he was remarkably powerless. He arose feeling as if he had been sifted through a beer strainer; he stepped out into a tentative dawn, the world not quite real. . . . Stop it, he ordered himself.

A company of horsemen waited outside the pavilion to escort them to the rites. Those chosen seemed well pleased with their task, anticipating what to them was a few days' recreation. The Sardians would never understand Sabazel. Andrion looked sourly for Patros.

The governor, appearing as much the worse for wear as Andrion, supervised the rigging of a litter for Toth. "Healing," Patros said, in a litany as much for himself as for the old servant, who seemed somewhat stronger this morning and lay looking about him with the bright insouciance of a sparrow.

"My lord," Patros said stiffly to Andrion, "how can I atone for the treachery of my kinsman Hilkar?"

"We do not choose our relations," Andrion replied, "or direct their actions. You have no atonement to make."

Patros sighed. "Thank you." He turned to confer with Nikander. "I should stay here with the army, with you."

"Go on to Sabazel." Nikander nodded sagely.

You deserve the blessing of Ilanit's touch, Patros, Andrion silently finished for him. And the dueling princes require supervision, he thought, noting Tembujin standing nearby, shoulders bowed as if expecting a blow. Several soldiers hovered with dubious expressions behind him, ready either to guard him or protect him; not even Andrion was sure whether Tembujin was a prisoner or a guest.

Andrion was obscurely pleased to see the Khazyari wearing a tunic and breeches cobbled together out of tent canvas, and some officer's cast-off boots. Yes, the man had lost a measure of his manhood, which was all to the good; but he had also lost his fighting trim. The odlok's proclivities being what they were, Andrion thought reluctantly, he could perhaps regain some confidence at the rites of Ashtar. Dana's friend Kerith, now . . . He sighed, steeled himself, caught Tembujin's eye and beckoned.

Tembujin looked around, realized Andrion was summoning him, slouched across the open area before the pavilion. He passed Bonifacio, stonily ignoring the priest's shudder and gesture against the evil eye. But he was caught up short by Dana's emergence from a nearby tent.

The two stared at each other a long moment. Then Dana grinned. "What happened to your hair, Khazyari?"

Tembujin essayed a grin of his own. "And yours?" He walked around her, staying well out of reach. Dana turned her back on him. Miklos came around a corner leading Ventalidar; he saw Tembujin and stopped dead. Then he, too, steeled himself. Andrion was relieved to see that the young man's face was hard but not sullen. Dana began a quiet conversation with him, close under Ventalidar's flaring nostrils.

"Are you well enough to ride?" Andrion asked Tembujin, assuming a veneer of courtesy.

"Ride where? To Sabazel, with you?"

"Yes." Why, by Harus, was he pleased to see a spark in the beast's eye? Keep goading him. "Yes. To test your abilities."

"Ah," snapped Tembujin, goaded.

Toth was watching them, not wistfully, but with an odd humor. Suddenly his face froze. Andrion followed the direction of his gaze. The morning vitrified into shards of glass, each stained with its own image, clear and yet distant. Not the faintest breeze stirred the encampment.

Shurzad, her eyes burning black brands, advanced from the opposite side of the open area. Even before the legionaries she went unveiled; her face was clammy white, her lips slitted over sharp teeth. Valeria walked behind her as if pulled on a leash, her eyes vacant above a lopsided veil. The gray cat was a slinking shadow beside them, its tail erect and crooked at the end, its topaz eyes intent on its prey.

Shurzad's left hand clutched white-knuckled at her amulet. Her other hand was concealed in the drapery of her skirt. Toth struggled to rise, failed, exclaimed, "By Ashtar's eyes, my ordeal has destroyed my wits!"

Tembujin saw the amulet. His head went up, alert.

Dana parted from Miklos. "Kerith would be pleased to befriend you."

"Thank you, my lady, but I shall stay here."

Patros, his back to Shurzad, was still speaking to Nikander. Bonifacio found a stain on the hem of his robe and called a servant to sponge it.

Toth grabbed for Andrion's hand. "Raksula. The Khazyari witch. Hilkar gave her an amulet just like that one, one that Shurzad gave to him. My lord, forgive me, I did not realize until now; the amulet is the sign of Qem, and Qem is an aspect of the Khazyari—"

"Khalingu's wings!" exclaimed Tembujin. "The woman is possessed!"

Andrion hurtled through spinning stained-glass splinters, splinters that pierced him, tore his mind, opened it, bleeding, to the truth. His hand fumbled for the hilt of Solifrax, moving as slowly as if through thick honey. His tongue stuck to the roof of his mouth.

Shurzad was a few paces from Patros's back. Her mouth curved in a malevolent smile. Her eyes did not blink. Valeria struggled. The cat dropped into a crouch, stalking. Gods! Andrion shouted mutely, gods, make someone move, make someone turn around! But each person-shape was a painted image, unmoving, unconscious.

His mind wrenched, seizing control. The sword leaped from the sheath spitting flames, brighter than the pale dawn sun. He lunged, cloak billowing, plume floating, slowly, slowly, and soldiers scattered before him.

Shurzad pulled a dagger from her dress. "Go to Sabazel," she shrieked. "Go, and be damned!" Patros turned. Nikander raised his arms, Dana's eyes started from her face, Miklos's mouth fell open in alarm. Shurzad's dagger darted toward Patros's heart. Shocked, he did not dodge.

"Ashtar!" Andrion cried, striking. Solifrax sang and Shurzad's dagger flew from her suddenly bloody hand to land quivering in the dirt before Bonifacio. The priest recoiled and tripped over his servant. Ventalidar reared, jerking Miklos, who sprawled into the dirt. The cat whisked under Shurzad's skirts. Toth collapsed on his litter, gasping for breath.

Tembujin appeared in the corner of Andrion's eyes. He snatched the amulet from Shurzad's throat. She screamed as if he had torn the living heart from her body, clasping her hands to her throat, buckling to her knees. Valeria moaned and swayed; Nikander caught her as she fell.

Curious soldiers rushed up. Nikander growled an order, and just as quickly they disappeared. Shurzad's forefinger lay in the dirt. Blood flooded the front of her gown as she crouched, whimpering like some small animal pinioned by a trap. But it was her throat she held, not her hand. Droplets of her blood stood in hard scarlet dots across Patros's cuirass. He did not move, did not speak, stricken.

Dana lurched forward, ripping the hem of her new cloak, and laid a scrap of cloth over the severed finger. Then she began binding Shurzad's hand. Shurzad's vacant eyes rolled toward her, passed by without recognition, stared into the distance. Dana's face was as tightly closed as a flower nipped by frost. It was she, Andrion recalled, who had brought Shurzad here.

He gestured sharply to Tembujin; Tembujin threw him the amulet. It left a faint trail of smoke in the air. Andrion caught it on the tip of his sword and raised it high. "Harus, Ashtar, an offering." His arm quaked, his hand burned, the charm sparked into flame. He let it fall onto the scrap of cloth and the finger. They sizzled, emitting a cloud of acrid smoke, and the scent of burning flesh fouled the morning air. Then only black ashes remained. A breeze pealed through the encampment, sweeping smoke and ashes into the vault of the sky where a falcon drifted, its eyes seeing all.

The stunned faces of the watchers moved, waking from vision. Tembujin looked at Andrion with a certain cautious awe. Impressed? Andrion asked him silently. And then he realized where he was, and who, and what he had just done. He had mutilated Patros's wife. He had called down divine fire. His arm was numb. The bitter smoke still clotted his throat.

The silence was broken by a muffled howl from Shurzad's skirts. The cat erupted from its shelter, dancing as if its paws were on fire. Tembujin plucked it up by the scruff of its neck. "So," he said. "A small snow leopard. Shall I kill it?"

"No," Andrion responded, swallowing. His voice sounded strange to his own ears. "Even it deserves healing. Return it to its cage, and bring it to Sabazel. Bring us all to Sabazel."

Sabazel, said the wind in his ear. His fingers tingled on the sword. My strength or yours? he asked the polished blade, he asked the wind. But neither offered a reply. Power ebbed and flowed about him, through him, within him, but he could not be frightened by it. He would not.

"Oh," said Bonifacio. "Sorcery." Hurriedly he began a prayer. Nikander called for Valeria's and Shurzad's serving women. Patros turned to Dana, looking at her as a condemned man would look from his solitary cell. She bit her lip deeply and embraced him. Andrion sheathed his sword. He found himself wondering when Patros's hair had gone so gray, his head sable and silver against Dana's golden one.

Shurzad and Valeria and the cat were carried away. A wide-eyed Miklos presented Andrion with Ventalidar's reins. "If we have the same enemy," asked Tembujin with a puzzled frown, "are we friends?"

Andrion did not even try to answer. Aching in every limb, he mounted Ventalidar and turned him toward Sabazel.

Raksula shrieked in pain and outrage both. She threw the amulet away from her burned and blistered hands and watched, cursing, as it disintegrated into ash. Odo made some sympathetic noise; she turned on him, scratching at him until he ran in terror from the yurt. She collapsed in a pile of skirts and spite, sobbing in frustration, swearing vengeance upon Andrion's auburn head.

Chapter Seventeen

SARASVATI SQUINTED AGAINST the sunset, searching for the walls of Iksandarun. But the city was still too far away. Soon, though, the little band would be there. And then what?

The plain rolled to the horizon like a golden sea. Only the straight line of the Road pierced its monotony. Only the huddled yurts and horses and camels of the small encampment, perched on a hilltop, broke the indigo sweep of the sky. A scout rode into the west, the hooves of his pony drumming against the ground. A falcon wheeled overhead, feather tips brushing the silver egg of a waxing moon.

Sarasvati eyed moon and falcon hopefully, but they offered her no sign. She turned back to her yurt. Hilkar stood there, smiling in thin-lipped, heavy-lidded malevolence, an expression he had no doubt copied from Raksula. A shiver, rising hackles, rippled through Sarasvati's body as he seized her arm. "Let me go," she ordered him.

"Now, now, my lady," he said. The honorific was a sneer. "You are hardly in a position to give orders, are you?"

She wrenched her arm away. "Slimy beasts like you are made to be trodden upon. Traitor."

"Ah?" His other hand whipped from a fold in his cloak. It held a long Khazyari dagger. Sarasvati's eyes narrowed but she did not step away. "Who is the traitor?" Hilkar whined. "You betrayed the father of your child, did you not? Who is the worse, my lady, you or me?"

She spat in his face and spun toward the shadowed doorway of the yurt. With the howl of a jackal, Hilkar leaped after her. The knife caught a last slanting ray of the sun and glittered.

One watching sentry nudged another. The second strolled away.

Hilkar and Sarasvati fell together into the interior, a flurry of cloak and skirts on the rich Mohendra carpet. Sarasvati clasped Hilkar's wrist in both her hands, holding the knife away from her. Its sharp tip circled her face, and her eyes glinted corundum blue. "So you still serve Raksula," she gasped. "Every witch needs a toad for a familiar."

They struggled for the knife in a silence punctuated only by sharp intakes of breath and muffled curses. At last Hilkar, perspiring with effort, brought his knee deliberately into Sarasvati's stomach.

She cried out and her face went stark white. Her hands slipped. Crowing with delight, Hilkar knelt over her, knife upraised.

A shadow blotted the doorway. In one stride Obedei seized Hilkar's clothing, jerking him away from Sarasvati, tore the blade from his fingers and set it against his throat.

Groaning, clutching her belly, Sarasvati sat up. Her hair lay in long red wisps across her damp face, her chest heaved. She raised her hand as if to stop Obedei, and then let it fall.

"No, no, governor," Hilkar gabbled, plucking at Obedei's boots. "I am under Raksula's protection. Raksula did not tell you to slay me. . . ."

Obedei shook him, snarling, perhaps more at Raksula than at Hilkar himself. "Guard him," he said to Sarasvati. "No attack you no more." He dragged Hilkar ignominiously from the tent. Yelps penetrated the felt as the nuryan kicked him.

"Ah, Obedei," murmured Sarasvati, "would you help me if you knew how I betrayed Tembujin?" She sank onto the carpet, considering the intricately twining leaves and vines of the pattern. Suddenly she tensed. Her fingers felt the faintest stirring within her belly, like the flutter of tiny wings. "Ah," she exhaled, "poor fatherless bastard. It is your mother who must be strong."

She lay a long time, curved around the helpless body of her child, as the light failed and darkness filled the world.

They moved slowly, burdened by Toth's litter and the wagon carrying Shurzad and Valeria, and came to Sabazel at sunset.

Dana looked up, up, to the heights of Cylandra wreathed in mist. The familiar sight lifted a burden from her shoulders; she felt herself breathing more deeply than she had for days. The sun sank behind the mountain, spreading translucent

shadow across the plain. The company passed the boundary
between light and darkness and was encompassed by gleaming
twilight. Lights sprang up in the city, and the brightest flared
before the gates. The shield, glowing in welcome. Dana urged
her horse into a gallop.

Ilanit held the star-shield before her; Dana could not tell
whether she supported it or it her. And yet she laughed in
delight as her daughter leaped from her horse and embraced
her. Ah, Dana thought, sanctuary in a mother's arms. They
looked at each other hungrily, hoping to see that nothing had
changed. But Ilanit's face was taut and keen, worn with care,
as if she had stood on this spot ever since Dana and Andrion
left two months before. Dana knew that her own face had
changed no less.

"What happened to your hair?" asked Ilanit lightly. "Did
you cut it yourself, in contrition for your misdeed?"

"Mother . . ." Dana began, but she could not carry the jest,
so she answered truthfully, hating herself for making Ilanit's
face grow even tighter.

When the rest of the company arrived, Ilanit raised the
shield again, letting its glow touch every face, inspecting each
for similar reassurance. She did not find it. Patros looked at
her with anguished eyes, her young brother Andrion nodded
stiffly in his new armor, Shurzad and Valeria gazed at her with
haggard, beaten faces, no longer able to hate her. One face
was old and ill, and one was a young Khazyari's, staring at her
as curiously as she stared at him. The soldiers of the escort, at
least, seemed as soldiers always did, exchanging ribald jests in
anticipation of the rites. Ilanit sighed—how few men really
understood—and gestured, and the Horn Gate opened.

Torches filled the temple square with dancing shadow
shapes. A group of men, waiting to one side, rose to their feet
with good-natured grumbles. Kerith waved eager greeting to
Dana. Lyris leaned on her javelin, watching the newcomers
with jaundiced resignation. Andrion swept her a bow and she
saluted expressionlessly.

"We waited for you," Ilanit said to him, "as you asked."

"Thank you," he answered. "We need this moment, Ilanit;
a deep breath, the sanctuary of a mother's arms, before the
struggle begins."

"But the struggle has already begun, has it not?"

He smiled, grateful for her perception. "Yes indeed." He

drew Solifrax a handsbreadth from its sheath; the bright metal hummed, and the shield answered in subtle resonances of power.

Ilanit touched its rim to the sword and considered the twin sparks they emitted. "Sword and shield ride together again. Good. I grow tired of watching it gather dust."

"You lie," Andrion told her affectionately. "You want nothing more."

Ilanit smiled. "Go on. Our mother waits for you." But he would not go until the others were cared for.

"Welcome," Ilanit said to Shurzad and Valeria. Valeria managed a faint nod, her eyes huge at finding herself in this legendary place. Shurzad stared blankly ahead, her face unpainted, unveiled, ravaged with twice her years. With despair, perhaps, at finding herself in the hands of the woman she had always perceived as her enemy. Or perhaps she simply did not know where she was.

Dana told their tale, and the stories of Tembujin and Toth; Ilanit consigned all three invalids to the care of temple priestesses. Shurzad and Valeria plodded away, leaning together for support, the cat peering with drooping disconsolate whiskers through the bars of its cage. But Toth lay gazing about him, transfigured with joy. Odd, thought Dana, that this place should mean anything to him.

Ilanit turned quizzically to Tembujin. He glanced from Dana to her mother and back, comparing their blond, green-eyed charms. A pensive smile shaped his mouth, a small boy surveying a tray of sweets, unsure if he will be permitted to have one.

Ilanit chuckled. "Will you offer to the goddess Ashtar?"

"She seems," said Tembujin, smile tinted in gall, "to be stronger than my own deity."

"Then join the other men, and listen well when I give the rules."

Tembujin hesitated. His bright black eyes turned to Dana, too proud to ask, but needing too much to pretend indifference. Dana looked away, unprepared to see such a depth in him.

Ilanit came at last to Patros. She needed no words to greet him; she simply set her hand on his cheek and secured him. The shield brightened for the length of a heartbeat, bathing them in its golden glow. The intensity of the look they shared struck Dana like a stinging slap. Like Danica and Bellasteros, they had chosen the complications of the heart, at times completing, at times draining them. Such compromise was never easy.

Dana glanced at Andrion as he turned alone up the street toward Danica's garden. Compromise, indeed. She started after him, stopped. Tembujin still watched her. His uncertainty gnawed at her; this fine, sleek animal could not live with such self-doubt. "Ashtar!" she said under her breath, "give me strength!" She sped after Andrion, hoping to outrun her importunate thoughts.

The darkness was a velvet drape over Sabazel. Andrion's footsteps rang on the pavement, counterpointing the distant strains of a lyre and song. As he bounded up the steps to the garden, a breeze caught his cloak and unfurled it like a glistening cloud behind him. For a moment he paused, looking toward the bright ripeness of the rising moon. His face was the image of a young warrior-god etched by substance upon shadow.

He strode through the garden, opened the lamplit door of the house, stepped inside. His dark eyes shot one searching glance toward the bed. Yes, the quiet shape was still there, wasted hands folded, breast rising and falling with agonizing slowness. Andrion moaned softly, but his back remained lance straight.

Danica laid her quill upon the scroll unrolled before her. Her face was a palimpsest, vellum written upon and scraped and written upon again, layer upon layer of thought, feeling, experience. Her eyes sparked, reflecting the armor before her, and then quailed, realizing that this stern black-clad warrior was her son. "Great mother," she gasped, "what has he become?" But her question needed no answer. She glanced with a wry smile at Dana, the image of her younger self. Dana returned her look: Yes, I fear he has become a man.

Andrion drew Solifrax and held it out to his mother. Lamplight cascaded down the curve of its blade and it hummed, a low note of latent power.

She shook her head. "No, it is not mine. It was never mine."

Silently Andrion turned, knelt, and offered the sword to his father. But his father slept on.

Bellasteros's face was translucent, suffused with the sheen of sword and shield; a pure, clear light untainted by the sorcery that had brought him low. For one long, breathless

moment, he seemed to Dana to be that image of his younger
self that had consecrated Gerlac's tomb. Her senses stirred,
her nape pricked. Bellasteros had never chosen the easier path;
now he clung stubbornly to life and duty until his duty was
done. Later, he would earn the death he deserved. Danica, in
choosing this fate for him, worked to some greater purpose. . . .

Andrion did not sense the reassuring vision. His face twisted
with grief and anger and inexpressible weariness. With a muttered curse he stood and thrust the sword back into its serpent-
skin sheath. The skin rippled in circles of light.

Together Dana and Danica lifted the black-plumed helmet
from Andrion's head, unpinned the black cloak, unbuckled
the polished armor, and left him clad only in a chiton. Dana
took the sword from his unresisting fingers and gave it to
Danica, who set it gingerly next to the dusty imperial diadem.

"Go and make your offerings," she said to Andrion and
Dana both, "and take what blessing you can. Forget time and
the rumor of war. Rest in the love of your mother."

Andrion kissed Danica and held her close, letting her stroke
his hair, her own son once again. Then he and Dana turned
hand in hand toward the temple square. Ah, Andrion, Dana
mourned, compromise, always compromise. That he heard;
his hand tightened on hers and his mouth firmed. Neither
would he choose the easy path, only the best one. The wall between them thinned, became transparent, dissipated into
moonlight as clear and hard as crystal.

Ilanit was just concluding the rules of the rites, who might
approach whom, which women were not to participate. Andrion placed a garland of asphodel around Dana's neck,
marking her as a participant; they kissed, but their lips did not
need to touch. They let each other go, silently, without promises, but not without hope.

The games began. Andrion ran and leaped and hurled the
javelin, his face tight with effort, burning as brightly as the incandescent moon above. Dana's heart ached for him, her
body ached for him, her thought swirled and spilled into
resolve; I, too, must play this game, for more than Sabazel.
She turned to Tembujin, took his hand, and led him to her
own little house.

Kerith had strewn the bed with sweet-smelling herbs. The
trembling light of a small oil lamp ignited the shadows with
suggestion. It did not escape Tembujin, but he stood stiffly

just inside the door, confused and wary.

Dana poured a cup of mild pink wine from the pitcher on the table and tore a chunk of bread from the waiting loaf. "Here. Fortify yourself."

"He will no longer fight for you?"

Poor innocent barbarian, knowing only how to take, not how to receive. "He does not own me. And you are no longer our enemy."

Tembujin sipped at the wine, nibbled at the bread. "Why, then?"

"Odd as it may seem, you excite me." And I would rekindle that fire your own people quenched, Dana thought. But if he knew that, he might deny his own lust out of spite. She drained her cup, letting the wine blunt thought, enhance sensation; a furtive pleasure, to permit herself to want him. She approached him, spread his tunic, and set her hands against his chest. Thin, but warm.

He edged away. "You will tease me and then kick me again."

"You deserved that kick," she told him, pursuing him until his back was against the door. She traced the sharp line of his collarbone and noted with suppressed glee that his pulse throbbed in his throat. "You had to be taught never to take a woman by force."

"I have never taken a woman by force," he muttered indignantly.

"No? And you would expect Sarasvati, say, to resist you when your army stands armed to the teeth beside your bed?"

Tembujin frowned, too intelligent to misunderstand her, too stubborn to agree with her. Good, she thought, stubbornness can be fanned back into confidence. She kissed the hollow in his throat, tasting the salt sweetness of his smooth golden skin.

"Sarasvati," he said in a small, taut voice, as if the name discomfited him, "was mine by right of conquest."

"Then you," Dana replied, "by right of conquest are mine." She took the cup away from him and set her lips against his. Yes, it was the kiss she remembered, only now she was the one that devoured his mouth and he—no, he did not resist. His arms closed around her, not in dominance, not in surrender, but in truce.

This was not Andrion, who could freeze her with a frown, who could thrill her with a glance. This was exotic meat, to be savored. She laid him upon the bed and undressed him. He needed more flesh upon his bones, she decided with a calculating glance, but he was naturally lean.

A moment later she found that Tembujin was still strong, so eager to prove his accomplishment in the pleasing arts that she had only to spread her limbs and listen bemusedly to the squeaks and sighs of her own voice. She smiled, and his face blossomed with elation.

It was she who took him, riding him like one of his own ponies, laughing at the irony, at the justice, at the joy of their coupling. The name of Ashtar burst from his lips, stirred the shadows, and called the night wind to caress them both.

Andrion raced among his soldiers, among the local peasantry, among traveling merchants. Burning with rage, he left them all behind. What weakness, he told himself, to think for even a moment that his new toy sword would rouse Bellasteros—and to hope for even a moment that it would not. What weakness to think that he could lie quietly with Dana and forget who he was. He sold her to his enemy to buy allegiance. No, he told himself with a mighty heave of a javelin that earned admiring glances from the other men and from the watching women, and shattered the torchlight into streaming amber pennons —no, it was her choice, and a necessary one. Tembujin could no longer be an enemy. The mother was all-forgiving.

Dana was leading the Khazyari away. Andrion stared at him, forcing the black eyes open with the intensity of his gaze: I give you my friendship freely; we shall see if you are worth it, barbarian.

The muscle in Tembujin's cheek jumped as he tightened his jaw, understanding. Andrion turned, pleased and yet distrustful of his pleasure. Was his lust for power greater than his lust for Dana? he asked himself savagely.

He threw again, flaring with scorn and wounded pride. The spear whistled through the air and struck Sabazian earth with a thud.

Ilanit and Patros walked close together, away from the square, into the night. First they would go to Bellasteros, and the knife would turn again in Patros's heart. Then Ilanit would heal him; after these many years their love was less passion than comfort, soothing, not searing. Another hazard of maturity. Lyris, wearing a garland of asphodel as warily as though it might explode any moment, watched them go with shuttered eyes. Jealousy, Andrion asked himself, or envy? But she had the grace to let them go alone.

The games were over and still he burned, a futile yearning scalding his muscles, his senses. He looked for Kerith and saw her accepting the attentions of one of his own soldiers. He spun, leaped up the steps into the temple and found a guest room with food and bath ready; steam did not, surprisingly, rise from his body as he settled into the water.

Andrion tried to damp his fever by sipping desultorily at a cup of Sabazian wine, but he remained turgid with conflict and desire. At last he blew out the lamp and lay naked on the pallet, contemplating the temple atrium through the doorway. The moon was at its zenith, and while the strains of music had died away in the city, the moonlight itself was music, distant trills spilling down a silver shaft of luminescence into the atrium and the small pool. The pool reflected the light in a wavering glimmer, shaping warriors and gods against the night. And do even the gods know, Andrion wondered, what tomorrow will bring to me, to Dana, to anyone?

A shape blocked his view, and he started. Lyris set her spear against the doorway and stepped into the room. Her angular form was somehow softened by the moonlight, but her words were abrupt. "Has anyone scraped you down?"

"No. I am alone this night."

She knelt down beside him and reached for a nearby strigil. "Then allow me." The scraper rasped his shoulder, raising gooseflesh.

"Why, Lyris?" he asked, gazing back into the atrium. Now the moonpath was dancing, slow and sinuous, like a woman promising rather than teasing.

"I would not have you think," Lyris stated, "that because I am for Sabazel I am against you."

"Now why should I think that?" The light dazzled his eyes. The scent of asphodel filled his nostrils. The strigil scraped the muscles of his back and buttocks. Her hand rested upon his thigh, as neutral a touch as that of his cloak. But, to his amused chagrin, his body responded. Gods, have I no shame? And he reminded himself, This is Sabazel, and the rites of Ashtar, and Lyris wears the garland.

He placed his hand behind her head, drew her down to him and kissed her. Her lips were stiff; not encouraging, but not cold. Had she intended to arouse him, knowing that she was bound to celebrate the rites, and choosing him as a harmless partner? Would this be her penance for her harshness that morning after the cavern? He was not sure if either alternative flattered him. He was not sure if he were making a fool of himself. He did not care.

No amusement shaded her eyes, only incredulity and, perhaps, a furtive longing. "So," she said, sitting beside him and laying down the strigil, "you can give me what no man ever has?"

"I would not be that presumptuous," Andrion replied. "I can only ask: May Gerlac's bastard grandson repay his insult to you, proving that not all men are animals?"

Her lips curved in a wry smile. "I know that some men are honorable. I see Patros's tenderness to Ilanit and to me; I see their passion and realize that Gerlac's demon ghost cauterized that part of me, so that I cannot feel it."

Andrion saw again the twisted body of the old king. His hatred had devoured many, but in the end it was his own soul to which he had laid waste. Tentatively, in apology, he stroked Lyris's face.

"Your audacity intrigues me, my prince." Matter-of-factly she removed her clothes.

Andrion realized what it was Tembujin must be feeling, swollen with need and yet wondering whether he would receive release or a swift kick. That was not far, probably, from what Lyris felt. She lay beside him, and he touched her as gently as he could.

She tolerated his efforts with a forbearance partly grim and partly amused. Andrion had never felt so clumsy. At last, growing impatient, she lifted his shoulders and drew him up between her legs. He found himself enclosed by those strong thighs he had once admired from a less advantageous position. This was too much; sparks blotted his mind and he succumbed to the demands of his body. Every frustration of the last months, of the last hours, knotted within him, tighter and tighter, and he could think nothing, reason nothing, only strain to break that tangle. Then every fiber in his body snapped, the knot burst into tendrils of flame, his breath sobbed the litany and the words were caught by the moonlight and consumed.

Andrion lay wheezing into Lyris's hair. Yes, his muddled thought told him, it was Lyris and not some vivid dream. She had been beautiful once, before an evil priest fed a demon with her maidenhood. Now she was a bleached bone, her spirit an offering to the relentless caprice of the gods. Her eyes, focused beyond him upon the atrium and moving moonpath, sent her faith to the goddess. That, at least, no one could deny her.

She looked around, saw Andrion, gently but firmly rolled him away from her. Her garland was crushed to pulp, smeared pink petals clinging to his damp chest. He stretched, groaning; his mouth was dry, and he swallowed. And suddenly he saw himself and laughed. "Ludicrous, all that gasping and heaving. Ashtar has a sense of humor, to take such as an offering."

"Indeed," Lyris returned, allowing herself a chuckle. With a comradely pat she picked up her clothing and dressed. "It must have been easier," she said, "when all men were enemies. When Sabazel stood alone. I came here too late."

"No, you came here to serve the days of change, the most important of all." He sighed. "Thank you, Lyris."

She glanced down at him, not without sympathy. "Thank you." Hoisting her spear, she was gone.

His body was like lead, inert, and his mind floated free. He drifted up the moonpath, toward a gleaming image that opened its arms to him, blond hair like spun gold and eyes as green as jade. . . . He fell into Ashtar's, into Dana's eyes, and smiling, he slept.

Dawn spilled through the shutters. A hummingbird whirred outside, its swiftly moving wings stitching light to darkness. Dana roused herself and glanced at the sleek body of the Khazyari prince beside her. The legendary lion of the Mohan, she thought with approval, bronze and black and strong.

Andrion, she told herself, was bronze and black and strong. She sent her thought toward him but sensed only silence.

Tembujin stirred, opened his eyes, found Dana's face. His expression was slightly glazed.

"Are you well?" she asked. She nibbled his ear, half concealed behind tangled ends of black hair.

His face suffused with lechery and caution. "Yes, of course."

"No longer weak from your ordeal? Last night you told me you were not at peak form."

He cleared his throat. "Hm. You surprised me then. Now I am no longer surprised."

Dana laughed. Poor barbarian, she thought; does your

courage hide between your legs? His hands closed firmly in the tangled ends of her blond hair. But no, she told herself as he guided her mouth to his, your courage is more complex than that. I give what I can, and you must find the rest within yourself.

His eyes glinted, firelight on jet, a hunted lion turning at bay.

Andrion sat beside Toth's bed, listening intently. When the faint, reedy voice faltered, he held a cup of herbed wine to the old man's lips, lips that were pale iris blue. "You should rest," Andrion told him. "We can talk later."

"Now," the old man insisted. "You must know everything now."

Gods, Andrion sighed to himself, Toth has given his life for me, for Sarasvati and Tembujin. How subtly the gods work. How cruelly.

The words went on, forming images of Baakhun, of Raksula, of Odo and Vlad. Images that tore at each other, jackals fighting over the same piece of carrion. No, not carrion, Andrion reproved himself. They fought for power, as he did. They fought for the Empire.

When the weak voice finally stopped, Andrion felt dirty, caught in a spider's web. The strands, gummed with the remains of the dead, clung to his face and hands. The strands bound his necklace with an unbreakable knot. Tembujin made him angry, but never dirty.

"Thank you," Andrion said to the ancient face on the pillow. "I shall bring a priestess to give you some strengthening brew."

Every breath Toth took was shallower than the last. "Bring me Danica, if you please," he whispered. "Your mother, Danica."

"Certainly." He stepped from the small room into the atrium of the temple. Sunlight glanced across the surface of the pool, and doves preened themselves, cooing, in the rafters. Andrion asked himself abruptly, How does Toth know that my mother is Danica, not Chryse? But he remembered the images of the Khazyari; Toth was a shadow, moving silently just at the fringes of others' lives, never living any passion of his own.

Andrion grimaced; the gods only knew what else Toth had discovered about his family in Iksandarun. Miklos's and

Sarasvati's innocent passion, for example. He really should say something encouraging to Miklos. For his bravery, offer him Sarasvati's hand, after victory—if they survived the spider's web.

He found Danica setting an incense burner close beside Shurzad's sleeping form. The woman's features were drawn fine and clear, a portrait sketched but not colored, surface but no depth. Andrion said a silent prayer for her, and for Patros, who leaned over her and touched her face with sad solicitousness, forced to play out his agony before the world.

Danica settled a coverlet around Valeria's fragile body. The girl smiled at her with the adoration of a child for a kindly grandmother. But her face was no longer innocent; something in the set of her mouth and chin told of her own anguish, played out mutely but no less painfully. And I had a part in that, Andrion chided himself. Patros knelt beside his daughter, kissing her with a tenderness that struck Andrion's heart like a sharp dart. Hatred was easier than love; like strong drink, it first exhilarated and then deadened the drinker.

The burner emitted a silver tendril of smoke. The room filled with the scents of lavender and valerian. Danica led both Patros and Andrion into the atrium. A breeze ruffled the surface of the pool; the mosaic on its bottom seemed to dance, at one moment jumbled squares of color, at others clear, precise pictures of a burning city, of dark horsemen, of a sword flaring in its bearer's hands.

"The possession was broken," Danica told Patros, "when Andrion destroyed the amulet; Valeria was, of course, caught in her mother's spell. Shurzad paid with her own flesh, and is now cleansed."

Andrion thought, I did something right? He remembered the tingling in his hand, the bitter taste of burning flesh in his throat. But he could not be frightened of this power.

As though hearing his thought, Danica took his hand between hers. "I had power once. It was pleasant, and it was terrifying as well. And yet it was still my own decision, how to use that power." She glanced at Patros. "Care for yourself, my friend; I could no longer heal you of a mortal wound, as I did once."

"But you have, today," said Patros, "by healing my family."

"I can heal their bodies. Whether Shurzad wakes filled with remorse or despair or anything at all, I cannot tell. She lived for her spite. Now she knows its futility, but what else does she have?"

"She has my love," Patros protested, "but I could never convince her of that. It is my fault, Danica, that she fell to evil."

"No, no." Danica released her right hand and took his. Slowly Patros's anguished features smoothed and his dark eyes filled with the atrium's light.

Andrion held Danica's left hand, strong and delicate as the wing of a bird, which had once borne the star-shield. She had carried it and her worries and his own infant body all the leagues to Iksandarun. And suddenly he knew that she should come again to Iksandarun, carrying Bellasteros. The wind murmured the name like an anthem, like a dirge.

The sunlight shimmered on the water and the mosaic shifted; a young man, sitting beneath a tapestry stitched with the outspread wings of Sardian Harus, his rich brown eyes considering with a wary pride the tall queen before him.

Andrion reclaimed his hand. But this is my battle! he thought with his own pride. The image shattered and he was immediately contrite. No, this is a battle for all of us—for the Empire, Ashtar, and Harus. Patros bowed his thanks and went in search of Ilanit. Andrion told his mother about Toth.

The old man was dying. His wasted face was touched by shadow, but his eyes were calm. "At last I have returned," he whispered as Danica knelt beside him. "I was born here; here shall I die and offer my soul to Ashtar."

Born here? Andrion repeated to himself.

Danica glanced up at him in bewilderment; he shrugged. She looked back at Toth. "What do you mean?"

"Do you not recognize me, my lady?"

The old man's face seemed to shift somehow, filling and smoothing. Danica gasped. "Tethysinia!"

Toth cackled in pleasure. "One and the same. I rode beside you on the embassy to Iksandarun, when you were little older than your granddaughter Dana. Do you remember?"

"Yes, but . . ." Danica almost stammered in confusion. Andrion shook himself. Toth? The old palace eunuch he had known all of his life? Tethysinia, a Sabazian?

Toth still looked Danica in the face, sparing himself—herself—nothing. "I lusted for an imperial soldier; I would not grace that feeling by saying I loved him. I left our camp to go to him, and I watched from the walls as you were attacked so treacherously by imperial troops. I saw you take the star-shield from your mother's dead hands, and I knew then I had lost Sabazel."

"But you could have returned," Danica frowned, "made atonement, taken up your life where you left it."

"No. I betrayed you, and I earned exile. The soldier died in a fight over a tavern wench and so paid the price, however unwittingly. I cut my hair and took a eunuch's robes and served the palace." Toth's voice was only a wisp of sound, her face drained into transparency.

"Why did you not reveal yourself to me when Bellasteros took the Empire," Danica choked, "when I entered the city at his side? Or later, when I visited his court so many times?"

"I was not worthy, my lady, of you or the conqueror. But I thought I could redeem myself by serving your son, named beloved of the gods." The pale, gentle eyes turned to Andrion.

Andrion felt like a fish pulled suddenly from water to gasp upon the riverbank. He knelt beside his mother and Toth, groping for soothing words. "You have served me, all my life. You served my sister in her hour of need, and you have served us all by bringing Tembujin to us." Gods, to hear his voice say such words. "Toth, Tethysinia, your loyalty is greatest of all."

The old woman smiled, face glowing, wide eyes shimmering with light like the pool in the atrium. And her eyes stayed wide and clear, reflecting the depth of the sky, utterly at peace. Danica sighed and touched the now lifeless hand. "Mother take her soul. She played her role, and now it is over."

Andrion swallowed hard. And I thought he had never felt passion, he mused. "Is nothing real?" he asked. "Is everything I believe only illusion?"

"Perhaps," Danica replied. A breeze keened, crisp and cold, through the temple. A corner of Toth's coverlet fluttered and then flipped neatly over the smooth alabaster face, concealing it. "We must believe in Ashtar, in Harus, in the beneficence of the gods, or we can believe in nothing."

"Beneficence and peace . . ." Andrion swallowed again, and managed to smile.

Arm in arm, Danica and Andrion walked slowly back into the atrium. The day was still glittering bright, etched in crystal and gold and blue, the last gleam of summer. "We shall lay her on a pyre," said Danica to the pool, "and give her the honors due a Sabazian."

The pool splashed, the mosaic rippled. Shurzad's cat crept up to the water, peered in, and patted its reflection with a velvet paw. The reflection was simply that of a domestic cat, innocent and carefree. Danica held out her hand for it to sniff; it rubbed its cheek on her wrist and folded itself around her legs. Danica tickled its belly, and it purred playfully. Andrion could not believe it had stalked the halls of Sardis with such a sinister air. "Qem, small trickster," Danica said to it, accepting no pretense, "welcome to Ashtar's sanctuary."

The third day was cooler, but still clear. Andrion, Dana, and Tembujin stood on a boulder-strewn slope of Cylandra, looking over the breadth of the world. The horizon smoked, blotted with gathering cloud, land blending imperceptibly into azure sky, as if the world contracted around Sabazel.

Tembujin exhaled in a sigh of determination. He sat down on a handy rock and laid out his supplies; horn, sinew, wood, and a pot of lacquer. "So the old creature was really a woman?"

"Yes," said Andrion. He tapped a short Sardian sword against his thigh and eyed Dana, questing for her emotions. Dana eyed him similarly.

"He saved my life," said Tembujin, "by giving me his own food; for that I actually find myself grateful." He, too, glanced at Dana, a brief sideways gleam, and set a strip of horn against the wood. "He served Sarasvati." His hand tightened on the frame of the bow. "Are you aware, Andrion, that Raksula now knows who Sarasvati is?"

"That had occurred to me," Andrion replied with a grimace. "All the more reason to secure a swift victory." And he proffered the sword to Tembujin.

Tembujin took it, cocking his head to the side. "You would trust me with these weapons, bow and sword?"

"Yes."

Tembujin cleared his throat. "I shall make a bow for you, Dana, as well. That long bow is not good enough." He snapped wood and horn and they sang, piercingly sharp.

"Ah?" asked Dana, with some amusement.

Good, Andrion told himself dispassionately, he finds himself; he is too fine a beast to waste. Tembujin glanced up at him, and their eyes met and held. The black eyes gleamed with a wry humor of their own. That bow is not good enough for Dana, those eyes said, but you, Andrion, are.

Andrion bowed. Turning, he laughed quietly at himself, at the game he played. He took Dana's hand and together they walked down the mountain slope, leaving Tembujin alone. The persistent creak of horn and wood followed them. A falcon circled far above, watching, and they saluted it.

Dana's little house was cold and silent. She lit a fire in a brazier; the coals hissed and snapped like Solifrax leaving its sheath. No, Andrion thought, today I am the sword and Dana my sheath. . . . You are incorrigible, he informed himself with a smile. Still smiling, he took Dana in his arms. "I shall never love another as I love you," he said. There, choose complication, and accept it.

"No one and no thing can break that which binds us," she returned. Her eyes opened to his, clear gemstones reflecting everything, hiding nothing.

They fed each other small bites of summer fruit until it was gone. They hid under the coverlet and made love with an intense, bittersweet joy. They lay knotted together, warm and content, and for a time they were one.

Outside the room the day faded, overtaken by cloud. The overripe harvest moon, beginning to decay, tried futilely to flee the racing clouds of winter and a wind tainted with the tang of cold iron.

Chapter Eighteen

ILANIT'S SENTRIES HAD saluted her as she and her Companions left the high plain sacred to Ashtar and entered the world of men; now they remained hidden in the folds of land leading toward Cylandra. Cylandra itself was a silver and lavender suggestion to the west, a memory at the rim of a smoked-glass sky.

The imperial encampment resembled an efficient termite hill. Shurzad and Valeria were consigned to their servants; Nikander ushered Andrion and Patros, Ilanit and Lyris into the great cloth-of-gold pavilion. Miklos, his face hard and sober, took his place by the doorway. Even in the early afternoon the braziers flared with glowing coals, forming a pocket of warmth against the chill.

Andrion sat gingerly back in his father's chair; to that, he thought, he was also becoming accustomed. And yet the still, sleeping face of the emperor seemed always just in the corner of his eye. His hand twitched Solifrax up and down, smacking it gently across his thigh, the serpent-skin sheath glimmering in brief rings of light. He caught himself, stilled his hand, and a moment later found himself twitching it again. Lyris smiled thinly at him, making some silent if not exactly complimentary remark on his manhood. He ignored her, focusing on Nikander's words.

"The Khazyari cannot take us by surprise, but neither can we surprise them. Two scouts have disappeared; we must assume they were taken."

Andrion winced. Patros nodded gravely, his dark eyes never leaving Nikander's face, letting no personal pain come between him and his duty.

"Our new cavalry units are training well," Nikander went

on, "and we should find ourselves much more flexible than in the days of the phalanx."

The phalanx, Andrion thought. The square of legionaries bristling with spears against which the Empire had dashed itself to bits. Around which the Khazyari ponies could run circles. "Your plan has worked," he said approvingly to Patros. "The barbarians, complacent, believe us to be ripe for the plucking."

Patros bowed, grateful for the compliment, but troubling to point out, "Tembujin says that the Khazyari do not like the heat of summer here, and that, taken with their uncertainty as to our moves, also slowed them."

The whistle of a bowstring came faintly through the sides of the pavilion. Then another, followed by a solid double smack. Tembujin's voice cried out in approbation. Dana studies her new weapon, Andrion told himself. It begins. Solifrax flicked across his leg and his blood drummed in his ears.

"If I may," said Ilanit courteously to Nikander, and he deferred to her. "I would not like to meet the Khazyari horsemen on the open plains, new cavalry units or no. Can we not draw them into the rougher country on our southern borders, into the valley of the Galel?"

"If they cannot use horses to advantage there, neither can we," said Patros. "Even our chariots would be useless."

So much for my fond image of myself astride Ventalidar, leading a cavalry charge, Andrion thought.

"We are not as accomplished with horses as they are," Nikander said. No one disputed him.

"We have an advantage," said Andrion, and every face turned to him. He wanted for one irrational moment to glance behind him; surely Bellasteros stood there, drawing those respectful looks. But he did not. "We know this land. We have another in that the best Khazyari officer is now loyal to us. He should, by the way, have a white horse to ride, befitting his rank."

"Ah," said Nikander sagely. And to Miklos, "See to it."

Miklos stood a moment, disbelieving. Then he executed a tight about-face and disappeared. Andrion's wrist flexed in irritation; I have swallowed my anger until I choked on it, why can you not? Solifrax slapped his thigh and stung his flesh.

Another flight of arrows outside. Ordered marching steps and a complementary patter of hooves. Shouted commands. A breeze jangled, faintly but perceptibly, through the pennons above the pavilion. Andrion laid his sword beside him and leaned forward, intent.

"I have sent half a legion up the Jorniyeh, past Azervinah," said Nikander, "to intercept the Khazyari as they retreat from Sabazel."

Lyris's face darkened. Yes, of course, Andrion thought, to her and to himself as well, they will retreat.

Dana bent her new bow. It was smaller than her other one, but more powerful; the hum of the string was like the hum of her body when touched by a man—no, she scolded herself, the rites are over. She narrowed her eyes, gauging the tide of her blood. Too fast, pulsing in dread and anticipation mingled. Between heartbeats she flicked her thumb. The bowstring snapped and the arrow hissed, cleaving the chill air, into the wooden target.

"Good," said Tembujin beside her. He raised his own bow and sighted, glancing upward; the scarlet and purple pennons above the pavilion lifted and began to stream outward in a breeze. "The wind," he protested, "is the bowman's worst enemy." He loosed his arrow and it went wide of the mark.

"No," Dana chuckled. "For us the wind is a friend. Work with it." She nocked an arrow, sighted. The rushing tide of her blood, and the wind murmuring through her hair, guiding her . . . There. Perfect shot. She turned with a grin of triumph to Tembujin.

With an exasperated roll of his eyes, he bent his bow again.

Andrion and the others were leaving the pavilion. Patros gathered his officers and lectured them, his right hand marking cadence in his left palm, every head nodding rhythm. That is the Patros my mother loves, Dana thought with a smile. That is my father.

The Companions stood attentively as Lyris explained the tactics; their mothers had trekked with Ilanit and Danica, with Patros and Bellasteros, once before to Iksandarun. Dana's smile faded into a sigh.

Andrion stood alone, isolated by a shell of rank and manner, less severe than sardonic. Several passing legionaries, some Sardian dark, some imperial fair, whose fathers had like as not been enemies, nudged each other and exchanged wide-eyed, awed asides. One young man almost tripped over a tent brace, so intent was he on the solitary figure of the prince.

Nikander turned to pursue some question tendered by a centurion. Patros dismissed his officers. Ilanit leaned close to him and said from the corner of her mouth, "So Sabazel rides again to the aid of Sardis. We have played this game once before, have we not?"

"Not quite the same, my lady," he returned. "Now we are one." He touched the rim of the star-shield and it rang gently.

Tembujin, at Dana's elbow, muttered an oath. She looked around. Miklos stood there, offering Tembujin the reins of a horse. The odlok set aside his bow and took the reins, cautiously, as if fearing they were poisoned. Miklos turned on his heel and strode away. Andrion frowned slightly at the stiffness of Miklos's departing back.

Tembujin stared in pleased surprise. Then, realizing how much his expression revealed, he assumed an air of indifference. He offered his hand to the horse. It snuffled curiously and snorted, accepting him. Tembujin proceeded to inspect the horse's legs and flanks, skilled fingers testing each muscle and tendon. The beast was a tall gelding, silver-white in the misty light; Tembujin noted the animal's lack of virility and turned, one eyebrow arched high, to Andrion.

Andrion bent in a stiff, formal bow. "A token of my friendship, Prince Tembujin."

"And a warning to respect those women you protect, Prince Andrion?"

Andrion grinned.

"My thanks," growled Tembujin, not without humor. He scratched the horse's neck. It rubbed its muzzle against his tunic; if it had been a cat, it would have purred. Tembujin smiled.

Andrion rocked back on his heels, pleased with himself.

"I need no man's protection," Dana said, nettled, to no one in particular. She loosed another arrow, which narrowly missed Bonifacio as he strolled through the range, surrounded by servants and acolytes like sweeping robes. He started, glared at her. She smiled blandly back.

Nikander murmured an order, and immediately the legionaries gathered in orderly rows. Miklos brought the remaining bronze falcon from the pavilion and grounded its pole beside Andrion. Bonifacio lifted Bellasteros's helmet from a box. A brief ray of sun sliced the clouds, laying a golden aureole about it. The crimson plume rippled in the wind as if it were a living creature, a hatchling, trying its wings.

No, there was the hatchling, Dana mused. Andrion's eyes
absorbed the glimmer of light on the helmet and on the falcon, a mingled flame of pleasure and horror filling their
depths. His own black plume fluttered, and his black cloak
billowed about his slender body. A body taut with a complex
beauty . . .

Bonifacio began the prayer, "To victory, and the embrace
of Harus." To Ashtar, Dana thought, and she abandoned her
musings.

Day passed almost imperceptibly into night. Andrion tried to
sleep. The darkness around him bristled with black-barbed arrows; through them came Tembujin, his face stretched tight to
the bone, riding a pale horse.

Andrion woke. The world was consumed in the crimson
folds of Bellasteros's cloak, red flames leaping from the neat
rows of tents, from the pavilion; greedy flames hissing upward
to stain the moon with blood.

He was still dreaming. He struggled again to wakefulness.
The moon was a silver blaze overhead, and the Companions of
Sabazel danced naked in its light, their supple limbs spangled
with the star-sheen of the shield.

Still he dreamed. He moaned, tossing on his narrow camp
bed. He saw through the opening of the tent the rising sun, a
thin crescent of gold like the blade of Solifrax. The moon contracted, became a many pointed star at the tip of the sun, and
the horizon was a gold chain binding them together. The
horizon clotted, and tendrils of smoke coiled upward to
become a thick-cabled spider's web encompassing sun, moon,
star, and bringing them down into the mud outside the inn in
Bellastria.

Andrion awoke and sat trembling among tumbled blankets,
waiting to see what new manifestation would greet him. The
darkness outside was thinning to a gray shot with rain. The
chill ate to his bones; he could hardly sense his own body, as if
it were not really his but a corpse's.

The tent flap moved. Andrion tensed; Miklos looked in.
"Ah, my lord, you are awake; the legions are forming, my
lord."

So he really was awake this time. He wondered if he perhaps
preferred one of his nightmares to this chill reality. He
wondered if his title in Miklos's voice became a sneer.

The young soldier blew flame into the smoldering coals in a

nearby brazier. In the sudden scarlet light his face was clear and steady. No, he did not sneer. Is loyalty the greater, Andrion asked himself, when it is so hard to bear? Groaning, he rose to his feet and reached for food, clothing, weapons.

Ventalidar's coat steamed. Gratefully, Andrion mounted his broad, warm back and turned his head toward the gathered officers. Behind them the legionaries were wraiths in the hazy dawn light, illusions of men, not flesh and blood. Ilanit's shield was a dull brass disk. The bronze falcon drooped upon its perch.

Tembujin was, indeed, a vision of death. His damp black hair matted his forehead and temples, and his cheekbones were sharp below brittle eyes. "You wish no armor?" Andrion asked him.

"Perhaps I was meant to die at the hands of my own people," Tembujin returned, lips stiff. "Perhaps you only delayed the inevitable."

Andrion could not reply. We are all fey, he thought; death no longer frightens us. But we must prevail.

He drew Solifrax and flourished it with an arm so tense it shivered. The sword was a quick stroke of lightning, flaring and then gone. Trumpets brayed, flat under the lowering sky, and with a mutter of resignation the imperial army moved. There should be more than this, Andrion thought; I have anticipated this day for three months and more. Banners should be flying, the troops should sing raucous war hymns, a falcon should screech overhead. But even Ventalidar plodded like a plow horse through the mud. His blood was torpid in his veins.

He laid Solifrax along his thigh, where it hummed faintly beneath the weeping of the rain. Perhaps it, too, steamed. He would let himself believe so.

The great khan seemed shrunken, his face darkened by decay; his high plucked forehead was as furrowed as if some nightmare fouled even his waking hours. His massive shoulders slumped and his huge hands trembled. He surveyed the damp, chill dawn absently, not quite catching its significance.

"You have drunk too much kviss these last months," Raksula hissed. She was dressed in the tunic, breeches, and long dagger of a warrior.

Baakhun turned ponderously. He did not recognize her. With a grunt he turned back to the people arrayed before him.

He tried to straighten his back and failed.

The sun was a bloody stain on the horizon. To one side huddled the burdened camels, the herds of sheep, the families of the Khazyari. To the other waited the ranks of warriors beneath their standards. The only breeze stirring was their muttered thirst for battle. Odo stood before them, a scarlet dagger in each hand, grinning over the mutilated bodies of two imperial scouts. "To a successful conclusion to our hunt!" the shaman squealed. "To victory, death, and the embrace of Khalingu!"

Raksula's face, ferret-thin, ferret-sharp, was engraved with a scowl. The scouts had said remarkably little before they died, considering the persuasions she had used, but they had been unable to conceal the presence in the imperial army of the black prince and his sword of power. Raksula flexed and loosed her hand as if it still stung from the burning amulet. Her mouth tightened to a pitiless slit.

Vlad stood beside Baakhun, slack-lipped, watching the army like toys gathered for his amusement. The carved plaque of the odlok hung lopsided on his tunic. With a muttered imprecation, Raksula straightened it. He cleared his throat and spat onto her boots. She tweaked his small, scrubby tail of hair, and he scuttled like a spider onto his pony.

Slaves hitched ponies to the cart carrying Khalingu's image. Odo clambered up and seized the reins. He began a tuneless chant, eerie rising and falling phrases that rose and then fell back, at one with the chill and damp of the dawn. The cart lumbered over the bodies of the scouts.

Voices took up Odo's chant, wailing of the blood and death that would warm such an unpromising day. The song swelled. The plain shuddered.

With a screech of ecstasy a young woman threw herself beneath the cart. It bumped over her body, leaving the muddy grass mottled with scarlet. A warrior leaped, and then a woman threw her child into its gruesome path. Odo's voice wound upward again, shrill enough to pierce the cloud, and the shrieks of the Khazyari followed it, consuming, compelling. Baakhun watched stolidly; Raksula licked her lips in anticipation. "Bring me the necklace," she murmured. "The necklace, and then the sword and the Empire. Qem has betrayed you, but I shall not, I am your most loyal servant."

The hangings around the god were as dense and gray as the sky. From within came a brief scrabbling, as of claws unsheathed and then drawn back again, and the smack-click of yawning lips and teeth. The rain fell in gauzy veils, shrouding the bodies of the sacrifices. The chant wavered across the plain and the cart rolled on.

The day swirled, steadied, swirled again. Time ended. To Andrion the world was the cold north wind that cut through cloak and armor and flesh. It was the hard rock against his shoulder and the tantalizing scent of damp earth in his throat. His hand was clenched so tightly on the hilt of Solifrax that it had long since ceased to feel it. Ventalidar huddled aggrievedly behind him, Patros knelt beside him; the Sabazians crouched in a knot across a narrow gully, Dana's slender form beside Kerith's, Lyris leaning over a rock with spear poised, watchful as a hunting wolf. Tembujin stood beside his horse, slapping the reins across his leg, features revealing nothing.

The valley of the Galel lay before them, serrated stone stretching past a watercourse to a murky horizon that could as well have been the far rim of the world as the far rim of the valley. Soggy tamarisk clung like moss to the tumbled rocks; a discordant wind moaned around stone spires like the ruins of an ancient city. Runnels of water splashed gently at the edge of perception. A snake poured down a nearby crevice and disappeared into the underworld.

Andrion realized then that not only was he hearing wind and water; distant shouts echoed through the tiered rocks. Nikander's force had engaged the enemy and drawn them hither; the armies, lumbering behemoths, jockeyed for position. He released Solifrax, flexed his hand until the blood flowed again, drew the blade from the sheath. It rang faintly and thrilled to his touch.

The sides of the valley seemed to ripple as the waiting soldiers stirred into alertness and the wind clattered with metal striking metal. Ilanit lifted her shield and the star pulsed in slow rivulets of quicksilver.

A fine chill mist sifted over the valley, obscuring the far rim. Then dim shapes materialized in the hazy distance. Andrion squinted and saw his own soldiers moving slowly, deliberately, through the rocks. That horseman was Nikander, no doubt; the old turtle orchestrated his "retreat," moving just fast enough to entice but not lose his pursuers.

Patros whispered hoarsely, a handsbreadth from Andrion's ear, "Nikander rides into the thick of battle as if riding to an inspection, and emerges not only unscathed but victorious."

Victorious, Andrion repeated silently.

Nikander's legionaries melted away. Khazyari warriors and ponies, tenuous beetle shapes, spilled with unearthly shouts down the watercourse and overran a few laggard imperial soldiers. Nikander appeared beside Andrion, who started, his teeth snapping, his sword jerking. Diplomatically, Nikander did not notice. The keening of the Khazyari resonated in the stones, in the air, in Andrion's blood. The mist was a chill mantle deadening the world, but he was not cold.

Tembujin leaped onto his horse and leaned over to Dana, saying something; she grasped her bow, steadied her quiver, pulled herself up behind him. The white horse faded into the underbrush.

Where were they going? Andrion ran his tongue over dry lips. It was too late now to doubt Tembujin's loyalty. The Khazyari were here, beginning to hesitate, to become suspicious. From Toth's vivid descriptions, Andrion recognized the bulk of Baakhun in the vanguard; that weasel-faced woman beside him, coiffed with a multitude of tiny plaits, must be Raksula. And beside her was the bloated form of Vlad, Tembujin's half-brother. The Horde was not crimson but black, a flood filling the valley, their ponies picking a path among the water-smoothed rocks of the stream.

Andrion glanced at Patros, at Nikander, at Ilanit. They awaited his signal. A flame kindled in his belly, a hot and consuming hatred. He rose, raising Solifrax, stretching toward the sky. Now! "In the name of the god!" he shouted through clenched teeth, calling no god by name. He leaped onto a boulder. The crystalline blade of the sword gathered the light of the shrouded sun and blazed, ringing him with a nimbus of fire. With echoing shouts imperial soldiers erupted from every shadow.

Arrows hissed like angry wasps past his ears. Yes, he thought dispassionately, I make an excellent target. One of those bows could shoot a shaft right through my carapace. He seized the hilt of Solifrax with both hands and jumped into the surging throng of soldiers; they buoyed him up, carrying him toward the Khazyari.

The barbarians were fast, Harus, yes; they turned with gleeful shouts and swarmed toward their attackers. One warrior was pulled from his horse and cut to pieces. And another; Solifrax shrieked and the dark face was colored suddenly red.

The sword seemed to move of itself, striking as fast as a venomous snake. Andrion grasped one thought plummeting through seething senses: vengeance at last.

The Khazyari boiled around him. The legionaries disappeared and he stood beside Ilanit, sword and shield pealing in fierce melody, icy wind pealing above them and sweeping the air free of rain. His body stretched and coiled, burning in an ecstasy of power. He was Solifrax, he was death; the glow of the sword and the wings of his cloak encompassed the world. "For Bellasteros!" he shouted, and Lyris on his other side screamed, "For Sabazel!"

The Khazyari slipped in the mud, fell over rocks, became waving equine and human limbs tangled in one bloody mass. But they kept coming, bronzed faces, black eyes in narrow slits. . . . Andrion's mind howled. He knew nothing else.

Dana and Tembujin stood on a ledge that wound along the rocky side of the valley. The sound of the battle, the shouts of men and the screams of horses, eddied upward and burst about them. There was Andrion, black cloak flying, sword darting like a tongue of flame. There was the star-shield of Sabazel shining like the face of the moon beside him. Their weapons were so bright they cast shadows, drawing the Khazyari like moths to the flame.

The Horde swarmed over the valley. Dana set arrow to bow, searched for a target in the indistinct mass below, fired. The arrow blossomed suddenly from the chest of a warrior and he fell into the melee. An odd feeling, Dana thought, to kill a man; I do not really like it. Tembujin stood somberly beside her, offering no comfort.

For every Khazyari horse that slipped and fell in the mud, so did an imperial soldier. Dana could not see that either side was the more powerful. She fired again and again into the confusion, until her arm ached and sweat began to trickle down her face. Ashtar! Andrion, Ilanit, Kerith, Patros . . . Silently Tembujin handed her most of his arrows. He leaped onto his horse and guided it along the ledge.

Imperial troopers blocked the ravines leading from the valley, forcing the Khazyari back upon themselves. Miklos propped the falson standard beside Ventalidar and plunged into the fray, shouting frenzied curses. From the depth of the Khazyari, Raksula saw the shining crescent of Solifrax and the shining disk of the star-shield. She, too, turned toward them, mouth open, eyes gleaming. Vlad clung desperately to his horse. A thin string of spittle hung from the corner of his mouth.

Baakhun's slightly vague eyes snapped into focus. Through the mist and rocks lining the valley gleamed a white horse, carrying a black-haired man with the bearing of an odlok. "Tembujin!" cried Baakhun. "He haunts me; I betrayed him and he haunts me!"

For a moment it seemed as if the entire struggling mass halted, frozen. Tembujin and his horse winked in and out, a taunting phantom above the battle. Tears streamed down Baakhun's sagging cheeks and he forced his way through his guard, seeing nothing but the shape of his dishonored son. "Tembujin!" The wind took the name and repeated it, over and over down the rocky galleries.

The Khazyari quailed. Andrion glanced at Tembujin's ghostly shape and laughed with a feral joy, urging his own soldiers forward. Ilanit began the Sabazian paean and he repeated it, their clear voices penetrating the battle and becoming one with the song of the wind. Solifrax blazed. Raksula spun in a circle, torn between sword and stunned Baakhun, cursing imperial soldiers and Khazyari warriors alike. The dagger she held leaped out, again and again, splattering her hand with blood.

Tembujin slipped from his horse and knelt beside Dana. "There," he said, his voice oddly strangled, "the lion standard of the khan. See, Baakhun, who was my father." Dana glanced at him, wondering if she should be frightened of his mood, his face and eyes radiant with hatred. But it was an intoxicating mood, and her head spun dizzily with it.

She nocked an arrow, as did he. Simultaneously they aimed. Baakhun's upturned face did not falter. But Tembujin's hand did. For just a moment his cheeks paled and his lips parted, uncertain. Raksula grabbed Baakhun's bridle and began to lead him back into the midst of his guard.

"He will escape!" cried Dana, hardly recognizing that urgent voice as her own. The wind pummeled her; her heart leaped. Her thumb snapped. Tembujin's bowstring shrieked. Two arrows arced through the air and one of them struck deep into Baakhun's chest.

With mild surprise the khan noted the arrow. He smiled, and died. Raksula screeched in rage. With hysterical strength she dragged Baakhun's inert body from his horse to hers. Vlad turned to see his father's face staring vacantly at him, blasted clean of regret and sorrow. Vlad wailed in dismay and jerked his pony around, overrunning his own warriors in his haste to be away from the battle. Raksula followed him with the body of the khan, screaming in an apoplectic frenzy, "They think we shall meekly retreat, but we shall strike and strike again! They cannot beguile us with evil sorcery, parading an image of the dead before us!" The Khazyari fell back.

Tembujin bent double over his bow, as though the arrow lodged in his own heart. Dana stopped herself in the midst of a victorious gesture. Her mind spun; love, death, loyalty, and sacrifice. She touched his arm but he did not respond.

The muddy course of the Galel suddenly filled with swirling brown water. Many of the Khazyari ponies were swept from their feet, and the warriors they bore smacked into the water and could not rise before imperial troops were upon them. The river flowed on, streaked with scarlet.

Nikander leaped onto his horse, ordering soldiers to follow him. They poured down the valley, pursuing the fleeing Khazyari, leaving a flotsam of mangled bodies behind.

A shaft of sunlight sliced beneath the clouds. The distant rim of the valley leaped into clarity, a sharp brass edge against a sky sketched in harsh chiaroscuro. Then the light failed, and the rain fell again.

Andrion's throat was raw. His arms and shoulders trembled. His armor seemed to be scummed with ice. His thoughts tumbled like brush in the torrent of the Galel. Harus, the battle lasted all afternoon, it seemed but a few minute's work. My nightmares had more substance. . . .

Baakhun had fallen. Whose bow had fired the arrow, Dana's or Tembujin's? Or did it even matter? The deed was done.

Ventalidar stood behind him, watching him. Solifrax fell from his nerveless fingers. He laid his face against the horse's warm, richly scented shoulder, and concealing himself with a crooked arm, sobbed.

Ventalidar nuzzled him. The spate of tears ended as quickly as it had begun; his mind steadied. Andrion wiped his face with a corner of his cloak and rescued Solifrax. He looked sheepishly around. Lyris leaned against a nearby rock, tight-lipped, as Patros wrapped a bloody cut on her thigh.

"Did we win?" Andrion croaked.

Patros was pale but composed. "Since they withdrew, and since their leader was killed, I suppose we won this battle at the least."

"This battle," nodded Andrion. "At the least."

"Why in Ashtar's name," said Lyris, "did you rush into the thick of the fray like that? We thought we should surely lose you."

"Ah," Andrion said. "Did you think you were protecting me?"

Lyris shrugged, and thanked Patros with a strained smile.

Andrion looked down at himself; his hands were caked with blood, but little of it seemed to be his own. He had suffered only a scratch or two on his arms. The curved blade of Solifrax was as clean and bright as ever. In that moment he hated its hypocrisy. He thrust it into its sheath, but it hung heavy with reproof at his side.

The brief flood drained away, leaving blood- and mud-mottled bodies heaped behind it. The slaughter of the Khazyari ponies was appalling; they lay everywhere, limbs askew, great dark eyes staring into a spectral sky. And was the slaughter of men any less appalling? Andrion demanded of himself. Soldiers, too, lay everywhere, some crying in feeble voices, too many silent.

Kerith was a bloodied shape nearby, her face twisted in agony, teeth sunk into her lower lip. Dana held her friend's head in her lap as Ilanit carefully bound the wound. And when had Dana come back, her quiver empty?

She looked up, her eyes meeting Andrion's. They swam in grief and horror. Is this the battle you wished for in the tomb? he asked her mutely. A clean battle in the open air? Her eyes fell, her face concealed by the hard shell of her helmet. He cursed himself for mocking her.

Tembujin leaned as if sorely wounded over the neck of his horse. Was he? But no, he sat up, forcing his back erect with an almost audible crack.

Andrion tried to summon vindictive glee—your father for mine, barbarian—but there was no glee left in him. The same game devoured them all. He mounted Ventalidar and went to help the gathering of the wounded.

Shadowed day clotted into lightless night. The torches of burial squads and the pyres of dead horses flickered crazily along the valley of the Galel, driven by a moaning wind. Andrion stood at the edge of the encampment as the Sabazians prepared to take their dead and wounded home. "We have lost five," Ilanit told him wearily, her shield muted on her arm. "I shall bring twenty more to ride beside you to Iksandarun, now that the enemy has been turned from Sabazel."

Andrion could think of nothing to say, so he said, "Thank you."

Dana set her hand on his stubbled cheek, searching his eyes as if to touch the ragged edge of his soul. Their breaths were mingled clouds of frost in the cold night. Not even a waning moon lit their faces.

Then the women were gone, leaving only the sound of hoofbeats to echo with uncanny clarity down the wind. Patros sighed and turned his harrowed face to Andrion. "Are you well?"

"Yes." They parted, each to his own duty.

Andrion's eyes seemed to be filled with half the rocks in the Galel. But he walked doggedly through the encampment, letting wounded soldiers touch the hilt of Solifrax, making weak jests with exhausted ones, soothing the grief of the camp followers whose men had not returned. The night fluttered, torchlight streaming about him, worshiping faces smearing into garish, tragic masks.

The bronze falcon followed him, borne by a haggard Miklos. He saw as in a delirium that Shurzad worked with the surgeons, her nine fingers splashed with blood and bile. Her kohl-rimmed eyes above her veil were dazed by the knowledge of the suffering of the soldiers who quieted at her touch.

Andrion dismissed Miklos. He turned, disoriented by his own camp. He saw Tembujin sitting cross-legged, shoulders bowed, alone and aloof outside his own tent. A torch guttered above him, and its uncertain brazen light made glistening tracks of the tears on his cheeks.

And I expected him to be battle-hardened, Andrion thought. Soon, I may see my own father die.

A gray shape flowed through the shadows. Shurzad's cat wrapped itself around Tembujin's legs. The Khazyari did not react. Then another shape appeared, a slender woman, large liquid eyes peering guilelessly above a carefully tied veil. "Ah," said Valeria's soft voice, "there you are, you naughty beast. I am sorry, my lord Tembujin, if he annoys you."

Tembujin hastily rubbed his sleeve across his eyes. "No, my lady Valeria," he said, clearing his throat. "He does not annoy me."

Valeria swept the cat into her arms, where it lay as relaxed as a fur drape, its far from guileless amber eyes smirking at Tembujin. "Ah," the girl murmured, "good night, then." She retreated with a rustle of linen and a faint odor of violets. Tembujin stared after her.

So she, too, tends the wounded, Andrion thought. Why not me? Because I am strong, strong. He plodded to his own quarters, the pale faces of the dead following him. I am not wounded, he told them. More battles lie before me, Iksandarun must be taken, this is but the beginning. . . .

He sat for a long time contemplating the purity of Solifrax, not bothering to wrap his cloak around him or light the brazier; nothing could turn the chill of this night. He ended the day the way he had begun it, cold and numb, caught in the coils of nightmare.

Chapter Nineteen

A FALCON CIRCLED a sky of deep, clear, brittle sapphire. Ashtar's eye, Andrion told himself. The depth of her thought suspended a spectral waning moon, a wisp of light that was like her mercy. . . . If I cannot believe in the gods, he decided, I shall have to believe in myself. I cannot believe in nothing.

Even here, at the borders of Sabazel, ashes swirled in a gentle wind and the acrid scent of the funeral pyre lingered, the last traces of the Sabazians dead in the battle of the Galel. The Sabazians dead for me, Andrion thought. And for him. Several women bore a litter toward a waiting ox cart, the body of Bellasteros carried at last from its sanctuary.

No, Andrion wanted to scream at the solemn faces, no, this is not a funeral, he will yet wake!

The wind rippled the banners of a waiting honor guard. The cart received the litter. Ilanit raised the shield in salute, and the morning sun hissed across its surface like wind stirring water in the bronze basin. Danica pressed something into Andrion's hand. It was the diadem of the Empire, a gold circlet newly polished and so cold it burned his fingers.

What did she mean? He fought in his father's name, not his own. And yet . . . "Would it be easier," he asked his mother, "if he had died a hero's death in Iksandarun, as he intended before I forced him to run away, before I brought him to this?"

"No," replied Danica. "The goddess has her purposes."

The crisp green eyes were calm, resigned, but to Andrion they were shadowed by the image of the black warrior, Bellasteros's mortality. He spun about, went to the cart, lifted the protective hangings and placed the diadem on Bellasteros's silver hair. The crown no longer fit him; it was

219

too big, and tilted rakishly over his brow. His closed eyes
did not open, and the crescent shadows of his lashes on his
hollow cheeks did not waver.

"The diadem is yours, Father," Andrion whispered so that
only Bellasteros could hear. "But the sword is mine now; the
horse has always been mine and never yours. . . ." He inhaled
with a shudder, wondering if he uttered blasphemy. "Father, I
carry your burden, I fight your battles, have I not earned the
sword?" The still face did not change. The falcon screeched
overhead, and the hangings snapped in the breeze. What did
you expect? Andrion asked himself.

Tembujin peered over his shoulder. "The emperor, your
father?"

"Yes," Andrion replied, too dull to resent his curiosity.

Tembujin's mouth twisted in a wry smile. "Toth did not
keep me alive with food alone, but with tales of gods and ancient heroes and the exploits of your parents before you were
born." He glanced at Danica cautiously, suspecting, perhaps,
what it meant to spring from such stock.

"I am sorry, Andrion, I had a part in bringing him to this."
Tembujin stooped to inspect one of his horse's hooves, pretending to find some pebble imbedded within.

Ah, thought Andrion. So you try to be my friend. He was
not sure he liked that thought. But it was little enough to forgive another man, when the gods themselves were ultimately
unforgiving.

Ventalidar snuffled the cool, clear air and shook his mane
as though to say, enough of this maudlin introspection, let us
dance across the world. Andrion had to grin as he leaped onto
her back. Danica, with the plump turtledove of Shandir beside
her, sat ready behind the oxen. Lyris frowned down at her
sword, debating whether it was sharp enough for the task
ahead. Ilanit contemplated the sky, listening to resonances
in the wind.

Dana reined up beside Andrion. "Is Kerith well?" he had
enough wit to ask her.

"Well enough," Dana replied, "so long as she stays here."

"I shall return you to her side before the snow flies," he
said, and was warmed by Dana's smile.

The ox cart creaked, bearing the weight of his past. The
Companions of Sabazel turned away from their own borders
and followed him over the rim of the world.

●   ●   ●

Andrion had realized, even as he gave it, that his promise to Dana was a rash one. The snow would probably fly well before they could even approach Iksandarun, let alone before the Sabazians could return to their home. But such rash promises were, it seemed, part of the language of love.

The imperial army moved laboriously south. Scouts brought word that the Khazyari had indeed been turned away from the pass; suffering from the loss of so many of their ponies, the barbarians seemed to turn tail and run. But as Nikander took the trouble to point out, they could well have learned the virtues of playing dead. Patros kept scouts, the questing senses of the legions, moving briskly into the great southern plain.

Was Tembujin, Andrion wondered, galled by his people's seeming meekness? He looked up from burnishing the bright blade of Solifrax, across the gold pavilion to where Tembujin made some minor adjustment to his bow. "We should move faster," Andrion said to Patros, seated at a writing table nearby. "We must harass them, give them no time to regroup."

Patros laid down his quill, but it was Tembujin who answered. "Having you behind them should be harassment enough."

Andrion exchanged a glance with Patros; Tembujin spoke of his tribe in the third person. "Governor," he said, "what shall we do with the Khazyari? Reinstate Tembujin to his proper role as khan?" He gestured expansively. "We could settle them on the moor north of Iksandarun, calling it Khazyaristan, perhaps. The Empire has room for a nomadic tribe."

The odlok glanced up, fully aware he was being tested. "You would not kill them—us—all?"

"I would rather free the Khazyari of Raksula's evil influence," Andrion replied. Tembujin's face darkened and his fingers snapped the bowstring in a short, sharp gesture.

"We have to defeat them first," said Patros. "Then we can be magnanimous."

"To a khan I can trust," added Andrion.

Tembujin's eyes were glittering slate, opaque, unreadable. "Have you not yet learned to trust me?" he said to Andrion and Patros both. "I know what ambitions I can now afford, and what my loyalties must be. Building is much harder than destroying, but in the end more profitable." For just a moment his eyes widened, letting Andrion see within. Then Tem-

bujin tucked one corner of his mouth into an ironic smile and
bent again to his bow.

Andrion leaned back in his chair, almost breathless. Solifrax hummed across his lap, glistening with a brief aura of
light. Beautiful, Andrion thought. As beautiful and as compelling as death.

The moon died, was swept away by the sun, appeared again as
a glaucous sliver riding the morning sky to the army's left. The
days were punctuated by violent but inconclusive skirmishes as
the Khazyari faded before them. The world was sustained in a
russet haze of autumn, the plains like rippling fluid bronze,
the sky a blue so crisp it made Andrion ache.

Tembujin resumed tying his hair into a short, stubborn tail.
Thank Sarasvati, thought Andrion, for trimming his manhood so nicely. The new moon after the fall equinox was
Sarasvati's birthday, noted by a prayer to the crimson-plumed
helmet: Bellasteros, protect your younger daughter, give her
strength. He gives us both his strength, Andrion told himself.
And we pray to him as if his apotheosis were already accomplished.

The quarter waxing moon marked Valeria's birthday; a new
Valeria, who initiated conversations with Andrion and Tembujin both, and contemplated the world with firm chin and
clear eye. She is no longer a fragile flower, Andrion thought,
but fruit ripened as I have been, by ordeal and the love of her
parents. Tembujin paid her polite and correct attentions, more
formal than the jests he shared with Dana or with Andrion
himself; Patros watched, partly sceptical, partly amused.

Shurzad stayed close beside her daughter. Her mutilated
hand reached as often for her naked throat as Andrion
reached for his. Her eyes still held some trace of that creature
struggling to be free. Or perhaps she found it, and did not like
what she saw. Her hair was carefully ringleted, her eyes
shadowed with lavender and kohl, but still she seemed to Andrion to be an edged weapon blunted.

Patros watched his wife through sad, wary eyes, and as
often as he shared a smile with Valeria, he smiled at her as
well. But it was Ilanit with whom he often talked, in the elliptical sentences of conversations already long concluded. And
one evening Shurzad came to Ilanit in the camp of the Sabazians.

Lyris tensed, her hackles rising. Andrion, seated with Dana, looked up. Ilanit offered Shurzad a rock to sit upon as graciously as if she opened the Horn Gate to her.

Shurzad remained standing, ill at ease but driven from within. "My thanks, Queen Ilanit, and to your mother, Danica, for helping me. Despite my often . . . unkind words about you and yours."

Ilanit bowed. At her knee the shield sparked gently.

"It was your goddess, was it not, who told you to succor me?"

Ah, thought Andrion. She seeks assurance that the gods do indeed look over us.

"No," answered Ilanit. "I chose freely to aid a wounded soul."

"But you are not directed by the voice of your goddess, certain in all that you do?"

"No." Ilanit cocked her head to the side, as if finding either the question or the questioner to be slightly pitiful. "My mother once bore the power of the goddess, but I never have. Ashtar reserves her strength to herself now, and leaves us mortals to find our own certainty."

"Ah. I see." Shurzad's face fell and she turned away.

Andrion stood, intercepted Shurzad, took her poor hand and bowed over it. "Forgive me, lady, for wounding you."

She stared at him, uncomprehending. "With the lock of hair you gave Valeria I enspelled you to come to Sardis, so that I could use you."

"No, no, lady," he returned, hastening to reassure her. "I dreamed I should come, in Ashtar's cavern at the full moon after midsummer's moon."

"And my spell was laid as the moon waned." Her face contracted in pain, her voice faltered. "So, even that effort was for naught." She turned and blundered away.

Andrion realized not what he had said, but what she had heard. "Harus! I did not mean to rub her nose in her helplessness!"

"She waits for redemption," Ilanit said, shaking her head.

Yes, Andrion said to himself. So do I. And I shall find it only in duty. He touched Dana's cheek lightly with his forefinger, bowed to Ilanit and the shield, managed a wink for Lyris. And he, too, went into the night, not blundering but striding as stiff as any soldier.

The full moon drifted, a gleaming disk, above the Khazyari

camp. The sounds of revelry were muted, as if Baakhun's pro-
digious appetite had eaten the spirits of his warriors and taken
them with him into death.

Raksula sat beside Vlad at the head table. He wore the
plaque of the khan, and the lion skin now waved above his
head. But he paid no attention to them; Raksula plied him
with delicacies, candied figs, lemon curd, roasted lark.
"Imperial foods for an emperor," she told him with an in-
gratiating smile.

A nuryan bowed before Vlad, inquiring about the posting
of the guards. His mouth full, he nodded toward his mother.
Her smile glistened as she gave the orders herself. Odo started
to amend the order and was quelled by an evil look from
Raksula. His face tightened and darkened like an overripe
plum. He handed Vlad another skin of kviss, asking with ex-
aggerated courtesy, "This, my lord, or some of that wine?"

Vlad muttered some sneer at Odo, spraying Raksula with
particles of fig. Her smiled froze into a bare-toothed snarl. He
grabbed the skin, drank, wiped the dribbles from his chin.

Something gleamed in the folds of his tunic. Raksula's eyes
widened so far that the whites glistened. With an oath she
lunged, seized the object, held it up. It was a necklace, a gold
crescent moon with a gold star at its tip. "So," she breathed,
"you have it."

Vlad tensed. The voices stopped. A sudden wind moaned
about the great yurt. With one clawed hand Raksula seized
Vlad by the collar. "Where did you get it!" Realizing that the
Khazyari watched her, she softened her voice, smiled again.
But her eyes were points of jet. "Where?"

"My father," he glowered. "He carried it in his tunic and
talked to it. It is pretty, so I took it; I am khan now and it is
mine." He scrabbled at the necklace but she whisked it away
from him.

Odo's stubby fingers opened and closed in midair. Raksula
thrust the necklace into her own bodice and hissed, "That
weakling Baakhun, bleating over the necklace his precious
Tembujin wore. But he is gone now, they are both gone, and
my time has come!" She scrambled up, dragging Odo with
her. He quickly wiped a sullen expression from his face and
replaced it with obsequious eagerness. Raksula giggled with
malign glee and issued new orders, a surprise attack on the imperial camp to coincide with her sorceries. The chieftains of

the Khazyari leaped up with new energy.

Raksula stalked from the great tent, Odo bobbing in her wake, and hurried to her own yurt. From charred bags she took herbs and arranged them in an arcane pattern around a tiny lamp. Odo began a chant, spitting rough, harsh words at the flame. Raksula lifted the necklace. She was a wizened gargoyle, teeth glistening, talons grasping a sparkling cascade of gold. The gold passed through the fire and dimmed.

Andrion was dreaming of the full moon, and Sabazel, and Dana's enlaced limbs warming the chill of the night, when the moon seemed to waver and wink out. He shifted, his senses crawling with dread. Something, somewhere, had gone terribly awry. . . .

He awoke. The camp was silent, the wind chiming softly around his tent, charcoal settling with little creaks and pops in his brazier, Miklos's steady tread outside marking the cadence of the night. The moonlight was a hazy corona between the flaps of the doorway, fluttering as if shadowed by sinister dark wings. He sat up, alarmed; then the alarm dulled, his mind sinking into lassitude, his thoughts moving painfully, slowly, through a cold torpor. He fumbled for Solifrax, every muscle groaning.

There. The sword, hard in his numbed and heavy hand. For a moment he saw himself, a reverse reflection in still water, clear and distant; then the water rippled, disturbed by a touch, and his image melted away.

The coals in the brazier hissed, smoked, flared into life. Fangs of flame, of ice, leaped before his eyes. He could not blink. He could not speak, his tongue frozen in his mouth. His ears rang with an infinite silence; no, a faint chant hung like a mist about him. He struggled to remember his own name—an important name, he had heard it before. . . . Valeria, he thought suddenly, enspelled with cold fire like an icy venom. Like this. His thoughts faded again, sucked from him by the chant.

The brazier seethed with flame, but no heat emanated from it. He fought against the torpor. Think, he ordered himself, try to think . . . the something wrong was within himself, writhing like a great snake in his heart, in his belly. His mind steadied, spun, steadied again. He saw Bellasteros's drained eyes, imagined his own eyes as blank and hollow. With a moment of clarity he thought, They found my necklace. He raised his hand to throat and snatched it away, his own flesh burning cold.

Andrion tried to call out, but his voice was only a shallow breath, a shallow wind devoured by the night, dying before the implacable face of time. But time slowed, halted, froze into bright glittering moments like jewels forever beyond his reach. Fangs of cold flame opened before him. His hand pulled Solifrax from its sheath, and the serpent skin slithered away, slow viscous scales absorbed into shadow. The blade of the sword was crystalline ice, reflecting no flame, as cold and remote as the face of the moon, a perfect death's head. Ashtar! he thought, and for a moment the name cleared his head. Ashtar, Dana, Ilanit, Danica, help me!

His mind fell through echoing nothingness and spattered into sparks. His hand stroked the sword. A thin trail of red glinted across his palm. He leaned his face into his hand and tasted the sizzling sweetness of his own blood. Blood and fire and the blade, sharp and sweet, compelling—it would pierce him through—no, it would be like a woman receiving a lover, filled . . . his blood would flow crimson over the blade and it would dissolve, it would be seized by clawed hands in some place filled with a gibbering darkness. . . . Of course, he told himself. I shall no longer want it. I shall be free of it. Andrion turned the sword, pressing its curved tip against his chest. It cut the linen of his chiton, each individual thread parting with a tiny snap.

The icy flames illuminated his face, his eyes hollows of desire and despair. Death, deliver me from the harsh borders of this world. . . . The blade pricked his flesh and his mind convulsed, screaming, *Dana!*

Between one moment and the next Dana started into tense alertness. Something, somewhere was terribly awry. She jumped from her bedroll and stood trembling. The moon, she thought, the moon wavered oddly, barred by a floating mist as dark and dense as Andrion's black cloak. A cold wind rippled through the grass and brush, rippled through the stars, swinging them like bells. Faint on the air she heard a cry, *Dana!*

Andrion! She seized her bow and dagger and screaming a warning ran from the camp. The Sabazian sentries leaped up. Danica thrust aside the hangings of the cart. Lyris and Ilanit tumbled out of their tent, grasping their weapons.

Dana plummeted into the imperial camp. *Dana!* came the cry again, sharp and urgent, dying abruptly. She brushed aside several surprised sentries and almost trampled Miklos at the door of Andrion's tent. She burst inside.

He sat on the edge of his bed, staring into the sullen red coals of his brazier. But his dark eyes reflected leaping white flame, cold flame, fangs of ice. He held the shining blade of Solifrax reversed against his own chest. He leaned into the blade, his face suffused with a grim ecstasy, and a coiling trickle of blood smoked down the brightness of the sword.

"Andrion!" Dana cried. "Gods, no!" She seized his hands, trying to pull the blade away. She realized then that a miasma hung about him, the chill sour odor of sorcery, sorcery turning the power of sword on its bearer. His flesh burned her fingers, but she did not let go.

He looked toward her without the least hint of recognition. His lips drew back in a snarl. With uncanny strength he knocked her to the floor, leaped up and raised Solifrax over her. Like a frozen lightning bolt the sword fell. She rolled away, knocking into and spilling the brazier. "Andrion, in the name of Ashtar!" He struck at her again, his face that of a mindless demon.

Miklos leaped at him from the side, bearing him down. The sword flew from his grasp and he howled in outrage and terror mingled. He fought, scratching and biting at Miklos, and the young soldier, his eyes rolling with uncomprehending terror, tried only to avoid him.

Dana scrambled up. Together she and Miklos pinned Andrion to the floor. The prince stared beyond them to the roof of the tent, through it to the darkening sky, his body jerking in uncontrollable spasms. Strange syllables issued hoarsely from his throat, the echo of some evil chant. Solifrax lay among the ashes of the spilled brazier, its brightness stained with blood, muted.

Ilanit stood in the doorway, the shield a fiery disk on her arm, her eyes and mouth circles of appalled comprehension. "Mother!" she gasped. "Not him, too!"

Andrion's chiton gaped, his chest smeared crimson, his bared throat pulsing with an angry red image of his necklace. "Mother," Dana repeated, not knowing if she called on the goddess or on her own mortal parent. Andrion's body trembled in her arms, his familiar body strange and distant.

Ilanit knelt and laid the shield over Andrion. His voice
stopped with a gurgle. His eyes closed and he became suddenly
still. Then Danica, too, was there, her strong but delicate
hands resting with her daughter's and granddaughter's on the
rim of the shield. The three faces, avatars of the same bone,
the same flesh, set in the same intentness, were sketched in
vivid relief by its clear light. A cold wind purled through the
doorway, drawing the spilled ashes into swirls of luminescent
particles. The sword hissed, flared, and faded.

Miklos edged away, his face struggling with fear and confusion. Then shouts spilled through the encampment, and he
fled.

Dim shapes crept toward the imperial encampment, curtained
by a dark haze. The sentries stirred uneasily, and more than
one sleeper muttered in the grip of nightmare. The moon
darkened as though veiled by gauze. Lyris, standing with
Shandir beside Bellasteros's litter, watched Danica disappear after Dana and Ilanit into gathering shadow and drew her
sword slowly across her thumbnail, frowning, shaking her
head. "Sorcery," spat Shandir. "Evil sorcery."

With unearthly shrieks the Khazyari attacked. Some sentries
were swiftly and mercilessly overrun. But those who had been
startled by Dana's rush through the camp gave the alarm.
Trumpets blared.

Fire arrows streaked through the air and tents blossomed
into flame. Ponies pounded through the crimson-streaked
night and legionaries died as they ran from their tents. Patros
appeared clad only in a chiton, naked sword in hand, calling
his soldiers to him. Nikander hitched up his robe and began
organizing the legionaries as laconically as if the tumultuous
camp were the parade ground by the walls of Farsahn. The
soldiers of the Empire steadied and returned battle.

Tembujin leaped onto the bare back of his horse and
grasped its halter in one hand, his bow in the other. His face
was that of an archaic statue, hard planes and sharp angles
untouched by the dancing light of the flames. He slipped
from light to shadow and back again, and many Khazyari died
in terror.

A cordon of Sabazians stood about Bellasteros's litter,
Lyris cursing with disgust at being saddled with a defensive
position. But she stood steadfast. Shandir knelt in the doorway, eyes narrowed, dagger ready to defend the sleeping king.

Ilanit and Dana roused and started up, then turned back, torn, toward Andrion's stark, white, pained face. Danica lifted his head into her lap, lifted Solifrax into her own hand. "We choose this man, too," she said, her voice breaking. The shield sparked. The sword sparked in reply. Dana wiped cold tears from her cheeks and followed her mother into battle.

Shurzad and Valeria huddled together beside their cart. Khazyari raced with gleeful whoops through the tangle of camp followers, seizing women and booty indiscriminately. The great ursine warrior—he who had escorted Tembujin to his supposed death—leaped from his pony and grabbed Valeria, saying something that even in Khazyari was obviously obscene. She struggled, but his huge hands could almost span her waist.

Shurzad leaped upon him, screaming, clawing, fighting for her daughter. Ponderously, as if to see what insect annoyed him, he turned. Several other Khazyari paused to watch, shouting taunts at warrior and women equally. Shurzad's cat scrambled up the man's felt-clad leg, every hair on end, tail like a brush.

An arrow cut the night. The warrior, his face set in innocent amazement, looked down at the shaft protruding from his tunic and then up. Tembujin, ghostly on a spectral horse, cursed him in his own language. The great warrior's eyes bulged. He fell, struck down by fear as much as by the arrow, dragging the women and the cat with him. His colleagues screeched and collided with each other, some rushing forward, some back.

One of them leaned from his pony and seized Valeria's arm, attempting to lift her up. Shurzad scrambled after them, wrenched her daughter away, interposed her own body. Tembujin swept the girl onto his horse. She clung to him with one arm, leaned precariously out and reached for her mother.

The Khazyari grasped Shurzad and threw her like a sack of meal over his horse. One of Tembujin's arrows struck him but he did not stop. The cat, clinging desperately to Shurzad's skirts, yowled. Valeria screamed. Shurzad's stunned face, a white oval tinted with flame, glinted over the warrior's leg and was gone.

The wrath of Ilanit's blazing shield and Dana's crimsoned dagger, the threat of icily gleaming Solifrax, turned the battle from Andrion's tent. Legionaries lunged in counterattack, led on one flank by Nikander, on the other by Patros. Bonifacio, clutching the plumed helmet, looked fearfully from his tent, but the shouts and screams of battle were already retreating into murky distance. Dim shapes began fighting the fires, and the ruddy glow faded. The Sabazians leaned on their swords, the sleeping emperor unscathed. The moon cleared and became again a pale orb, remote and silent, drifting to the west and drawing dawn behind it from the east.

The cold light of day was a shroud over the shattered encampment. Even the wind seemed to moan in pain. Smoking ruins of tents lay in hummocks along the avenues; search parties divided the soldiers lying in the churned, red-stained dirt into piles of bodies like cords of wood, into twitching tortured figures borne away to places of rest.

Tembujin gave Valeria into the circle of her father's arm and turned away before she could tell him the tale of Shurzad's capture. The odlok found Dana sitting wanly beside the bed where Andrion muttered in delirium, starting up in a cold sweat, lying back as still as death. Danica sponged his brow, her face shuttered and chill. Ilanit's shield hummed beside her, singing some private dirge; Solifrax, silent, lay at her hand. She glanced at it again and again, perhaps in resentment, perhaps in respect.

"Your barbarians have his necklace," Miklos said to Tembujin shortly, from his post by the door. "That you gave them."

Tembujin scowled. "Can you not stop the spell?" he asked Danica. She looked at him with a terrible patience. "I can protect him from its full force. But I cannot stop it, no. The necklace holds too much of him."

"So," Tembujin muttered, "I owe him life." He spun, his fists clenched at his sides, and brushed aside an approaching Sabazian without even seeing her. Dana looked after him, frowning, seeking after some nuance of his thought. But it escaped her, and he, too, was gone.

The Khazyari camp was traced by the mists and smokes of a bleak, cold dawn. Warriors milled about, quarreling over their booty, binding their wounds. A nuryan, seeing Shurzad huddling numbly by the body of a dead warrior, relieved her of her jewelry and silk gown and delivered her to Raksula. "A lady of quality," he announced. "Perhaps she has information."

Shurzad, clad only in a thin shift, shivered with fear and

cold. But when Raksula's sharp fingers grasped her chin and jerked her face to the watery sun, she did not flinch.

Raksula's eyes were bruised with exhaustion and her many braids straggled unheeded. She was a cornered scorpion, sting poised to attack all who came near. She snarled at Shurzad, "I know you. You failed me."

Shurzad nodded in dull recognition, unsurprised. "You are she who led me to the betrayal that stains me still."

Vlad, puffed with self-importance, prodded the soft curve of her flank. Odo stared sullenly at Raksula. Raksula ignored them both and leaned close to Shurzad, spraying her face with venom. "Ah, but you followed me. You and I are alike, our plans thwarted at every turn by the power of Sabazel."

Again Shurzad did not flinch. A tiny, angry tremor tightened her mouth, perhaps at Raksula, or at Sabazel, or even at herself.

To the assembled warriors, Raksula called, "Build a fire. This is the lady of the governor-general of Sardis; she will be sacrificed to Khalingu, that our fortunes may be restored." She smiled, every pointed tooth glinting, and released Shurzad's chin with an acid caress.

Shurzad's face went even whiter. She swayed, caught herself. The cat padded through the watching throng, eyes bright, tail lifted alertly. Slaves brought loads of brushwood and piled it high.

"So," Raksula murmured, seeing the cat, "a small Qem, Khalingu as snow leopard. Did you know, Shurzad, that you worshiped the god of the Khazyari?"

Shurzad stared blankly at her, not quite hearing her, listening to some other voice. The cat folded itself around her leg.

Raksula pulled the gold necklace from her dress and thrust it into Shurzad's face. "See my power? I hold the life of your prince in my hands." Odo's fingers twitched. Vlad frowned petulantly. The gold was reflected twofold in Shurzad's somber eyes, a distant brightness like the glow of moon or sun through a rift in cloud.

On the outskirts of the crowd a sentry fell without a cry, taken from behind. A dark figure quickly assumed his tunic and fur cap and stood watching. Icy rain spattered the morning, and the people huddled closer to the pile of brush. Someone threw a flaming torch into it. With a slow crackle, fire danced among the branches.

Odo grasped Shurzad's unresisting form and began a wail-

ing prayer. She closed her eyes, sighed deeply, opened them
not on to despiar but on to decision. The cat crouched. Unnoticed, Tembujin set an arrow to his bow and then lowered it,
grimacing in frustrated loathing as Raksula stepped forward
brandishing the necklace, and was concealed by several children. The fire roared upward, smoke and flame licking at the
shrouded sky.

Then with a shriek the cat leaped onto Raksula, its claws
raking long furrows into her forearm. She shrieked in turn and
threw the beast away from her. In one smooth movement
Shurzad wrenched herself free of Odo's grasp, seized the
necklace from Raksula's fingers with her own maimed hand,
and threw herself into the incandescent heart of the pyre.

Brush crashed and sparks flew. She screamed, less in pain
than in ecstasy, "Qem, I commend myself to you. Harus,
Ashtar, have mercy!"

"Gods!" Tembujin exclaimed. His bow leaped up. An arrow like a hissing brand struck Shurzad cleanly in the heart.
Her hair was a torch, her clothing ash, her body a golden
image traced in fire, but she was already dead; Andrion's
necklace was melted gold in the melted flesh of her hand,
purified. The expression on her face, hopeful at last, remained
an afterimage among the flames.

The cat, a gray shadow, disappeared. The Khazyari stood in
utter silence, even Raksula struck speechless. Gouts of flame
seared her face of any human expression, leaving only the
cold, vacant sneer of a reptile. A wind pealed across the sky,
too cold to spread the scent of death.

Tembujin raised his bow again. As if sensing his presence,
Raksula jerked about. Her eyes were knives flaying his
disguise from him, peeling his every motion down to the hard
kernel of hatred in his soul. Her bloodstained hand pointed at
him. She screamed in hysterical denial, incoherently. Vlad
screeched excited orders, Odo shouted, the Khazyari cried out
in dismay and confusion and surged in grotesque shapes about
the roaring, all-consuming fire. Raksula was swallowed by the
crowd.

"Seethe in your own wickedness, witch," Tembujin
shouted. Cursing her, cursing himself, he ran on the heels of
the wind to his horse and raced into the uncertain light of day.

Chapter Twenty

IN THE THIN light of the waxing moon the walls of Iksandarun were as stark as dried bone. Raksula stalked up and down, up and down, beside the small smoky fire outside her yurt, as if by an effort of her will she could lay those walls waste and return the Khazyari tribe to its high water mark in the north. Beside her stood the dark hump of Khalingu's cart, stirred with the fitful rattle of unsheathed claws.

Voices drifted on a cold wind, warriors, women, children, slaves, fighting over what store of food could be found in this already drained land. The jewels and silks and fine porcelain looted from Iksandarun at midsummer could not now, at midwinter, buy food where food did not exist.

Raksula looked with loathing toward the shadow-tipped mountains to the south. She shook her fist toward the implacable black prince and his army, advancing from the north.

Her arm was scarred by angry red scratch marks. In the pale light of the quarter moon, in the flickering light of the fire, her cheeks were flushed and feverish. Her eyes glittered. When Odo approached she snapped at him like a jackal. "Well?"

"My lady," he said, with arid courtesy, "the khan wants to go south. He fears we could no longer win a battle with the legions."

"He fears everything. Khalingu, why give me such a son!"

Odo grimaced, the flesh of his face crumpling like stained, used linen. "If we return to the Mohan, claim our tribute, regroup—"

"No! I rule this tribe. I say we stay and fight and slaughter those who would push us from this land we have won!" The whites of her eyes and her teeth glistened with a phosphorescent pallor, fire and ice eerily mingled.

233

Odo stared at the toes of his boots, dull and resentful. Two guards approached, escorting one figure, dragging another. Raksula clasped her arms about her, her clawed fingers fondling and soothing herself.

Obedei sketched a polite if wary salute. "My lady, welcome. Iksandarun opens its gates to you and the khan."

"Khan Vlad," Odo said under his breath, tasting the words and then spitting them out in disgust.

"Yes," said Obedei stolidly. "I received your message, of the glorious death in battle of Baakhun. Surely he sits at Khalingu's feast."

Raksula snarled some irritated courtesy. Her bulging eyes raked the figure held by the guards. Hilkar essayed a sickly grin and tried to prostrate himself. Obligingly, the guards dropped him. He fell face first into the dirt.

"Well?" Raksula demanded.

"Most noble lady. Ruler of the all-powerful Khazyari. All-seeing, all-knowing. I ask reward for my services. . . ."

"Did you kill Sarasvati?"

Obedei's brows tightened as he strained to follow this conversation in the common tongue.

"My lady," Hilkar squeaked, "I . . . Governor Obedei would not let me."

"Baakhun told me to bring her to Iksandarun," Obedei said with stiff reasonableness.

Raksula glared at him, holding back scathing words. She kicked Hilkar in the ribs. He yelped and squirmed. "You worthless idiot," she shrilled. "I wanted her dead, you piece of carrion!"

Obedei's eyes clouded. Odo, elaborately disdainful of the entire exchange, contemplated the still, opaque hangings of Khalingu's cart. Hilkar tried to scrabble away but confronted the bent bows of the guards.

"Go away," shrieked Raksula. "If I see you again, I shall kill you!"

Hilkar fled in an awkward crablike scuttle. Raksula turned to Obedei, seized his tunic in her talons and spoke, close enough that her saliva sprayed his face like hot sour wine. "I want her dead, do you hear me! She carries Tembujin's spawn, and I want her dead!"

"Yes, my lady," Obedei replied, eyes hard, jaw set. "Those are the khan's orders?"

Raksula cursed him and stumbled into the dark shadow cast

by her yurt. Her voice remained, circling on the wind like the
distant howling of a feral animal, "I rule here, I rule this tribe,
I order the future!"

Obedei stared after her. He clasped his hands before his
chest and then opened them, as if wondering if they contained
anything. He tightened his mouth to a guarded slit.

Odo ran his fingers through the amulets he wore. They
jangled faintly. The wind jangled a response and carried a
tang of sleet through the disheveled encampment, across the
scarred walls and into the desolate streets of the city.

A thin gray cat whisked across the open space, its topaz eyes
glinting, and disappeared beneath the walls of Iksandarun.

Sarasvati stood on a battlement, watching the fires leap in the
vast Khazyari encampment. Small fires, they seemed, tentative
flames shredded by the wind, not the great bonfires of the
night Iksandarun fell. The wind was cold, jangling in her ears.
She drew her cloak more tightly about her shoulders and in an
instinctive gesture stroked the mound of her belly. "Tembujin," she sighed, "surely you deserved your death."

The rooftop garden behind her was a wilderness of dried
stalks and shattered filigree. Obedei stamped down the brick
path, his boots crunching through the drifting leaves, his hand
tight on the hilt of his dagger. Sarasvati turned to greet him,
saying acidly, "How fares your people? Do they enjoy the
taste of defeat?"

"No fair mock me, lady. Vlad rules, Raksula rules. I fear
for all."

Sarasvati regarded his bleak face, and begrudged him a
smile. "Do not fight, Obedei. Hide until the battle is over."

"No, lady." He shook his head, a controlled shudder. "I
am Khazyari."

"Chained by your birth, as I am chained by mine to those
people you call slaves. Have they food and fuel to see them
through this cold night?" Something caught her eye; she
turned to see a scrawny cat limping down the path. It paused,
fixed her with guileless topaz eyes, meowed piteously.

Sarasvati, cooing sympathy, picked it up and cradled it in
her arms. It raised its paw, patted softly at her breast, leaned
its furry cheek against her and purred. The lines of care at the
corners of her mouth melted into a smile, as awkwardly as
though she had forgotten how to smile.

Obedei eyed her ripening stomach. He clutched white-knuckled at his dagger and then released it. He threw his hands outward, flinging away the treason of what he could not do, torn between loyalties. "I go, see that slaves are fed, warmed, as you wish." He strode back across the wasted garden, kicking in violent bursts of frustration at the leaves in his path."

Sarasvati turned back to the battlement, to the sheer wall plunging into black shadow, to the sullen fires of the invader, to the sky. The stars were muted, veiled by thin cloud; the moon was cleft as precisely in half as if it had been sliced by the blade of Solifrax itself. Her smile wavered, her eyes were polished with a sudden moisture. "Andrion," she whispered. "Father."

The cat propped its chin on her forearm, fluffed its whiskers, gazed contentedly out into the night. It almost seemed to be smiling.

Andrion sat on his great war-stallion, finding a furtive pleasure in the sunset. Before him were great banks of startlingly pink cloud, licked smooth by the wind like cliffs licked by the sea. An elliptical moon hung like a great pearl just at their edge. Behind him his escort waited discreetly. He knew he should be contemplating the campaign. But the planning, the worrying, had worn deep aching ruts in his mind, not unlike the dull ache in his gut when he passed the ruined caravanserais, villages, and farms of the southern plains. How dare the Khazyari tear down what his father had built?

My father, Andrion thought, transmuted into godhood while still living, worshipped by thousands. He sat often by his father's bedside, presenting the problems of the campaign as if Bellasteros could counsel and commend him. Every now and then Danica's voice would complement his, remembering other battles. But Bellasteros did not wake.

Andrion never wondered anymore whether he wanted him to wake, just as he never wondered what would happen when he did. The people in their simplicity acclaim me, follow me, he thought; perhaps the sword does not, in the end, matter. . . .

No. He touched the hilt at his hip and it tingled under his fingers. The blade was now etched with a curling tendril of roughness, the path of his own blood on that night of hopeless delirium.

In a few days' time would be the full moon of midwinter,

Andrion's nineteenth birthday. Damned Khazyari, if they would only stand and fight and end this ordeal! But he knew they would stand at Iksandarun. He did not dare reckon the cost of victory. He was haunted by a vision of himself seated on the peacock throne, wearing diadem and sword, attended only by the shades of the dead. But then, the throne was not his. He shifted on Ventalidar's reassuringly solid back; at least that was not ambiguous. The wind murmured soft nothings in his ear, playing with his black plume and his billowing black cloak.

Ventalidar shuffled his feet in an intricate dance step, toying with his shadow, and jangled his harness. Andrion felt his face crack into a smile. The sun sank, a crimson wound, toward the horizon.

I should go back and practice my weapons, Andrion told himself. But Lyris refused to spar with him anymore, finding his desperate, deadly assaults embarrassingly difficult to turn. Miklos could not refuse; for that reason Andrion would not force the young man to submit to him again.

Tembujin and Dana approached the solitary figure of the prince, followed by the odlok's own escort, the hulking Khazyari warrior he had shot the night of Shurzad's death. Tembujin, yielding to some obscure sentiment, had demonstrated how to use the man's silk shirt to withdraw the arrow; reassured that the odlok was not some evil phantom, the warrior had attached himself to him and followed him like an adoring hound. Andrion's escort, not to mention Lyris, looked askance at the man's presence; but no matter how large, he was only one.

Tembujin said something in Khazyari. Obediently the warrior halted, tilting his face to the sunset. In the rosy light he seemed an innocent if overgrown child. Andrion's brow quirked with irony; did the man realize that the implacable black prince now before him was the boy he had thrown in the mud in Bellastria?

Dana reined up beside Andrion. "Patros sends his respects, and asks if you are ready for the evening meal. We are fortunate; a scouting party brought down some antelope."

Andrion allowed himself the pleasure of contemplating Dana's precise face. She was somewhat pale; she had been pale for . . . how long now? Ashtar! It had been almost three months since the autumn rites!

She smiled secretly and let her lashes shadow her eyes. Tembujin leaned back, propping his leg on his saddlebow. "Now, Dana," he said, his chin raised with expectation.

"I would not speak to him alone," Dana explained. Andrion's heart plummeted. His mind repeated the words as she said them: "I am pregnant."

Tembujin's eyes crossed with Andrion's in a look somewhere between the clashing of swords and a wary handshake. "You cannot know which of us is the father," he said aggrievedly.

Dana shrugged. "I know who is my child's mother."

Andrion searched himself for some reaction. Damn Tembujin, grappling with every woman he loved, filling her with his own—no, that was not the right reaction. "What pleasant news," he stated.

"Indeed," said Tembujin. He looked north. Andrion looked south. Dana sat between them, turning her head from side to side, and at last she laughed. Yes, Andrion thought, another twist to my fate. Another path chosen, again the most difficult.

As they swished through the dried grass toward camp, Andrion found himself exchanging a self-conscious chuckle with Tembujin. "How we must amuse the gods," Andrion said. "They play with us, today a favor, tomorrow a blow."

"The ordeal would be the same," returned Dana, "whether we believe in the gods or not."

"Is there any purpose to life and its indignities?" Tembujin asked caustically.

"I want to think so," Dana replied.

Even the daughter of Sabazel knew uncertainty. Andrion was almost cheered. But then, why did they persist in trying to grasp the ungraspable? His thought spiraled downward, disappearing into an elusive mist, finding no answers. Perhaps there were no answers to find. The riders approached the outskirts of the camp. Tired sentries brightened at the sight of their prince and saluted; he returned their courtesy.

Miklos stood poised with the bronze falcon before the sunset-tinted pavilion, looking expectantly at Andrion. Forgive me, Andrion thought to him as they dismounted. I have no answer except duty.

The gold pavilion was bright with torchlight reflected again and again off Sardian bronze, an amber-rich sunrise, certainly, not a sunset. The image of the falcon seemed to preen itself on its pole; Bellasteros's helmet, set in honor on the central table, gleamed as though a living head turned it back and forth, watching the diners with calm benignity.

Dana sat upright on her couch, her stomach intolerant of reclining. Valeria sat with her, unveiled, as she was frequently now, regarding Dana with wide eyes. "You are with child?" she whispered, making of it some dark secret. "How do you feel?"

"Queasy," said Dana. "Bloated." But that is not the question you really ask. "Would you like to come to Sabazel for the rites?"

Valeria colored. "I am not quite ready for that."

Are you not? Dana silently asked, but thinking it would be unfair to press her, she laughed gently. "I tease you. Forgive me." Valeria was a butterfly broken free of its chrysalis, delicate and beautiful and sad at realizing how transitory was its life.

Dana felt eyes upon her; she glanced up and saw Tembujin watching them both. Valeria flushed even more deeply while trying to hide a smile. So, Dana thought, the son of the lion is indeed loose among the flocks. The gods move in subtle ways.

Andrion watched from his place at the head table, glowering with amusement and annoyance, too proud to compete. His dark eyes guarded their depths, allowing only glimpses of the lambent flame that illuminated them. His mouth was bracketed with fine tight lines like controlling reins. Tembujin may be exotic meat, Dana thought, but you, Andrion, are my male half. She tipped him a salute of her rhyton, despite the fact that it contained only water. He smiled, and his face was transformed, lit brilliantly from within. How beautiful that smile, she thought with a pang; doubly so for being so rarely revealed. If only he could discard for a moment the Empire that he carried, a heavy shell, upon his shoulders. But then he would not be Andrion.

Beside Andrion, Ilanit talked quietly with Patros. Patros, Dana sighed. An oak tree blasted by lightening, scarred but still standing tall. His hair was almost completely gray now, his face furrowed deep. But his eyes rested on Ilanit, finding sustenance in her strength even as she hoarded her strength to share with him. Dana could just hear his voice. "I should not have brought Shurzad to the battlefield."

"Andrion and Dana asked you to bring her," Ilanit reminded him.

"It was my inattention that turned her to evil," he insisted.

Ilanit hushed him, reminding him that he did not suffer alone. He looked up, saw Dana and Valeria side by side, and his weary face creased with a smile.

Nikander sat beside Lyris; their laconic remarks were pebbles thrown down a deep well, one at a time with long pauses between. The old turtle offered Lyris a date. Gravely she accepted.

Dana looked down at her own plate, sighed, pushed it away.

Iksandarun lay at last on the horizon. The forts guarding the pass to its plateau were dark blotches in the fitful light. As Andrion glanced up, a scurrying cloud covered the face of the moon, casting a translucent shadow across the land. Tomorrow, he thought, the moon will be full. He urged sable Ventalidar into the night, and his small band followed him, Tembujin on a dark horse, Dana with her bright hair tucked under a helmet, Miklos cloaked to the eyes against the cold.

Patros had not been pleased to hear, at the staff meeting, Andrion's plan for the night. "You will creep back into the city?"

"Yes. I want to see if the water tunnel can be cleared, letting our troops open the gates of the city from within. Justice, do you not think?"

"Indeed," the governor had sighed. "I shall not waste my strength arguing with you, Andrion, to let someone else go in your stead."

Andrion almost wished Patros had argued with him. It was sobering to be thought infallible. The party crept across shadow-dappled plain, a chill south wind bearing the muffled sounds of their horses away from the city. At last Andrion's straining eyes picked out the limber branches of the willow grove. He had come home. But this place, too, was changed from his memory of it. The trees creaked like crones, whispering querulously.

An ethereal silver light stirred beneath the trees, the bare branches an intricate lace across a starry sky. The small band tied their horses and walked up the stream to the great leaning stones. Miklos lifted the dried thorn branches hanging over the entrance to the tunnel. The water was icy cold on Andrion's feet, the darkness shifting and stirring as if black torches guttered within the corridor. He set his hand on the cold, tingling hilt of Solifrax.

"So this was how you escaped," Tembujin said. His quiet voice echoed, faded, died. "Not the divine intervention I had assumed."

"I would not be so sure of that," said Andrion, thinking of Toth.

They huddled inside the entrance as Miklos opened his tinderbox and lit a torch. The sudden light was a blinding radiance. Blinking, Andrion took the torch and lifted it. The flame flickered in a chill draught. "See," he said, as much to himself as to the others, "there must still be an opening." Close together they splashed on, slipping, colliding, parting with muttered excuses.

The pool was dim watered silk, softened by swirls of mist. The rough-hewn ceiling of the chamber was a wilderness of shadow. Not like Ashtar's cavern, Andrion thought irrelevantly. Dana eyed the ancient specters thronging this place, not threatening, but not welcoming either. The torch seemed to have shrunk into a mere pinprick of light.

Andrion started up the stairs, slipping in the tumbled rocks and dust. Soon he was blocked by large boulders. He inspected them carefully; it would never do to survive the odyssey of the last months only to die in a landslide back where he had begun. There, he decided, that stone. Silently he handed the torch to Dana and set his shoulder against the rock. It was cold, draining heat, draining strength. Miklos and Tembujin pushed beside him. The rock moved. With a mighty rumble and crash it fell.

The wind gusted through the opening and the torch guttered wildly. Four shadows leaped and danced upwards. They scrambled out of the hole, doused the torch and stood, weapons ready, waiting for someone to come and see what the noise had been. No one came.

The wall of the palace was a jagged rim against a sky that at one moment spewed chill rain, at the next cleared into star-embroidered gauze. "Come," said Andrion. He lifted Solifrax before him, its blade a curving glimmer driving back the darkness, and he led the way into corridors filled with dust and debris and tattered cobwebs.

The palace spun past Andrion like a distorted dream. He wondered suddenly if he would wake and find himself still young, still secure, the ordeal having been only nightmare. The cold, musty corridors were like a tomb. His footsteps, the footsteps of the others, were a faint ripple through the silence.

A rat scuttled in front of them and they all started.

It was not all silent. A reedy voice crooned in an anteroom of the throne chamber. Andrion and Tembujin shared one long, wary look, and peered around the corner.

Hilkar held an oil lamp above a figure crouched at his feet, a ragged woman clutching a baby. "Please, lord," she said. "I have no jewelry for you; they took it all. Please, I need food, if not for me then for the child." The baby wailed faintly, no louder than a kitten. The woman's free hand grasped at Hilkar's robe. Andrion saw then that he guarded a basket filled with bread.

"What a shame," Hilkar said without sympathy. "You must have something to spend in order to buy. Go scratch in the streets; perhaps the high and mighty Khazyari dropped something of value there. Sell yourself to them. Or, perhaps. . . ?" His scrawny hand reached toward her.

"Is that he?" asked Dana's breath in Andrion's ear.

"The traitor," Andrion and Tembujin answered simultaneously. And Tembujin added, "So he has come back here. Could Sita . . . Sarasvati. . . ?"

"Please," the woman begged. Hilkar smirked, savoring his morsel of power.

Sparks spun behind Andrion's eyes, a blazing fury blinding him as surely as had the sudden flare of the torch. Spitting an epithet, he stepped around the corner. Hilkar started violently at this apparition in black and bronze. The lamp jerked, sending Andrion's shadow streaming up the soot-stained wall like some all-consuming wraith. "Who, what?" Hilkar gasped. The woman's pale face turned with hope and fear mingled.

"Your evil past," snarled Andrion, "come to haunt you." He threw his cloak back. The winged brooch glittered no less brightly than his eyes. His armor gleamed. The sword Solifrax flashed, and its light drained Hilkar's face of color, leaving it as pale as the skull beneath the skin.

The man's eyes bulged from their sockets. "Andrion!"

Andrion lunged, the sword singing in his hand. Hilkar, for once rendered speechless, dropped the lamp and collapsed like a deflated bladder. The lamp sputtered out. The woman reeled back, seized the basket of bread, fled. Her running footsteps and the tiny wail of the baby faded into the night.

Hilkar sprawled beneath Andrion's foot, his eyes crossed and fixed upon the shining blade lifted above him, his mouth

open, containing only abject terror. "Murderer!" Andrion
snarled. "I swore, I swore to . . ." What had he sworn? That
boy who had cursed and cried in this very room as the enemy
pounded at the door was no more. He had drunk deep of the
cup filled with hatred, and there was only a bitter aftertaste in
the mouth of the man he was now.

Tembujin knelt beside Hilkar, drawing the man's eyes to
him. The eyes froze in their sockets, and Hilkar moaned like a
sick animal. "Think upon it," Tembujin purred. "Your be-
trayals have betrayed you in the end, for they brought enemies
into alliance against you."

Hilkar's eyes rolled back, becoming only glistening white
crescents beneath shivering lids. His body trembled violently
and squeaks emanated from his throat, pleas for mercy
perhaps. Andrion's stomach crawled; the room spun, drawing
a cold wind across his hot skin. His eyes cleared and his fury
chilled into shards of ice. This pitiful creature, he thought,
devoured by his own hatred, a wasted shell of a man. If I
could even for a moment pity Gerlac, I can pity Hilkar.

Tembujin glanced up, one eyebrow arched. "You will not
kill him?"

"No," said Andrion.

Tembujin stood, his mouth tight as he, too, tasted the bitter
dregs of revenge. Deliberately he turned his back on Hilkar's
cowering form and dusted his knees. "Pathetic worm, is he
not?"

Swift footsteps echoed down a nearby corridor. A light
glimmered, setting the shadows dancing. Andrion lifted Solifrax again.

A cloaked figure paused in the doorway of the anteroom,
bracing one hand on a column, firm and yet poised for any
eventuality. A woman's figure, Andrion realized. "Hilkar!"
she demanded. "How dare you come lurking here?" His heart
leaped into his throat. It was Sarasvati.

Tembujin stiffened. Miklos stepped forward and then back.
Dana shot a swift, intrigued glance at each of them. Hilkar
scuttled like a giant cockroach away from the lifted lamp and
into a side corridor. "Let him go," said Dana, as the men
spun about, torn. "He has bought his fate."

"Let him go, then." And Andrion turned away, his face
opening into a radiant grin. "Sarasvati! It is I!"

The lamp did not move, its small flame did not waver. Her

hand grasping the cloak loosened, and it fell. Her coppery hair gleamed with rich amber highlights, her eyes were the shining lapis lazuli of deep evening, reflecting and magnifying the glow of Solifrax. Her eyes swam. "Oh," she said, her voice suddenly small and choked.

Andrion was at her side in one bound, sweeping her into his embrace. Her hand faltered, and Dana leaped forward to take the lamp just as she dropped it. Andrion swallowed the tears that clogged his throat; how long had it been since he had wept in joy? His hand held Solifrax angled across his sister's back, for a moment forgotten.

She clung to his shoulders, wondering perhaps when those shoulders had grown so broad. She searched his face in the shadow of his visor, noting what strengths had been incised there since they last met. His eyes were the eyes of the emperor, dark and rich, flickering with a distant flame. "Andrion . . ." Her belly stood up tautly rounded between them.

He laid his fingertips on her lips. "I know. I know."

Sarasvati looked from the shelter of Andrion's arm to each of the figures behind him. She paused in pleasure at Dana's smiling face; in grief at Miklos's features, as contorted as if her look were a sword thrust through his vitals. When she came at last to Tembujin's locked and shuttered eyes, she blanched. "Gods! He has come back to haunt me!"

"No," Andrion assured her, "he is quite alive."

The lamplight and the light of Solifrax touched her face with a sheen of gold and sorrow. Tembujin alive, and Bellasteros's sword carried in Andrion's hand; "Ah," she said, accepting all.

Andrion led her into the throne room. The peacock throne had been gouged of its precious stones, and some of its fine carved wood was hacked into splinters. The walls were stark stone, unsoftened by any tapestry or fresco. The past had been erased; the room was a parchment, waiting for new hands to write upon it.

Andrion seated Sarasvati upon the throne. "No," she protested, "it is not my place to sit here."

"Yes it is," he replied. He sat at her feet and laid Solifrax across his knees, where he could see its shimmering refractions play across the vacant chamber, catching an occasional spiderweb like a misty jewel. Dana perched on one arm of the throne, holding the lamp, her other hand placed on Sarasvati's shoulder. Miklos stood at quiveringly taut attention in the doorway. Tembujin scouted the walls, pretending great interest in nothingness.

"So," said Andrion. "Tell me."

Sarasvati spoke in brief phrases, filling in the gaps left by Toth's and Tembujin's accounts of the woman Sita and the necklace of the moon and star. Then Andrion and Dana spoke in turn of Sabazel and Sardis, ailing Bellasteros, the sword Solifrax, the rescue of Tembujin, the deaths of Toth, Shurzad, and Baakhun. The palace seemed to stir around them, a hungry beast waking, ready to feed.

"Gods," Sarasvati said at last, whether a prayer or a curse Andrion could not tell. "Obedei told me what he knew, and I feared our father was wounded—"

"Obedei?" asked Tembujin from a far corner. "He is here?" And scathingly, "He would not defend me against Raksula's charges."

"Of course he would not," Sarasvati shot back. "Like me, when I came willingly to your bed, he chose life over honor in the hope that honor would in time prevail."

Tembujin scowled, his features veneered with a petulant arrogance, and advanced to the throne. "You would have me ask forgiveness of you?"

Miklos's sword fell from his hand with a crash, as though he threw it away rather than slash Tembujin with it. Sarasvati searched his face; frowning, she looked back at Tembujin, pinned him with her eyes, ripped the veneer from him. "You have been to Sabazel, and still you can ask me such a question?"

Dana's foot began to tap, a quick, uneven rhythm. Solifrax flared in Andrion's clenched hand. Tembujin shut his eyes. The words were dragged from a depth he may not have known he possessed. "So then, forgive me, my lady. . . ." His voice thinned and died. He had just swallowed something cold and slimy, it seemed, and struggled to keep it down.

Dana exhaled and grinned at him. "Your sensibilities grow finer by the day, my odlok."

He offered her a ripple of his mouth that might have been a smile. Sarasvati glanced calculatingly from Tembujin to Dana and back. "You, too?"

"Yes," Dana said. "I am with child, his or Andrion's, we know not. But I chose them both."

"And that is the difference." The side of Sarasvati's mouth crimped at such a choice. "Surprising as it is, Tembujin, I am

pleased that despite my best efforts you are not dead. But
then, I am no longer bound to you, and I need never touch you
again.''

Tembujin turned away, too proud to admit defeat.

"By law," Andrion said, "I should order Tembujin to
marry you, Sarasvati. But that would hardly remedy the situation.''

Sarasvati nodded emphatic agreement. Committing herself
to a difficult task, she turned to the stiff shadow in the doorway. "Miklos, I am pleased to see you well.''

"Thank you, my lady," he returned, biting off each word.

Andrion waved Solifrax as if cutting the tension. A bubble
swelled within him, smooth bright colors glinting from its surface. He stood. "Miklos," he announced, "let me offer you a
reward for your service. The hand of my sister Sarasvati. If
she so pleases," he added quickly. Ah, he thought, preening
himself, a fine idea come to fruition.

Miklos stepped forward stiffly, called to parade before his
commander. "My lord, my lady, I—"

"Andrion," said Sarasvati in a faint voice, "I think perhaps . . .''

Dana laid down the lamp, leaving her face suddenly in
shadow. Tembujin strolled away until he collided with a wall.
He leaned against it with his face concealed by his crooked
arm.

"My lord," said Miklos, pulling each word tighter and
tighter, "this is such a great honor—thank you very much
—but I cannot, I cannot." He turned abruptly away and went
to retrieve his sword.

"Why did you do that to him?" Sarasvati asked Andrion
wearily. Her dark blue eyes shone with tears.

Of course. His bubble burst into a rain of needles, piercing
him to the quick. Of course Sardian Miklos would recoil from
a woman stained by rape. The young soldier had learned a
definition of honor so narrow it choked him.

No, it was not fair. What was? Andrion slashed the air with
Solifrax and the blade sent light glancing across the room. The
complications of the heart, damn them all. Miklos stood
bowed in the doorway, patiently waiting for Andrion to come
and kill him. Tembujin leaned against the wall, denying any
part in this travesty. Dana, her mouth slitted with irritation,
glared at the flame in the lamp. Sarasvati sighed; she reached

for and secured Andrion's hand, at the moment the stronger of the siblings.

A shadow stirred in a far, dim corner. A gray cat padded up the length of the room like an ambassador seeking an audience. It meowed courteously to Dana and to Andrion, and leaped onto Sarasvati's lap, draping itself around her belly. She started, and then smiled at it.

Dana and Andrion glanced at each other, shaken from the somber moment. "That could not be—" Andrion began.

"Qemnetesh," stated Dana. "Shurzad's cat."

Sarasvati plucked it up and held its face to hers, seeming to expect it to talk to her and reveal the truth. "It appeared only two days ago; it must have come with the Khazyari."

"No doubt as a little spy for the gods," Andrion said dryly. He reached out and ruffled the beast's ears. It smirked at him. He might have been angry or sad or merely tired, but he could not afford the luxury of reflection. "We must return to camp, Sarasvati. We shall attack tomorrow, from without and within."

"Justice," nodded Sarasvati, turning also to duty. "Very good. I have been hoarding weapons; the slaves, our people, will rise against their oppressors. Bring yourself and the sword, and they will fight for you."

"But are you not coming with us now?"

"I must stay here," she said, admitting no other possibility. "The people need direction. I shall see you on the morrow."

"Or in paradise," Andrion returned. He shivered. It was in this very room that Bellasteros had taken leave of Aveyron with almost those words. . . . No, the price had been paid, and paid again this night; the victory would be theirs. All he had to do, it seemed, was be in two places at once.

Gravely he kissed his sister. Dana embraced her. Tembujin bowed jerkily and fled into the hall. Miklos looked at Andrion, almost pleading for hatred; then he squared his shoulders and turned to Sarasvati. They stared at each other, divided by the length of the chamber, divided by the length of the Empire. He saluted her, and with a clash of his armor vanished. She let him go.

They left Sarasvati sitting on the battered throne in a pool of lamplight, thoughtfully stroking the cat. The cat lay with its forepaws tucked, whiskers alert, ears pricked for any echo of battle.

The group walked in glum silence through the deserted corridors. They spread splintered boards from the ruined stable across the opening to the well. They lit the torch again, and followed its small sputtering crimson light to the willow grove. The wind had died; the trees were still, each branch an engraved pattern against a steel-gray sky. The horses stamped restively, eager to be away.

Andrion sheathed Solifrax and climbed onto Ventalidar. He saw Sarasvati's glistening eyes before him, and his gut cramped cruelly. He glanced over at Tembujin, who would be his friend, and he said matter-of-factly, "You bastard." Miklos's white, pinched face looked around, thinking, perhaps, that the prince spoke of him. Dana winced.

"Ah," returned Tembujin in acid tones, "but my parents were wed. It is you who are—"

Andrion growled, "Hold that handsome tongue, Khazyari, or I shall be pleased to shorten it." His voice spun itself out and broke. Ventalidar leaped forward.

Tembujin jerked his head so that his tail of hair danced, but he said nothing more. The grove fell behind them. The dark mound of Iksandarun seemed to shift and stretch, its eyes, the fires of the Khazyari, blinking. The streets began to resonate with the rumor, with the promise, that the black prince had come at last, and that he carried his father's sword.

Hilkar ran, his scrawny neck outthrust, his robes fluttering, through the city, past the guards at the gate, into the Khazyari encampment. He stumbled to a halt, wheezing, and demanded of the guard outside Raksula's yurt, "I must see her. I have news, important news, a warning." He rubbed his hands together as if feeling riches between them.

The fabric doorway was ripped aside. Gouts of shadow poured from the blackness of the yurt into the fitful firelight, eclipsing it. Raksula's sharp-angled face, thin lips, glittering eyes, were those of a cobra peering angrily from its den. "What do you want?" she demanded.

"My lady," he gabbled, "Andrion was in the city tonight. He carries the sword Solifrax, and with it he rouses the slaves!"

"What?" Odo appeared at Hilkar's back.

Hilkar turned and grasped Odo's amulets so that they jangled with a brief, muted trill. "Andrion. He was in the city tonight." Odo removed Hilkar's hands.

Raksula's braids writhed. Her lips dripped venom. "What game is this? Maggot! You think you can play both sides?"

"No, no, my lady." Hilkar dropped to the ground, flattening himself at her feet. She stepped back. "I saw him, he saw me, he threatened me with the sword!"

Odo looked at Raksula. Raksula looked at Odo. Odo leaned over and grasped what few hairs still adhered to Hilkar's skull, pulling his head up. "Andrion saw you, and he did not kill you? Come now, such a pitiful story is not worthy of your villainy."

"No, no, lord," Hilkar gulped. His hands fluttered, broken wings, against the ground. "And Tembujin was there, with Andrion, as an ally."

Raksula screamed like an animal suddenly caught by a swooping raptor. "No, no you did not see him; it was only an evil vision. No one has seen him, do you hear, no one! You cannot fool me with such a lie, he is dead, moldering, gone!" With an effort she controlled herself, wiping the foam from her lips. Her chest heaved.

Odo stood staring at her, grated by some edge in her voice. For a moment his face clouded in suspicion; perhaps he wondered what she knew that he did not, what it was she so hysterically denied.

Hilkar lay sprawled, quivering in terror. "I told you," Raksula snarled slowly, savoring each word, "that if you came to me again, I would kill you." Hilkar spewed protestations of loyalty and innocence. She laughed at him. "And you are stupid enough to think I would believe this tale. Pathetic fool." She gestured to the guard. He drew his dagger.

Hilkar squeaked, trying to wriggle away. Odo's cloud coalesced into anger. He grasped one of Hilkar's arms, the guard the other. Raksula turned back into her lair. Her voice, still laughing, still screaming in agony, arched higher and higher and sliced the night into shivering gobbets of darkness.

Hilkar wept and pleaded as they dragged him to Khalingu's cart. No one listened. Odo took the dagger, raised it, and the thin weeping voice stopped abruptly. But nothing stirred inside the cart, as if the god disdained this offering, as if Raksula's shrill screeches offended even him.

Odo turned, frowning; he wiped the red blade of the dagger on Hilkar's scarlet-stained robes and returned it to the gaurd. The hangings about the cart remained as flaccid as Hilkar's body. The sky was opaque and airless.

Chapter Twenty-one

THE NIGHT LASTED forever. The sun, the moon, the stars faded into a dark featureless eternity. Andrion huddled on his narrow bed, caught in that uncertainty between midnight and dawn, between waking and sleeping.

He saw Sarasvati's lapis lazuli eyes filling with lamplight, burning like Valeria had once burned in his arms; he saw Tembujin's tail of hair fall from his head and writhe like a snake across the dim flagstoned floor of the throne chamber in Iksandarun. He saw Solifrax fall into a star-muddled basin of water, inscribe a trail like a glowing crescent, slice the sky into tatters of light; he saw it plummet with a hiss into Gerlac's sarcophagus, and nestle there safe in the golden billows of Dana's hair.

He sat up, cold sweat congealing on his body. The night was dark and airless. Solifrax lay silent beside his empty armor. He lay back down. His body was armor, a hard, dry husk, unfeeling, unseeing, hearing only expressionless voices planning strategy:

"Danica," Ilanit said, "teased Bellasteros about rebuilding the forts at the head of the pass, asking who would dare attack him. It is we, it seems, who would attack Iksandarun."

"We shall have to bludgeon the Khazyari into submission," said Nikander. "A clumsy strategy, a waste of good men. And women."

"The Khazyari can simply retreat into the city and close the gates," Lyris pointed out.

Patros's even voice replied, "But Andrion can lead troops into the city through the old tunnel, rallying our people. That would not only distract the Khazyari long enough for us to breast the pass and overrun them quickly, that would prevent their retreat.''

"Andrion can lead the army to the gates of Iksandarun.''

"Andrion can lead our people in revolt and open those gates.''

"Andrion can easily be in two places at once.''

Andrion twitched and groaned. Yes, that was the plan, formulated before he had walked again in Iksandarun or after he had returned, bleak and cold; he could not remember. He remembered the shuttered eyes of Tembujin, and the desolation on the face of Miklos. He saw the mound of Sarasvati's belly, only it was Dana who sat, waiting, pregnant with the future.

And Bellasteros the conqueror slept, serene in Danica's hand. And Bellasteros slept. And Bellasteros, Bellasteros, Bellasteros . . .

"Andrion!"

Andrion started up into a glancing light. No, it was only a small oil lamp, held in Lyris's hand. A woman, he was awakened yet again by a woman. "The battle begins," he said thickly, reaching for his sword.

"No, not yet." She pulled the covers from him and jerked at his arm. "Your . . . your father . . . Danica sends me . . .''

Andrion had never thought to hear Lyris stammer. "What?" he demanded, a ripple of cold tightening his spine.

"Bellasteros wakes and calls your name."

The words seeped like a fiery liquor through his veins, and he heard himself gasp. The tent receded, rushed close, receded again. Then his body fired with a fierce joy and sudden sorrow; he seized the sword and burst running from the tent, sweeping aside his guard. It might have been Lyris at his heels, it might have been fate; he did not turn to see.

The night was still shadowed, the sky flat, unyielding, black. The camp of the Sabazians stirred with small points of light like stars held in safekeeping. The women were wraiths plucking at him as he ran by. He plunged into Danica's tent, leaving the world shredded behind him.

The tent was filled with the yellow light of lamps, the red light of a fire in a brazier. It was warm and fragrant with healing herbs. Bellasteros sat propped on pillows like an effigy;

Danica sat beside him, her green eyes fixed upon his face, greedy for every small movement, every nuance of expression. Shandir hovered nearby. Ilanit and Dana stood side by side, the shield between them. Its light cast a gentle glow on the face of the king. Or perhaps it was his face drawing a glow from the shield.

His dark pellucid eyes fell upon his son. He smiled.

Andrion knelt beside his father's bed, his face upturned as if to the sun. He knew he was smiling, he knew his smile was tight with petulant, shameful resentment: Now you wake. Now, when I have learned not to need you. But no, that is not true, I shall always need you. . . . Bellasteros raised a wasted arm to touch his hair, reassuring himself that Andrion was a living being, not some figment of his long, long dream.

Bellasteros's face was gaunt, almost as gaunt as the skull Andrion had once held. His hair and beard were smooth shining electrum, the same color as Danica's hair; the glow of the diadem was camouflaged by it. But Bellasteros's eyes were rich dark brown, their depths stirred with many surfaces, many lights, internal reflections repeated over and over into infinity. His eyes were clear, untainted by sorcery.

Bellasteros's face blurred, and Andrion blinked. He saw himself mirrored in his father's eyes, he saw what his father saw, a man, not a boy. "So," said his father's faint but precise voice, "you have been busy, I hear. Leading my army, finding your sister Sarasvati, taming our enemy."

"I did it in your name. . . ." His throat closed. Andrion drew Solifrax from its sheath. It rang, and the shield of Sabazel behind it rang in greeting. The filigree hilt fit his own grasp now, the perfection of the blade was marred by his own blood; he sank his teeth deep into his lower lip and offered the hilt to his father's remaining hand.

Danica looked down on Andrion with a wry amusement. Bellasteros, with an effort, raised his hand and touched the sword. It sparked for him, a slow swirl of light motes raining upward to kiss his face. And he let the sword go. "It is now yours."

Andrion tried not to snatch it away. He held it before him, between them. "Father . . ." he said, but there was nothing else to say.

The corners of Bellasteros's eyes crinkled with his smile, fine lines etched on his face as they had been upon Danica's by years of decision and light. "Andrion," he murmured, "beloved of the gods." His voice was a fine thread of sound, savoring the name. "Again I come to Iksandarun. Again Iksandarun must be taken. I would ride at the head of the army one last time. I would be young again, and strong." His face tightened in regret and then cleared.

Patros knelt beside him, his face struggling with hope and fear. For just a moment Andrion saw Bellasteros and Patros as the boys they had once been, brothers setting off together across the world before its width divided them. "Marcos," Patros said, calling his friend from the hazy borders he approached, too noble to hold him back if he wished to go.

Bellasteros clasped Patros's hand, comforting him. "I entrust your friendship to my son. He can have nothing stronger."

Patros's composure cracked, his face twisting in anguish. But he allowed only one tear to course like a shining drop of amber down his cheek. Bellasteros set his hand gently down. Danica took Bellasteros's hand and held it between her own, her face as brittle as fine porcelain.

A pole appeared beside Andrion, clasped by Miklos's white knuckles. The bronze falcon swooped over the emperor, wings glittering.

Andrion bowed in pain over the sword. It flamed before his face; his cheeks were hot with it. In the corner of his eye the shield of Sabazel stirred in response, lovers murmuring together.

Then Bellasteros grinned, white teeth flashing in his pale beard, rousing from his pillows as if drawn to some vision. Twenty years fell from his face. Andrion floated down into the cool fire of his father's eyes. He saw a red plume and a crimson cloak and Solifrax flaring under a crystal blue sky. He saw the garden of the gods, Ashtar holding Harus safe upon her wrist, Solifrax growing from the earth itself beneath the Tree of Life. For a moment he heard the wind chiming in the branches of the Tree, rippling through its green leaves and golden fruit. Green and gold, Danica's, Ilanit's, Dana's eyes . . . The distant reflection diminished, faded, and was gone. The light in Bellasteros's eyes went out, and his head fell heavily onto Danica's breast.

Andrion felt the sword sear his hands and then cool. He saw the shield flash and then dull. He felt his mind reel through some great space, fall, shatter against the hard cold surface of death.

Danica's emerald gaze splintered into sharp, tearing shards. Patros bent his face into hands and crouched, his shoulders shaking. The falcon seemed to droop above Miklos's ashen face.

So, Andrion told himself, with a few banal words the conqueror dies, and takes his numinous cloak from this world to another. Yes, to another world; Andrion was certain of what he had seen in Bellasteros's eyes. He reached to his mother's breast and closed the blankness that had been his father's eyes. The flesh was waxen, already transmuted to some other substance.

Danica's face was patched together with line and shadow, her features subtly changed, one important facet of her expression gone. With the greatest reverence, she laid Bellasteros's head against the pillow and regarded it with a distant smile. Andrion sensed her thought, sparks in the basin of water: We shared the fruit that grows beyond the world, you and I. We shall never be truly separated.

Slowly he stood, groping through his tangled thought: relief, that his father had at last left him; resentment, that Bellasteros had abandoned him to the task ahead. To speak of leading the army again . . . His heart writhed with sobs that could not pass the hard shell of his throat. I already cried for you, he thought, the night when they took your right arm.

He saw Ilanit and Dana, eyes downcast, leaning together. He saw Patros grim and still. He saw Shandir clasping her hand to her mouth. He saw Nikander, standing to attention, tears rolling down his hollow cheeks. He saw Tembujin, of all people, hovering just inside the doorway of the tent beside a white-lipped Lyris. The Khazyari let Andrion see a kind of taut horror-stricken sympathy shadow his dark eyes, then hid his face. Miklos glanced around and scowled.

Danica lifted the diadem from Bellasteros's head as she had set it upon him, at the full moon of midwinter nineteen years before. She turned the coverlet over his calm, quiet face. She whispered, "The king is dead. Long live the King of Sardis, Emperor." Andrion thought for a moment that her eyes filled with tears, filled with weary anger that she should even care about this event in the world of men. But they filled instead with that infinite green-gold shimmer, that certain vision of peace.

With a sigh, acknowledging implacable time, Danica set the diadem upon Andrion's brow.

He had expected the diadem to be heavy, but it was not. It was barely a caress upon him, a brief dizzying tingle through his body. He could see himself in Patros's and Danica's eyes, the band of gold rippling in tiny flames across the bright embers of his hair.

The tent swayed. Tembujin vanished. Patros knelt before Andrion, saying, "My fealty, my lord"; his voice leaped from one octave to another, but his upturned face was determinedly calm. And Nikander knelt, and Miklos. The falcon nodded gravely. The shield of Sabazel flared in friendship, and friendship only; who can ever know, Andrion thought to Ilanit's green eyes, what Sabazel really is to me.

He should be numb. He should be dazed by grief. But there was a shimmer in his own mind. His senses were distressingly clear, every color, every shape sharply engraved. Every sound, the creak of leather, the sigh of coals, the varied breaths, fell as distinctly upon his ear as the chime of a bell. Every fiber of his body sang, and his thoughts spun in great shining circles like scythes on the wheels of war chariots, cutting their way to a scheme so mad he did not at first trust his perceptions. But if he could not trust himself, he could trust no one.

So this is why you lingered so long, he thought to the shade of his father, only to wake now, and die. Bellasteros, the proud king, would never surrender to weakness. Bellasteros, my father, would never abandon me before I was ready to see him go. Bellasteros, the master strategist, would throw himself one last time into the game. Pride and love and duty stronger than sorcery and death.

Everyone was watching him. Andrion tightened his teeth until his jaw ached. He took the diadem from his head and set it, a glowing ring, upon the coverlet. He embraced his mother, commending the symbol of the Empire to her. He plunged Solifrax into its scabbard, hiding its whispering light. He summoned his followers and led them from the tent.

The darkness was impenetrable. For a moment Andrion could see nothing but the gentle green and gold motes of light that floated in his own mind. Then they spiraled away and vanished, and the dim outlines of the imperial camp coalesced before him. A figure stood there, bobbing and bowing. "My lord, no one woke me, forgive me." It was Bonifacio. Andrion was not the only one who had forgotten all about him. He muttered some courtesy and waved Bonifacio into the tent.

The night was silent, every small noise absorbed by the flat steel-gray sky, by the harrowing chill. Andrion realized without surprise that hundreds of people were grouped politely if warily on the borders of the Sabazian camp. Only their eyes glinted in the darkness, reflecting the watchfires, waiting.

Bellasteros had been the spindle upon which these people spun their hopes, weaving them with legends of the past. How could he dash that expectancy from them? Andrion raised his chin, confident in his plan; stubborn, some part of him said, and he accepted that as well. His mind sparked with tiny snaps, as if the diadem still graced his brow.

He stepped forward and raised his arms. "Bellasteros is well," he called, his voice firm. "He will lead us into battle tomorrow!"

A great cheer erupted from the crowd, shivering the sky, calling a brief breath of icy wind to lift Andrion's hair from his perspiring brow. He grinned lopsidedly, ashamed of himself, pleased with himself. "Go back to your quarters and get what sleep you can. Our destiny is upon us!"

Again the people cheered. With many happy speculative murmurings they dispersed. Andrion turned to those dim forms standing behind him, and his grin faded into a long exhalation. Nikander's brows were halfway up his forehead. Patros's mouth hung open in astonishment. Lyris, Ilanit, and Dana were three blank, stunned faces. How fortunate, Andrion thought, that this is a dark night, and no one can see their expressions giving me the lie.

He opened his mouth to explain and then stopped, hearing a muttering of angry voices. He turned and saw, a few steps away, Miklos grasping the pole of the standard as if it were a mace. Tembujin's hands were raised, palms outthrust in cautious warning. The ursine warrior stood behind him, frowning at the tone of the words he could not understand.

Miklos growled, "You had no right to intrude upon the emperor!"

"You have no quarrel with me," Tembujin replied placatingly.

"No quarrel!" Miklos exclaimed. He lunged forward, the bronze falcon flashing in the firelight. The huge guard deflected him with a mighty arm. Tembujin did not move.

Neither did Andrion. "Stop it," he said in a quiet voice that penetrated the darkness like a javelin thrust. Miklos pulled himself to clanking attention, his eyes rolling aggrievedly toward Andrion. Tembujin shrugged his tail of hair and slouched as if unconcerned. But his eyes, too, turned in silent question to Andrion. "Give Governor Patros the falcon," said Andrion to Miklos. "Go, bring me Ventalidar."

Miklos handed over the standard and hurried away. Andrion looked after him with an inward groan; always the same questions of love and honor and reality, inescapable. Bonifacio came backing out of the tent, intoning a prayer, and Andrion interrupted with brisk orders. "Bring me the red-plumed helmet. Find me a crimson cloak. In the name of Harus, tell no one that Bellasteros is dead."

Bonifacio, too, stared in amazement. "Go on," Andrion said, making a quick shooing motion. With many a dubious backward glance, Bonifacio went.

Patros and Nikander, Ilanit, Lyris and Dana, still waited, trusting if bewildered. Andrion beckoned Tembujin and asked them all, "Would it not be a terrible blow to see the emperor die, wasted by sorcery, on the eve of battle? Would the people not prefer to see him die powerful in victory? Would he not himself choose to die strong and confident, in duty's saddle?" Each face was rapt, unblinking. "Let us then set him to lead the army before Iksandarun, as he did once. And I shall then be freed to take Iksandarun from within." There. It sounded ridiculously simple. It sounded impossibly macabre.

Nikander and Patros exchanged a wild-eyed glance. "But if anyone deserves now to rest . . ." Patros ventured.

"I know that you mean no disrespect, my lord . . ." essayed Nikander.

Andrion pulled them closer, held them fixed with the intensity of his eyes, his voice. "He asked for this, did he not, with almost his last breath? How can we deny him, deny his land, one last hour of youth and strength? Bellasteros always wrote his own rules, even for me. . . ." He gulped, but his eye did not waver.

"Of course," Patros sighed. "He did ask. How he would enjoy the irony of it." Nikander seemed almost dazed, turning the scheme in his mind, approving it. Ilanit nodded slowly, and the shield glimmered in her hand. Dana glanced at Tembujin, and he shook his head. "Such audacity," he murmured. "Worthy of the falcon indeed." Lyris stared at Andrion as if he had gone mad. Then she checked herself, looked right and left at the steady faces around her, and shrugged acceptance.

Andrion began to breathe again, and doled out his orders.

Everyone scattered, gray ghosts in the night. No, the night was lightening toward dawn, a faint glow in the east giving each tent, each weapon, a crisp silver edge.

Tembujin remained. His black eyes flashed as if to say, Come now, anyone capable of such humor can surely be my friend. "Well," Andrion said to him, "I suppose that we bastards should work together."

With a short laugh Tembujin, too, disappeared, his bearlike escort shambling behind. Andrion's smile grew tighter and tighter until at last it broke. His scheme slithered through his mind; the price of the Empire indeed: my youth, and my father's life . . . Only then did he wonder whether Tembujin had meant to name him the falcon.

The dawn glimmered behind a sky plated with blue-gray cloud like chain mail. The wind rang coldly from some profound depth. The moon was hidden. It will return tonight, Dana thought, at the full. And I am not in Sabazel, not in Andrion's arms celebrating the day of his birth. I celebrate death. But then this day is the meeting point of light and dark, when the sun begins its return to summer, when hope dies and is reborn.

She tucked her lengthening hair under her helmet, and laced on her breastplate. No, her belly was not yet round enough to thrust protestingly against it. She searched her thoughts, seeking some tendril of the Sight, but her senses were as numb as the sky.

Andrion loomed up beside her, darker than dark in his black cloak. "No point in asking you to stay behind and protect our child," he stated.

"Your mother carried you into battle the day you were born."

"Marking me with death," he said. Dana darted a sharp glance at him; he was not bitter, not fey, not even worried about the fortunes of the day. She kissed his cold and stoic lips, their helmets clashing together, and drew from him a grave smile.

Behind them Ventalidar stood as tremblingly still as one of the paintings in Ashtar's cavern, his eyes rolling in bewilderment at the stillness of his burden. His burden was Bellasteros, as straight in death as he had been in life, integrity instilled in his very bones.

Danica stood at the horse's head, crooning reassurances, glancing up again and again at the carven features framed by the red-plumed helmet. Her lips tightened in some wry humor between tears and laughter, but her eyes gleamed with an uncanny patience, as if for once she knew the ending of the game and had only to wait for it to be played out. Her firm, fragile hands spread the crimson cloak across Ventalidar's haunches, settled the reins around the wicker stand that braced Bellasteros's back, snugged the ropes that bound his legs to the saddle.

The morning lightened, a sun like the fading embers of a watchfire reddening the haze. Andrion stepped to his father's shining greave and said with a quiet, resigned humor, "For months now I have had visions of riding this horse, my own god-given horse, in a bravura charge against the enemy. But it is you who will do that."

Andrion pulled Solifrax from its sheath. What? Dana asked herself. The cloak was pinned over Bellasteros's mutilated arm; he could not carry the sword even if Andrion gave it to him. But Andrion moved with the assurance of one who has plumbed the depths of doubt and found a solace beyond.

Solifrax etched an arc of fire in the mist. The flare of light was so bright that for a moment Dana could see nothing. Faint incandescent shapes seemed to move before her, the walls of Sardis, the wings of Harus, young Bellasteros. . . . The light faded. The emperor's features were cleanly chiseled, the angle of his chin softened by a neat sable beard; his mouth was tightly closed, set firm with the habit of command. One dark-lashed eyelid shivered into a wink—ah, the demands of the game we play—but no, it must have been some aftereffect of the light emitted by the sword. But his eyes remained open, dark, clear gemstones.

Danica emitted a short, strangled cry of recognition. Bellasteros was strong again, and whole; broad shoulders filled the crimson cloak, two hands grasped Ventalidar's reins. Not breathing, not living, but whole. The cloak billowed in sudden tolling wind and Dana smiled.

Andrion waved Solifrax in salute and with a flourish sheathed it. He glowed with exaltation and power; he glanced around at the watching faces, not ashamed to exult. He patted Ventalidar's quivering shoulder, and the horse calmed, no longer wary of its burden.

Danica, smiling in fierce satisfaction, kissed Bellasteros's right hand and closed it about a polished Sabazian saber.

Nikander and Patros appeared from the murk, startled by

this image of their emperor, alive and well and determined to
achieve victory. Awed and pleased, they, too, saluted. Valeria
slipped from her father's horse and regarded Bellasteros without flinching, her unveiled cheeks pink, her eyes bright with
the courage of those who must stand and wait.

Bonifacio hovered behind her, muttering prayers and protests. A breath of wind brought the word *sacrilege* to Dana's
ear; she glanced around even as Andrion did. Andrion's keen
eye fixed the priest, and he flushed beet red; Andrion's eye
discarded him and he turned, almost colliding with the phantom shape of Tembujin's white horse. Bonifacio made the sign
of the evil eye. Tembujin, jerking himself away from Bellasteros's cool, almost arrogant features, cordially returned it.

The odlok left his guard with a terse Khazyari phrase at
Danica's side. Evidently his loyalty was not to be tested in
battle against his own people; Tembujin asked that only of
himself.

And here was Miklos, bearing the bronze falcon yet again.
His features were sharp, pared to the bone with elation and
resolve. "My lord," he said to Andrion, "may I lead the
emperor into his last battle?"

"Why?" Andrion asked. "Ventalidar has wit enough to
carry him."

"To prove my loyalty to you," Miklos stated.

"I have never doubted your loyalty."

"Have you not?"

Andrion's eyes burned with a chill flame; the emperor's
eyes, subtly refined. "Is this the greatest gift I can give you?
Go then, with my blessing. And may you feast this night in
paradise."

"My thanks, my lord." With a salute of the falcon, Miklos
turned away.

So, Dana thought, the playing pieces move onto the board.
Andrion braced himself like a legionary preparing for inspec-
tion. "Iksandarun waits for deliverance," he said to Dana, to
Danica, to all the watching faces. And to his father as well.
Bellasteros's handsome features remained serene and certain.

And it is this, Dana thought to Andrion, that delivers you.
She caught the brilliance of his eye, nodded, and turned away.
The dawn stirred with muted voices, turning wheels, hoof-
beats, as the army lumbered forward.

Andrion led his troop of a hundred picked veterans, Lyris
and twenty Sabazians, to the grove, through the tunnel, out

into the palace without really seeing anything around him. Willow branches, water, stone were all the same gray shadows. The surreptitious whispers of the soldiers might as well have been the distant humming of insects. He saw a prancing black horse bearing a crimson plume and a crimson cloak, he heard the blaring of Sardian trumpets, a resonance of Iksandarun's past as strangely altered as a dream. His hand clutched Solifrax, as though if he released it, he would disintegrate into a figment of his father's vision. But the hilt thrilled against his damp palm, sensual, cold; the vision was his.

Sarasvati waited, wearing a chiton, a modestly draped cloak, and a Sardian stabbing sword. Her tied-up hair was a sleek copper helmet, her eyes points of blue fire. Briefly she greeted Lyris and Andrion and introduced them to her officers, ragged men and women armed with knives and scythes, bricks and sturdy staves, hatred and determination.

It would be useless to ask her to stay behind, Andrion told himself. He told her quietly of Bellasteros's death and transfiguration; she swallowed any grief, any surprise. "Later," she said, and he nodded. Later, the leisure to reflect and comprehend.

With dour approval Lyris found Sarasvati a coat of mail large enough to encompass her waist, and a leather cap. Andrion organized his troops; soon the ragtag army was flowing like turgid water from the palace and through the city. The turbulent sky diffused a thin sunlight over city and plain, casting no shadows. The wind raced in cold muted chimes around each corner, down each street. Wailing cries echoed eerily as the Khazyari moved toward the pass. Dully pealing trumpets echoed in reply. Camels bellowed.

The crowd slipped across the amphitheatre as silently and as inexorably as wind scouring stone. Andrion remembered sitting there laughing at comedies, sighing at tragedies; he had a sudden vision of his father's life, his own life, becoming in the end only a garbled drama played before thousands of remote faces. Andrion Bellasteros, the man of honor.

Every alleyway, every building, disgorged more people. A few tossed bodies of Khazyari warriors like so much garbage onto rubbish heaps. The vengeful wave swept to the gates of the city. The huge doors were supported by pylons carved with reliefs of fabulous beasts, enameled eyes staring. Here, Andrion thought, Hilkar stood on a midsummer's night, throw-

ing back the bolts and writing the heart of that drama. Surely
the gods were amused that a worm would have so much power
over the life of Andrion Bellasteros.

The slaves and soldiers rushed forward, slaughtering what
few Khazyari stood about the guardhouse. Now it was Andrion's own hands that released the bars; with a hundred eager
hands beside him, he opened the city to the world outside. The
Khazyari encampment lay in bedraggled lumps before him,
and beyond that a dim mass seethed with the faint sparklings
of weapons, rumbled with shouts and cries.

Sarasvati gasped. Andrion turned and started. There, a
fragment of evil memory, was Hilkar himself. Or Hilkar's
body, rather, pinioned upside down to the front of the gate,
with arrows through hands and feet. His mouth was gaping in
horror, mottled with blood. Andrion noted bleakly that his
throat had been cut; so, his death had been more merciful than
he might have received from this mob.

Shouting curses, the freed slaves, the citizens of Iksandarun, threw bricks and stones with sickening thuds at the
body. The arrows loosened, and the scrawny form fell and was
torn apart.

Lyris's stance seemed to say, such is the fate of traitors. But
Andrion averted his gaze, and Sarasvati's complexion turned
slightly green.

At last the jeering shouts died away. Subdued, the people
turned again to Andrion. He felt his face hewn of frosted
stone, not applauding them, not criticizing them. He drew
Solifrax and thrust it, a clear crystalline flame, toward the sky.
He told his army, "Let the women and children live. Let any
warrior who lays down his weapons live." He knew they
would obey.

He allowed himself a thin smile. He let his eyes reflect the
flame of the sword. He raised his voice in the Sabazian paean.
Now, now! Lyris's keen white face broke into fierce glee, her
arid voice climbing beside his. The wind swirled, the clouds
swirled above them. The makeshift army streamed with fell
songs into the Khazyari camp.

"What!" Raksula shouted. "Do not jest with me!"

The panting messenger stood firm. "Our camp has been attacked from behind. Not just the slaves in the city, but imperial soldiers led by the black prince himself and the fiery
sword of the emperor."

"No!" screamed Raksula.

Another messenger fought his way through the mayhem. "The Emperor Bellasteros himself leads the legions, with the odlok Tembujin at his right hand. They cannot be stopped!"

"No!" Raksula howled. "No, it is not so!"

Odo jerked his pony around and overrode her shrill voice with his own orders. The messengers hurried away. The Crimson Horde eddied, uncertain, and began to fall back. Vlad, bouncing like a sack of meal upon his pony, disappeared into the mass.

Raksula screamed curses at Odo. He ignored her and followed the retreating Khazyari, trying to keep their uncertainty from becoming a rout. She glanced around, saw the shining falcon, the red plume, the shield of Sabazel that glittered despite the gloomy day, advancing implacably up the throat of the pass. The Sabazian paean rang down the wind, was caught and magnified and altered by the imperial army that came to reclaim its own. She spun her horse about and galloped back to the camp, back to the shelter of Khalingu's cart, laughing and weeping hysterically.

Chapter Twenty-two

THE HORDE FELL back toward Iksandarun. Sprays of arrows filled the air like showers of clattering rain. Andrion's small band found themselves almost overwhelmed; frenzied faces spun by, daggers flicked, and one tore Andrion's black cloak. Another left a gleaming scratch along Sarasvati's mail; her own blows were enthusiastic but much too clumsy. Now, Andrion told himself, now is the moment to turn. Solifrax blazed. The attackers fell back. Andrion and Lyris bracketed Sarasvati and led a wedge of their followers through the smoke of burning yurts toward the city.

A hoarse voice shouted, and a Khazyari nuryan dove through the swirling legionaries straight at the black cloak, the falcon brooch, the sword, the unmistakable signatures of Andrion. Andrion thrust Sarasvati behind him; Solifrax leaped, whistling through the air, and the man's tunic was suddenly laced with red. He fell, his face twisted with pain and despair. Lyris was upon him, sword lifted—

"No!" Sarasvati screamed. She pushed Andrion aside and lunged at Lyris. Lyris, startled, missed her blow and her sword struck sparks from the cobblestones. Several other warriors froze in midstroke.

The slumped Khazyari looked up, some measure of sanity stilling the maelstrom in his eyes. "No, lady," he gasped, "I die now."

"Nonsense, Obedei," Sarasvati told him. She kicked his dagger skipping across the stones and bent to help him; overbalancing, she fell.

Lyris stood in an awkward stance, sword half-extended, mouth open. With a snap she shut her mouth and looked indignantly at Andrion.

Obedei. The name was not a strange one. Andrion extended his hand to his sister, signed to two legionaries, and had Obedei hauled inside.

Willing hands slammed and bolted the gates before the astonished faces and horrified screams of the Khazyari. They dashed themselves against the walls, turned, were crushed by the tide of the imperial army.

Andrion leaned on his sword, considering the dirty and exhausted face of the nuryan. "He helped you?" he asked Sarasvati.

"Yes," she said. "He is a man of honor, loyal to his own people."

Tembujin, thought Andrion, saw beyond his people to a greater loyalty. "Your lord Tembujin is still alive," he said to Obedei, "and reclaims his title. Will you serve him?"

It took a moment for the words to penetrate. Then Obedei's features collapsed into a crooked grin. "Surely, lord, surely." Lyris shrugged, and sheathed her sword.

Sarasvati wiped the perspiration from her brow and looked with wide eyes at the rust-stained sword she held. "Gods," she whispered. "So that is battle. My respects, Lyris, for choosing it as your profession."

"It was forced upon me," Lyris growled.

"Indeed." Sarasvati draped Obedei's arm across her shoulder, and with a grateful look at Andrion, led him away. Andrion saluted them.

He and Lyris watched the battle from a walkway above the gate. An occasional arrow whistled by them; one, its force spent, bounced off Andrion's cuirass. He hardly noticed, so intent was he on the scene before him. He held Solifrax across the parapet, its blade unstained by any blood it had shed save his own. Its gold glowed beguilingly against the stained brick, and Andrion wondered whether he loved it or hated it.

Below, in the square before the gate, huddled several Khazyari women and children who had escaped inside during the altercation with Obedei. Andrion glanced down; yes, the townspeople were reassuring them and leading them to safety. He felt he should smile at this small favor, at the sparing of Obedei, but his tendons were knitted too tightly to allow even that.

Warmth poured over him and he looked up. The clouds fractured into glades and rills of blue, Ashtar's eyes contemplating the arrayed pawns of her vast and complex game.

Sudden shafts of sun raked the battlefield, picking out one
struggling knot of figures, dimming, picking out another;
smoke swirled in the sunlight like starfire in the bronze basin.
The swaying forms on the battlefield were only faded frescoes,
indistinct figures caught in stylized attitudes, their movement
an illusion in the corner of the eye. Their shouts and cries were
less real than the low notes of a dirgelike wind. Perhaps, Andrion thought, this is truly one of the battles of Daimion, or
the triumph of young Bellasteros, not my own clumsy ascen-
sion.

Andrion leaned over the parapet, straining toward the distant mass of men; he felt himself on the battlefield, Ventalidar's muscles flexing and loosing between his thighs, the
wind tugging at his black plume and black cloak. There, in a
strand of sunlight so thick and golden it looked like an amber
stairway leading upward, was Bellasteros. The red plume and
red cloak streamed behind him, and Ventalidar's black coat
shone with echoing hints of red. The bronze falcon rode the
wind just ahead, circling, swooping on its prey, avenging its
brother smashed on the day of defeat.

And there, in another thread of light, was the shield of
Sabazel, the embossed star pulsing in quicksilver swirls, illuminating Patros's grim face. That calm figure, a rock in the
midst of a torrent, was Nikander. That tiny form was Dana,
clambering with several Sabazians up the turf-covered mound
of an earlier generation's dead Sardians.

Some Khazyari, their backs to the wall, fought berserkly on
and died. But others . . . Andrion squinted. Yes, there, on the
far edge of the Khazyari camp, was a scowling Tembujin, bow
upheld over the prone bodies of supplicants, white horse ca-
pering. A squat figure scurried furtively through the smoldering piles of felt that had been yurts. He had seen that face
before, in a nightmare, but the name escaped him.

He was not on the battlefield. He waited helplessly, the
struggling armies beyond his reach. His hand slapped Solifrax
on the parapet; the sword scored the great block of stone into
myriad tiny fractures.

But warmth touched him again, a dazzling ray of sunlight
caressing his head and then fading. The bronze falcon was at
the gates of Iksandarun, followed closely by the scarlet and
purple pennons. The battle, the world circled around him. He
bounded down the stair, Lyris at his heels. Again Andrion
opened the gates with his own hands.

Miklos rushed by, hand clenched on the standard, armor bloodied, eyes staring wildly ahead. Ventalidar rushed by, miraculously unscathed, the form on his back still erect and tall. Andrion thought for one scalding moment that Bellasteros's pallid face was the youthful one of his visions: short hair, beardless chin, rich brown eyes surveying the width of the world, taking it as his own, bequeathing it to his heir.

Legionaries and Khazyari poured struggling through the gate. Miklos and Bellasteros were gone. Andrion spun for a moment, senses reeling. Then he sternly collected his scattered wits; his duty lay outside. Lyris was waiting. "Come!" he shouted.

Lyris called her Sabazians, Andrion shouted orders at his centurions. He commandeered horses from the first cavalry riders he saw. They surged through the mass outside the gate into the ruined encampment. Their horses stumbled through fire and smoke and mud, past dead camels and ponies, past an appalling number of sprawling dead people, horror-filled eyes looking beyond the turbulent iron-gray arch of the sky. The very ground seemed to shiver with an eerie sound, wailing high-pitched trills, like but not quite the Khazyari song of victory that had harrowed Iksandarun at midsummer; this song spiraled down, down into an abyss of fear and despair.

The full moon of midwinter, Andrion thought. Midwinter. The winter kings, Andrion and Tembujin, struggle toward the spring.

There was the shield, radiant not with sunlight but with moonlight and star-sheen. Solifrax flamed, seeming almost to leap from his hand toward the shield, its mate. Unerringly, cutting down anyone in his path, Andrion fought his way toward it.

Dana and a group of Sabazians sat atop the earthen mound of the Sardians dead in Bellasteros's victory nineteen years before. She set her last arrow to her bow, raised it, stopped. Her mind writhed, sliced suddenly by a fiery blade. *No, save that arrow!* She gulped, lowered the bow, looked frantically around for some clue to her vision. The wind kissed her fevered cheeks and slackened.

The small, distant figure that was Patros sent pages scurrying. Ilanit's shield gleamed at his side. A company of cavalry pounded by, pursuing Khazyari mounted on lathered ponies. A crimsoned sword gestured, and one of them fell and was trampled. Chariots skimmed across the plateau, harvesting death. The gates of Iksandarun opened again. The crimson plume vanished inside, the black plume and the fiery arc of Solifrax reappeared. So, Dana thought, time swallows the one and spits the other into play.

Nikander materialized out of swarming soldiers, Tembujin at his side, shouting something to Patros. As one Patros and Ilanit, Nikander and Tembujin wheeled. Encompassed by a guard of Sabazians and legionaries mingled, they plunged into the Khazyari camp. Women and children scattered before them like a covey of pheasant, their cries a weird resonance in a failing wind.

A thick golden thread of sun fell upon the camp, glancing through the haze of smoke, seeming to burn it away. Then the camp was dim, indistinct, a remote sketch once again.

A squat man draped with amulets waited in the midst of several imperial soldiers, hands upraised, shielded eyes rolling from face to face. He cringed as Tembujin leaped down, grasped the front of his tunic, and shook him like a lion shaking a bloated carcass. The odlok drilled the man with a few words of Khazyari; his fleshy cheeks quivering, the man responded.

Tembujin's words, droplets of gall, seared Dana's mind. The shaman Odo, she told herself. He says he will surrender the Horde. Odo's body seemed as boneless as jelly; his eyes rolled up in his head, leaving only a rim of glistening white. In contempt, Tembujin dropped him.

Nikander spoke to the waiting soldiers; they formed a ragged circle, a dike holding back the ebb and flow of battle. At the edge of the circle, Dana noted, was a small two-wheeled cart curtained with opaque gray hangings. Or perhaps it was curtained with smoke. The wind had stilled itself, and yet the hangings moved in and out as if stirred by slow breaths.

Then her ear picked up a shout, one clear voice overriding all others. There was Andrion, buoyed up by Sabazian helmets, by the glow of Solifrax. Ashtar! Dana thought; to her keen eye Andrion's face was melted gold freshly poured from its crucible, burned free of all pretense, all caprice, all lingering youth. She saw, heard, felt him rein up beside Ilanit. "Well met, my sister."

"Well met, my brother," Ilanit responded. She lifted her shield. He lifted his sword, the sword that was a part of his own body. They touched. Their light was lightning striking up, rending the coulds, drawing down a sunbeam that was also molten gold. The crescent of the sword, and the star of the shield; the necklace, Dana felt Andrion think. I have almost forgotten that necklace. The sword rang the shield like a bell, and Ilanit grinned.

The sun went out. Dana shivered, her perceptions flowing from her mind like water from her body. She cursed the Sight that took her unaware and used her as its vessel. The camp, the circle of soldiers, the figures in their midst were distance pieces upon a gameboard. And still she watched, unable to move, the hair prickling on the back of her neck, her bow prickling in her hand. There is the shaman. Where is the witch?

Andrion saw his officers waiting. He saw Odo, still crouching in the dirt. His eye touched Tembujin's and considered the controlled rage within it. He dismounted onto the churned and bloody ground. Ilanit and Patros followed; Nikander and Lyris remained mounted, leaning forward with great attention. Tembujin stirred Odo's flabby body with his toe. He asked, no doubt, the same question: Where is Raksula?

Odo seemed to grope through clouds of fog, his face twitching with a tic. He said nothing.

Nikander regarded Odo as if he were a dead fish washed up on the shores of the Jorniyeh. Tembujin slapped his sword against his leg, before Odo's face. Dana's mind strained tighter and tighter toward the scene below. But she could not move toward it. She would break, she thought wildly, panting; she would burst into shivering strands of flesh and thought and dissipate down the wind. . . . But there was no wind.

Then a frenzied shriek shattered the air, the smoke, the sunlight. Raksula leaped like a crazed leopard from beneath the cart. A long dagger glinted in each hand, her many braids streamed out from her head, her eyes bottomless wells of madness, as flat and dark as a moonless midnight, seeing everything, but recognizing nothing.

She fell upon Ilanit. The shield arched up. The daggers rang against the emblazoned star and the ringing echoed into the sky.

Ilanit's sword struck one braid from Raksula's head, spun, feinted, struck again. But Raksula's scrawny body seemed to carry the miasma of the battlefield around it, she was never quite where she appeared to be. She fought with an uncanny strength and speed, screaming as she struck, "Sabazel chokes my every plan, denying me my rightful place. Sabazel be damned!" Ilanit swung and parried; frowning, she gave back one step, then two.

Every watching eye was drawn to the swirling forms, mesmerized as surely as a moth by some gleaming candle. Patros's teeth glinted between drawn-back lips. Tembujin swayed as if fighting a sudden dizziness. Nikander and Lyris leaped from their horses and froze, weapons poised. Andrion stood with a suddenly dimmed Solifrax upraised, eyes transfixed by the dancing shapes before him, blades weaving an intricate pattern of light and shadow, clashing again and again with dull thuds. He grimaced. The sword glimmered before him and then faded.

Dana leaned from her horse, screaming, "Sorcery, it is sorcery, the witch has a spell about herself!" Her entire body was one quivering strand of awareness, arcing swift and sure to where the small doll-like figures circled; her body was bound to the saddle of the horse and she cried in a paroxysm of frustration, "Wake up! Wake up!" The Sabazians about her jostled each other, sharing alarmed glances.

"All your fault, all yours, not even any of your concern . . ." Raksula screeched in Khazyari and common tongue both, her lips flecked with foam.

"Loyalty," gasped Ilanit. "Love." Her eyes narrowed in concentration, as if replaying every practice session, every battle she had ever fought; her finely knit body bent and swayed. Still she gave way, uncertain whorls of light eddying across the face of the shield.

Every face was drawn to Raksula, Odo forgotten. He pulled a dagger from his tunic. Raksula's eyes, glittering jet, snapped in command. Odo threw himself toward Andrion's back. The dagger flared as sunlight spilled again over the battlefield.

Dana saw the distant figure rise and move, slowly, slowly, a fly struggling through golden resin. Her thought exploded into white-hot sparks. Her hand ripped the last arrow from her quiver and flung it against the bow; the bow leaped. One shot, now, or another king devoured by bloody Iksandarun, all this agony for nothing. . . . Andrion, flesh of my flesh, blood of my blood. "Ashtar!" she screamed, and the bowstring sang high, clear, strumming the air itself.

The thick golden rays of the sun were shattered into prismatic dust by the shriek of the arrow. With the hideous sound of a melon splitting open it struck Odo's back, passed through his body and sprouted in bloody petals through the amulets on his chest. In utter astonishment he fell face first into the dirt, the dagger still in his hand.

In that moment Raksula howled and spun, slicing Patros's arm from shoulder to elbow. Ilanit shouted. Raksula whirled, striking again; her other dagger shattered against the star-shield into glowing shards of metal.

Someone cried out in pain. It was not Patros, Dana realized, but she herself. Tears blurred the world before her. She threw the bow onto her shoulder and urged her horse, scrambling and slipping, down the mound.

The shriek of the arrow broke the spell. The shield rang and flashed in rays of fire, clearing the air. Ilanit shook herself, settling her perceptions in the glow of the shield. Solifrax fired in response. Everyone moved at once, Lyris clasping Patros as he crumpled, Tembujin and Nikander coiling, Andrion surging forward, cloak flying, sword cleaving the sunlight with a bright white light of its own. One sideways glance showed him Dana hurtling down the side of the mound. Gods! he thought, I let myself be blinded, I let down my guard! Dana, you are my other half.

Raksula spun, drunk on her own hatred. Ah, Andrion thought, it is indeed exhilarating. He felt his teeth bare themselves, his eyes burn.

She struck. Andrion struck faster. Solifrax sang and Raksula's right hand flew from the end of her arm, still clutching her dagger, and hit the hangings around the cart with a thwack. The hangings rippled violently. Raksula screeched and clutched the stump of her arm to her breast, dark vermilion blood staining her tunic. Her features contorted, at one instant recognizably human, at the next shuddering in malign bestial rage.

Hatred! howled Andrion's mind. If I hate anyone it is you! And yet, and yet . . . He caught himself, braced himself, sword upraised and thrilling through his entire body. Ilanit appeared on his right, shield pulsing with the same power. Tembujin appeared on his left, head lowered, eyes narrowed, a lion poised for the leap. Nikander stood just behind, ready for anything.

Dana burst through the surrounding cordon and stopped, her horse rearing, her eyes flicking from Lyris stanching

Patros's wound, to wary Nikander to Tembujin and Ilanit and Andrion standing side by side, shining warriors.

Raksula recoiled, eyes glazed. She scrambled onto the tongue of the cart and ripped away the hangings. The statue of Khalingu, wings furled, claws sheathed, tail curled, looked at her with eyes of adamant.

Her hoarse voice began muttering a prayer, a spell perhaps, incoherent words pouring like bile from her mouth. An echoing purr filled the air, mocking her rough words. She stopped, lips parted, eyes staring. There, on Khalingu's lap, lay the cat Qemnetesh. The beast's fur shimmered with quicksilver and its topaz eyes glowed. It yawned, its flicking tongue red and sharp, and it crossed its paws in lazy, insulting indolence.

"Qem," murmured Patros, "an aspect of Ashtar."

Andrion felt the gleam of the beast's eyes. He raised Solifrax like a scepter before him. Silence fell over the battlefield as if a lid had been clapped upon it. Dana's nostrils flared. "Not sorcery," she murmured, and a breath of wind carried the words to Andrion's ear. "Magic, the touch of the gods themselves." Her voice faltered.

A shaft of sunlight struck the cart with an audible peal. In reply the statue of Khalingu glittered, filling with swirling motes of light. It wavered and faded and changed. It became the figure of a cloaked woman holding a falcon upon her arm. Her eyes and the eyes of the raptor were a blue so piercing that Andrion felt they could see right through him, as though his flesh, his very soul, were no more substantial than the wind or the sunlight and could be molded at will. Whose will? he queried silently. Whose?

A serpent rose from beneath the woman's feet, spread its hood, shadowing Raksula's appalled face. The sheath of Solifrax writhed at Andrion's side.

Unnoticed, Odo crawled to his knees and then staggered to his feet, a decaying corpse reanimated, clutching a dagger in its scabrous hand. He fixed Raksula with eyes yellowed by a sick, sour spite.

The cart filled with mist, glimmering silver smoke shrouding the images of the gods. Raksula collapsed, hand outstretched, wailing demands and imprecations. The shapes flickered with tiny golden flames and crumbled, leaving only sparks to float down upon her face.

Her eyes cleared. She glanced behind her, at the icy faces, at the shining weapons. Her thin lips wavered, into a sneer perhaps, or perhaps a smile; defiantly she cursed the gods themselves. Odo threw himself into her embrace. The dagger flared and buried itself to the hilt in her breast. Odo and Raksula fell together into the burning cart and were consumed.

A wind rang suddenly down the sky, unfurling Andrion's cloak and snapping it like a banner. In the wind was a taut, clear note of music, a serenity beyond this world. Even as the note faded from his ears it hung, quivering, in his mind.

Andrion's cold carapace shivered into thousands of tiny fissures, revealing the raw, naked, mortal creature beneath. Tears rolled hot down his cheeks, draining him of rage and hatred. He was filled with the music, ripened by it, his awareness vibrating like a plucked lyre string. He stared into the sky, every sense extended. The westering sun drenched the battlefield and the walls of Iksandarun with light as thick as the finest honey. A wind scented with ice and asphodel rolled up the clouds and swept them away. The distant but distinct call of a falcon echoed down the wind, repeating that same note that trembled in his body.

Andrion inhaled deeply of the cool, clean wind. "So," he said quietly to it, "do I pass the test? Or have I merely won this game for you?" This day, the long-anticipated ending, was nothing like he had ever feared or hoped. His mouth tucked itself into a rueful smile. He sheathed his sword, sheathing his bewilderment and his strength. He turned to the shapes around him, recognizing them, his blood and his flesh.

Every face was set in the same god-struck awe. He had not imagined that note of grace. "Our faith is rewarded," he said to them all, and laughed at the complacent certainty in his voice. Only death was certain.

The cart burned in waves of heat, but it emitted no smoke, no smell. The gray cat padded to Andrion's feet, meowed up at him as if to say, And that is that, and slipped like a whorl of mist away.

Patros's head rested against Lyris's breast, his expression strained but at peace. "My congratulations, lord, on your victory," he said, and he attempted a bow, caught himself, blanched. Ilanit knelt beside him and soothed him with a touch.

With a rush the world toppled the surrounding dike, admitting the flooding stench and screams of battle. Tembujin advanced warily on the flaming cart, his own hatred burned to

ash. Dana slipped from her horse and came to Andrion, her
steps tentative, her eyes hesitant, even fearful; despite the
watching eyes, he took her hand and set it against his face,
under the cold metal rim of his helmet, and drew from her a
grave smile.

A shape scuttled from under the blazing cart like a weevil
popping out of a rotten pomegranate, tunic smoldering, voice
squalling. Tembujin started violently and then rolled the
plump figure in the dirt. Vlad, dirty, smudged with soot, slob-
bered onto Tembujin's boots and begged mercy.

Tembujin snatched the plaque of khan from Vlad's throat
and wiped it off on his own shirt. He looked around and met
Andrion's eye with an exultant and embarrassed pride.

With a gracious bow Andrion set the plaque over Tembujin's sleek black head. Do I look quite like you, slightly dazed?
Andrion asked mutely. But he had the wit to declaim to every
waiting ear, "Hail the ruler of Khazyaristan, my ally, the
lion."

"My thanks," Tembujin said. He did not add *my lord*.

Andrion's brows rose and he stifled a grin. Really, the
man's arrogance was . . . refreshing. "Our work is just beginning," he said firmly.

Tembujin glanced with queasy resignation at his brother,
picked him up and shook him. "Yes, I suppose it is now my
duty to teach you some manners." Vlad whined fealty.

The burning cart collapsed into smoldering embers. The imperial trumpets sounded, harsh and clear. Nikander and Ilanit
turned to their waiting soldiers and led them back into the
melee. The Khazyari writhed a few more moments, like the
body of a beheaded serpent, and then threw down their arms.
Dana sent messengers for Danica and Valeria and Shandir; she
helped support Patros into the city. Andrion and Tembujin,
with Lyris just behind, wove the torn and dangling threads of
the battlefield into one great multicolored tapestry.

The sun set, taking the day into the past. The wind murmured a low victory paean. Iksandarun's gates stood open to
the new emperor.

Chapter Twenty-three

THE SKY WAS an overarching bell of crystalline indigo. Its rim, the temple square and the surrounding buildings, was a rich gold filigree; its vault held the stars, cold, remote, unstained by battle. The west swam in roseate honey, the east lightened with ripples of quicksilver as the full moon made ready its entrance. Andrion stood gazing around him, each image as pure and distinct to his eyes as a jeweled icon.

The ruined temples, spilled bricks, charred wood, waited only for willing hands to rise again into shrines for ancient deities. In their midst was the high altar, a huge slab of limestone hollowed and stained by the centuries; stained by the blood of traitors the night Andrion had been born, and had almost died. The night Bellasteros had banned human sacrifice. Now Bellasteros himself lay on the altar, an icon of cinnabar and bronze, an offering to the caprice of the gods.

Andrion knelt, set his helmet beside his father's head, laid the curving blade of Solifrax at his father's right hand, rested his forehead against the stone. The stone was chill, and yet surprisingly forgiving. It shimmered against his flesh, ancient voices murmuring, *The summer king, sacrificed that the winter king might live, and living, secure. . . .* He started up. Surely he heard only the wind in his ears. But he wondered, secure Sabazel? Secure the Empire? *As the seasons pass, so pass the generations of men.*

Bellasteros's face in the waning light of the sun was translucent, no longer of this world and its passion. But it was the passion of this world that had hewn that face. And Andrion had loved it. "Farewell, Father," he whispered, "until we meet again in some far realm."

As Andrion rose, he sensed the eyes of the gods upon his

back, judging him, approving him. He was tempted to turn
and flip them all a rude gesture, but thought better of it. With
a sigh he retrieved Solifrax and thrust it firmly away. It purred
in its sheath, complacent, but he could no longer hate it.

A few paces away Danica, an icon of electrum and jade,
bound Patros's arm. Valeria wiped his brow, alternately beam-
ing upon his gray head and upon Tembujin's supple form
nearby.

Tembujin was an ivory icon, a barbarian image now inter-
preted in familiar terms. The hulking bear stood nodding, no
doubt receiving detailed instructions from Tembujin's incisive
voice; the warrior's huge hand clasped Vlad's collar as if the
boy were a wayward puppy.

Sarasvati sat with Miklos's head in her lap, Shandir binding
his wounds. Superficial wounds, except for the one in his eyes
as he looked up at the lover he had abjured. "I had hoped to
die, lady."

"Nonsense," Sarasvati said as brisky as she had to Obedei.
She met Andrion's eye. "Can Nikander not use such a loyal
centurion in Farsahn? One who would be happier at his own
end of the world, I daresay."

"Indeed," said Andrion. And, to Miklos, "Thank you."

The young man relaxed into their mercy. Miklos and
Sarasvati, Andrion thought, a statue broken and reassembled
in a different pattern, imperial lapis lazuli too fine for Sardian
granite.

Someone called his name. He turned. There stood Ilanit and
Dana, with Bonifacio fussing at their heels. Ah, he thought
wryly, if Harus could survive Gerlac's devotion, he can certainly survive Bonifacio's. Andrion set his face in an obliging
smile and went to them.

The star-shield rang and subsided to a genteel gleam. You,
too, he thought, pretending innocence. But Ilanit's face,
Dana's face, glowed at him; icons of emerald and shimmering
pale gold set in the glory of Sabazel. He bowed to each of
them, and in afterthought, to Bonifacio.

The gates of the temple courtyard were thrown open as if by
a gust of wind. Lyris and Nikander—her expression unim-
pressed, his impassive—waited outside. Beyond them the
population of Iksandarun gathered, face upon face shadowed
by the twilight into one expectant mass. Andrion stepped to
the top of the stairway, steeling himself; the legends were
already rife of how he and his sword had called fire from

heaven and singlehandedly defeated the Khazyari god.

They waited for him to speak. "The emperor Marcos Bellasteros is dead," he called. "Dead for you, this day of victory."

A solemn sigh rippled through the people.

He set his teeth, thought, Go on, say it.

"Will you have me, then, as your emperor?"

Cheers, shouts, pandemonium.

Beyond Andrion lay Bellasteros's mortal shell, a stark outline against the great blood-tinted face of the rising moon. Before him the moonlight glinted in a thousand eyes. Ilanit and Bonifacio scuffled surreptitiously, each reaching for the diadem Dana held. "Tradition," hissed Ilanit, "for the queen of Sabazel to crown the emperor." Lyris rattled her sword. Bonifacio desisted.

With a grin and a flourish, Ilanit placed the diadem upon Andrion's brow. Again it sparked gently against his skin, a light weight, perhaps crushingly heavy. The people cheered.

Nikander came forward leading Ventalidar; his seamed face, amazingly, split into a brilliant smile. The horse danced as if his day had been spent strolling in the stable yard. Andrion patted him, received an approving snort, and leaped into the saddle. The moonlight glanced down upon them both, black horse and black-and-bronze rider touched with crimson.

Torches flared along the street. Cheers rolled upward and dashed against the serenely gleaming sky. Andrion was a clear glass vessel, it seemed, scoured clean, filled with the mingled light of sun and moon. His dark pellucid eyes reflected them both.

The names the people cried ran together, "Andrion Bellasteros, Andrion Bellasteros!" The world tilted, righted itself, and spun in orderly whorls under Ventalidar's prancing hooves.

The petitioners were gone, officials bowing extravagantly, soldiers saluting. The audience was over. Andrion glanced up at the bronze falcon propped beside the throne. It seemed to smirk at him, as if it could hear his stomach rumbling. He let himself dwell for a moment on the prospect of spring lamb basted with honey and lemon; but no, times would be leaner yet before they grew better.

The gaunt form of the governor of Sardis appeared, his arm in a loose sling. Behind him stood his daughter Valeria, and beside her, his black eyes busily inspecting the ceiling, stood the khan Tembujin. Beyond them Sarasvati and Dana stood giggling together. So, the time had come to unravel a few complications. Andrion tried to look stern and solemn, but laughter bubbled inside him.

"I ask your permission, my lord. . . ." Patros said with a bow, and stopped, suffused with wry resigned amusement.

"My lord," Valeria chirped, her lovely blue eyes glinting as brightly as a steel trap. "I would ask permission to marry the khan."

Tembujin's gaze crashed to the floor. Andrion could have sworn the man was seized in a fit of shyness, rather than concealing his triumph. Gods, what was the man's appeal to these women? Andrion cleared his throat. "Ah, an alliance, very good. We can put together some kind of feast, I daresay."

Tembujin looked up. No, by the beak of the god, he was not triumphant. He had indeed learned the limit of his ambitions; Dana and Sarasvati stood smiling blandly upon his back, ever ready to remind him of it.

Valeria flashed Andrion a glittering smile, then turned that smile upon Tembujin. Food, she seemed to be thinking, was not the feast she had in mind. Andrion allowed himself a chuckle. "When you are ready," he said, to Tembujin, "you may lead your people north, where there is ample space for you to dwell in peace."

"My father need never have fought," sighed Tembujin. "The land was there for the taking."

"For the giving," Andrion amended. Their eyes met, and for a moment they struggled. Then the khan looked away, no longer needing such contests.

Andrion leaned back and crossed his legs before him. The cat Qemnetesh oozed purring over his ankles, and he started, looking suspiciously at it. But it remained a cat. Sarasvati turned and beckoned, and Obedei entered the door carrying a roll of fabric. "My wedding gift," she said to Tembujin with a sly sideways gleam.

He gasped as Obedei unfurled the rich and complex pattern of the Mohendra rug. "I . . . ah . . . ." It was his turn to clear his throat. "My thanks, lady."

Dana caught Andrion's eye. He blew her a rash kiss even as he thought, I, too, know the limit of my ambitions.

•   •   •

A frosty dusting of snow, gleaming ethereal pink in the rosy light of dawn, lay across the plateau, concealing the graves of the imperial dead. The Khazyari dead had been returned to the elements under Tembujin's grim supervision, given to the jackals and the ravens, as was their custom; not even their bones remained. Rebuilt yurts dozed to one side of the Road, the smoke of their cooking fires fragile silver tendrils reaching to a fragile waning moon.

Dana considered Andrion's profile, a clean edge carved in the silver sky. His features were marble, shaped and polished by time and fate. His dark eyes gleamed with ever-shifting depths of thought, with courage tempered by sensitivity. His test, she thought, will never be finished, any more than his father's was.

The young emperor's eyes rested on the mound of stone that would soon be Bellasteros's tomb. But only the conqueror's fleshly shell was there in the cold quiet darkness. He lived still in some warm and shining otherworld, waiting until Danica, his female half, finished her own test and joined him.

Andrion turned to his mother. Danica embraced him, her eyes stirring with a serene green-gold shimmer that seemed to melt the white ice around her, shading it with the colors of spring. When she released him, she left that shimmer reflected in his face.

The Companions waited. Lyris and Shandir, holding the disgruntled cat in a wicker cage, were already mounted. Ilanit lifted the weight of the softly glowing star-shield and turned away, the good-byes repeated yet again.

Patros and Andrion between them handed Sarasvati onto her horse. Of course, Dana thought, she should have been given to Sabazel at birth, traded for Andrion himself. In that, too, had Danica and Bellasteros shaded the law. . . . Andrion bent over his sister's hand, hiding his expression, and she smiled down at him. "It is for the best," she assured him.

"Yes," he returned. "Yes, indeed." With a sigh he let her go.

Dana stood alone between Andrion and Patros, allowing herself one last moment of masculine warmth; they wore no armor, and nothing came between them. Even Solifrax was quiescent at Andrion's side.

Her belly stirred with a touch as gentle and tentative as that of a butterfly testing its cocoon. She caught her lip between

her teeth, keeping herself from leaning against Andrion and
murmuring something foolish.

The company of women turned away from the world of
men. Iksandarun dwindled behind them into the brightness
of the morning. A flare of light before the gate was Solifrax,
raised in salute and then sheathed. If the grief was perfect,
then so was the joy, ever changing, ever enduring; Dana set
her face to the northwest, toward the borders of Sabazel and
home.

The wind purled across the plain, cold and fresh and yet
bearing within it a distant breath of spring.

Andrion leaned in nervous weariness against the parapet and
surveyed the rooftop garden. Now, at midsummer, the pomegranate and apricot trees that had been planted so hopefully
the winter before last were laden with fruit. Beds of flowers
and herbs lined graveled walks, and an arbor of flowering
broom shaded a bench. Wind chimes concealed in the fret-
work of the palace trilled. Or perhaps it was the wind itself,
tickling his hot cheeks, that chimed reassuringly in his ears.

He glanced again over the parapet. The horizon rippled with
banners and light refracted off polished armor, prisms of
color reflected into the blue dome of the sky. With a sigh he
turned back to the garden.

Tembujin stood beside him, looking not at the garden but
over the rooftops of the city. Now, two years after the
Khazyari attack, Iksandarun was still the worse for wear; new
buildings and empty lots filled with rubble stood cheek by
jowl, like an idiot's gap-toothed grin. At least it was a grin,
Andrion reflected.

Beyond the city the plateau lay in golden silence under the
afternoon sun. A few knots of activity marked rising farm
buildings. And yes, in the last moment the procession had inexorably advanced, elephants glistening with painted patterns,
sistrums playing a counterpoint to the wind.

"Damn you, Tembujin," said Andrion.

The khan glanced around, brows rising. "What have I done
now?"

It was Dana who answered. She looked up from where she
sat beneath the bower of golden broom, smoothing the horn
and sinew of her bow. "Do not blame him," she called.
"Blame your advisors, who place such stock in sons."

Ah, Andrion thought, Tembujin and I both were sons, once. But that grief was oddly old and fragile, no longer needing examination.

"Behold," said Tembujin, with a sweeping gesture toward the procession. "Your bride."

Andrion's throat went suddenly dry. Gods, why had he agreed to this? But he knew why; he was alone, filling the duties of emperor and general and father of his people. He was only twenty years old. . . . Dignity, above all, dignity.

Tembujin's teeth flashed in a grin, his black eyes snapped. A sleek coil of hair nodded behind his head. "Cheer yourself," he said. "She is a princess of the Mohan, and Mohendra blood makes one meek and unassuming."

Andrion glared at him. He subsided with a laugh. A page called from the doorway, "My lord, the ambassadors and the princess approach."

"I know," Andrion snapped irritably. "I have eyes." The page vanished. Andrion cursed himself. Unworthy of a king, to make a subordinate suffer for his own nervousness. He turned and watched Patros lead the honor guard with purple and scarlet pennons flying to the procession. He imagined the courtesies exchanged. He imagined the princess looking through the canopy of her howdah, every bit as curious and fearful as he was. An absurd game, strangers brokering themselves in marriage. He prayed that it was her choice to come here, that she had some spirit and was not a placid cow.

If all his life had been planned by the gods, then this was, too. And if there was no plan, then this event, too, he would make his own.

Solifrax murmured at his side. He set his hand on the hilt, reassured by its familiar tingle. Just a symbol now. He checked the draping of his cloak, the angle of the falcon brooch; his cheeks were smoothly shaven, his hair trimmed in a neat fringe across his forehead. The diadem of the Empire was hot upon his damp brow, sparkling, clean and bright.

"I have a gift for you," said Tembujin. "A wedding present."

Dana laid down her bow and came to join them. "It is from me as well," she said, her solemnity belied by a twinkle in her eye.

Tembujin produced something from his tunic, something that glittered gold in the sunlight. The wind caught it, and it emitted a low note of music. A necklace, Andrion saw. A golden crescent moon with a golden star at its tip. His throat closed, but he managed to stare with mock severity from black eyes to green and back. "It is about time you made good your peccadillo."

Dana looked at him as if his face were transparent glass, garishly painted with his every emotion. Smiling, she took the necklace and secured it around his neck. It thrilled gently against his skin. Tembujin swept into a low bow. Andrion laughed and thanked him.

Sweet voices, innocent of death and desire, floated down the wind. Andrion, Dana, and Tembujin turned to see Valeria and four children moving like bright flowers through the garden. The eldest was a boy, over a year old, walking with studied intensity. Next were twins of about a year, trying to decide whether to walk or crawl. The youngest arched from Valeria's arms, wanting to join its . . . cousins? The bloodlines became tangled.

"Damn you, Tembujin," Andrion said with a certain rueful humor. Of the children only one was a girl, one of the twins, a tiny sprite with flaming red hair and eyes the indeterminate blue-brown of the sea. The other three were boys, all of them black-haired, sloe-eyed, and bronze-skinned, already moving with the suppleness of their father. "Three of them, you had to have three of them. And my councillors make worried remarks behind my back, for I have no heirs at all."

Tembujin glanced over the children with the air of a farmer inspecting his crop, and grinned. "I have my talents."

Andrion's brows rose in exasperation. Dana touched his arm. "The goddess gifted us," she said to both men. "I was honored to bear you each a child. Our daughter, Andrion, is the heir to Sabazel."

Ah, well, yes; he should sacrifice that much to the Goddess. But Ashtar! Dana would take the girl and return with her to Sabazel, and there tell Sarasvati how their sons were safe in their father's . . . yurt.

Valeria hugged her baby, her plump cheeks glowing next to the glow of the little face, laughing as the little hands entwined themselves in her hair. "And that child is the heir to Khazyaristan?" Andrion asked.

"His mother," said Tembujin, "is the only one of my sons' mothers to whom I am legally wed."

Dryly, "Indeed." Andrion had considered making Saras-vati's son, his nephew, his heir. But the boy looked too much like his father to suit the still wary councillors. Hence this wedding he himself faced—gods! the procession must be entering the city! He spun about.

The populace cheered raucously as the parade advanced through the streets toward the open gateway of the palace. This stranger, Andrion thought, will bear my sons.

Elephants swayed ponderously under the arching palace gate. In the richest howdah sat a young woman. Her hair was silken black, her great brown eyes flamed with intelligence. She wore a sari of crimson silk woven with gold threads; her jeweled headdress jingled softly with the movement of the elephant, with the caressing touch of the wind.

Andrion leaned over the parapet, almost tripping himself with his sword. The princess looked up. Her generous lips curved into a smile, shy and yet pleased. Her eyes sparked with the light shining from the diadem. Her eyes—he could fall into their depths and nestle there. Just as the elephant passed under the gateway, eclipsing her shining face, she shrugged gracefully.

Andrion leaned precariously farther, drawn by that smile, by that wry shrug. Tembujin's firm hand closed on his cloak and pulled him back. He shook himself, disoriented. Dana dissolved in laughter. "I can see you already suffering."

With a plump, Andrion's daughter sat down in the pathway. She found and gravely tried to consume a caterpillar. She gagged. Andrion bent to the child's side and fished the creature from her soft little mouth. She glared at him, not at all grateful, and set up an indignant wail.

"The world is a bit much to swallow," he agreed. "But we choose to try." He stood, straightening his garments. He looked with glazed benevolence on these people, his family, and went to meet his bride.